GRACE TURNER

SOMEWHERE to STAY

CONTENTS

Content Note   vii

Chapter 1   1
Chapter 2   13
Chapter 3   23
Chapter 4   39
Chapter 5   51
Chapter 6   71
Chapter 7   81
Chapter 8   89
Chapter 9   103
Chapter 10   113
Chapter 11   123
Chapter 12   133
Chapter 13   143
Chapter 14   151
Chapter 15   165
Chapter 16   179
Chapter 17   191
Chapter 18   199
Chapter 19   209
Chapter 20   219
Chapter 21   235
Chapter 22   245
Chapter 23   259
Chapter 24   275
Chapter 25   289
Chapter 26   297
Chapter 27   311
Chapter 28   319
Chapter 29   327
Chapter 30   339
Chapter 31   351
Epilogue   363

Acknowledgments   369
Also By Grace Turner   371
About the Author   373

To anyone who thinks being called a slut in the bedroom doesn't sound like a good time.

Theo is here to prove you wrong.

CONTENT NOTE

This book is intended for adults and contains sexual situations. *Somewhere to Stay* is a super spicy book that contains degradation/humiliation, spanking/impact play, forced orgasms, anal sex, and exhibitionism. The book also contains mention of gambling addiction/compulsion, past homelessness (off-page), and previous suicidal thoughts (alluded to, non-graphic).

If you have any questions about the content of this book, or feel anything should be added to this list, please feel free to reach out to me on social media (@graceturnerauthor) or email me at graceturnerauthor@gmail.com.

ONE

HOME SWEET... FUCK

Theo

THE CHILD THAT DARTED OUT IN FRONT OF MY TRUCK WAS LUCKY.
My reaction was quick enough that his head didn't meet the
bumper.

The tires squealed, piercing the quiet, picturesque scene of
the suburban neighborhood.

I held my breath until a woman rushed out into the street.
The woman I assumed was his mother scooped her child up in
one arm and grabbed the little tricycle he'd been riding with the
other. If the scowl she shot my way as she stalked off was any
sign, she thought the near miss was my fault.

Not the best way to begin my hopefully short stay in the
godforsaken neighborhood. I already didn't want to be there.
Actually, I wanted to be anywhere but there, if I was being
honest.

But I didn't have a choice.

Cautiously and itching to shoot the woman a gesture I knew
would only deepen her scowl, I continued down the street. I
watched my best friend's car turn right down a street several
houses down and blew out a frustrated sigh.

I was extra vigilant, my eyes whipping back and forth across the street, prepared to slam on the brakes again at a moment's notice.

Each house was similar to the next. They all had pristinely mowed lawns and brick mailboxes. There were yard signs and garage sale posters. Many of them had American flags hanging somewhere on the exterior, and there were children *everywhere*.

All of it made me want to turn back around. I already felt out of place. I didn't think that their lives were perfect. I knew better than that. But they could at least fake it and pretend that they were. I didn't even have the ability to pretend like my life was anything but a disaster.

I also knew that with one look at me, they would go running. And it wasn't because of the tattoos covering most of my body, even traveling up my neck and across my hands and fingers. It was like the remnants of my poor circumstances clung to me just as the tattoos did. Even if, unlike the tattoos, they couldn't see them, most people still knew they were there.

I took the same right Ryder had moments before and spotted his car turning into a driveway halfway up the street.

Trying not to grind my teeth, I pulled into the open space next to him and stared at the house I'd be living in for who the hell knew how long.

Ryder, being the friend and person I knew, had immediately offered up his childhood home to me when I'd realized I didn't have another option. He was moving back for the fall semester to be closer to an internship he'd snagged.

Just me, Ryder, and his mom. That wasn't a recipe for disaster or anything.

I'd been on my own for so long that the idea of someone else telling me what I could or could not do felt juvenile.

Ryder had gone on and on for the week leading up to the move about how his mom was cool and understanding. That she'd been young when she got pregnant with him and they'd always been close.

But she was still his mom. My hopes weren't high.

I knew that his parents had divorced a few years before, and now it was just his mom living in the house he'd grown up in. He'd told me not to worry so many times that I'd begun to worry more. Like every time he said it, he was trying to cover up how worried I should actually be.

Through the windshield, I stared up at their house. Unlike most of the homes we'd passed, their house had character. The house itself was mostly white with dark blue shutters, which wasn't as eye-catching as the abundance of flowers springing up from the flowerbeds and the bright green front door.

Ryder immediately jumped out of his car and grabbed his duffel and large suitcase from the backseat. I did the same, grabbing my duffel from the seat behind me before meeting him at the bottom of the porch.

"That kid seriously had a death wish," he said, jerking his chin down the street.

I grunted in response and shook my head.

"My mom's not home yet," Ryder said, taking the two steps up the porch and crossing the short distance to the door. "She works downtown, so she usually doesn't get home until after six."

With an easy smile, Ryder pushed open the door, and I stepped inside behind him.

He'd always been like that—he was the happy, carefree guy who was rarely without a smile. If Ryder hadn't been so insistent that we were supposed to become friends, we wouldn't have. And that would've been a shame, because often he was one of the only positive things in my life.

Freshman year of college, he'd spent our entire history class trying to convince me to be his friend. He sat down next to me and didn't shut up the entire semester. After months, I finally wore down, and we've been inseparable ever since.

"Welcome home," he said, waving to the house and shutting the door behind us.

Fuck, I couldn't believe I was really doing it. Standing inside the entryway, it all suddenly became real.

Ryder nudged my shoulder with his. "I know that look, come on." He brushed past me, and I scowled at his back as I reluctantly followed.

"I don't know what look you're talking about," I mumbled.

We walked farther into the house, passing a room that looked like an office with french doors on the right and, on the left, a long table set against the wall displaying several photos of what I assumed were Ryder's friends and family.

Ryder scoffed and tossed his duffel on the stairs. I took his lead and set mine down next to his.

He pulled open the fridge and grabbed two water bottles, throwing one to me and twisting the top off of his own.

"It's your *'I really want to bolt'* look."

I shook my head, flipped him my middle finger, and considered the rest of the room. To the right, where Ryder was again looking through the fridge, was the open-concept kitchen. There was a large island in the center with a butcher block countertop and cabinets the same shade of green as the front door. The rest of the kitchen counters were lighter granite, and the cabinets lining the walls were white.

There was a small eating area at the back of the house with windows that looked out over the sizable backyard.

One space seamlessly transitioned into the next, and I surveyed the living room to the left. The couch was a light gray and covered in colorful blankets and pillows. There were even more pictures placed on the built-in shelves surrounding the TV.

It was nice and homey and clean and the feeling that I didn't fit yet again began to rear its ugly head. And I would never admit it out loud, but Ryder was right. That urge to fucking run was strong.

"Wanna go see upstairs?" Ryder asked, yanking me from my thoughts and popping one of a handful of grapes into his mouth.

I really wanted to *leave* but knew I couldn't. And I only grew more angry every time I was reminded that my options were limited to one.

But I refused to be without a roof over my head ever again.

So, I nodded and grabbed my bags to follow him up the stairs. There were three bedrooms and two bathrooms on the second floor. The bedroom to the left was Ryder's, apparently, and the one directly across the hall was mine. His mom's room was at the end of the hall.

"My mom said it's all ready for you," Ryder said as he opened the door to what was supposed to be my room. "New sheets and she cleaned out the closet. Towels and all of that are in the bathroom next to my room. Umm…what else do you need to know?"

The room was a decent size with a queen-size bed and a large dresser. Most of it was decorated in various shades of blue, and there was a window on the opposite side that looked out on what I assumed was the backyard.

There was a blanket tossed over the chair in the corner of the room and new clothes hangers hanging in the closet. Behind that chair and next to the closet door, there was a new fragrance plug-in that filled the entire room with what I thought was vanilla or something similarly sweet.

"So, what do you think?" Ryder asked, interrupting my perusal of the room. He was standing in the doorway, watching me warily yet expectantly.

"It's a room," I said, and he blinked once before he chuckled. I didn't mention, because Ryder already knew, that it was the nicest room I'd had in several years. That urge to run was itching at my skin like a bad fucking rash. Especially when I noted all the ways his mom had prepared it for me.

"Okay, well, I guess get unpacked and we can figure something out for dinner. My mom will probably want to eat with us."

I nodded, and he walked the few feet to his room across the hall. He immediately turned on the same rock playlist he'd been listening to for the past two years and busied himself with unpacking his own shit.

I just stood there, though. I didn't think there was a point in unpacking the few things I did have left, especially if I was only going to be there as long as I absolutely had to. Long enough to replenish my savings and get my own place, or at least an apartment with a roommate.

I was already working four to five nights a week at Haven City Tattoos, but I'd find another job if I needed to. It would be a lot, working two jobs and taking a full course load, but I'd make it work. I'd done harder shit.

I trusted Ryder implicitly, but I hadn't yet met his mom. And she was bound to decide—maybe sooner rather than later—that it wasn't worth it to let me stay. Especially rent-free, which was still a sore topic between Ryder and me. Trusting anyone like that felt as foreign to me as that damn room did.

But I unpacked anyway. Because if I didn't, I'd have to hear about it from Ryder. It took me all of three minutes to empty my duffel. Two of which I spent deciding if I should split up my socks and briefs into two separate drawers to make it appear like I had more than I did.

I was sitting on the edge of the bed, idly scrolling through a job search site when Ryder appeared at my doorway.

"Hey, man. All unpacked?"

"Umm…yeah."

Hearing the hesitation in my voice, Ryder stepped into the room and leaned against the wall. He crossed his arms over his chest and leveled me with an unimpressed look.

"Don't give me that look."

"Oh, you can read my looks now, too?"

"Yes, asshole. It's your *'you're being difficult'* look."

He chuckled and dragged his hand through his dark hair.

"Yeah, it is. But seriously, I promise this is going to be great. It's going to be like living with two roommates instead of one. And both my mom and I are *way* better than fucking Colby."

The anger I had to check when I heard my old roommate's name tasted bitter on my tongue. Colby had not only been dirty, loud, and nosy, he'd also kicked me out when I was at my lowest.

Saying that Ryder and his mom would be better than Colby wasn't saying much.

"Just give it a chance, okay?"

I took a deep breath and nodded. At the same time, we both heard the door downstairs.

"Mom?" Ryder called a second later.

I wasn't nervous to meet his mom; I couldn't remember the last time I'd been nervous for anything, actually. But I was a little on edge. I wasn't a "meet the parents" type of guy, whether it came to my friends or girlfriends. The tattoos always evoked polarized reactions, and they took my silence as disrespect.

I didn't enjoy talking.

Most of the time, people weren't worth the effort it took to have a conversation. And small talk made me want to cut off my own ears and rip out my vocal cords.

"Nope!" a voice from downstairs yelled back, and Ryder smiled.

"Let's go."

I hesitated for a moment, but stood nonetheless and followed Ryder back down the stairs.

Rip the Band-Aid off. I only had to meet her for the first time once. She'd welcomed me into her home, I just had to not make her want to kick me out.

Frustration buzzed along my skin. My throat was thick with it, too, as I was reminded once again that I was at someone else's mercy.

Each time my boots hit the wooden stairs, the sound echoed

louder. Halfway down, I could hear Ryder already talking a mile a minute, but I didn't look up. I stared at my worn, scuffed boots until I was four or five steps away from the bottom. When I finally looked up, all I could see was Ryder's back. From where I stood, it looked like he was talking to an empty kitchen.

But the bottom step creaked slightly, and he turned at the sound.

"Took you long enough. This is my mom, Natalie. Mom, this is Theo."

Finally, he stepped to the side and revealed the woman he'd been speaking to.

And I nearly stumbled back.

Her smile hit me square in the chest, and all the oxygen was sucked from the room. Her straight, white teeth were surrounded by full lips.

Struggling to stay standing, my eyes, with a mind of their own, slipped over her body like I had any right to look.

She was still wearing the clothes she'd worn to work—a flowy deep blue top tucked into a black pencil skirt that formed to every single one of her curves. Her legs were bare, and her calves were toned. Lower, I noticed her black heels were fairly high, and they clicked across the dark, hardwood floors as she approached me.

Never had I been so instantly attracted to someone. And my reaction was fucking unsettling.

I realized when she stuck out her hand that I'd been transfixed, openly ogling her as she approached.

My eyes snapped up from where I'd been eyeing the small part of her waist to meet her startling blue eyes. Her black hair fell in waves around her shoulders, and it was a stark contradiction—the darkness of her hair compared to her light eyes.

Like I was on autopilot, I stuck out my hand and clasped hers. Her hand was small, much smaller than mine, but the warmth of her palm pressed against mine was heavy.

"Hi, umm…it's so nice to meet you, Theo," she said. Her

voice was low and breathy, and hearing my name roll off her lips made blood surge to my cock. My entire body pulsed to the tempo of my name on her tongue.

Well, fuck.

I had to clear my throat twice before I muttered a quiet, "Hi."

That was all I could manage as my thoughts wandered without my permission.

I shook my head like that would dislodge the thoughts and immediately let go of her hand that I was holding hostage.

But her eyes didn't leave mine. My menacing look, as Ryder called it, didn't seem to scare her at all. And I swore that I saw something glimmer behind her blue irises. Something bright and sweet. It couldn't have been interest, but fuck did it look like it.

Yet as quickly as I'd noticed it, the spark was gone.

Then Ryder asked from the kitchen what we were going to do for dinner. Interrupting the perfect mental image I'd dreamed up: his mom on her knees with tears running down her cheeks to meet the drool pooling around my engorged cock that was wedged between her lips.

Natalie quickly turned and walked back into the kitchen. And it took more effort than I would've liked to not watch her ass sway.

This wasn't fucking happening. This could *not* be fucking happening to me.

Fuck, fuck, *fuck.*

I rolled my neck along my shoulders, but it didn't relieve any of the tension. Just like stuffing my hands in the front pockets of my jeans didn't stop them from itching to reach out and touch her.

The swift, sudden reaction wasn't something I'd experienced before.

Talk about wanting to fucking run. If there ever was a reason to get out, she was it.

"Yeah, that sounds good. Theo, how do you feel about—"

Ryder began but stopped abruptly, fishing his phone out of his back pocket. He looked confused when he peered down at it.

"This is my adviser at school. Umm...one second," he said quickly, and went out the sliding glass door into the backyard as he answered.

Leaving me and Natalie alone.

TWO

BUFFER, PLEASE

Natalie

I DIDN'T KNOW WHAT I IMAGINED RYDER'S FRIEND TO LOOK LIKE, but I hadn't expected *that*.

My long day at work had been followed by an even longer commute home. I genuinely enjoyed my job. Most of the time. And as much as I also liked the people I worked with, it was a lot.

But I'd looked forward to coming home and seeing Ryder, who'd been on campus most of the summer taking classes. And I was also interested to meet his friend, who would be staying with us for...who knows how long.

Ryder hadn't told me much about his friend, Theo. He'd said that due to circumstances outside of his control, he needed a place to stay. He didn't have any family to speak of and really had no one else to turn to.

And maybe I was naïve—or, as my best friend, Caroline, liked to call it, a pushover—but I couldn't let him just live in his car or on the street. I'd once been in a similar position. Although I was much, *much* younger when I got pregnant with Ryder, I still didn't have many options. Had it not been for my ex-husband's parents, I likely would've ended up on the street.

I understood better than most what it was like to run out of options, and I wasn't going to let that happen to anyone. No matter what, I wanted to lend whatever support I could.

Then he walked in.

It was everything I could do to keep my breathing steady and the smile on my face as I shook his hand. But all I wanted to know was if those tattoos running up his neck and over his fingers were *everywhere* else, too.

He had messy, curly brown hair that fell over his forehead and deep brown eyes that closely watched my every movement. He had to be about a foot taller than my five-foot-two frame, and the way his black T-shirt pulled across his chest and his worn jeans hugged his thighs, I was sure there was plenty of muscle hidden beneath.

But it was something else, not his size and stature, that made it feel like he was taking up the entire room. Like all of the energy—and in turn all my attention—was siphoned directly to him.

I knew it had been a bad idea the moment I offered him my hand. But I was trying to be polite and welcoming, even though I'd somehow known that when he grasped it, it would only intensify every feeling. And that's exactly what had happened.

Like I'd been ripped into his orbit, I could only stare up at him as he muttered a quick "hi" and dropped my hand like it was on fire.

As quickly as I could manage while being confused by the onslaught of foreign feelings, I turned and walked back into the kitchen, putting as much distance as I could between us.

The entire interaction was wholly unsettling, and whatever it was was going to stop just as quickly as it started. If I didn't give it any power or thought, then it would eventually go away.

Easy.

I turned my attention back to Ryder, whom I was ecstatic to

have back home, even if it was for a few months. Ryder's dad, Mark, and I had been divorced for over a year, and the house was oddly quiet when it was just me. I was happy to have people around again. I didn't mind the quiet, but I didn't like it all the time.

Ryder and I discussed dinner and quickly decided on the same restaurant we'd been going to since he was a kid. It didn't really require a discussion, but I could tell he was worried about making sure Theo felt welcome, which meant he overthought every single decision.

My thoughts drifted back to the man behind me, still standing near the stairs where he'd been since he'd come down. I could feel his eyes on my back, like they were as real and physical as his hands. I imagined them sweeping over me, and a shiver buckled down my spine at the phantom touch.

Ryder was saying something to him over my shoulder, but then he stopped abruptly, pulling his phone from his pocket and excusing himself to take the call outside.

I tensed, suddenly realizing that he'd left Theo and me alone. I figured I had two options: hurry upstairs to change like the coward I was, or try to push past whatever just happened and start over.

The first option was much safer and the one I should have taken, but instead I turned around and put on the best unaffected look I could muster.

"What Ryder was going to say is that he wants to go to his favorite little hole-in-the-wall burger place. We've been going there since…well, since forever."

I glanced at Theo long enough to see that he was leaning against the wall, one shoulder propped against it, his arms crossed over his chest, and one ankle over the other. His entire demeanor was casual, calm, and as unfazed as I was trying to act.

God, I was losing my mind.

I couldn't have made it all up—the weird, intense pull. That wasn't possible. I wasn't that delusional. But it didn't matter because I wasn't thinking about it. We were starting over.

Spinning, I kicked off my heels next to the kitchen island and nearly moaned at the relief in the arch of my foot. Breaking in new heels was the bane of my existence, and if I never had to wear them again, I'd be happier for it. Only I enjoyed the confidence boost the additional few inches gave me.

Theo still hadn't said anything, so I tried a different tactic.

Without looking back at him, I asked, "Are you unpacked already?" I busied myself loading a few of the dishes left in the sink into the dishwasher and was surprised when I heard Theo finally mutter a quiet "yes."

Okay, we were getting somewhere.

"That's good." More silence followed. I closed the dishwasher and glanced out the back door. Ryder was pacing up and down the patio, one hand wrapped around the back of his neck and the other still holding the phone in a tight grip against his ear.

I silently urged him to come back inside and play buffer between me and his friend. But I wouldn't give up easily.

"Did you like the room?"

I chanced another look up at Theo. He was still standing in the same position, appraising me with dark eyes and slightly inclined his head in response. My lips pursed in thought, I braced my hands on the island in front of me.

"You and Ryder have been friends since freshman year, right?"

He nodded after assessing me for another moment.

"Are you enjoying college so far?"

His brown eyes narrowed, and his shoulder lifted an inch. The movement was so quick and small that I would've missed it had I not been watching him so closely.

"Did you grow up around here?"

And of all the questions I asked, I didn't expect that one to garner the biggest reaction. You would've thought I asked if he kicked puppies or spit on babies with the way he flinched and straightened.

I was looking for a reaction, a response, *something*, but that was the last one I expected.

I couldn't even begin to identify what about that question would spark such an insidious fire behind his brown eyes. The tension in the room climbed higher the longer we stood staring at one another, neither of us speaking. I stayed silent for fear that whatever else I might say would cause even more of a reaction.

Yet I was suddenly invested in knowing more about him. I needed to know why he flinched when I asked where he grew up. I wanted to know what sparked that fire behind his eyes that I couldn't force myself to look away from.

Searching for anything to change topics or lighten the mood, I glanced around the kitchen until my eyes landed on the junk drawer. A receipt was sticking out the side, and when I opened it, I accidentally pulled out an old birthday card, a paint swatch, a battery, and a phone charging cable, along with the keys I'd had made. I untangled the key ring from the chord and shoved the rest of the stuff back into the drawer.

I cringed at the keychain that was dangling from the set of keys. A dark pink heart with my name, *"Natalie,"* written in the center in white, loopy text.

I wasn't sure where it had come from, but it was the only keychain I'd had. I couldn't change it right then, so I hoped he would at least accept the set and change it later.

Hesitantly, I crossed to Theo and held the keys out in front of me.

"These are yours. One for the front door and one for the garage."

His eyes bounced between me and the keys for a moment. Long enough that I considered he may not take them. I held my breath. After what felt like a millennia, he held out his hand.

What I should have done was drop them into his

outstretched palm. Quickly getting rid of them and stepping back out of his space. But I didn't.

Instead, I set them in his hand and let my fingers linger over his palm. I wasn't expecting his skin to be soft, and I definitely wasn't expecting the electricity that shot up my arm at the small, unassuming touch.

I swallowed down the gasp that lodged in the back of my throat and dropped the keys in his hand. I yanked my hand away, the feeling lingering against my fingers and shooting up my arm to my shoulder. Curious if he felt it too, my eyes darted to his.

Brown, honeyed eyes stared back at me, narrowed in a glare so intense that I could feel it bone deep.

"You can change the keychain," I blurted out. "It's just all I had. You can throw it away if you want. I won't be offended if—"

"It's fine," he said, cutting me off before my nervous rambling could ensue.

Too lost in my thoughts and Theo's glare, I didn't hear the back door slide open or Ryder step inside. I jumped back from Theo, and my attention quickly shifted when I noted the worried look on Ryder's face.

My heart dropped, and my thoughts immediately swung to the worst possibility.

"What's wrong?" I asked, the worry evident in my voice.

"Nothing's wrong. It's actually really good news. Umm..." Ryder's gaze bounced between me and Theo, and even Theo's dark brows were furrowed in confusion and concern.

"That was my adviser, and she apparently submitted my application for an internship at NASA. I originally told her not to submit it even after I filled it out because they only covered part of the living expenses and the minimal money I'd make from the internship wouldn't cover the rest. But I didn't tell her in time. I had no idea, but she'd already submitted it and decided to see what would happen. They hadn't contacted her, so she didn't think I'd gotten it. But they just contacted her. Someone dropped out at the last minute, and they offered their position to me *with* an extra stipend to cover the rest of the living expenses."

My excitement was instantaneous. "Ryder, that's amazing!" I cheered and rounded the kitchen island to congratulate him, but stopped short when his expression remained forlorn.

"You're right, that's great news. So, what's with the face?" I asked, and he took a deep breath, scrubbing a hand over his mouth and again glancing between me and Theo standing behind me.

"It's in Texas, and I'd have to leave in two days."

The excitement I felt a moment ago was still there, but it was muffled by the nerves that shot through me with that last very important piece of information.

With Ryder gone, I'd be living alone with Theo for an indefinite amount of time. And without the buffer that I realized we'd both desperately need.

But the opportunity was life-changing for Ryder. He couldn't say no. I wouldn't *let* him say no.

"You can't say no to this, Ryder. You have to go," I said, and he stared at me for a moment. I could see it in his eyes that he didn't want to say no. He was trying to come up with a solution that meant he didn't have to. His eyes lifted to Theo, and I turned just enough to spot Theo in my peripheral.

His jaw was tight, and there was even more tension in his shoulders. His tattooed hands were fisted at his sides, and his eyes were fixed on Ryder. I could've guessed that living with me *without* Ryder was the last thing he wanted to do. He was probably already hesitant about the entire setup, even with his best friend in the mix.

"You've gotta go," Theo finally said. "I'll figure something else out."

Ryder laughed and shook his head. "No, you're going to stay here." He looked down at me like he was questioning whether or not to say anything more but still continued, quieter, "You don't have anywhere else to go."

Theo rocked back on his heels, like the truth of the statement nearly knocked him over. He pushed a hand through his curly hair, and I could see that he wanted to fight and argue. Although I didn't understand the circumstances surrounding his inability to find somewhere else to go, I couldn't imagine it'd been easy—whatever he'd gone through to get him to that point.

Just based on the little I did know about him and our very brief interaction, I was sure he wasn't the type of person to ask for help.

"I don't think—" Theo began, but Ryder shook his head and began speaking over his friend.

"No, just no. Do you think I should take this internship?"

Theo rolled his eyes and nodded.

"Then I'll take it *only* if you promise to stay here."

But even that didn't dim the fight in Theo's eyes. Having also noticed it, Ryder turned to me.

"What do you think, Mom? Should Theo stay while I'm in Texas?"

"Yes." My answer was automatic because there wasn't any reason to contemplate it. I wasn't going to kick him out. That wasn't even an option. And for some reason, I really wanted him to stay. Which was honestly more of a reason to say no and find another solution.

But I didn't listen to my common sense or all the alarm bells aggressively ringing in my head.

Instead, I turned to Theo, whose expression was unreadable. His full lips were set in an unmovable straight line. I swallowed before I said, "You need somewhere to stay. You should stay."

THREE

HOLY FUCKING SHIT BALLS

Natalie

"Hold on, I think you need another one," Caroline, my best friend, said, standing from where we were both reclined on the couch to find the other bottle of wine we'd opened.

She'd known that Ryder and his best friend were moving in for the fall semester, but after a whirlwind few days, I hadn't had a chance to fill her in on how everything had completely changed.

It had been less than a day since Ryder left, and Theo had agreed to stay with a quick, solemn nod. I couldn't tell if he was annoyed or relieved that I'd taken Ryder's side, but he hadn't continued to argue. We'd still had dinner that night, Ryder and I holding most of the conversation and Theo only jumping in when he was asked a question directly.

Ryder didn't appear put off by Theo's behavior, so I assumed it was the norm for him.

On the awkwardness scale, it wasn't as bad as I thought it would be, and afterward, we'd immediately begun preparing Ryder for his internship. He had an apartment the company provided as well as a roommate who was also part of the internship program.

He had most of what he needed already, but I did buy him a larger suitcase.

He'd left thirty-six hours after he received the phone call. And Theo and I were officially alone.

Suddenly my house felt both too big and too small. Which was why I invited Caroline over. Another decision I was worried I'd grow to regret.

"He's here, right?" she whispered. I offered her my empty glass, and she poured a generous amount of rosé before she reclaimed her spot beside me.

We should've met at her house, but she said something about painters working when I suggested it. Theo was upstairs, and if I knew anything about my best friend, it was that she had a hard time being quiet on her best days.

I nodded and glanced back toward the stairs before taking a long sip.

"What's he like?"

I shrugged. "Quiet. Tall." *Gorgeous, mysterious, confusing.*

She rolled her eyes at my lackluster answer. "Besides tall, what does he look like?"

I tried to hide my expression before it slipped free. But it was futile, she'd seen my reaction before I could properly suppress it.

"Wait a second." She set her own glass on the coffee table and readjusted so she was facing me. "That face means he's either butt fucking ugly *or* he's gorgeous," she said too enthusiastically and excited for her own good. "Oh, please, please tell me he's gorgeous."

She pressed her hands together in front of her chest like she was praying for the second option.

"He's...gorgeous," I sighed, resigned to the fact that I would have to tell her. She would've figured it out eventually, and it was better to let her get it all out when it was just the two of us.

She squealed, and I shushed her while she bounced up and down in her spot.

"Okay, I can't wait to see him and meet him. But until then, tell me everything. I want every detail."

Caroline was only a few years younger than me. At thirty-two, she owned a successful event planning business she'd opened right out of college. She hadn't found a company she wanted to work for, so she decided to make one herself.

That was the kind of person the outgoing and driven blonde was. In her work, she was dedicated and hardworking. But outside of the office, she loved to let loose and live her life to the fullest.

We'd become fast friends when she moved into the house down the street several years earlier. She'd attended the annual Fourth of July barbecue, and we bonded over the stupidity of a few of our neighbors. What better way was there to become friends than to talk shit and gossip about others?

She was headstrong and opinionated. She rarely had a filter, and I envied her for it. It was one way I wished I was more like her. I would've loved to be more carefree and opinionated.

But unlike Caroline, I *did* want a committed relationship. She'd claimed on more than one occasion she didn't see the point of it.

Getting married again was still a long way off for me, but I wanted to find someone else. *Eventually*. I thought that maybe my forever person was still out there.

I downed the rest of my wine, and Caroline's gray eyes widened.

"He's tall," I said again, beginning with his most obvious and inconspicuous features, and before I could say anything else, she asked, "How tall?"

I rolled my eyes, knowing exactly how the conversation was going to go—no matter what I said, she'd want more details.

I held out my hand, and she glowered at me from beneath

her lowered lashes. "Please save your questions until the end," I requested.

She let out an exasperated sigh but nodded while simultaneously waving at me to hurry the hell up.

"He's six foot two, maybe? I know he's got to be at least a foot taller than me. He has curly brown hair and brown eyes. And...tattoos. He's *covered* in tattoos."

A slow smile spread across her face, and her eyes lit up with a mischievousness I knew all too well. Nothing good came from that look.

"I knew it was only a matter of time before you fell for a bad boy type." She winked, and my stare remained flat. "Anyway, how would you know that they're everywhere? That they cover his entire body?"

I threw my head back and groaned toward the ceiling. "Okay, fine. I don't technically know, but they go up his neck and over his fingers. I feel like it just makes sense that they would be...everywhere."

She nodded her agreement and refilled my wine. I sipped it idly as she pursed her lips.

"So, you're attracted to him."

I nearly choked, and the burn made my eyes water. "He's twenty-three," I croaked out.

It was Caroline's turn to roll her eyes. "Age has nothing to do with it, babe. He's well over eighteen, and that's all that matters. And he's not the same age as Ryder?"

"He took some time off of school or something. I don't know, we didn't get into specifics. But you call five years 'well over'? He's still fourteen years younger than me."

She shrugged. "He can buy a beer, and he likely knows how to use his cock by now, too."

"Holy shit, we are *not* having this conversation right now," I whisper-yelled and glanced again at the stairs. Theo was in his room, likely with the door firmly shut, but the last thing I needed was for him to overhear anything Caroline had or would say.

Theo and I hadn't spoken since Ryder left the evening before, and I didn't want to make matters worse by him overhearing my best friend talk about his cock.

"Oh hell yes, we are," she said, at least a little quieter. "Don't lie to me."

"Yes, he is hot. Are you happy?"

The grin that split her face was obnoxious, and all I wanted to do was wipe it off. Her teasing and prying were not helping anything. I was already self-conscious about my one-sided attraction, I didn't need her making me feel worse.

"I'm not sure why you're so upset about a hot guy living under your roof."

"Please, stop. This cannot be happening to me…"

"What? Being attracted to your son's best friend?"

I smacked her in the arm, and all she did was laugh at my antics. "Can you not say it like that?"

She only winked, and I wanted to throttle her right then and there.

"I…" I began and decided the truth was the best option. "I don't know if it's even *him* so much, as it's been almost two years since anything has happened with anyone."

Her eyes widened in shock, and she clasped one of her hands around mine. All signs of joking gone, she asked, "Honey, are you serious?"

"Why on earth would I lie about something like that?"

"Okay, fine, you're right. So, what are we going to do about this little issue?"

I shook my head and pulled my hand back, burrowing farther under the blanket I'd draped over us both.

I wasn't sure anything could be done. I'd slept with one guy after Mark moved out and before the divorce was finalized, thinking that since I'd known the divorce was imminent, I was ready to move on. Except I wasn't.

One of my coworkers had set me up with him, and the date

had gone well enough that I decided to rip off the metaphorical Band-Aid and jump in bed with him. It was when he was panting on top of me like we'd just run a marathon, reeking of the garlic we'd had for dinner, that I knew I'd made a mistake.

I'd faked an orgasm just so it would be over.

He fell asleep almost immediately. I left in the middle of the night and spent an hour in the shower when I got home trying to scrub the feeling of his hands from my body.

That was almost two years ago. I'd gone on a few dates since then, but they hadn't turned into anything more than that. I hadn't been on a date since the papers were signed and the courts made it official. I'd nearly given up on dating altogether.

"What can I do?"

I honestly didn't think being single was going to be so complicated. But I wouldn't change my decision—our divorce was for the best.

I never wanted to marry Mark, but when you're freshly sixteen years old, pregnant, and homeless because your parents kicked you out, you do what you have to do. Mark's parents were willing to let me live with them if we got married, so that's what we did.

We lived with his parents until we could afford our own apartment, and then eventually bought the house I still lived in.

We weren't miserable the entire time, though. There were times, years even, when I was almost happy. Ryder made life so much better; he was the light of my life. And I stayed with Mark because of him.

Two years ago, I finally decided I was done being almost happy sometimes, yet often miserable, and told him I wanted a divorce.

Mark didn't even act surprised. We didn't *fit* anymore.

And even if it was the right thing for all of us, it still fucking sucked.

"When was the last time you went out on a date?"

I thought for several seconds, but it didn't take long for the memories to come rushing back. "I think the last time was when I went out with your sister's friend, maybe?"

"Oh! You mean the one that smelled like cabbage?"

I nearly gagged at the memory. "Yes, cabbage guy." He worked with Caroline's sister's boyfriend or something like that, and she'd never actually met him before setting me up.

We'd texted and talked on the phone a few times, and he seemed nice enough. He picked the restaurant, and when he leaned in to hug me, I was overwhelmed by the smell of freshly cooked cabbage. It was all I could focus on the rest of the night since the stench had seared itself into my nostrils.

I couldn't even remember the guy's name and only referred to him as "cabbage guy" if I referred to him at all.

"That was so long ago. Okay, yeah, we're going to have to fix this. Now that I know you're interested in dating and fucking…" She paused, waiting for my confirmation, which I begrudgingly gave with a nod of my head. "Then let me set you up. I know exactly the right guy." The conspiratorial smile and gleam in her eye made me immediately want to refuse.

"Don't look at me like that," she warned. "I've actually met this guy on more than one occasion. He's in his midforties, a widower, and has two sons, I think, that are around Ryder's age. And he is a total DILF."

"And how do you know this guy?"

She shrugged and said, with a cavalier nonchalance I envied, "I fucked his brother a time or five."

"Oh, good. I get the ugly brother then?"

She tossed her head back and laughed loudly. "No, they're both extremely attractive. Their entire family won the genetics lottery."

My prospects were so few that I considered letting Caroline set me up. The idea of going out to a bar to meet someone or joining a dating app sounded more miserable than letting my friend pick someone out for me.

"I can tell you're overthinking it, but just listen, if it doesn't work out, then oh well. It won't make it awkward for me, and you never have to see him again. And maybe he will be at least decent enough to break your two-year hiatus *and* get your mind off of Theo."

Nervously, I fidgeted with the edge of the blanket, pulling at a stray string and contemplating her argument. I really needed *something*. I needed a change to pull me out of my rut. And maybe a date with—

"What's his name?"

"Umm...Tanner."

Maybe a date with Tanner would at least be a good start.

"Theo is definitely a much hotter name than Tanner," she said, almost absent-mindedly, and I narrowed my eyes at her.

"Let me think about it."

"Sure, you go ahead and—"

Caroline's eyes were wider than I'd ever seen them and transfixed on something just behind me. Without looking, I knew what—or better yet, *who*—caught her attention.

I cursed under my breath and chanced a quick look over my shoulder. Apparently neither of us had heard the stairs creak as Theo descended them. Caroline only noticed him when he'd stepped into view and frozen mid-motion on the second to last step. I guess he hadn't heard us either, which was a relief given our topic of conversation.

His hair was still damp from the shower, and I swore I could smell his body wash even from several feet away. I silently chastised myself for wanting to investigate further, to bury my face in his neck to see if that's what I smelled and what it was exactly. My cheeks flamed at the thought.

Theo's attention bounced between me and Caroline, who still sat gobsmacked with her jaw slack.

"Didn't mean to interrupt," he said quietly, taking the final two steps down the stairs.

He didn't wait for a response from either of us before continuing into the kitchen and pulling open the freezer.

"Holy fucking shit balls," Caroline whispered. "I'm speech-less. Do you know how hard it is for me not to come up with words?! I always have something to say!"

She tried to reach for me, but I smacked her hand away. I grabbed my wine at the same time she called to Theo, "I'm Caroline, Nat's best friend, and you're *definitely* not interrupting anything."

I whipped my head toward her and gave her my most unim-pressed look, which she blatantly ignored. There was no missing her flirty tone or lilt to her voice.

"Oh, shit," Caroline muttered, quickly finishing off the one glass of wine she'd allowed herself. "Sorry, I have a meeting with potential clients in like an hour. I have to go." I mentally did the math on the odds of me being able to convince her to reschedule her meeting so she could be my new buffer.

But I already knew the answer: zero.

She jumped from the couch, toed on her shoes, and kissed my cheek before I even realized what was happening.

"I'll text you later, Nat," she said, but paused at the bottom of the stairs and watched Theo in the kitchen. She bit her lower lip, and her gaze lazily perused his body. "And I'm sure I'll see you soon, Theo."

Mortifying. My best friend was mortifying, and I was going to kill her for it.

The front door gently clicked closed behind her, and yet again I was faced with two options: talk to him or disappear upstairs into my room like the teenager he made me feel like.

I acted like it was a toss-up, but it wasn't, and my curiosity won out.

Standing, I hadn't realized how much the wine was affecting me until I felt my legs wobble underneath me. I steadied myself against the couch and finally walked into the kitchen.

Theo leaned back against the counter, staring at the floor and waiting for whatever he put in the microwave to finish warming. I noticed last night that he'd put a couple of frozen dinners in the freezer and a few drinks in the fridge. That was the extent of the groceries he'd purchased unless he was keeping snacks up in his room.

That thought kind of made me sad. I should have been doing more to make him feel welcome, but it was hard when my skin heated and my heart raced when I was near him.

Pushing away all other thoughts, I took a seat at one of the barstools and tucked my legs underneath me. I propped my elbows on the counter and said, "Heating up dinner?"

He tilted his head up, brown curls falling over his forehead as one side of his mouth curled slightly.

"Very perceptive."

I cocked my head yet smiled at his sarcasm. At least he'd responded.

"I was planning on cooking tonight..."

"I have to work," he said quickly and turned to fetch his meal from the microwave.

While he stirred it, I asked, "Where do you work?" I couldn't believe I hadn't asked that simple question yet.

"Haven City Tattoos."

"You're a tattoo artist?"

He replaced the meal in the microwave, tapped a few buttons, and then turned back to me. He again leaned back against the counter, arms crossed over his chest. He was wearing what I'd realized was his usual attire: black T-shirt, worn jeans, and black boots. It was like his uniform. I hadn't seen him in anything different since he moved in. Although I had no issue with it. It definitely worked for him.

He lifted his eyebrows as if to silently say, *"You don't believe me?"* I didn't mean to sound surprised, because I genuinely wasn't. I was intrigued.

I had to swallow before I responded. The challenge in his eyes stirred something within me that I couldn't tamp down even if I wanted to.

"I guess that explains all the ink then. Have you ever tattooed yourself?"

"Once or twice."

I nodded and readjusted my position on the barstool.

"So you probably work pretty late then," I inferred, and he only tilted his head slightly. "That must be hard with school."

The microwave beeped, and he pulled out the steaming meal. With measured steps, he crossed the kitchen to the trash can and disposed of the plastic film before walking back.

I *couldn't* stop watching him. Everything he was doing was so menial, yet I was wholly enchanted by the way he moved. His muscles flexed, and his attention stayed firm on each task at hand.

I especially enjoyed watching his hands. Beneath the tattoos, there were veins running the length of his hands, and his fingers were thick. But they were also steady and gentle and…

Stop staring at his hands, Natalie.

"I guess you pay for school yourself, then?" The words flew out in a rush before I could consider that maybe that topic was also off limits, just like the one about where he grew up. So, I continued speaking, trying desperately to backtrack and sound less judgmental and accusatory.

"I got an associate's degree, but that took me four years," I began, staring down at the butcher block counter and fidgeting with a piece of junk mail. "It's kind of challenging going to school and raising a toddler. My ex-husband got a bachelor's degree, and I stayed home while he did that. But I eventually got a job, and I have a great job now, so I guess it all worked out. However, I do think college is a really good idea if you can manage to go or if you want to go, because I know it's also not for everyone. I think I would have liked to go for all four years. I really like learning new things…"

My words finally trailed off when I realized I'd been rambling like a lunatic. I'd also folded the piece of paper in my hands over and over again until it was an eighth of its original size.

Theo was standing on the other side of the island, hands braced on the counter, and an amused smirk playing on the corners of his lips. It was the first whisper of a smile I'd seen from him.

My heart jumped into my throat at the playful light in his eyes that accompanied the small grin.

"Now I know where Ryder gets it from," he said in a voice that sounded like warm honey.

"What?" was all I could come up with. My brain was literal mush. I couldn't focus on much else besides the way his hands gripped the edge of the counter and how his eyes scanned every inch of my face.

"You talk a lot."

I flushed at the comment and fumbled for the right words, which was ironic since he was right and I couldn't shut up when I was nervous. Finally freeing my gaze from his, I looked up to the ceiling and chuckled. "Yeah, I kind of ramble when I'm nervous."

"I make you nervous." Not a question but a statement. I jerked my chin back down, once again meeting those intense brown eyes.

I didn't realize I'd been holding my breath until my lungs began to burn. And that was why my next words came out all breathy. At least, that's what I told myself. It had nothing to do with how I suddenly felt lightheaded under his attention.

"Kind of. You don't really say much, so…"

He took the last bite of his food and pushed the empty black tray to the side. Bracing his elbows on the counter, he leaned forward further, stretching the fabric of his T-shirt even tighter around his biceps.

I couldn't decide if I wanted to inch closer or try to put as much distance between us as I could. Actually, I knew what I *wanted* to do, and it was taking all my energy to refrain from doing it.

"The fact that I don't talk much makes you nervous?"

"Yes," I answered automatically, and his gaze immediately shifted to my lips. Unconsciously, I licked at them and then bit the lower one between my teeth. I watched him swallow like he had to force it down, and then his eyes shifted back to mine.

Maybe I'd been wrong before. Maybe the connection flaring alive between us hadn't all been in my head. I didn't know if that was worse, though. If we both felt it—whatever *it* was—we'd both have to ignore it. Especially if he felt it as intensely as I did.

It was easier to manage if it was one-sided. It was easier to pretend it didn't exist that way.

"Why?" he asked.

I shifted once again. "Because I don't know what you're thinking. Honestly, I couldn't even guess."

Something about my answer made him smile. But it wasn't a normal smile, it was a grin laced with a mischievous, conspiratorial edge. It made my hair stand on end.

"Trust me, Natalie."

I startled at my name on his lips, but he continued like he hadn't noticed my reaction.

"You don't want to know what I'm thinking."

And with that, he straightened and tossed the remnants of his dinner in the trash before he rounded the island. He headed upstairs without a glance back.

When I heard his bedroom door shut, I finally took a breath and relaxed back into the barstool. But I couldn't fully relax. I didn't think that was possible with Theo in the house or even with the knowledge that he was living there, too.

When he wasn't around, he still lingered.

And my heart rate refused to slow because I replayed his words over and over again.

"You don't want to know what I'm thinking."

Their meaning would have been ambiguous if not for the way he'd spoken them. His deep voice was earnest yet simmering with barely controlled restraint that was reflected in his eyes and the tense set of his jaw.

And it only made me want to know more. I wanted to know every single one of his thoughts, especially those he'd just been thinking. The ones he swore I didn't.

I wanted to know if they matched mine.

FOUR

A SKULL WEARING A COWBOY HAT
SMOKING A CIGARETTE

Theo

THERE WAS THE FAINT HUM OF CONVERSATION AND THE BUZZ OF guns throughout the studio, but it was still relatively quiet for a Friday night. I had an appointment later, and it would likely pick up after ten, but until then, I was sitting up front, staring out the windows at the street beyond.

Cars passed beneath the street lights, and every once in a while, a few people walked by on their way to or from the bus stop a street over. I tried to focus on those people—I tried to think about what they were doing or where they were going. I tried to think about *anything* else. But it wasn't working.

I'd already cleaned my room—which was located in the back corner of the studio—and mindlessly scrolled through social media that I rarely used for anything besides showing off my latest work.

I'd even offered to help everyone else with anything they needed in an attempt to keep my mind occupied and off the one fucking person who had begun tormenting me day and night.

It'd been a little less than a week since our run-in in the

kitchen. We'd spoken briefly in passing since then, but that was the extent of our interactions.

She'd told me I made her nervous, and *god*, I wish she hadn't.

I loved that I made her nervous. She squirmed under my attention, and the blush that stained her cheeks was the same shade as her lips. Plush lips that she had a tendency to bite and lick when she was nervous, too. Even during our brief interactions, I'd been able to learn that much.

She had these cute little ticks, like the lip biting, that were hard to miss once I'd finally noticed them. She tucked her long, black hair behind her right ear again and again and rambled like she had an endless amount of words and thoughts.

Her deep blue eyes flitted here and there, refusing to stay on mine anytime she was feeling apprehensive.

She was confident yet coy. She carried herself like a woman who knew what she wanted and how she'd get it, yet there were moments where she seemed thrown off and unsure.

The contrast was captivating.

I imagined that the confident woman was who most people saw. I liked to think that I was the only one who was able to make her unsteady enough to reveal the rest.

And that was the exact thinking that was going to get me in trouble. I already craved her little reactions, knowing I could easily pull them from her if I wanted to. It was taking all my self-control not to do it, which was why I decided to keep my distance altogether.

But keeping my distance didn't prevent me from remembering her sitting at the kitchen island with her elbows braced on the butcher block counter and her tits inadvertently pushed together. No matter how hard I tried, I remembered every single breath, expression, and movement she made.

How much I wanted to talk to her was honestly the most unsettling part. The fact that I didn't say much made most people nervous, and I was usually content to sit in silence. There weren't many people I'd met that said anything worth responding to. Ryder had been an exception, and so had my boss, Robbie. But Natalie…she was an exception all her own.

She didn't have much of an issue carrying on a conversation with herself if necessary, but unlike most people, I wanted to respond. I wanted to hold a conversation with her and answer her questions. I wanted to hear all of her thoughts. Maybe she'd be content in the silence, too, but I didn't feel like silence was the only option.

And knowing that made *me* nervous.

As I began spiraling further into my thoughts, Robbie stepped out of his room with Cam right behind him.

"Just normal aftercare. You know the drill," Robbie instructed, and Cam nodded.

"Hey, Cam. What'd you get?"

They donned a large smile and stuck out their arm. Robbie had really knocked it out of the park. On their forearm was a black widow spider that was realistic enough to make me a little apprehensive. The shading was perfect, and the shadow underneath it made it appear like the spider was sitting on top of their arm.

"That's seriously insane. You've got some of the coolest ink," I said, and Cam smiled wider.

"You're fucking telling me," they said.

Cam was covered in ink and only wanted more. They came in at least every month or two for something new. They'd even given me some new ideas to add to my legs and stomach—the only two places where I had any substantial amount of skin left to cover.

Cam waved and said their goodbyes before heading out the door.

The bell above it chimed, and Robbie looked at me.

"What are you doing up here?" the big guy asked. Robbie was a large man covered in ink he'd collected over his fifty-five years. He was the owner of Haven City Tattoos and the only person to take a chance on a stupid seventeen-year-old kid with nowhere to go.

Thanks to Robbie I only had to live in my car for about a month. After I got kicked out of the house I'd been squatting in, I parked in random lots with little to no foot traffic. Then I got arrested again for sleeping in my car. Similar circumstances and the same asshole officer. Without another option, I found a new spot in another random lot. It had been a total coincidence that I'd picked the lot behind the studio. He'd spotted my truck after he'd closed up and found me sleeping in the backseat, freezing my ass off. He banged on my window, scaring the shit out of me and waking me up out of a restless sleep. When I'd finally rolled down the window, he told me to follow him down the street, or he was calling the cops.

Terrified of going to jail, I did as he asked. I followed him to his apartment and put up a hell of a fight when he offered to let me stay. Not long after, he offered me a job as his apprentice. He got one look at my notebook filled with sketches and drawings and told me that he wouldn't let my talent be wasted.

After we negotiated rent that barely even covered his monthly utility bill, I ended up staying with him until I went to college at twenty. I had been working for him ever since.

When shit hit the fan with my roommate this time around, I'd contemplated asking Robbie to let me stay again, but I couldn't. His daughter was living in my old room, and he'd already done more than enough for me.

That was how I'd ended up living with Natalie.

And just like that, I was thinking about her again.

Fuck me.

"Waiting for my next appointment," I finally said to Robbie, who was tapping away on his phone.

"Somebody new or..." he said, only looking up long enough to glance at me with a knowing smile.

I rolled my eyes and flipped him off rather than answer him. He had the same reaction every time she came into the studio.

He chuckled and patted me on the shoulder. "Just don't get caught again. I'm heading out. See you tomorrow."

Robbie quickly grabbed his stuff from his room and pushed through the front door at the same moment Ava walked in.

"Hey, Robbie," Ava said, batting her eyelashes in faux flirtation. She loved trying to get a rise out of my boss, and it was fun to watch her try.

He shook his head and hollered, "Be good, kids," before the door shut.

Ava didn't let the lack of response affect her, instead, she continued toward where I sat behind the counter.

"Ready?" she asked with a smile.

I nodded and followed her as she led the way back into my room. Half of her blonde and pink hair was in two twin buns on top of her head, and I watched them bounce as she hurried down the hallway.

Her black skirt twirled around her thighs and showed off the fresh ink we'd finished on her calf only a month before. If Ava wasn't in my chair at least once every month or two, something was seriously wrong.

That's how I'd met her—she'd walked in two years ago for a piece on her upper thigh, and she'd kept coming back. And after a few appointments, she'd made it obvious she was interested in more than just new ink.

We started fucking that night, agreeing that it would never be more than a hook-up. The agreement had worked out flawlessly and had been just what I needed. We almost always ended up messing around in the back of her car or my own after her session—hence Robbie's warning not to get caught again—and I doubted tonight would be any different.

I wasn't delusional enough to think it would completely cure my hang-up on Natalie, but it would be good enough to at least take the edge off and keep my mind focused on someone else for a while.

I turned the corner to find Ava already whipping her white T-shirt over her head and eyeing the bare spot on her inner arm where she wanted the art.

"A skull wearing a cowboy hat smoking a cigarette, huh?" I asked, and she shrugged.

Whirling around and plopping down on the chair, she draped her arm over the armrest and smiled. "I thought it was fun, and the design you came up with is too fucking cute."

"Yes," I said, prepping the area and laying down the stencil. "Because that's how I want everyone to react when they see my artwork."

She rolled her eyes and tried to reach over and smack me. I darted out of the way before prompting her to double-check my placement in the mirror.

She leaned over, looked at it quickly, and then laid back down.

"Looks good. And as long as I like it, that's all that should matter."

I was mostly kidding because I did agree with her—as long as the person in my chair was happy, then I couldn't complain. Besides, I did enough big, badass pieces that a cute little skull in a cowboy hat wasn't going to hurt my reputation.

We fell into our normal routine, her talking my ear off about her life since we last saw one another while I silently got to work. The familiar hum and vibration of the gun was cathartic. It lulled something in me and quieted my racing thoughts. All that mattered in those moments was the permanent art I was inking on my client's skin.

When I was so wholly focused on my task and the buzz of the gun, it was easy to shut out the world. It also kept out the darkness that liked to descend upon me whenever it felt like it.

Less than an hour later, I was done, wiping the area clean and applying the bandage after she inspected it in the mirror and squealed with excitement at the finished product.

While I cleaned and straightened my area for an early start the next day, Ava lingered in the doorway. Her fingers were flying quickly over her phone screen as I closed the last drawer and turned off the additional lamp in the corner of the room.

She shoved her phone into her purse and looked up at me with a small smile. She hiked her thumb over her shoulder, and without words, I knew what she was silently asking.

Yet I hesitated. It was only for a moment, but I'd still thought about telling her no.

That one moment of hesitation was more telling than I wanted it to be. I couldn't remember the last time I considered telling Ava no.

Quickly, I shook off the moment's hesitation and gave her a shallow nod instead.

Shoving down any remnants of that uncertainty, I followed her out the back of the studio and across to her car, where she'd parked at the back of the lot. We were the only business still open, and there weren't any lights that far back, so we couldn't be seen. I contemplated telling her that we should go back to her place, but she had a weird ass roommate who had apparently walked in on her one too many times.

A hotel also wasn't a possibility because I still could barely afford food.

I gritted my teeth against the thought of taking Ava back to Natalie's house. The thought was thankfully fleeting, but it made me move faster toward the car all the same.

Ava drove an old Toyota 4Runner, so there was plenty of room in the backseat. Gripping her upper arm, I tugged her along quicker. Her boots clicked faster against the asphalt, and she didn't argue.

I swung open the backdoor, and she immediately hopped in, tossing her purse up to the front passenger seat and settling with her back against the door across from me. Although the backseat was bigger than some, I couldn't jump in as she had. But as quickly as I could, I slid onto the seat and locked the door behind me.

Ava didn't delay, the moment I turned back to her, she was

on top of me. Her legs straddled mine, and her hands clasped my face. Her mouth was on mine in another second, and she groaned as our tongues tangled. Reflexively, my hands found her hips and guided her to grind against me.

Then a thought, like a blinding flash of light, stalled my movements.

For a split second, it was Natalie, not Ava, whose hands were running down my chest and slipping beneath my T-shirt. It was Natalie's long, dark hair my fingers were threading through, gripping and pulling for easier access to her mouth. It was Natalie who was eagerly grinding down on me and searching for some sort of friction and release.

And it was the thought of Natalie, imagining her under my hands, that lit a fire inside of me and made my cock harden beneath her.

She felt so good. Natalie felt *so good*. She was—

Fuck. My eyes popped open, and I reared back. But Ava didn't catch the movement, she just diverted her lips from my mouth to my neck as I tried to remain in the moment.

I looked down at her and focused on the woman on top of me. Her hands were soft and urgent. Her mouth was warm and eager. It all felt good, but for some reason, I couldn't do it. My hands went limp, and I opened my mouth to say something, but she beat me to it.

"I already know it's not me that's the issue, so what the hell is going on?"

I groaned and scrubbed my hands over my face. I couldn't even make it one fucking minute without thinking of Natalie.

"My head is just all over the place." My voice was muffled behind my hands, but when I dropped them, her gaze was assessing and unrelenting.

"Ha!" she scoffed and peered at me incredulously. "All over the place or on someone else?" she asked, and I froze.

"Who is she?"

"Fuck, Ava. I'm sorry," I said as she shook her head and slid off my lap.

"No, don't be sorry. The fact that we've been doing this for two years and this hasn't happened before is already crazy. But you've gotta tell me what her deal is since whatever it is has you so messed up you can't even get it up for me."

She motioned to my mostly soft dick, and I let my head fall back against the headrest. The car's ceiling was more intriguing than her stare. Knowing how preoccupied my thoughts were, I should've never even gotten in the car. The hope I'd been feeling leading up to that moment was delusion.

My head was so fucked.

"It's nothing."

She choked out a disbelieving laugh. "Bullshit. Tell me."

I rolled my head to the side and gave her my most annoyed expression. "I can't explain it to you when I barely understand it myself."

"Oh," she said, the surprise evident in her voice.

"Oh?"

She hid her smile behind her hand and folded her legs underneath her.

"Yeah, *oh*. So it's definitely something big."

I shifted on my seat and contemplated leaping out of the car to escape her scrutiny and the vulnerability she was expecting. I hated that feeling, like someone was seeing more of me than I wanted them to.

"It's nothing," I repeated through clenched teeth.

She gave me another disbelieving look and shook her head. "And let me guess, you're not going to do anything about it."

I scoffed, which was all the response she needed to know my answer.

"Well, Theo, if the feelings are that intense, they're likely not going to go away, but whatever," she said and shoved at my shoulder. "Now, if you're not going to fuck me, get the hell out of my car."

She continued shoving me while I fumbled for the door handle and stumbled from her car into the warm night air. Ava climbed out behind me and straightened her top and skirt.

Suddenly, I felt bad for the way everything went down, and I stopped her before she could open the driver's side door.

"Ava, I'm—I'm sorry," I said. She smiled and patted my arm.

"No big deal, Theo. Maybe after you figure out your head we can pick up where we left off."

I didn't respond as she climbed back into her car, drove across the lot, and disappeared around the building. I didn't say anything because, as usual, I didn't really have anything to add. But I also didn't want to tell her that getting my mind straight was likely going to be impossible.

Short of making good on all the dirty and devious thoughts, I didn't know what else to do.

And I couldn't do that. I couldn't touch her.

I repeated that to myself as I walked back inside.

Keep your thoughts, and your hands, to yourself.

FIVE
FLYING DEMONS

Natalie

I SAT IN MY CAR FOR ABOUT TWENTY MINUTES, MUSIC PLAYING quietly in the background while my eyes flicked between the front door and Theo's black truck parked beside me before I finally decided to go inside the house.

I hopped out of my car and waved to our neighbor, Ms. Morris, who was checking her mail and staring over my head at Theo's truck. Better yet, she was glaring daggers at the truck like it had personally offended her.

"Natalie, is that boy behavin'?"

I plastered a fake, cordial smile on my face. Ms. Morris was lonely, so I tried to give her the benefit of the doubt. Her son had moved out years ago, and her husband was rarely home. Neighborhood gossip, it seemed, was the only thing she had left to look forward to.

I just didn't like being the topic.

"Yes, Ms. Morris."

She pursed her lips and narrowed her eyes like the truck was a symbol for Theo's delinquency.

"Well, you let me know if you need anything."

And the way she said that was like she expected me to be banging down her door sooner rather than later. Instead of snapping at the judgmental broad, I hurried into the house and quickly closed the door behind me.

I loved my house. I took a deep breath when I was finally inside, and a sense of calm washed over me. My house was great, but some of my neighbors were assholes. Nosy assholes who were too curious about Ryder leaving and Theo staying.

I leaned back against the closed front door and banged my head against it like it would dislodge the Theo-filled thoughts.

But of course, it didn't. I walked further into the house and dropped my purse and laptop bag onto one of the barstools at the kitchen island. Two seconds later, I kicked my heels off, scooped them up, and headed up the stairs.

Halfway up, I paused momentarily to glance down at my phone. Ryder had responded to my earlier message, asking how he was doing. We'd talked a few times since he'd left, but they'd only been short conversations touching on the high points. He was busy, and I didn't want to bother him too much.

> Ryder: Everything's great! Working on a big project. Tell you about it soon.

I smiled and told him I couldn't wait to hear about it before continuing upstairs.

Theo's room, previously our guest bedroom, was the first door on the right. My steps slowed as I approached. The door was closed—as it usually was—and I didn't hear any sounds or movement emanating from the other side.

After almost two weeks of living together, we'd both learned each other's schedules fairly well. It was Friday night, which meant he'd had class that morning and was likely getting ready for work.

We didn't see much of each other since I worked while he

was at school, and he worked several nights a week, usually from six-ish to well past midnight.

Which meant we also hadn't spent much time together. There was the occasional "hi" or "bye" as we passed each other, but that was the extent of our interactions. And I was still more curious than I should've been about him.

Rather than stand outside of his door like a fucking weirdo, I continued to my room at the end of the hall. Closing the door, all I could think about was washing the week off. We'd hired three new attorneys and a new legal secretary, which meant my week was filled with onboarding and training and paperwork and utter chaos.

Thinking about stepping under the warm water and letting the lingering tension and stress wash down the drain made it my top priority. I tossed my heels into the closet and clumsily stepped out of my clothes, leaving them in a messy trail between my closet and the shower. I pulled open the glass door and turned the water on until the handle was pointing all the way to the left, and the water was bound to singe my skin when I stepped in.

I let it warm for a minute or two and dimmed the lights slightly. It was one of my favorite rooms of the house. I'd hand-picked the dark gray, nearly black tile that covered the shower floor and ran up the walls. I'd also refused to waver on the rainfall showerhead we'd installed and the dimmable lights.

It was the perfect place and as close as I would ever come to having a spa retreat in my own home.

Grabbing a clean towel from the closet, I hung it on the hook affixed to the glass and stepped inside.

Only to be dive-bombed by the largest flying insect I'd ever seen.

I was screaming before I even fully understood what was happening. Suddenly I realized it wasn't just any insect, but a giant fucking roach that had targeted me and landed directly on my chest.

A secondary scream burst from my lips as I flailed, my hands frantically beating against my chest to remove the giant creature. In my attempt to brush it away, I tumbled backward, hands flying out, aimlessly reaching for something to stop my fall. The only thing I was able to grab onto was my towel, which was no help and ended up falling on top of me as my ass and back hit the tile with a resounding thud.

I bit my lip to keep from crying out in pain but quickly remembered the reason I'd fallen in the first place. Pain be damned, I gripped the towel around myself and scooted as far as I could away from the shower, scanning the floor the entire time for the stupid asshole bug.

"What the—"

The voice drew my attention from the shower to my bathroom door. Theo was standing in the doorway, his face contorted in shock and concern.

My cheeks immediately heated with embarrassment as I gaped up at him. I'd screamed, so logically, he'd come running.

"There was—there was a roach."

The words left my mouth, and in an instant, his worry morphed into humor. The corners of his mouth tilted upward, and I appreciated that he at least rolled his lips to keep the impending smile at bay.

"All of this over a roach?" he asked, stepping farther into the bathroom and peering into the shower. The flying demon was scuttling across the ground near the rug, and as I frantically looked for any sort of weapon, Theo stepped on it.

He cut his eyes to me for a moment before he grabbed two tissues from the counter and scooped the crushed remnants. He crossed the small space to the toilet and unceremoniously flushed it.

Good riddance, motherfucker.

"It landed on me," I said when he reappeared a second later. Did I love cockroaches or any insect that unsuspectingly flew at me? Absolutely the hell not. I didn't think anyone really did, and therefore my reaction was completely understandable. For some reason, I really wanted him to know that, if only to eliminate some of my embarrassment.

"It landed on you?"

I nodded and tried to stand while carefully keeping the towel covering all my important bits.

Theo averted his eyes as I stood, but he did so slowly. He stepped back toward the door, stuffing his tattooed hands in his front pockets, as I secured the towel around my middle.

When I turned back around to face him, I immediately realized how close we were. We were only a few feet apart in the small space, and I was nearly naked.

"Yes," I finally said, my voice wavering slightly. "It attacked me."

He again tried to stifle his smile, and I felt like I was in high school again, feeling the flush on my cheeks spread down my chest.

"Hence the screaming," he said, and all I could do was roll my eyes.

"Thank you for killing the stupid thing, but if you're going to chastise me, then you can leave."

One of his eyebrows lifted, and his playful, amused expression morphed into something a little darker. And suddenly I was flushing for an entirely different reason.

"What are you saying, Natalie? I could stay otherwise?"

I froze and turned his words over in my mind a few times before I was able to breathe again. His light brown eyes were expectant and steadfast on me, considering my reaction with intense scrutiny.

No matter how long I stood there, gaping like a fish out of water, I wouldn't have come up with a decent response. I felt like I was glitching. Like his presence was short-circuiting my brain.

Finally, he took pity on me and turned to leave. But before he could completely close the door behind him, I said, "Thank you, Theo."

He paused, hand gripping the doorknob so tightly his knuckles were white. He didn't move his head, but his eyes bounced back to me for a second, like he was reconsidering leaving at all. But his second of hesitation was only that—a second of contemplation before he closed the door.

I heard my bedroom door close as well over the sound of the shower feet away.

Immediately, I hung the towel back on the hook, scanned for any other little creatures, and stepped under the hot water quickly steaming up the bathroom.

It wasn't nearly as soothing as I'd hoped it would be. The entire interaction was wholly unsettling, and I could still feel Theo's gaze, like a lingering sensation that was vibrating over my skin.

The water was doing nothing to make it disappear. I honestly didn't think anything would.

I cut my shower short by at least twenty minutes. All I thought about while I was standing under the spray was what would have happened had I told Theo he could have stayed.

That's what I'd wanted to say. The curiosity clawing at the back of my mind whenever I thought about him urged me to push, but those were also the type of thoughts that were guaranteed to get us in a shitload of trouble.

I so badly wished Caroline hadn't ditched me that evening. I was supposed to be cooking for the both of us, but one of her favorite guys she only saw every few months called and let her know he was in town for the night. One night meant our dinner would have to wait.

Before heading downstairs, I threw on my favorite pair of sweats—that were worn and far past their prime—and a long-sleeved T-shirt. I'd planned to make myself a drink, cook one of my favorite meals, and try to put any thoughts of Theo completely out of my mind.

But my plan was immediately abandoned when I walked downstairs to find Theo standing in the middle of the kitchen.

He was staring down into the freezer drawer, likely contemplating which frozen meal he'd prepare that night.

I continued down the stairs, hitting the third stair that always squeaked slightly and drawing Theo's intense stare from the freezer up to me.

I blew out a breath and cleared my throat before I said, "I was going to cook tonight if you want to eat with me instead of eating…" I pointed to the open freezer door.

Rounding the kitchen island from the other direction, so I didn't have to pass him, I grabbed the whiskey and aperol from the bar cart near the kitchen table.

"Is bourbon the main course, or are we skipping straight to dessert?"

I slid both bottles onto the island and considered how it looked, pulling two bottles of liquor out after stating that I was cooking. After the long week I had, it honestly wasn't outside the realm of possibility.

He closed the freezer and turned to assess me, crossing his arms and leaning a hip against the counter.

"It's the appetizer," I volleyed back. I pulled two glasses from the cabinet and set them next to the liquor. With a brow raised, I looked back up at him in silent question.

One side of his mouth tilted upward, and I took that to mean he wanted one too.

He slid into one of the barstools on the other side of the island as I set to making the cocktail. With Theo watching me closely, I fumbled through making the drink more than I normally would have but finally managed to pour it from the shaker into the two glass tumblers.

I tapped my phone and connected to the Bluetooth speaker in the kitchen at the same time Theo took his first sip. Eyes still locked on me over the top of the glass, he pressed it against his lips and tilted it back.

The music filtered through the air and filled at least parts of the silence.

An unreadable expression passed over Theo's face, somewhere between a smile and a grimace. I sipped my own drink wondering if I'd done something to mess it up, but the orange and lime flavors burst on my tongue, followed by the savory, smokiness of the bourbon.

"Do you not like it?" I finally asked.

He leaned back and tapped a tattooed finger against the glass as he shook his head. "I love it...and this song," he said, and I smiled. He returned my smile with a small one of his own, and I was thankful that some of the tension dissipated with it.

Ignoring the way even his small smile sent butterflies fluttering in my stomach, I started collecting ingredients from the fridge. It took more effort than I hoped it would to ignore the giddy anticipation when it was the first time I'd felt that way in...forever. I couldn't even remember the last time I felt half of what Theo made me feel with a simple compliment and a small smile.

"I was going to make chicken parmesan," I said casually over my shoulder as I pivoted and opened the cabinet to my left.

After considering which bowls I needed, I stretched up onto my toes and reached as far as I could. My fingers still barely grazed the edge of the porcelain, and rather than risk breaking the dish, I dropped back down flat on my feet and braced my hands on the counter, preparing to jump up on it.

When I was too lazy to grab the step stool I kept tucked in the hall closet, I boosted myself onto the counter and retrieved what I needed. Which happened more often than not.

The granite was cool beneath my fingers, but as I began to press up, bracing myself to hop onto it, a warmth blanketed me from behind. I sucked in a sharp breath and stilled as Theo stepped up behind me. He easily reached up into the cabinet and grabbed all three bowls.

He kept some distance between us. His chest was the only part of him that brushed against me as he took the bowls in hand, but I could still feel the warmth and enormity of his body.

It seeped into me like he'd wrapped his arms around me and pulled me into his chest.

As quickly as he appeared, he was gone, and I shivered at his absence.

"Thanks," I murmured, trying to hide my reaction.

He'd set the three bowls next to each other on the island and began sifting flour in the first one.

My eyebrows nearly hit my hairline at his initiative. He glanced up in time to catch my expression and shrugged as he continued to the second bowl, where he cracked an egg.

"Are you surprised I can cook?"

"No," I responded quickly. But he cocked a dark brow at my rushed answer.

Immediately I turned my attention to…anything else. I needed some sort of distraction from him. My kitchen wasn't necessarily small, but Theo seemed to take up any of the free space.

I set the chicken on the counter and started working on the pasta and the sauce. We cooked in companionable silence for several minutes. He dredged the chicken in the flour, then the eggs, and finally in the breadcrumb and parmesan mixture he'd mixed up and I'd seasoned.

Every once in a while he'd ask me where specific utensils were, but I was surprised he knew where almost everything else was. We easily moved around and with one another. Never once did it feel awkward or strange.

As it had been since he moved in, it took more effort than I liked not to watch him work.

"Do you have to work tonight?" I finally asked. We were only halfway through cooking, and it was already later than he usually left.

"Later," he said, standing next to me at the stove. I stirred the pasta as he tossed a breaded chicken breast into the hot pan.

"How are your classes?"

He cut his eyes at me as he grabbed the tongs from the

holder. Whether he liked it or not, I was determined to learn more about him. I wanted to get him talking.

"They're good."

"What are you studying?" I asked, hoping that the question would lead to more than a one- or two-word answer.

"Business."

Well, that backfired, but I also couldn't hide my surprise at his answer. That was the last thing I expected him to say, and I was considering a follow-up question when he commented on the expression I couldn't manage to keep hidden.

"That's surprising, too?"

"Yes, I expected you to say something like—"

"Art?"

"Yes!"

He chuckled, and I smiled, turning my focus back to the pasta instead of appraising the black tattoos running up the length of his neck.

"I umm…" he trailed off, his eyes going distant. For several seconds, he stared at the digital clock on the oven, but I could tell he wasn't invested in the time. There were a million other thoughts plaguing him. I could almost see the memories flitting behind his eyes.

"My boss, Robbie, wants me to take over the studio after I graduate or soon thereafter."

"So you're studying business to take over the business?"

He nodded and flipped the chicken, which was perfectly crispy.

"And you enjoy it?"

He choked out a humorless laugh and shook his head. "I don't, but it's going to get me where I want to be, so that's all that matters."

That concept I understood better than most people. When I was only a teenager, I had to consider how to end up where I wanted to be. I was a teenager with a toddler, so all I could manage was an associate's degree that took me four years of night classes to complete, but it allowed me to apply for the jobs I really wanted.

Maybe it hadn't been totally necessary looking back, but at the time, it felt like the only possibility.

"So, you really love tattooing?"

I already expected his answer, but what I didn't expect was the earnestness with which he spoke or the seriousness in his expression.

"More than almost anything."

"What do you love about it?"

He was quiet for a few seconds, moving the cooked chicken to a clean plate and replacing it with another piece in the pan.

"I like the creative aspect. It's also insane that people trust me enough to ink something permanent on their skin. But when I'm tattooing…it's easy to let everything go. When the gun is in my hand, nothing else exists."

I liked listening to him talk about it. There was a reverence in his voice that I hadn't expected. It was also the most I'd ever heard him speak. The most words he'd strung together.

I swallowed around thick emotion clogging my throat and traced the sharpness of his jaw with my eyes. My fingers itched to reach out and run my hand against the dark stubble dusting his chin as his eyes found mine.

Clearing my throat, I turned the burner off, removed the pot from the heat, and drained the pasta into the colander in the sink.

"What do you do at the law firm?" Theo asked.

"I pretty much run the place, make sure it doesn't burn down, that kind of thing."

"Sounds important," he commented, and I couldn't help but laugh.

When I turned back around, Theo was smiling, like *actually* smiling at me, and my heart collided with the inside of my chest. Then his eyes swept down my body, and an entirely different feeling washed over me. I was self-conscious under his attention, but I was frozen in place.

I didn't think I was unattractive by any means, but fresh out of the shower, my hair still damp and wearing a pair of threadbare sweats, I also wasn't anything to look at. But you wouldn't have known with the way Theo's attention lingered over me.

Our gazes collided. His eyes were brimmed with something that towed the nearly invisible line of friendly and *more*. And all his unwavering, undivided attention settled between my thighs.

It was all I could do not to press them together and relieve some of the incessant pulse.

The desire startled me enough that I broke our connection and turned on the water to rinse the pasta. I wish I could've splashed some on my face without looking like I'd lost my mind more than I already had.

"I guess you could say it's important. I know the place definitely wouldn't run right without me," I said.

"How long have you worked there?" he asked, turning back to the chicken and adding a new piece to the pan.

"Umm..." I muttered. It had been so long I had a hard time doing the mental math. "Fifteen years?"

"You're dedicated."

I chuckled but shook my head. "I guess so. They were really flexible when Ryder was younger. I could take off however much time I wanted and as often as I needed to. And the company's still really great so that's hard to leave."

He nodded thoughtfully and plated the last piece of chicken on the platter.

I stepped around him to stir the sauce one more time and remove it from the burner.

"But you don't enjoy it anymore?" Theo asked as I grabbed two shallow bowls from the cabinet.

"No, I do, but it's also all I've ever known. Maybe I'll do something else eventually, but I'm not sure."

We both made our plates and sat down at the island. We each took a bite, and it was even better than the last time I made it.

I caught him looking at me out of the corner of my eye and peered over to find him staring at me with a slight curve to his lips.

"What?" I asked around a mouthful of chicken.

"You were dancing," he said, taking a sip of his drink and twirling the pasta around his fork. "Do you do that often?"

"Dance when I eat?" I hadn't even realized I was doing it until he pointed it out.

He nodded.

"Sometimes."

His eyes lingered on my face for another second before he turned back to his plate.

"This is amazing," he muttered between bites.

"It is really good. We did well," I said with a smile. "So, you're studying business and you're a talented tattoo artist. What else should I know about you?"

He narrowed his eyes in my direction and sat back in his stool. His large body made the chair beneath him appear so much smaller than it really was. "How would you know if I'm talented?"

"I don't think your boss would want you to take over his business if he didn't think you were talented."

He considered it for a moment and ran his finger around the rim of his half-filled glass.

"There's not much else to know," he said, and I gave a derisive snort. It wasn't very flattering, but I couldn't help it.

"You don't believe me?"

I shook my head. "No, not at all."

He took another bite and then took a deep breath, followed by a sip of his drink. "There's nothing you'd probably want to know."

It was on the tip of my tongue to tell him he was completely wrong, that I wanted to know everything, but I didn't. Instead, I tried to lighten the mood with the first question that came to mind.

"What's your favorite color?" I asked, and before he could answer, and while he was looking at me like I'd asked something completely abnormal, I said, "Let me guess: black."

He chuckled and peered around the room. "And let me guess, yours is green."

I also glanced around and noted all the pops of green I'd recently added. "Lucky guess. Favorite type of food?"

"Mexican. You?"

"Mediterranean."

"I don't think I've ever had it."

I dropped my fork and gaped at him. "Okay, well, we'll fix that. Favorite genre of music?"

He considered me for a moment, licking his lower lip and tucking it between his teeth. He leaned forward slightly, and our knees inadvertently brushed. The small, innocent touch was enough to send a burst of desire down my spine and twisting through my arms and legs.

The sensation made me lightheaded, and all I wanted was for him to touch me again. Not accidentally, but with purpose and promise. Because he wanted to know what I felt like under his fingers.

"This," he said, and it took me a second to remember what I'd asked. He pointed to where the Bluetooth speaker sat on the counter, and I furrowed my brow.

"Nineties or rock?"

He nodded and with a small smile, stated plainly, "Both. Any kind of rock, though, and from any decade, really."

"Well, I guess that's good that we both have the same taste in music," I said, and quickly added, "since you know, we live in the same house right now. That would really suck if either of us was playing music that the other didn't like. That could be…annoying."

He smiled like my babbling was entertaining, and I rolled my eyes, eating the last bite of my food and pushing the plate away.

Theo was out of his barstool in the next second, grabbing both of our empty plates and loading them into the dishwasher.

"Oh, you don't have to—" I tried to say, but he waved me off, loading the rest of the pots and pans we'd used into the dishwasher as well.

He worked quickly, and while he did, I made myself another drink and asked him more pointless questions like what his favorite animal was and his favorite sport.

"Golf?" I questioned, gobsmacked, as he started the dishwasher cycle and closed it. He wiped his hands on the towel and turned to me, leaning back against the counter and appearing much more at ease than he was an hour earlier.

"Golf cannot be your second favorite sport."

He shrugged and tossed the towel onto the counter.

"I guess it doesn't require much talking, and you're supposed to be quiet, so for those reasons, it makes sense," I said, and he shook his head.

"Did you play golf?" I asked.

His smile fell, and I immediately wanted to retract the question, but instead of withdrawing as I suspected he would, Theo sighed and crossed his arms over his chest.

"When I was younger, my dad and I would go all the time. He'd take me and my older brother at least every few weeks, so I got pretty good. He even put me in lessons for a while. But I haven't been in several years."

Just that short answer—well, short for the average person—included so much more information. He had an older brother and, at one time, had a close enough relationship with his dad that they did things like play a round of golf.

But I noted the way he forced the word "dad" out like it was hard for him to say.

He cleared his throat and stepped forward to where I was leaning against the island. Two steps and he was in front of me, close enough that the knuckles of my hand gripping my drink grazed the fabric of his black shirt.

We were so close I could smell his clean masculine scent and see the ring of yellow surrounding his pupil. His amber eyes were steadfast on mine, and I had to tilt my head back to maintain eye contact. Maybe I imagined it or only saw what I wanted to, but when his lids lowered, there was a hunger churning in his gaze.

In my peripheral, I saw him reach out, and I stuttered a breath. His fingers brushed against my arm, and against my will, my eyelids fluttered slightly.

But then I heard his keys sliding against the counter, and he quickly stepped back. He twirled them around his fingers but didn't release my stare.

"Thank you for dinner, Natalie," he said, his voice lower than it had any right to be.

"You're welcome," I said automatically, but it was breathy, and when he smiled, I knew he heard it too.

He turned to walk away, and that was when my eyes caught on his keys and the dark pink keychain that was hard to miss. He hadn't yet gotten rid of it, the keychain with my name on it. The one that had been on the keys when I'd given them to him. He'd added the two house keys to his car keys and hadn't removed the keychain.

A strange mix of emotions tumbled through me. Maybe he just hadn't had the chance, I reasoned. It wasn't high on his priority list. Maybe he'd forgotten. He'd been in a rush to add the keys or something like that.

His boots softly thudded against the wood floor, and when the door closed and the lock clicked, I finally released a breath. Hurriedly, I found my phone and texted Caroline immediately.

Me: You think Tanner's free tomorrow?

Since our first conversation, Caroline had asked me nearly

every other day if I was ready for her to set me up. I was so vehemently against it that I even downloaded one—or all—of the dating apps to try to find my own date.

I knew I wasn't ready for that, though. Two seconds into trying to create my profile, I completely gave up.

But spending time with Theo had been the motivation I needed. As was the needy pulse between my legs he'd left me with.

Caroline responded immediately.

> Caroline: Okay, so don't be mad, but I already told him you were free tomorrow. Actually, you can't be mad because now you want to go out with him! I was just tired of you blowing me off.

> Caroline: I'll send you the details later. After I've been fucked within an inch of my life.

I should have been more surprised that my best friend took it upon herself to set me up when I told her not to. But I wasn't. It was how Caroline showed her love.

> Me: I'm so happy for you.

I added the middle finger emoji and hit send. Two seconds later, she sent back the same emoji with a kissy face.

I groaned into the empty house, crossed my arms over the counter, and laid my head on top of them. It was insane, the turn of events that had gotten me to that point. I hoped the date wasn't a complete dud, but I also didn't have high hopes that it would lead to anything more.

When you didn't get your hopes up, it was harder to be let down in the end.

I knew it wasn't the healthiest way to live life, but it was easier to protect myself that way. No expectations meant no reason to get upset. Caroline called me guarded, but I considered myself cautious.

Except with Theo. There was something about him that made me want to throw that all away. He made me not want to consider what other people thought or how I might get hurt. Even more reason I needed to go on the date. I needed to pivot my thoughts.

I groaned again and began making another drink.

Maybe the bourbon would douse my desire. Then again, maybe it would ignite it and burn us all down along the way.

SIX

NO NICE GUYS

Theo

WHEN IT CAME TO NATALIE, WHAT LITTLE SELF-CONTROL I STILL maintained was holding on by the thinnest of threads. The night before had been a form of cruel and unusual punishment.

The way she screamed, I was terrified I'd run into her bedroom to find her laying bloody on the ground. I was thankful that hadn't happened, but knowing only a thin towel kept me from finally seeing every inch of her was nearly enough to make me waver.

Then I'd been stupid enough to stick around and cook dinner with her. But I couldn't tell her no. The thought hadn't crossed my mind. It hadn't even been a possibility. I *wanted* to spend time with her.

And had I not gotten out of there when I did, the night was guaranteed to end completely differently. Likely with something I would make sure she would enjoy in the moment yet regret afterward.

I'd spent the night at work trying to erase the memories of her flushed skin and clean, freshly-showered smell. I'd tried to combat the memory of her quick breaths, striking blue eyes, and delicious curves with the vibration of the tattoo gun in my hand. But with every mark I made against someone else's skin, I wondered how hers would feel beneath my fingers.

I wondered if she would be just as sensitive to my touch as she was to each of my movements and my stare. If she would be just as eager for it as she was for my words.

And when the gun hadn't worked, when the rhythm and control ceased to have its usual effect, I spent a restless night imagining what would happen if I crawled into her bed, or better yet, if she gave in and crawled into mine.

Then I woke up early and went to a coffee shop to catch up on some schoolwork as an excuse to get out of the house. And when I realized I'd done everything and even worked ahead in more than one class, I went back to the house long enough to grab what I needed for the gym and leave.

Three hours of running, lifting, and several rounds with the punching bag, I still wasn't any more under control.

I drove home from the gym with every window of my truck down and music blasting. Mostly to enjoy the last of the late summer weather, but it was also a pointless final attempt to get my mind right.

It was times like those when my mind was spinning and I couldn't handle being inside of my own head that I would've called Ryder or asked him to hang out. But he was eight hundred miles away, and for other obvious reasons, I wouldn't be confiding in him. I could have probably called him under the guise of just checking in, but he knew me better than that—two seconds on the phone, and he'd immediately known something else was up.

And the guilt that swirled in my gut told me enough that calling him was a bad idea.

I pulled up to the house with the green front door and cursed when I saw Natalie's car still in the driveway.

I contemplated driving past and figuring out another way to spend my time, but I had nothing left to do. Robbie had given me the night off, so I didn't even have that to fill my time. He'd said something about feeling bad that I'd been working so much and going to school that he wanted to give me a Saturday night free.

I fought him on it since my one friend was in another state, but he wasn't going to give in.

A night off should've been a blessing, but in reality—in my reality—it was nothing but a curse.

I was out of the truck the second I stopped.

Just get it over with, I told myself. The quicker I got into the house, the quicker I could hide in my room like a fucking teenager.

But the second I reached out, key in hand to unlock the door, it swung open before me. My heart jumped into my throat, and Natalie nearly screamed.

"Holy fucking shit," she muttered and steadied herself on her heels.

My eyes trailed up her body, eyeing the strappy heels on her feet and memorizing the fit of her black dress. It flared out at her knees but hugged the smallest part of her waist. The neckline was deep and showed off the delicate curve of her breasts. My mouth was watering by the time I noticed her curled hair that hung in black waves around her face, and the smokey makeup she'd applied around her eyes.

At once, all the blood in my body rushed to my cock, which quickly stiffened behind the thin material of my gym shorts. A slight breeze would likely have set me off. My perusal of her body was not one I hid, and the way her jaw slackened and her eyes glimmered with interest, I knew she'd noticed it for what it was.

"Going out?" I finally ground out.

She snapped her mouth shut, and she stepped around me out onto the porch, which was illuminated by the dim light next to the door and the final remnants of daylight.

She cleared her throat and brushed her hair over her shoulder. "Yep," was her only response, and I narrowed my eyes at her as she continued fidgeting nervously. She tugged down her dress and messed with the fabric at her collarbone. The material cascaded down each of her arms where it cinched at her wrist.

She chewed her lower lip as her eyes darted to her car. She was more nervous than usual, and a very sick part of me liked to watch her squirm.

"Ms. Talkative doesn't have anything to say now?" I smirked and leaned casually against the post to my left.

My comment had the desired effect as she rolled her eyes. And I was so fucked in the head that all I wanted to do was punish her right then and there for doing such a thing. I wanted to sit down on the bench just behind me and take her over my knee while any one of her neighbors could see. She'd have to be quiet as my hand marked her bare ass until it was so red and sore she'd feel me for days after. The burn would bring tears to her eyes, and that perfect makeup would end up smudged all over her soft skin.

Fucking the attitude out of her afterward was just as compelling.

"Yes, I'm going out," she said, pulling me from my fantasies.

"With Caroline?" I tried, because something told me I should ask.

Nervously, she shuffled from one foot to the other, and I knew it wasn't because her heels were already bothering her.

"Umm...nope. Not tonight."

Quietly and patiently, I waited for her to explain. Something I learned from always being the quiet one, most people wanted to fill the silence. The longer it went on, the harder they worked to ease the awkwardness that usually accompanied it.

One of the things I liked about Natalie was that she didn't always feel the need to do so. Like me, she was content with the silence. Unless I made her nervous, then she couldn't help but babble a little.

I thought it was endearing.

And just as I expected, she clarified, "His name is Tanner."

That was why she was being so coy and secretive. "You have a date?" I asked and was fairly impressed with the evenness of my tone. Especially when every part of me vibrated with the desire to do whatever necessary to keep her there.

"Yes, it's my first one in a while…"

All I could manage was a nod as I clenched and unclenched my fists and held back the demand for her to stay. Realizing I simultaneously couldn't demand that but eventually would if I kept standing there, I turned to walk inside.

But a small hand on my elbow stopped me in my tracks. Her nails, painted a shade that was almost as dark as her dress, dug lightly into my skin, and I wanted to feel them everywhere.

I jerked to a stop and turned to find her staring up at me with a deep furrow between her dark brows.

"Aren't you going to tell me to have fun or something? Maybe wish me luck?"

I choked out a hollow, surprised laugh. My jaw hurt with the way I ground my teeth as I contemplated my answer.

"Now, why would I do that, Natalie?"

She dropped her hand and shivered. I nearly smiled at her reaction to hearing her name. I already knew she wouldn't do that with Tanner. It was a reaction reserved specifically for me and stemmed from the nuclear connection between us.

"It's polite," she said, and I scoffed. Undeterred, she continued, "Okay, well, it's just a nice thing to do."

My laugh again was nothing short of hollow and cold. I took a step forward, and like she should have, Natalie took a step back, eyes wide and fixed on my face.

She was so much shorter than me that it was easy to tower above her without trying. And again, that dark part of me enjoyed the way she wanted to cower but didn't.

"I don't have any inclination to be nice, Natalie. And while it might be the polite thing to say, it wouldn't be honest."

In a move I didn't expect, she stepped forward and tilted her head higher to maintain eye contact. We were so close that if she breathed deeply, her tits would brush against my stomach.

I held my breath.

"And why is that?"

Because if you have a bad time, you'll be more eager to come back home to me.

I dismissed the thought as quickly as it appeared.

Everything about her had thrown me off. Her coy confidence left me ready to throw in the towel and cut all my losses. Another minute of verbal sparring, and I'd have her over my shoulder, heading up to her bedroom.

So, I caved and said, "Good luck, Natalie."

It wasn't the response she was expecting. Her slack jaw told me as much as I stepped back into the house and closed the door behind me.

Part of me wished she'd push back inside and demand to know what I meant. That she'd keep pushing me until we both broke. It wouldn't have taken much at that point. Everything she did was a taunting tease. A taste of the forbidden that I knew I would never have.

I tossed my duffel bag onto the steps and immediately pulled open the fridge, hoping there was something that didn't require too much work to prepare. The frozen meals I'd picked up were all I'd been able to afford, but they were beginning to taste like cardboard. Especially compared to the food Natalie and I had prepared together.

I scanned the contents ready to make do with whatever I could find, when my eyes landed on the middle shelf. In a clear Tupperware container were the chicken parmesan leftovers from the night before. On top of the container was a pink sticky note. I slid it out and read the note:

Your half of the leftovers.

It was signed with a heart and an "N." Immediately, I tossed the food back into the fridge and shut the door hard enough the condiments rattled on impact.

The moment I began feeling sorry for myself, though, there was a faint sound I couldn't quite make out. I glanced around the kitchen and heard it again. When it happened a third time, I saw Natalie's iPad sitting on the island light up with a new notification.

I crossed to it as it dinged a few more times and reached to turn the volume down. But I stopped when I saw my name in one of the messages that lit up the screen.

Her phone must have been connected to the device, and seeing my name, my curiosity got the better of me.

There wasn't a passcode, so it was easy enough to swipe open and find their most recent messages.

Caroline: Did you find your phone?

Natalie: Yes! It somehow wedged itself between the couch cushions.

Caroline: I love how you act like your phone did that itself.

Natalie: Fuck right the hell off.

Caroline: ANYWAY, good luck on your date!

Natalie: Ugh, thanks. I can't believe I let you talk me into this.

Caroline: Umm…no, ma'am. I didn't have to talk you into anything. You're the one that agreed after living with your son's best friend for like two weeks.

Natalie: Theo. His name is Theo, so please stop referring to him like that.

Caroline: Omg, that would be such a good name to moan.

Natalie: STOP! You are not helping at all.

Caroline: Right, right. So sorry. Well, I hope it all goes well! And maybe this will be enough to get Theo off your mind.

Natalie: We can only hope.

Caroline: Besides, I've heard he has a pretty big dick.

Natalie: How would you know?!

Caroline: Oh my gosh, Nat, TANNER—your date. I don't know about Theo...although I bet he's packing too.

Natalie: I'm done with this conversation. You're the worst.

Caroline: Love you, too!

I turned the volume down, set the iPad back on the counter, and stepped away. Knowing she was struggling just as badly as I was, that she'd even decided to go out on a date to get me off her mind, changed everything.

Knowing she was as affected by me as I was by her was too tempting and intoxicating to ignore. Reading those messages, my will to stay away completely disintegrated.

SEVEN

MINT CHOCOLATE CHIP

Natalie

THE WAITER PLACED OUR CHECK IN THE CENTER OF THE TABLE, AND before I could suggest splitting it, Tanner added his card to the bifold and handed it back to the man.

His smile told me he was enjoying himself, and I hoped mine reflected the same.

The upscale Asian fusion restaurant he'd chosen had been really good. The lights were slightly dimmed, and the music played at just the right volume in the background. Our waiter had been attentive, and the food was rich and flavorful.

And the man sitting across from me had also been…good.

Thankfully, I hadn't gotten my hopes up, so I wasn't disappointed when I realized there wasn't more of a connection between us.

It hadn't been a bad date. Tanner was a really good-looking guy with a strong jawline and disheveled salt-and-pepper hair. His blue eyes were nearly gray, and he smiled with his entire face.

He asked me more questions than I asked him, which I knew

was hard to come by, and he complimented me on more than one occasion. He didn't talk about himself *too* much, but I did learn that he'd been divorced—not a widower as Caroline had said—for four years and had three children he saw often. He and his ex-wife coparented well—according to him—and he worked in technology. The specifics of which I didn't quite catch.

Overall, it was a good date. But that was all it would be. I didn't make a love match, and I definitely couldn't see myself sleeping with him if I was being honest with myself.

The conversation continued seamlessly as he paid and we stood to leave.

"I had a really great time," he said with an easy smile as we approached my car, only a few spaces down from his own.

I returned the smile. "I did, too. It was fun," I said, and Tanner took the opportunity to interlace our fingers and step closer. I knew what he was about to do, and I frantically searched for the right words to tell him that I wasn't really interested without hurting his feelings.

But I was too slow, and before I could react, he leaned in and kissed me.

His lips pressed against mine, and I let it happen. I didn't push him away or rear back. Instead, I let him lead the quick, chaste kiss.

Before I knew it, it was over, and I was proven right once and for all—there were no sparks between us. But based on the elation on his face, he must have felt something. Or he was just excited that he got to kiss me at all.

"I'll call you tomorrow, and maybe we can set up something for next week." His voice was riddled with hope, and I couldn't find it within me to crush all of it in that moment. I'd act like an adult and wait until he called and let him down then.

I gave him a noncommittal "sure," and I was excited when he didn't linger.

Quickly, I jumped in my car and was already dialing Caroline before I even backed out of the spot.

"Was he perfect?" she said by way of greeting, and I groaned. She cursed, and then there was shuffling on the other end of the line. "Okay, hold on, I know it couldn't have been that bad."

"You're right, it wasn't bad, but we're also not meant for each other."

I turned right onto the main road, heading back home, as Caroline asked, "Not even meant enough for each other that you could spend a night in his bed?"

I rolled my eyes and came to a stop at a red light. My head hit the headrest, and I closed my eyes momentarily.

"No, unfortunately not."

She sighed, like it was just as hard for her, and said, "Okay, take me through the entire date," which I did, start to finish, as I drove home.

By the end of it, she agreed that we probably weren't ideal as anything more than friends but still maintained that sleeping with him would be fun.

"I don't think fun would be the word I'd use to describe it especially since I felt next to nothing when he kissed me."

I pulled into the driveway and ignored the way my heartbeat sped up when I parked next to Theo's truck. But I pushed past the nerves and anticipation and told Caroline I'd call her the next day and we could discuss my love life—or lack thereof—in as much detail as she wanted.

"Fine," she sighed. "Don't do anything I wouldn't do!" she added in a sing-song voice before hanging up the phone.

I mustered up the courage to get out of the car but held my breath until I stepped inside and heard the faint hum of music from upstairs. I continued into the kitchen with a one-track mind, which included myself, a spoon, and a pint of ice cream.

I discarded my heels near the barstools and quickly found the mint chocolate chip I'd been fantasizing about the entire drive home. Grabbing a spoon, I pushed up to sit on the counter and took a bite. I had to suppress a groan as the flavor burst on my tongue. It was exactly what I wanted, and I was so completely engrossed in my dessert that I didn't realize I wasn't alone until I heard the refrigerator open to my right.

Between bites, I glanced over and closed my eyes against the sight of Theo shirtless, tattooed back on display, muscles flexing as he reached for something in the fridge. The only piece of clothing he wore was light gray sweatpants that hung low on his hips.

I waited to open my eyes again until I turned back to my ice cream and slowly took another bite. All I had to do was focus on the cold, sweet flavor and not on the new heat pulsing between my legs. Not even the cooler countertop beneath me that was pressed against my thighs helped stifle the warmth.

Not looking up from where my eyes were fixed on the container in my hand, I still noticed Theo walking around the island, twisting the cap off of his water bottle as he stopped directly across from me. Leaning his back against the opposite counter, he took a swig of water, replaced the plastic lid, and set it behind him.

I could feel his eyes on me, and I pretended to act unaffected by his attention.

"You're home early," he mused, and I couldn't help it, my eyes snapped up to meet his. But not before I quickly scanned the muscular planes of his chest and toned stomach. His pecs were covered in the same black ink I'd seen on his back, but the lower down his abs I tracked, the more sparse they became. More tanned skin peaked through between the dark, intricate designs.

My eyes met his once again, and I swallowed before I said, "Not exactly. It's past ten."

I took another bite and watched Theo track the movement of the spoon as I slowly licked the remnants. His hungry gaze sent a wanting shiver through me. And the way he eyed my mouth, it was like he was imagining something other than the spoon between my lips.

He shifted, a hand scrubbing over his mouth as his attention jumped back to my eyes. The desire shining back at me was enough to make each subsequent breath more difficult than the last.

"Where did you meet this guy?" he asked so casually that I couldn't reconcile the burning desire in his eyes and the tone of his voice.

He wasn't one to normally ask many questions, so I said, "Caroline set us up."

"And it didn't go well?"

I narrowed my eyes and tilted my head slightly. He didn't balk at my assessing stare, and something inside of me wanted to challenge his cockiness.

"I never said that."

"You didn't have to."

I took another bite of my ice cream and decided to tell him the truth. I also didn't think I was a skillful enough liar to pretend like my date was anything more than *fine*. Especially pinned under his scrutinizing stare.

"There wasn't much of a connection," I said. "He was nice. He asked me a lot of questions and seemed genuinely interested in my answers. He was pretty funny and not bad to look at, but…"

"What's wrong with that?"

"Nothing."

He straightened and shifted his hands behind him so they were braced on the counter on either side of his hips. The movement made my eyes drop lower, and I traced the lines of his defined V peeking out above the waistband of his sweats.

I had to readjust on the counter and immediately felt the blush darken my cheeks.

"That's not good enough?"

"No," I finally managed to say. "Besides being attractive, those are all qualities I look for in a friend, too. There needs to be something more than that if I'm going to date someone."

And without missing a beat, he said, "To date someone or use them to get the dirty thoughts of your son's best friend out of your head."

EIGHT

THE DIRTY TRUTH

Natalie

THE SPOON FELL FROM BETWEEN MY LIPS AND CLATTERED ungracefully to the counter beside me as it bounced off my leg. The pint of ice cream almost slipped from my grip, but I was able to catch it before the worst could happen.

"What?" I croaked out around my panic.

How the *hell* had he known that? Unless he heard Caroline and me a few weeks ago, but even then, I didn't believe he'd wait that long to bring it up.

A wicked smile curved his lips as he explained, "Did you know that your iPad also receives your text messages? The sound was on when you left earlier, and when I went to turn it down, I noticed some very interesting messages between you and Caroline."

He pushed off the counter and took two slow, measured steps toward me. My knees brushed against his bare stomach, and I nearly spread my legs at the slight, inadvertent caress of our skin. That deep desire blazing in his eyes hadn't extinguished, and the closer he came, the more likely we were to get burned.

"Something about getting me off your mind?" he asked, sliding his tongue across his lower lip. "Have I been taking up too much space in that beautiful little head of yours?"

I attempted to swallow, to clear the nerves clogging my throat, but I couldn't. Most of the confidence I'd mustered dissolved as he surrounded me. He wasn't even touching me, yet somehow I felt him everywhere.

This wasn't happening.

Reaching for my last thread of courage, my own unwavering stare met his. He saw the challenge in my eyes, and his smile widened even further.

"It's not very nice to snoop."

His dark chuckle wasn't what I expected. Neither was I expecting him to reach out and pluck the half-eaten ice cream carton from my grasp. Eyes still fixed on my face, he slid the carton across the counter and leaned forward, bracing both of his palms on the butcher block on either side of my thighs. He was huge. Rugged, strong, and wholly intimidating.

He was effectively caging me in, and I had nowhere to go. Not that I was considering bolting anyway. In that moment, he was my only thought. Him and how far he might take it. My hands stayed clasped in my lap as he assessed me.

"Like I said before your date, I have no desire to be nice."

He shifted closer until his stomach was pressed against my knees, and it took more force to keep them closed than it would've to open them for him to step between.

"So, tell me, Natalie. Did the friendly divorcée get me off your mind?"

Worried I might shift and the outside of my thigh would brush his hand, I stayed so still my muscles ached. When I didn't respond immediately, his jaw ticced, and the kitchen grew infinitely warmer.

"No," I finally managed to whisper, and his smile was my reward.

"Well, what are we going to do about that?"

I shook my head, and he tsked at my response. He tilted his head forward until his nose softly brushed my cheek, and I couldn't even force my next breath into my lungs. With one small touch, all thoughts vacated my mind. I was no longer worried about who I was, who he was, or who we were to each other. My only thoughts were consumed by that moment.

"We can't have you going around thinking about me all the time, can we? Those dirty thoughts are doing no one any good locked inside your head."

His hot breath against my skin and the occasional brush of his nose was the sweetest form of torture. I didn't trust myself to respond. The moment I opened my mouth, I knew all that would spill from my lips were pleas, begging for him to touch me. To not leave one inch of my body untouched.

"Maybe we should set them free—play out every dirty thought you've ever dreamed. Even the ones you don't want anyone to know. The ones you're too scared to even let yourself think about."

He ran his nose up my jaw, inhaling deeply as he went.

Each stuttered breath I was able to suck into my lungs was filled with him. His scent was clean and masculine, and it made me dizzy with unending desire that pooled between my thighs until I was pulsing with need.

"What do you think about that?" he asked, and I was startled by the question. My hands were folded in my lap and my eyelids drooped, yet I continued staring at the cabinets behind him. His breath ghosted over the sensitive skin of my neck, and I felt the goosebumps appear over my entire body. "Answer me, Natalie."

"No," I croaked out. "No fantasies…"

Did I know what I was saying? Absolutely not. I'd left my body completely by the time his lips grazed my collarbone.

"Mmm…" he mused quietly, and the vibration of the sound penetrated my skin. "Well," he began shifting back and meeting my eyes again. With his voice so calm and level, it was his eyes that belied the inner turmoil that matched my own. "Then maybe we can use mine," he finished.

My eyes widened, and that smile graced his lips once again. One that promised gloriously sinful things.

"Yes, Natalie. All I've been thinking about since last night was getting you like this. Picking you up and setting you on the counter so I have perfect access to every part of you."

He shifted closer, but my legs still barred him from all of the access he wanted.

How could this be happening? What were we doing? And why didn't I care?

"So, don't lie to me again," he growled low in the back of his throat. "Especially when I already know the truth."

He reared back fully, and the absence of his body looming over mine momentarily sobered me enough that I managed to ask, "The truth?"

Standing at his full height once again, I leaned my head back enough to hold his stare. His brown depths scanned my face, and one of his hands brushed the outside of my thigh as he pulled back.

For a moment, I thought it was all over. That he'd stopped before we'd actually really started, and he was going to leave me there, needy and wanting, on the kitchen counter.

But then I felt his touch on the inside of my right knee. It wasn't tentative, but it was soft, barely a whisper of a touch as he traced that one finger slowly higher. I shivered, although it was so strong that it whipped through my body with enough force that my back arched at the sensation.

My dress had bunched up indecently around my waist, and I watched as the tip of his tattooed finger danced higher until he found the edge of the fabric. The dress moved as I squirmed, and his finger dipped beneath it just enough that my breath caught in the back of my throat.

He stared at that finger, so close to the apex of my thighs I could feel its heat, and he could no doubt feel mine, too.

"The truth," he said, his voice dripping in warm honey. "The truth is that if I lifted up your skirt right now, I'd see the little puddle on the counter that you've been making for me."

His eyes flashed to mine, silently asking permission, and finding no argument reflected back to him, he brushed his hands over the tops of my thighs as he pushed the fabric even higher. My warm skin was suddenly exposed to the cooler air around us, yet I couldn't find it in myself to care.

His palms hovered over my thighs, and I could feel the effort of his restraint vibrating through him. Our eyes still locked, he ordered, "Spread your legs."

And like they were voice activated, my legs parted automatically.

A deep sound of approval emanated from the back of his throat as he peered down at my black panties. "*Fuck*," he muttered under his breath as both hands clasped my knees and forced my legs even farther apart. His grip grew tighter the longer he stared down at me. His blunt nails dug into my skin.

"Look at these pretty panties," he mused, tugging me sharply to the very edge of the counter until my ass was barely balanced on the edge. Maintaining his tight grip, he shifted his hands higher, ascending my thighs with an appreciative yet determined touch.

"Did you put these on expecting to get fucked tonight?" he asked. The muscles along his chest and down his arms flexed with each small movement. "Who were you thinking of when you put these on, Natalie?" He leaned in closer, nose brushing mine, before he shifted and breathed against my ear, "And don't lie to me."

"It wasn't him," I panted. I was strung so tight I felt like I was going to burst at any second with the energy of a thousand suns.

And before I could react, one of his hands darted forward and bracketed around my throat. Shock rippled through my body at the impact, and I stiffened as his fingers settled against the sides of my neck.

His eyes widened, and I didn't think he'd meant to do it. At least not that way. And I saw the question in his eyes. *"Is this okay?"*

My answer was to lean harder into his grip. Balancing on the edge of the counter, I braced my hands behind me, giving them most of my weight, which in turn opened me wider for Theo.

He mumbled something that sounded like "beautiful" under his breath, but I couldn't make it out completely in my lust-filled haze.

My entire body jolted when his thumb brushed my throbbing pussy, tracing the outline of the wet spot on my panties that I felt pressing against me.

His touch was teasing. He rubbed lightly back and forth, back and forth, until I was a writhing mess on the counter. He petted the lace until I was nearly dripping, and I wouldn't be surprised if I *had* created a puddle beneath me.

The first time he brushed against my clit, I bit down so hard on my lower lip to keep from crying out that I tasted iron. His hand around my throat shifted until he clutched the side of my neck. One thumb teasing my pussy over the black lace, the other pressing against my pulse so he could feel the frantic rhythm of my heart.

It was the same incessant pulse I felt between my legs.

"These panties were so pretty. What a shame you've ruined them," he muttered.

He did one more pass with his thumb over the fabric before he moved them to the side and exposed my throbbing center. "But look at what those panties were hiding," he bemused. "Those are nothing compared to how fucking pretty your pussy is."

His golden brown eyes were focused between my legs as he ran his thumb through the dark triangle of neatly trimmed hair and spread my bare lips. His eyes darkened as he stared down at where I craved for him to really touch me, completely unencumbered by the thin lace.

My skin was heated, and my body felt like a livewire. Even the air against my pussy was too much to bear as I shook with anticipation. And just when I thought I would have to begin begging, the fervent pleas poised on my tongue, his finger brushed my clit.

The pad of his finger slipped over the needy spot, and I moaned.

"There she is," he said, voice deep and breathy. My back bowed, and my body hummed with excitement.

His pace quickened, rubbing me thoroughly into a quickly approaching oblivion. His grip on the side of my neck tightened. I was so wet his fingers easily slipped around my opening, between my folds, and dipping inside of me only far enough to tease.

My eyes had fallen shut somewhere along the way as I unashamedly gave myself over to the pleasure. But Theo's thumb pressed under my chin and tilted my head up.

I recognized his silent request and opened my eyes to find his locked on my face, only a breath between us. When his lips parted, I thought he'd kiss me, and my heart took on an entirely new, erratic beat. But he didn't. He leaned forward, peered down the length of my body, and spit onto my clit.

It was so unnecessarily filthy that I gasped and writhed harder against the counter as I watched it slide down to my opening.

His thumb found my clit once again and kneaded it in tight circles, applying the perfect amount of pressure to send me barreling toward an orgasm I knew was going to be life-altering.

I wanted to reach out and touch him. To trace the intricate artwork inked on his skin with my fingers and then my tongue. I wanted to dig my nails into his shoulders when I finally broke apart, but I worried the second I shifted my weight from my hands behind me, I'd collapse backward, and I too badly wanted to see everything he was doing to me.

Looking down my body, past the material of my dress gathered around my hips, I feasted on the view of him mercilessly teasing me. Until his hand shifted back to my throat, and I jerked my attention to his face.

The second our eyes met, he smiled and shoved two fingers deep inside of me.

I nearly screamed.

His thick fingers filled me, and my nails dug into the counter. Overwhelmed by the sensation and already on the precipice of an orgasm, my hips bucked forward, and I clamped around him.

He hooked those two skillful fingers upward and massaged my walls until he found that delicious spot that made me nearly carnal.

"God, you're such a little slut for my fingers. This pussy is desperate for me. I can't imagine how you'll look taking my cock."

An unfamiliar thrill shot through me at his mouth and the dirty words that he used so freely.

Slut.

I was surprised by my reaction to that normally derogatory term. It was a name I'd been called before, but never the way he said it. Like it was simultaneously something to be proud of, something to envy, and the dirtiest, most shameful thing you could be.

And he was right, I was a slut for his fingers. And surprisingly, I wanted to revel and bask in it. I wanted to hear him say it again.

Theo devoured every single one of my reactions and watched me intently as I fell apart around his fingers.

"That's exactly what you are, isn't it? Do you think you'd enjoy being my pretty little slut?"

I whimpered and lost myself in his eyes that were raging with desire. Muscles flexing as he mercilessly finger-fucked me, his body tensed as I clamped down around him hard and came.

"Oh, look at you," Theo said, his tone demeaning enough to make me flush with humiliation. "You're coming already. Use my fingers. God, you must have really needed this."

Like I was shot into the sky, climbing higher and higher, the orgasm grew until it crested not once but twice. Unspeakable pleasure racked through my body, and noises I didn't know I was capable of left my mouth.

My pussy convulsed around him, and I moaned his name.

It was never ending. I kept waiting for the pleasure to cease, for my orgasm to dissipate, but there was only wave after wave.

Slowly I fell back into my body, resituating myself within my skin, and tried to blink through the post-orgasm haze. The most intense post-orgasm haze I'd ever experienced.

The kitchen lights were too bright, and the counter beneath me was too hard. Things I hadn't noticed before were suddenly coming into focus. Without the pleasure clouding my thoughts, the ache in my arms from holding my weight was brutal, and so was the shaking in my legs.

Theo's fingers slipped free from me, and I shuddered at the loss. My eyes met his, and I watched his gaze flicker.

Like it happened in slow motion, Theo raised his hand to his mouth and placed the fingers he'd just had inside me against his tongue. He held my stare as he sucked the remnants of my orgasm from each digit, and I wanted to know exactly what he was thinking at that moment. If the orgasm he'd coaxed from me tasted as good as he hoped it would.

I leaned forward, shifting my weight from my sore hands and arms as he dropped his hand from his mouth.

"Good night, Natalie," he murmured, and in the next second, he was gone. He didn't look back as he climbed the stairs two at a time.

Legs spread, my breathing was barely back to normal when I heard his door close and the music turned back on.

Shocked by his sudden, cold departure, I sat there for far longer than I should have. Until my legs fell asleep and my eyes grew heavy.

Finally, I slid unceremoniously from the counter and cringed at the wetness between my thighs. My legs shook underneath me, and I stared at the spot I'd vacated.

And the wet spot I'd left behind.

I swore it grew larger, taunting me with the evidence of the sin we'd both committed moments earlier.

I closed my eyes and shook my head. That was not how I imagined the night ending, and my gut twisted as the realization dawned.

"Fuck," I muttered under my breath.

Reaching under the sink, I grabbed the cleaning spray and rag. But instead of wiping the counter, I stood frozen in the middle of the kitchen. Rag in one hand, spray bottle in the other, my mind spun and spun. And as my thoughts collided in a chaotic jumble, they wandered.

Staring unseeingly into the living room, my lungs struggled for a shaky breath.

Theo's hands, strong and confident against my skin, had felt better than anything I'd ever experienced before. He'd broken me apart so easily and known exactly how I'd craved to be touched. Each teasing brush of his lips, his stubbled cheek combined with the low rumble of his filthy words and the merciless cadence of his fingers inside of me was intoxicating. It was enough to make me forget why we shouldn't have done it and why it couldn't happen again.

But all I wanted *was* to do it again and shame burned hot against my skin. I wanted my son's best friend. I wanted the man who had nowhere else to go and wound up living in my house to fuck me into utter oblivion.

God, I was a terrible fucking person.

When my thoughts lingered on Ryder, I abandoned the cleaning supplies on the counter and headed upstairs. I paused long enough to turn the lights off in the kitchen and grab my phone before I hurried to my bedroom. I didn't stop until I was hidden behind my door. Not even when I heard the music emanating from behind Theo's door suddenly shut off.

Stepping into the bathroom, I took one look at myself and groaned. My hair was disheveled, and my cheeks were flushed. I looked like I'd had the most mind-bending, life-altering orgasm of my life.

Turning away from the view of my sated self, I stripped. There was a renewed sense of urgency pumping through me. An urgency that was screaming at me to wash it away. Wash away all the pleasure that clung to me like I was its lifeline. Hastily, I grabbed a new towel, turned on the water, and stepped under the scalding spray.

I lathered soap on my loofah and scrubbed viciously at every inch of my skin. But it didn't matter. Theo had already embedded himself so deep within me that any attempt to scrub him away was useless. Like one of the tattoos inked on his skin that I hadn't even had the chance to explore.

I hated that I'd liked it. I'd enjoyed everything he'd given me —the humiliation, the degradation, and the filthiness that had come along with Theo fingering me on the kitchen counter.

I didn't want to like it, but that didn't make it go away. And it sure as hell didn't temper the thoughts of what more he could do.

Would Ryder forgive me? The thought startled me, and I dropped the bottle of soap to the shower floor.

Theo and I were both adults with sexual chemistry that broke the measly little charts I'd become used to. But if Ryder ever found out about it…it's a line I never imagined I'd cross but found myself leaping over anyway.

That line was invisible when it was me and Theo. When it was us, I completely forgot that he was Ryder's best friend.

Did that really mean it couldn't happen again?

I shook the thought from my head the second it appeared. I

was miles ahead of myself since Theo'd left seconds after I'd come.

No doubt he thought it was a mistake, too. One he tried to distance himself from as soon as possible.

But he could have ignored the texts he'd seen. He could have stayed in his room when I'd gotten home from my date and left me to my pint of ice cream.

But he hadn't. He'd come downstairs with a purpose, and I had a feeling he wouldn't have left until he was satisfied.

And lucky for me, it had awoken something within me that I wanted so desperately to lean into. Something that made the guilt I expected to feel never appear in the first place.

He was everything I never knew I wanted and everything I couldn't have.

I was spiraling and fast, so I did what I could to shut off my thoughts.

I reached to turn the water hotter, but it was already as high as it would go. It was no use. My shame and desire were already burning me from the inside out.

NINE
SCAREDY CAT

Theo

"YOU GOING BACK?" ROBBIE ASKED, LEANING AGAINST THE doorframe of my room at Haven City.

I hadn't even heard him walk in, and judging by the unimpressed look on his face, he knew I was stalling.

All I could manage was a noncommittal grunt, so he stepped inside and sat down on one of the extra stools near the door.

"Look, you know I would let you stay with me if I had the room," he said, and I quickly waved him off.

I didn't want him to feel bad about anything. It was my fault I was stuck in the stupid situation I was in, and I knew Robbie would help if he could. It wasn't his fault that I couldn't keep my hands to myself.

"I know, and I appreciate that. I just need to get my head straight."

The disbelieving look crossed his face once again, and I pretended like I didn't notice.

I liked to think that if I hadn't seen those texts between Caroline and Natalie that I wouldn't have done what I did. But it was pointless to lie to myself. Reading those texts was just the push I needed to disregard every reason why I knew I shouldn't touch her.

And then when I came downstairs to find her on the counter, her legs swinging as she sucked ice cream off the spoon the way I imagined her sucking my cock, I snapped. I thought I would have had more self-control than that, but it turns out I didn't.

Unless she'd told me to stop, I wasn't going to. In that moment, touching her and feeling her come apart under my fingers was my only purpose.

And it'd been better than I could've dreamed. Each of her panted breaths and needy moans replayed in my head on a constant loop. As did the way she blossomed under my attention and humiliation. That turned her on. Laying her soul bare, she couldn't hide anything from me.

I had her close to falling apart before I even touched her. And that type of power over someone's body was addictive. *She* was addictive.

And therein was the issue: I could *not* be addicted to her.

"You want to tell me exactly what happened to get your head all out of whack? Make you come runnin' to my place late at night?" Robbie questioned. It was the same question he'd been asking me since I showed up on his doorstep at one in the morning two days ago.

The second I heard Natalie's bedroom door shut, I was out of the house. I was bound to seek her out if I stayed there for another second, especially with the smell of her still lingering on my fingers.

I hadn't confided in Robbie before because I was still trying to figure out how everything escalated to this point. And he'd given me the space to process it.

Sighing, I leaned my elbows on my knees and let my head fall into my hands.

"Is it your mom?"

"No," I said instantly through clenched teeth.

Robbie raised his hands in surrender and pursed his lips. Not sure why he even brought her up, but I appreciated that he quickly changed topics. The last thing I ever wanted to do was think about my mother, let alone talk about her.

"Did you fuck her?" he asked, and my head snapped up. Somehow, I managed a hollow chuckle.

Confusion, irritation, desire, and a whole host of other emotions I couldn't quite identify lanced through me at the reminder. It was one of two women—Robbie was smart enough and knew me well enough to figure that much.

"No, but I might as well have," I finally confessed. I didn't look at him, but I felt his disappointing gaze land on me.

He was quiet for a minute while I stared at the tiled floor beneath my boots.

"I knew you'd do something stupid," he murmured, and I cringed at the honesty of his statement. Stupid was an understatement. "And you're confused because she's your best friend's mom."

I groaned at the reminder and sat back. Thankfully Robbie didn't look as disappointed as I thought he would. Concerned was probably a better word to describe his expression.

"Thanks for the reminder," I chided, and he chuckled.

"Look, I'm not going to pretend like I haven't done my fair share of shit I regretted, but beating yourself up about it isn't going to help."

But that was the thing...I didn't regret it. I wish I did because then maybe that would keep me from wanting to do it again.

I did, however, regret having to keep a huge secret from my best friend. And that's the thought that kept me up the past two nights. If they weren't related, I would have been inside her so many times by now that I would've imprinted myself on her forever. She would crave me like I crave her. And who the hell was I kidding? That thought scared me, too.

"Ahh, I see," Robbie mused, drawing me from my thoughts before I was able to go deeper down the Natalie-sized rabbit hole. He laughed to himself. "You don't regret doing it, and you want to do it again."

I met his amused expression with one that hopefully conveyed my annoyance. All he did was chuckle again.

"Interesting…and I bet you're concerned not only about how it might impact your living situation but also your friendship with Ryder."

"Enough," I managed to ground out through clenched teeth.

"Okay, but you sure you don't want my advice? Would you prefer we skip that part today?"

Robbie was the only father figure I'd had in the past several years. I appreciated him and what he'd done for me more than words could describe. I'd forever be indebted to him for taking me in and giving me something to live for when I didn't really care if I took another breath.

But even so, I still hated the way he read me like a damn book.

I scrubbed a hand through my unruly, curly hair and considered him. He took my silence as his cue to continue.

"Don't fuck her just because you want to get your dick wet."

"Seriously, Robbie?" I questioned derisively at his crude words. Standing and pacing to the other side of the room, I pretended to busy myself with something else. I'd already reorganized everything three times, and the place had never been cleaner. That's what happened when I was avoiding going back to Natalie's house or the glaring reality of what a clusterfuck my life had come to.

I grabbed a few paper towels, the spray cleaner, and started cleaning the same spot I'd cleaned only minutes earlier. Until I caught a flash of pink out of the corner of my eye and tried not to flinch.

I needed to get rid of that goddamn keychain. Why I hadn't already, I honestly didn't know. I still needed the keys because I had to go back eventually—I'd only thrown enough clothes in my duffel for a night or two—but the keychain itself wasn't necessary anymore.

"Hey, now, I wasn't finished," Robbie argued. "You're usually so level-headed and thoughtful about every decision, I knew you'd fuck up eventually."

"This really isn't helping."

"And you know what the repercussions are if you continue this," he continued, unaffected by my interruption. "You just have to decide if they're worth it or not."

"You mean if possibly losing my friendship with Ryder is worth fucking his mom?"

My words were harsh, but Robbie didn't flinch at my tone.

He nodded and stood from the stool. "Look, I've met Ryder quite a few times, and from what I know of him, he's pretty understanding and laidback. But I don't think anyone would take their best friend sleeping with their mom too well. Maybe he'd come to terms with it eventually, but I wouldn't bet on it. This is a bad idea. You can't." He chuckled. "You can't unfuck his mom. Once you've crossed that line, there's no turning back."

"Wow, nicely said," I said, sarcasm dripping from my every word. We were both silent after that, the unspoken question loud around us.

Was that a risk I was willing to take?

Neither of us said it, but we were both thinking it.

Robbie was right. I was level-headed and rational when it came to making decisions. I'd grown up fast and learned that those were pillars of adulthood. But around Natalie, that all went out the window. There was no rationality when I was near her. It was like that part of my brain completely shut off, and all I wanted was to wrap myself up in her.

I'd been so focused on fighting those feelings for the past few weeks that I'd forgotten the real reason I'd let Ryder talk me into living there in the first place. It was supposed to be temporary and allow me time to get back on my feet and find a place of my own.

I needed to make that my priority. Maybe even find somewhere that wasn't temporary.

When I pulled into the driveway and Natalie's car was nowhere to be found, I thanked whatever deity made that happen. It was Labor Day, so I figured her office was closed, but she must've had other plans.

Hurrying into the house and up the stairs, I reminded myself to stick to my plan. I was going to pack my bags and crash at one of my other coworkers' apartments. I honestly wasn't looking forward to it since Jace partied more than any living person should and already had two other roommates, but I hoped it would be a better alternative.

I couldn't risk my friendship with Ryder, even if he would eventually forgive me. He would never know about what happened in the kitchen the other night, and nothing like it would ever happen again.

After I left, I'd text Natalie and tell her that although I appreciated her letting me stay, it was for the best if I moved out. And that we never tell Ryder about my momentary, one-time lapse in judgment.

But the second I entered the guest bedroom, my plan hit its first roadblock. I whipped my dirty T-shirt off and realized I needed a shower. Badly. And not knowing what the bathroom situation was like at Jace's, I knew it was safest to take one while I still had access to a shower that I didn't have to share with three other dudes.

Five minutes tops. That was how long I estimated it would take me to jump in and get back out. As I grabbed a new towel from the cabinet and turned the water on, I hoped that deity was still looking down on me and Natalie wouldn't get back before I was able to leave.

Stepping under the water, I quickly scrubbed my body and

ran shampoo and conditioner through my hair. It was work to not let my mind wander. I had to consciously not think about her, which was counterintuitive since I still ended up thinking about her, maybe even more.

I willed myself not to remember how perfect her cunt felt wrapped around my fingers or how delicious each of her sounds were. Or imagine how gorgeous she would look with the water running over each of her curves, her head tossed back as she let the water soak her black hair.

Just the momentary lapse made my dick harden, and I cursed under my breath.

I refused to jack off to the memory of her poised on the counter or to any of my other creative fantasies. Once I started that, I knew nothing else would ever do it for me. So, I'd been painfully hard for *weeks.*

Angrily, I shut the water off and grabbed the towel. I whipped the shower curtain open and dried quickly before I cracked open the bathroom door. I waited several seconds but didn't hear anything. Deciding it was safe and Natalie hadn't returned, I quickly crossed the hallway and pushed open the bedroom door as I tried to tighten the towel around my waist.

Staring down, I didn't realize I wasn't alone until the door clicked closed behind me and I was halfway across the room.

I knew my plan—to leave and never come back. That was the right thing to do. I knew my plan, and nothing would keep me from seeing it through. Except one thing. One person. And that one person was sitting in the center of my bed.

The moment I noticed Natalie, her white sundress spread around her, I stopped in my tracks. Her legs were tucked underneath her, and her hands were folded in her lap while she fidgeted with the hem of the dress.

Her black hair was in soft waves that flowed over her shoulders and past her breasts. Long, dark lashes framed her blue eyes, and as she watched me from across the room, I could see how nervous she was.

For several seconds neither of us said anything. I tried to figure out if she was just a figment of my imagination, an apparition of my deepest desires that came to fruition to test me.

Her eyes appraised me, running from my feet, over my towel-clad waist, and up my stomach. She unabashedly assessed each of the tattoos across my chest and down my arms. And when she'd considered every inch of exposed skin, she looked back at my face with a new flush to her cheeks.

"What are you doing here?" I finally asked, my voice sounding like gravel and belying exactly what finding her there had done to me. Much longer and the towel around my waist wouldn't be able to hide my rapidly stiffening cock. Then she'd know, without a doubt, how little I could help myself.

"Probably making a huge mistake," she said quietly. And I questioned if I heard her right.

I straightened and had no idea how to respond. Most of the time I didn't have much to say, but that didn't mean I was ever at a loss for words.

But Natalie didn't wait for me to say anything as she continued, "You left."

She straightened her spine yet continued to fidget with the end of her dress, and I wondered what would happen if I stayed quiet. I could see her apprehension growing the longer I took to respond, and I enjoyed watching her squirm.

She'd told me, and I'd experienced firsthand, that when she got nervous, her first reaction was to begin babbling. I wanted to know if I waited another minute if she would start—

"Okay, well, thank you for confirming this is a huge mistake. I've obviously lost my mind, and that will be the last time I ever look to Caroline for advice. I'm just going to go ahead and get the hell out—"

She pushed to her knees on top of the mattress as she spoke and was making for the edge of the bed before I interrupted her rambling.

"What do you want?" My voice was low, and the steady rise

and fall of her chest ceased the moment I spoke. Then her eyes closed slowly, like she was steadying herself to respond.

My dick twitched, and I had to clench my fists to keep from closing the distance between us and reaching for her. I wanted more reactions like that one. I wanted all of them.

Her eyes fluttered back open and settled on me once again. We were like two ends of a magnet—the tension and attraction between us pulling us together whether we wanted it to or not.

So caught up in holding myself back, I momentarily forgot I'd asked her a question until she finally answered.

"More."

TEN

PIERCED

Theo

MORE.

My entire body began thrumming with energy the moment the word left her lips.

Thinking I could outrun how she made me feel was pointless.

It was my turn. With one word, she'd laid out exactly what she wanted from me.

With that single word, my entire fucking plan imploded. And I knew I was about to make the biggest mistake of my life. Because once I had her, there would be no going back.

Without another thought, I closed the distance between us, stopping at the foot of the bed and reaching for her. She didn't hesitate to offer me her hand, and I pulled her to me.

With a gasp, she slid across the sheets until we were nose to nose. So close that her tits brushed my bare chest, her hard nipples poking through her dress, and I could feel each of her hurried breaths against my lips. We were so close that all I could smell was her. It was an intoxicating mix of warm vanilla and something spicier.

Our lips brushed once more as she pushed closer, but I

dropped my head, kissing down her neck and inhaling more of her heady scent. My tongue skimmed along her collarbone, and the gasp that left her lips was the sweetest sound.

Her hands were suddenly clutching my shoulders, and I had to know immediately if she tasted as sweet and potent as she smelled. I gripped the backs of her thighs, lifted her up, and dropped her back to the bed.

The bottom of her dress fluttered up around her, the white fabric coming to rest high up on her waist and showing me her intricate white lace panties. Dropping my head back, I groaned toward the ceiling and took a moment to compose myself.

The moment did me no good, though. The woman splayed out before me, breathing heavily, blue eyes wide, and staring at me like she was hanging on to my every move, was going to be my undoing. She was an offering I had no right to take.

"Is this the 'more' you wanted?"

She nodded, her hands gripping the blankets beneath her as I ran a hand down the inside of one of her thighs. They fell apart the closer I got to her center, and her hips pressed upward, searching for my hand or some sort of pressure or friction.

"So needy," I muttered, running my thumb down the center of her soaked panties.

Her hips surged again, and I looked up to find her biting her lower lip like she was trying to suppress those noises I'd been dreaming about. That wasn't going to work.

"Let me hear you, Natalie," I said, pushing her panties to the side and slipping one finger inside her wet, tight heat. She bucked up into my hand and released her bottom lip, letting a low, throaty moan free. "*Fuck*, yes. Let me hear how much you wanted this."

I added another finger, and another gasp was followed by a whimper as I slid against her G-spot.

"You poor fucking thing. This pussy needed attention, didn't it?"

She nodded, and I continued. "You wanted me to throw you

on the bed and finger your greedy little cunt until it's ready for my cock."

I didn't wait for her to confirm what I already knew before I was on my knees, my face eye-level with her perfect cunt. It took no effort at all to pull her to the edge of the bed.

The white lace was gorgeous and damp. Leaning forward, I inhaled deeply and licked her through the fabric. The taste of her soaking through the lace spoke to all of my primal and distinctly inhibited impulses. The roaring inside me to touch and claim and fuck.

With one quick tug, I pulled her panties down her legs and tossed them on the floor.

Seeing her laid out before me, willing and eager, stirred my most carnal and base desires. I peered up the length of her body and watched her face as I leaned forward and truly tasted her, completely unimpeded, for the first time.

Her exquisite taste exploded on my tongue, and I was obsessed. I flattened my tongue against her, and licked up her slit, from her opening to her clit, over and over again. I replaced my fingers, plunging two inside of her as I lapped her clit and sucked it between my teeth.

Her hand plunged into my damp hair, her nails scraping against my scalp as her fingers twisted. She tugged slightly, and I craved that sensation. Like she was giving herself over to the overwhelming need just as I had.

Her hips moved up and down, little movements that revealed she wanted more. I looked up again to find her attention on the spot where my head disappeared between her legs.

And when our eyes locked, I pulled back just enough to speak between licks as my fingers continued to work inside of her.

"Grind against me, beautiful. Ride my face and come all over my tongue and fingers," I instructed, and her eyes slid closed, her hand tightening in my hair. Her hips continued to move, only faster and more urgently.

I smiled against her cunt.

"*Fuck,*" she whimpered, and I added more pressure. My tongue deliberately stroked her aching clit while my fingers coaxed her orgasm nearer. I felt her clench a second before my name tumbled from her lips on a beautiful cry.

Replacing my tongue with my other hand, I stood and watched the ecstasy tear across her features. The orgasm seemed endless as she tightened around my fingers over and over again. And I swore it took all my focus not to release my own impending orgasm all over her stomach.

"You were so wound up," I observed. "It only took a few minutes to get you to come harder than you ever have, isn't that right?"

Her groan turned into a growl as her eyes popped open. She leaned forward and ripped her dress over her head before she said, "Fuck me, Theo."

My lips tilted in a smile, and without hesitation, I tore the towel from my waist. No longer obstructed by the weight of the fabric, my cock bobbed and settled, pointing directly at her.

She leaned back on her elbows, legs still spread and her pussy dripping, as her eyes devoured me. They traveled down my chest, over my stomach, until they suddenly stopped just below my waist.

"You're…" she began, sitting up to look closer. She stared at my dick like it was the eighth wonder of the world and then finally continued, "Pierced."

I nodded and swept my fingers through the mess between her legs, using her release to start jacking myself. The sensation of my own hand wrapped around my cock was almost too much. Especially when she was staring at it with awe and curiosity.

I let her stare for a second more before I climbed over top of her and guided her backward, farther onto the bed. I couldn't wait a second longer to be inside of her. There was an itch beneath my skin that wasn't going to go away until I felt her clamping around me.

"I have an IUD," she said as I reached for the bedside table to grab a condom. I immediately stopped.

I'd been tested a few weeks ago, and all of my results came back negative. Those results were still valid, too, thanks to the woman underneath me. I couldn't have done anything that might have changed them.

"My little slut wants to take my cock raw?"

She shivered, eyes closing momentarily at my words, before she nodded and fixed me with a newly confident gaze.

"There's something else you should know before we do this," I said, gripping my length in my hand and running it through her folds.

I paused and rubbed the head over her clit in little circles, using the metal piercing at the tip for extra stimulation. While I did, she fought for the words to respond and to keep her eyes open.

"What?" she managed to say, and I bent my head down, coasting my lips over hers. Still playing her clit with the tip of my dick, she craned her neck in search of my mouth.

I realized then I still hadn't kissed her. Our lips hadn't touched more than to brush against each other like they just had. And I was ready to devour her. But not before I was inside of her.

"There's no going back after this. No one else will ever compare after me," I murmured against her lips, pressing the blunt head of my cock against her opening.

She nibbled on her bottom lip, and I licked at her mouth, eager to hear the thoughts I could see stirring behind her vivid blue eyes.

"Tell me, Nat," I murmured, and her sigh was warm against my lips.

"Prove it," she said with a cocky little grin. One that I greatly enjoyed wiping from her face when I thrust into her less than a second later. She barely got the words out before I was completely seated inside her, my hips flush with her ass and my eyes threatening to roll back in my head.

"Oh, fuck," were the next words out of her mouth as her nails dug into my biceps. I stilled, giving her a moment to adjust to my size.

With our eyes locked, it was better than I ever could've imagined. Better than it had ever been before, and that thought spurred me to move.

I pulled out slowly, studying her expression and recognizing the first time she felt the piercing against her G-spot. She gasped as the metal slipped against her upper wall, and she tensed beneath me.

"Do that again," she muttered, and I did. I pushed back in, still keeping my strokes slow as I teased that little spot, and let her feel every inch of me as I pulled back out. I repeated the rhythm until she was panting and writhing beneath me. Her hands roamed over my arms and shoulders, her hips tilted upward to meet mine, and I let go.

My hips snapped in a deliberate, even tempo, driving all the way in and touching every part of her on the way out. Her face contorted in pleasure. Her mouth dropped open on a gasp, and I reveled in the noises spilling from her lips.

Her brow furrowed, and she rocked beneath me, still searching for more.

I dropped all of my weight to my forearm on one side of her head and reached for a pillow just behind her head. I pushed it beneath her hips and drove into her deep.

A few expletives tumbled out of her mouth at the change in position, and I smiled until she tightened around me, and I nearly lost it.

I was lost in her. She was so warm and wet and I devoured every single one of her minute reactions. I committed every noise and movement to memory. I would have them all memorized by the time it was over.

"How good does it feel, Natalie?" I asked, and she moaned, her hands diving into my hair.

"So. Fucking. Good," she said between thrusts.

"The cock you weren't supposed to have. The last person you were supposed to let fuck you. That's the best cock, isn't it?"

She didn't have to respond for me to know I was right.

My grip on her hip was punishing, and I snapped my hips in tandem with her eager, hurried breaths. Her tits bounced, and I leaned forward to lick over the curve of her breast before taking one of those pink nipples between my teeth. I bit and sucked and licked, and in the next second, she was gushing all over my cock.

God, did I want to extend it forever, but finally having her made it hard to hold back.

We would do it all again. I would have her again and again until we were both sated.

Kissing up her chest, I nipped at her collarbone and licked up her neck. In a few quick movements, I pushed my hands beneath her, crossed my arms behind her to grip her hips with the opposite hand, and pulled her up.

Without pulling out, I sat back and settled her on my cock. Her ass hit my thighs and drove me even deeper into her. Unaware that deeper existed until I found it.

Her arms fastened around my neck, and I tangled my fingers in her long, dark hair. It flowed down her back in simple waves, and it was too tempting not to run my fingers through and grip hard.

I tugged roughly enough to make her head snap back, giving me even better access to lavish kisses and bites along her neck. I pushed up into her at a punishing pace, and with each thrust, the tighter she grew. She was making a mess of both of us, the way she creamed all over my cock. With my free hand, I palmed her ass and guided her up and down over me.

She was so wet that I easily slipped in and out, and I felt my own orgasm barreling toward me at top speed. But I wasn't done with her. I needed one more.

Just one. *For now.*

"Such a good little slut, taking this cock like you were made to do it."

She clenched, but my movements didn't stutter, although it became harder to speak.

"You're so greedy for it, clenching so hard and eager to come," I growled into her skin. "Are you going to come all over my cock, Natalie?"

She tried to nod, but I still had a hold of her hair. I loosened my grip because I wanted to see her eyes.

Her head dropped forward, and her eyes locked on mine. She was drunk with pleasure, liquid in my hands, but still able to bounce and grind on top of me.

Skin slapping and our breaths mixing, I held her tangled hair in my hand so she had no choice but to stare right at me.

"This is only a taste of what it's like to be my little slut." She whimpered at my words, and I smiled. "*God,* I can feel you trembling. How long has it been since someone's fucked you right?"

Her eyes began to close, but I yanked on her hair. Startled, they flew open, immediately settling on me.

"Eyes on me, Natalie. I want to watch you fall apart on my lap."

Her nails dug into my skin, and she fought my grip on her hair to lean closer. I loosened my hold, and her teeth sunk into my shoulder as she tightened around my cock. I held her closer as she fell apart, just as I wanted. She pulsed around me, and she moaned into my skin. The pain from her bite was sharp and made the pleasure pulsing through me more vivid.

Through the first wave, she leaned back, closing her eyes and letting the intense pleasure wash over her. The sight of her completely coming undone sent me over the edge, too.

My own orgasm consuming me, I stilled as my release pumped deep inside of her. Perfect sounds were still spilling from her lips, and all I wanted to do was taste them. Finally, my mouth crashed down over hers.

Yes, yes, yes, I chanted in my head.

I cupped her cheek, brushing my thumb over her cheekbone as she tilted her head to the side.

She eagerly kissed me back, her fingers in my hair tugging me closer. And those sounds on her lips tasted better than I ever expected. Our tongues danced together as she continued to writhe on top of me, and my hands memorized every inch of her skin.

I kissed her possessively, a whirlwind of lips, teeth, and tongue. It was thorough, commanding, and reckless.

ELEVEN

HOW EMBARRASSING

Natalie

THREE ORGASMS. THEO HAD GIVEN ME THREE ORGASMS, AND EACH one was somehow better than the one before.

And that was saying something when the first one was utterly mind-blowing.

Our lips disconnected, and our heavy breaths mingled as he dropped his forehead to mine. We sat like that, still holding one another, for several minutes before he laid me back onto the bed.

My body was spent, and the soft mattress and blankets felt good beneath me. Theo's cock had slowly softened inside me, and I groaned when he finally slipped free. His tormented brown eyes swept over my body, and he watched himself pull out. Between my thighs, I could feel his cum leaking out of me, and I shuddered and groaned at the sensation.

Like he'd never seen anything like it before, he ran his finger down my slit, collecting his release and pushing it back inside with one finger. I gasped at the intrusion and shrunk away from his touch.

"Sensitive?" he asked with a smile, finally looking away from where his finger disappeared inside me.

"A little."

His smile took on a darker quality, and he pulled his finger free. Lifting his hand, his finger shined with our combined releases, and he pressed it to my lips. Greedily, I opened, and he slid his thick finger against my tongue. I sucked it like I imagined I would his cock. The salty, earthy flavor exploded on my tongue.

He groaned, eyes flaring with desire, and I saw that cock I so badly wanted in my mouth begin to stir back to life.

Short refractory period. Good to know.

He drew his finger from my mouth and stood from the bed. Captivated by the pure power strumming through his muscular, tattoo-covered body, I momentarily forgot how our last time ended—with him storming out of the kitchen and then leaving entirely.

"Are you going to run this time, too?" I asked before I could think much harder about the question. Or that I'd asked it because I didn't want him to run. The mix of emotions I'd felt the last time it happened were as surprising as the entire interaction—if that's what you wanted to call it—in the kitchen.

With a cocky grin over his shoulder, he opened the door and walked across the hall into the bathroom. He returned only a moment later with a damp washcloth in one hand.

I hadn't moved, and he kneeled on the bed next to me once more, using the cloth to wipe between my legs. He tossed it on the bedside table when he finished and reclined back onto the pillows next to me.

"Earlier, you said something about Caroline and the advice she gave you," he said, and I sat up. I found a blanket next to me and tossed it over myself, only for Theo to rip it off a second later.

"Don't cover up," he instructed, leaving no room for argument. "What did Caroline say?"

I shook my head and sighed. "Does it really matter?"

He was silent, and I glanced over at him to find him looking at me, waiting.

"I went over to her house this morning. She talked me into doing." I struggled for the right word and settled on—"this"— waving between the two of us.

"She convinced you to wait for me to get out of the shower and seduce me?" he clarified, and I couldn't help but laugh.

"Did I seduce you? I don't think you could really call it that." He shrugged, and I continued, "She pretty much told me to stop worrying about the morality of it or how *other people* might react."

The man of few words didn't say anything else.

My conversation with Caroline had gone exactly as I'd expected it to. She'd been preparing for her annual Labor Day party when I'd walked in unannounced, found a bottle of wine in the fridge, and opened it without a word. She'd stood there, brows raised and eyes wide, patiently waiting for me to explain as I took a few long gulps.

So I sat down at her bar and told her everything. Then I'd spent longer than necessary answering her very detailed and probing questions. And only after I'd answered every single one did she tell me to go for it.

She wholeheartedly believed Ryder would forgive me if he ever did find out. She told me that I needed to do something for myself. She berated me for not doing it sooner, for not focusing more on myself. She said all this while I stayed silent.

I guessed she wasn't wrong. I'd been predictable and dependable my entire life. Both at work and at home. Partially to make up for the fact that I'd been a teen mom and because my family needed me to be. I'd been so focused on raising Ryder, on taking care of Mark, on making sure we were not a statistic that I'd come last.

And now, I wanted to be anything but predictable and dependable. I wanted to be Theo's…slut.

Then Caroline reasoned—albeit badly—that the sex might

not even be that good. With an expression that told me she barely believed her own words, she said that the insane chemistry might fizzle out the moment we tumbled into bed together. Or that after the orgasm-high wore off, we wouldn't want anything else to do with each other.

I believed that about as much as she did, and that was when I realized it didn't matter. I'd truly gone to her not for advice or with the expectation that she would talk me out of it. I'd gone to her because I knew she *would* tell me to do it, and I wanted someone to agree. I wanted someone to tell me I wasn't a bad person for wanting him. Or for knowing it was a bad idea yet doing it anyway.

I'd already decided that I was going to give in, and I knew she would confirm my decision and feed my delusion.

What else were best friends for?

I left her house resolute in my decision. As much as going behind my son's back sounded like the worst possible outcome, staying away from Theo felt impossible.

And as I headed home, I hoped we could fuck each other out of our systems. I hoped that once we slipped apart, sweat slicking our skin and trying to catch our breath, that we would mutually agree to never do it again.

I thought about that possibility and the possibility that he'd think I was crazy, when I slid onto his bed. It wasn't until the shower shut off that nerves, so sharp and intense that I thought I might be sick, filled the pit in my stomach.

Now, I was staring at him, curious about the thoughts swirling behind his deep brown eyes, and I knew I'd want more. One time was nowhere near enough.

"You can't tell me you haven't thought about what...about how..." I stuttered over the words, struggling to find the right ones, but he understood what I meant.

"Why do you think I left?" he finally asked. His jaw worked, and I could feel the tension rolling off of him.

I opened my mouth to say what, I didn't know, but I didn't

get the chance. Before I could utter a word, Theo was back on top of me, forcing my thighs wide once again as his hard cock pressed against my cunt.

Need immediately began thrumming through me and climbed higher when his tattooed hand collared around my throat. His manly scent surrounded me, and with his weight on top of me, he was all-consuming.

I reached a shaking hand out to trace across his chest. My fingertips brushed down, stroking across his abdomen. Every muscle tightened, rippling with desperate need that I swore I felt too.

"I've thought about it all," he muttered, dipping down to taste my skin with his tongue. "But the only thing I'm thinking about right now is how gorgeous you looked coming around my cock. And how much I want to see it again."

He drug the blunt head of his cock along my slit, and I shifted under his weight, widening my legs. He skimmed the tip of his nose along my jaw until his lips briefly met mine. I pressed my hips higher as he nipped at my bottom lip once. The second time he bit me, it was hard enough that I thought he'd draw blood.

The combination of his cock teasing me, his hand around my throat, and his teeth at my lip made me moan and writhe harder.

"And that's all you should be thinking about, too," he murmured against my mouth and filled me in one easy thrust.

He stretched me unlike anything I'd experienced before, and the brush of his piercing against my inner walls was unfamiliar yet fucking phenomenal. Like he'd submitted to the pain of the piercing just for my pleasure.

His strokes were steady and deep. I locked my legs around him, crossing my ankles, and forcing him even deeper. My fingers brushed over the tender skin along his shoulder where my teeth had sunk into him earlier. The area was raised and red, and I'd somehow bitten directly between two dark, intricate tattoos.

He groaned and kissed me with the same fervor in which he fucked me.

"*Fuck*, you feel…" He trailed off, continuing to kiss me and quickening his pace. "You're going to enjoy being my slut, aren't you?"

"Are you saying you want more?" I asked. My nails drug down his back, leaving red lines and marking him further. "Already?"

He let out a carnal growl and rose up on his knees. The hand that had gone limp around my throat tightened once again. His other hand plunged between us and stroked my swollen clit, making me quiver with need. All other snarky comebacks poised on my lips quickly fell away.

"Tell me I don't hold your pleasure in my hands, Natalie," he growled down at me. "You would let me do anything I wanted to you because you're so desperate to be fucked by me."

My pussy clenched, and I could already feel my orgasm building and coiling deep inside of me. His pace was punishing, thrusts quick and hard as he fucked me thoroughly.

"Am I wrong?" he asked between clenched teeth.

I managed to shake my head in answer. Around him, it was like I was spellbound. In any other circumstance, I wouldn't have given him that power. But I liked the way it felt when he owned my body. I wanted him to use me, degrade me, control me.

"How embarrassing," he muttered, not easing the pressure around my throat, the circles on my clit, or the punishing thrusts. "You're creaming all over my cock like you enjoy being used. Do you like this, Natalie? Do you like being treated like my own personal fucktoy?"

My eyes fluttered, and my cunt constricting around his cock was answer enough that I didn't need words.

"Yes, there it is." His words were drawn out, and I scraped my nails down his chest, his stomach, and clutched his wrist where his hand was still around my throat. Not because I wanted him to remove it, which I saw in his eyes he contemplated, but because I wanted it tighter.

The pressure change was slight, but enough that it impeded my breathing and made me lightheaded.

"You're—you're so big," I babbled mindlessly. "And it feels so, so good. *Oh, fuck.*"

"Show me that pretty face when you come. *Show me,*" he growled, pounding into me. "Clench around my cock and come with my hand around your throat."

Three more merciless pumps of his hips and blinding ecstasy surrounded me. I gripped his wrist with both hands, hoping he would keep me grounded because I felt like I was going to float away.

The aftershocks were consistent, and I continued pulsing around him as he came inside of me. I loved the way his face contorted in pleasure. The way his brows furrowed and his eyes couldn't help but close. Every muscle in his body tensed, and his full lips parted as a groan shuddered through him. Watching the dark, beautiful man overcome by ecstasy was captivating.

Both of us were slick with sweat, breathing hard, and still clinging to one another.

As I had before, I felt his release slide out of me when he slipped out. Eyeing my leaking pussy, he pumped his fingers into me and watched my face as I gasped and moaned.

Finally, he stood and reached for the damp cloth on the bedside table. That was when I noticed the time.

"Oh, shit. I have to go," I said, quickly jumping from the bed and standing on wobbly legs that nearly gave out under me. But Theo was there to steady me with a firm grip on my hip.

"Now you're the one running?" he joked.

"No, Caroline is having a Labor Day party, and I was supposed to be there twenty minutes ago. Actually…" I said. And I didn't know what came over me, but I continued, "You should come, too."

His eyebrows rose, and he looked at me like I'd grown two heads.

"You live here, too. At least for now, and most of our neighbors will be there," I reasoned.

I could see that it was on the tip of his tongue to say no, but slowly a devious smile crept across his face. I stiffened because I knew that look couldn't mean anything good.

"Okay, I'll go. But on one condition."

Hesitantly, I asked, "Okay, what condition?"

"Don't shower. I want you to smell like me, smell like sex. And I want my cum dripping out of your pussy the entire time," he instructed, pressing his lips to mine one more time.

TWELVE
BEST FRIENDS

Theo

I SHOULDN'T HAVE GONE.

But I found myself agreeing before I even had a chance to think about it. And suddenly, I was walking down the street with Natalie, holding a bowl of something she'd made. It was too domestic for my taste, and all I wanted was to get back inside of her.

Natalie pushed open Caroline's front door, and I walked in behind her. She put her little white sundress back on and replaced her panties with another similar pair. I loved knowing that my cum was still inside of her and how messy her panties would be afterward.

The thought made me smile to myself as I shut the door behind me.

Caroline's house was slightly larger than Natalie's. Everything I could see was either white or black and a stark contradiction to Natalie's colorful home.

From the entryway, you could see all the way through the house and out the floor to ceiling glass doors leading out to the pool. A pool filled with children. *Screaming* children.

I wasn't morally opposed to children, but I also wasn't a fan when they screamed. Or cried. Or when they were dirty.

We didn't make it but a few steps inside before Caroline stepped into view just down the hall and beelined for us. Her blonde hair was tied up on top of her head, and she was wearing a sheer black dress over her bikini.

In one hand she held a wine glass, and in the other she was struggling to carry a cooler. She dropped the cooler in the hallway and continued toward us. Her eyes were appraising and wary, darting back and forth between me and Natalie before she came to a stop in front of her friend.

"You're late," she said with a smile, still leaning forward to give Natalie a hug. "And I hope it's for a good reason," Caroline whispered in her ear with a sly smile and a glance back to me.

I shuffled on my feet, not sure how I felt about anyone knowing exactly what had just gone down. It wasn't much of a secret if everyone knew.

Caroline stepped back and raked her eyes over Natalie from head to toe, like she was looking for signs that Natalie had heeded her advice. But I hadn't marked her anywhere Caroline would see. I'd wanted to, but I'd refrained in case anyone became too suspicious. The last thing I wanted was to put Natalie in an awkward position, having to explain away bruises and bite marks with ridiculous lies.

"Anyway," Natalie said, turning back to me. "I'm going to take this"—she plucked the bowl from my hands— "to the kitchen."

And she was gone before I could argue.

Caroline, however, hung back and appraised me as she had Natalie.

"It's nice to see you again," she said, a knowing smile tugging at her lips. Caroline was quite a few inches taller than Natalie and a few years younger. I didn't know much about her, but I did know that she was outspoken and confident. And she genuinely cared about Natalie.

She sipped from her drink as I nodded my greeting. Under her intense stare, I contemplated bolting. Between the children screaming and the number of other neighbors who would likely be confused by my presence, it was the last thing I wanted to do. The door was right behind me, too. It would have been easy enough to leave before hardly anyone noticed.

"I don't usually like this shit either," Caroline said, stepping up beside me and turning to face the chaos at the back of her house. Eyeing the crowd, I already felt out of place with my black boots and jeans. I'd swapped out my black T-shirt for a white one, but I still stuck out. Everyone else was in normal pool party attire—bikinis, swim trunks, flip-flops, weird-shaped hats.

"Most of these people annoy the crap out of me, actually," she continued, and I couldn't help but chuckle at her honesty. "But their drama? Their drama is worth putting up with their personalities."

Down the hallway, a man in American flag swim trunks and a button-down white collared shirt walked from the living room on the right into the kitchen on the left.

"Like him." She pointed to where the guy had just been. "His name is Ralph, and he lives two houses down from me. He's hit on me every single time I've seen him since they moved in a few years ago."

She took a sip of her drink and snapped when a woman with brown hair wearing a yellow swimsuit began yelling at two children splashing each other in the pool.

"Ooo, and that's Gina. Her husband, whose name I can't remember, lost his job a year ago and apparently can't find another one. She's had to go back to work while he sits at home all day doing God knows what. I bet in another year they're divorced," she sighed and looked back at me.

"So, it's much more entertaining than you'd think. And even if you still hate it, I bought good beer. It's in the fridge."

She walked off quickly after that, grabbing the cooler she'd dropped and heaving it back into the kitchen.

I could still feel the door at my back. Like it was taunting me with the peace and solitude I knew waited for me back at Natalie's. Along with a bed that smelled just like her.

But she'd be upset if I left. She'd wanted me to come, so I'd find a quiet spot away from the chaos, stay only as long as necessary, and hopefully no one would want to socialize with me.

Walking further into the house, I stopped in the kitchen and pulled open the stainless-steel fridge. Almost everyone was outside, crowded around the patio and Caroline's in-ground pool. Natalie had mentioned that we were about half an hour late, but drinks were already steadily flowing like they'd been there for hours.

Toward the back of the yard, I spotted a small bench tucked under one of the larger trees, and it was the perfect place to watch without being part of the chaos. I grabbed a beer and braced myself for the mayhem.

Pushing open the sliding glass door, the sun felt good on my skin. I found my sunglasses in my pocket and put them on as I trudged past a pool full of children. The sunlight reflected off the water while their parents sat at the pool's edge or at the tables and chairs on the patio watching. The children were screaming and splashing, and at the end of the day, there was bound to be more water outside of the pool than in it.

I held my breath until I sat down on the shady bench without anyone approaching me. I caught a few sideways glances in my direction from the few people who obviously didn't know how to hide their stares behind their sunglasses.

But I didn't care about any of them. I tipped the beer to my lips and scanned the yard for the person who held all of my attention and monopolized every single one of my thoughts.

I spotted Natalie among a small group, crowded around a table full of food in a spot safe from the sun's rays. She was talking to the woman wearing the yellow swimsuit, Gina. And like she could feel me watching, Natalie's face tilted toward me.

I wasn't too far away to see the faint smile tugging at her lips as she struggled to continue paying attention to the woman in front of her. For once, I didn't try to hide my own smile. She bit her bottom lip, shook her head, and turned back to the woman.

Fuck, she was perfect. Her black hair fell down her back in dark waves, and the round sunglasses that sat on her nose looked fucking adorable on her.

She looked the part of the innocent, well-mannered suburban woman with her white sundress, strappy sandals, and a sweet laugh that burst from her lips like a goddamn melody. But knowing that behind closed doors she became the exact opposite just for me, it made my cock stir behind my zipper. Which was unfortunate with the amount of people and children around.

I continued to watch her from a distance as she made her way around the party. Even from where I sat, I was sucked into her orbit and entranced by watching her interact with everyone else. She was kind and talkative and gave every person she spoke to her undivided attention. Until she couldn't stand but glance over at me, feeling my eyes on her and giving me a seductive, secretive smile.

At one point she was close enough that I heard her laugh over the dull roar of the other guests, and I wanted whomever she was speaking to to say whatever they'd said again just so I could hear the sound one more time.

It was while I was contemplating if it was too early to leave and take Natalie with me that my phone buzzed in my pocket. I smiled when Ryder's name and photo filled the screen, my normal reaction to speaking to my best friend. But my smile dropped, and my mouth went dry when I realized the enormity of the secret I'd now have to keep.

"Hey, man, what's up?" I tried to sound casual and normal as I answered, but there was a strained edge to my voice that he no doubt would have picked up on in person. Hoping the phone distorted the sound, I held my breath.

"Hey! Long time, no talk," Ryder responded in his usual

upbeat manner. And I was immediately overwhelmed by relief and guilt.

We'd texted a few times since he'd left for his internship, but he was so busy we hadn't spoken as often as we normally would have. It was good to hear his voice, yet anxiety outshined every other emotion. It was a tight ball sitting heavy in my chest and making it hard to think straight.

"Well, you've been super busy becoming an astronaut or something," I said, and he chuckled.

"Not an astronaut, but we have been working with telescopes, and a few other people are working on a project for the space station."

My best friend was so smart.

"Okay, so tell me then: are aliens real? I know you're probably sworn to secrecy or something, but I'm sure there's a clause for friends, right?"

He laughed again, and I fidgeted with the label on my beer bottle. It felt good—*normal*—to talk to him like this.

"I'm an intern. The best I know is that the director takes his coffee with one and a half sugars and a dash, specifically a dash, of cream."

"That's really disappointing. Maybe you should—" My words were abruptly cut off by a high-pitched scream. One of the kids decided to push another into the pool, which created an even more chaotic frenzy of splashing and rough housing.

"What are you doing? You at a party or something?" he asked, and I froze. I couldn't lie and tell him I was at his house or on campus.

And I would never go to a party without Ryder as my buffer.

Taking a deep, grounding breath, I decided the truth was probably the best bet. I decided I'd tell him the truth about everything that I could and would only leave out the parts that were necessary.

It was to be expected that Natalie and I would get closer,

maybe spend more time together. We were living in the same house. So it wasn't that strange, I tried to convince myself.

"Umm…yeah, Natalie dragged me to this party at Caroline's."

Ryder laughed, then groaned. "*Fuck*, Caroline. That woman has been my wet dream since I was like fifteen. But Natalie? You on a first-name basis with my mom now?"

Immediately, I ran over every single word I'd said—which hadn't been many—and couldn't come up with a reason why he'd think that was odd.

"I guess so. It would be weird if I called her Ms. Calaway all the time, don't you think? And it's not like I'm going to call her Mom."

There was some movement on the other end before Ryder said, "I guess so, but it's still my mom. Just a little weird. How's it been having her as a roommate?" he asked with a chuckle, and I cringed.

Playing along like nothing had changed was going to be more difficult than I imagined.

"Fine, we don't see much of each other." Not a lie, but also not entirely true. Had he asked me the day before, it would've been completely accurate.

But today changed everything.

"You're telling me she hasn't forced you to eat dinner with her or guilted you into a movie night?"

"Umm…no, not really." My eyes still hadn't strayed from Natalie, who had begun talking to one of the children. She sat at the edge of the pool, her feet dangling into the water.

"Hmm," he mused like he didn't totally believe me. "That's what she does when I'm home. Not that I'm complaining, but—"

"Well, I'm not her kid," I said quickly. Too quickly, based on the silence on the other end. I needed him to remember that, though. That was not our relationship at all.

"Yeah, right," he finally said, and I heard the hesitation in his tone. Quickly, I searched for a topic that would divert the attention from me and Natalie, at least for this conversation.

"How's Texas?" I tried, and he sighed loudly.

"Hotter than balls and so fucking humid. I swear, I can't breathe when I walk outside."

THIRTEEN
DON'T COMPLICATE IT

Natalie

I NEARLY SPILLED MY DRINK WHEN CAROLINE SNUCK UP BEHIND ME and slapped my arm.

"You slut, you actually did it, didn't you?"

I felt my cheeks redden under her scrutiny as she stepped in front of me. Since we'd walked in, she'd been pulled in every direction, so we hadn't had time to talk. But I knew I wouldn't escape without a conversation. Otherwise, she'd be banging down my door as soon as she could. She finally found her opening over an hour later and was getting straight to the point.

Trying to do so without her noticing, I glanced back to my right where Theo was still sitting beneath the same damn tree. And it was from that small bench that he'd been watching me the whole time.

A smug smile played at his full lips, and his sunglasses were perched on his nose.

I couldn't see his eyes behind the polarized lenses, but I'd felt them on me every single second. They followed me and tracked my every movement as I made my way through the party. Even when he'd had his phone out earlier, talking to someone for a while, he'd kept his eyes steadfast on me. I tried not to look at him, but I wasn't strong enough to escape his pull. That much I'd already learned.

"Oh my gosh, you can't stop looking at him even now."

I swung my attention back to her, shaking off the feeling of his eyes, before sipping on my drink.

"I don't know what you're talking about," I said coyly.

She scoffed immediately and looked over at Theo. "Don't give me that shit. Even from this distance, the sexual tension rolling off of the two of you is insane. And now, you're looking at each other like you've seen one another naked. *So, how was it?*"

"I'm not talking to you about this," I quickly said in a hushed tone. "At least not right now."

Although no one was nearby and everyone was still gathered around the pool several yards away, I worried that someone would overhear. I didn't want to become one of the many stories our neighbors passed around. Like we were the newest piece of town gossip to be shared over glasses of wine and between sniggered laughs.

"That's ridiculous," she argued. "I knew every detail of your and Mark's sex life. You told me when you attempted anal and how poorly it went. You told me about his leather phase. You even told me in explicit detail how he tried to—"

"Stop!" I angrily whispered, using my free hand to cover her mouth. Her giggle vibrated against my palm, and I raised my brows in silent question: *Are you going to shut up?*

Reluctantly, I removed my hand, and she immediately continued, "I'll only stop if you give me the details. Unless it was bad. Was it bad? I know we considered that possibility, but could you imagine that? Oh god, wouldn't that be awful? You have sex with your son's best friend only for it to be horrible."

I groaned. "It wasn't bad, and do not refer to him as that ever again. It makes me feel…"

"Dirty?" she supplied with a smile, and I rolled my eyes.

"Okay, so it wasn't bad? But that doesn't mean it's good either…"

"It was *incredible*," I sighed, and the smile that crossed Caroline's face was devious.

"What was incredible?" a voice asked from behind my right shoulder. I stiffened immediately but managed to force a smile onto my face and maintain my internal freakout.

"That dip you made, Tiffany," Caroline supplied smoothly. Tiffany was the nosiest of the bunch, and I could feel the smile I'd plastered on my face slipping. If she'd heard a word of our conversation, everyone else would've known in a matter of minutes.

"Oh, you're too sweet. I just wanted to say bye," Tiffany said, and I nearly sighed in relief. We said our goodbyes, and neither Caroline nor I said another word until she was well out of earshot.

"Okay, so it was incredible?"

Doing one quick glance around us to make sure no one else planned to interrupt, I nodded.

"Oh, thank God," Caroline said with relief. "But I need more than that. What's his dick like?"

"Jesus Christ, I can't believe we're talking about this right now."

Caroline gave me an unimpressed, impatient look, her blonde brows nearly hitting her hairline. "Stop acting like we don't talk about this shit all the time and spill."

She was right. It was normal for us to discuss her experiences, but I didn't always have something to share. And telling her about Theo almost felt too personal. Like it was something only for us—too special to be shared.

And that thought was terrifying enough to make me speak.

"It's perfect. *Big* and he's…pierced."

Caroline choked on her drink, nearly spewing it out of her nose as she tried to cough back her surprise. I rolled my lips to try to keep from laughing at her struggle, but I couldn't help it.

It took her several seconds to compose herself, but when she finally did, she said, "That's it. You're living my dream."

I never thought I'd hear anything like that from her. She'd spent the several years that I'd known her creating a successful career and dating whomever her heart desired. If anything, *she* was living *my* dream.

"Okay, but does he know what to do with his big, pierced cock?"

Suddenly, I was assaulted with memories from just a few hours earlier. The way he touched me, tasted me, and coaxed from my body more pleasure than I'd ever known, all while saying some of the dirtiest things I'd ever heard. It was enough to make me readjust where I stood and make my skin heat.

"Honestly, you don't even have to respond," Caroline said, pulling me from my memories with an easy smile. "It's written all over your face just how good it was."

I didn't have a chance to tell her just how right she was before her gray eyes went wide. She was peering over my right shoulder yet again, and I braced myself for another one of our neighbors to approach us. But it wasn't Stewart or Courtney who stepped up beside me.

"I'm heading back to the house. I have some assignments to catch up on," Theo whispered into my ear. An involuntary shudder ran down my spine as his hot breath hit my skin.

"Okay," I breathed out, unable to think of anything better to say and worried that if I turned around to look at him, I'd follow him out of the house and back to his bedroom.

I felt when he left. With his intense attention no longer igniting my skin, I turned back to see him disappear into Caroline's house through the sliding glass door.

"Not going to follow him?" Caroline asked quietly, and I whipped back around to glare at her.

She shrugged and finished off her drink. "Is it because you feel guilty?"

I considered how I was feeling in that moment, and I waited for the guilt to overwhelm me. But it didn't.

"No, I'm more terrified that I…I want it to happen again," I said quietly, staring down at my hands clasped in front of me instead of at my friend.

"You're both adults, Natalie, and…" She trailed off and it was unusual for Caroline to be at a loss for words. I looked up and I was even more surprised to see tears gathered in her eyes.

"Caroline, what—" I began but she waved me off.

"Just a momentary emotion, but it passed." She laughed and quickly composed herself. "I've just…I've only known you for seven years, but in that time, you've put everything aside for your family. You stayed in a marriage you didn't want to be in to raise Ryder and put your own ambitions and goals on hold to do it. You deserve something for yourself, and if Theo is that for you, then I'm all for it."

"Even if I'm going behind my son's back? Even if I'm putting at risk my entire relationship with him?" I countered.

She'd used the same reasoning when I'd spoken with her that morning, and I'd believed her then—I'd agreed with her then. But after actually being with Theo, everything had changed. The way I wanted him and the way we were drawn together felt like it was more than attraction.

And with feelings like that, it was bound to end badly.

"Does it suck that he's Ryder's best friend? Yes, absolutely it does. But like I said, you're both adults, and as long as you're both consenting, then what else is there?"

I contemplated her question, her reasoning for a moment, when she added, "Does the age difference bother you?"

It was hard to believe there were fourteen years between us. I was starting eighth grade when he was born. I was likely much closer in age to his mom than I was to him. When I considered those things, the age difference was hard to ignore. But most of the time, it felt like we were on level ground. Age truly was just a number.

I pushed my hand through my tangled hair and tried to steady the nervous pounding of my heart. "No, honestly, I've barely thought about that aspect of it. It doesn't feel like there's much of an age difference at all when it's just us. But someone could say that I'm taking advantage of him. He's living in my house because he has nowhere else to go. The age thing just makes it worse," I said, my voice getting louder until I took a breath and continued in an angry whisper. "What if he thinks the only reason he's allowed to stay now is because we're having sex?"

"Okay, now, you're just being ridiculous. Stop for a second and take a breath." Caroline didn't stop scowling at me until I did as she said. She talked me through three more deep breaths and then said, "Let's try this again. Do you really think *he* thinks all of that? That you're taking advantage of him?"

My shoulders dropped, and I hung my head. "No…"

"Exactly, so enough with that shit. It's just sex, Nat. It doesn't have to be complicated. Enjoy it while it lasts, and don't over-think it."

I didn't say anything more because I couldn't. A few of the other partygoers had left, while others looked like they were preparing to leave.

After everyone had finally gone, I stayed around to help Caroline clean up while trying to control my anxious thoughts. Thoughts that had centered around Theo since the day he'd moved in. More specifically, they were hung up on what would happen when I got home.

And the deadly spiral my mind had succumbed to didn't ease even when I pushed through the front door and nervously started up the stairs.

But the moment I hit the landing, my phone began vibrating in my hand. And when I looked down at the name scrolling across the screen, it was no longer a decision I could make: going to Theo's room or continuing to my own. The decision had been made for me.

Theo's door was mostly open, and I could clearly see him seated on his bed, books open around him, and his laptop propped on his knee. He turned his head the second I stepped into view and began to set his computer aside until he noticed my phone in my hand.

The muscles in his jaw jumped, and his hand tightened around the computer. I couldn't look away from him, and as badly as I wanted to ignore the call and walk straight to him, it was that feeling that made me answer even quicker.

"Hey, Ryder!" I said with real enthusiasm. Only a little louder and more exaggerated to help stifle the disappointment when I continued past Theo's room.

FOURTEEN

THE BEST WAY TO BLOW OFF STEAM

Theo

THE DOOR SLAMMED CLOSED BEHIND ME, AND I STALKED FARTHER into the house. The cool, calm demeanor I'd crafted was near crumbling from just one fucking phone call.

But that was all it took when it came to my mother.

I paced around the kitchen, circling the island, trying and failing to calm down.

Since I'd last spoken to her, she'd gotten a new number, and so had I. Thinking it could be someone calling about one of the several jobs I'd applied to or the apartments I'd inquired about, I answered the unknown number.

But it wasn't Susie from Human Resources calling to set up an interview. It was my mother, Kimberly Wilde, calling to "*check in.*" I hadn't the first clue how the fuck she got my new number, but nothing should have surprised me when it came to her.

I definitely shouldn't have been surprised that the call ended in a request for "just a little cash to get her by." In the past, I'd expected her calls. But I didn't think she had the courage to ask me for money anymore.

My mom was a compulsive gambler. She hid it really well for

a while until I was in high school. At that point, I was old enough to notice her mood swings and recognize that more valuable items around the house were going missing.

It was when she'd cleared out all their accounts and gambled away their savings that my dad decided he'd had enough. He left, and my older brother left not long after.

I was sixteen at the time and didn't have another option. Neither of them wanted to drag me along, so I watched over her for as long as I could. I lasted a year before I also couldn't take it.

On my seventeenth birthday, I moved out. I tried to help her for as long as I could, but nothing was working. I had to cut off all contact for my own sanity and well-being.

You would think that her entire family leaving her would make some sort of impact, but it didn't.

After I turned twenty, had a little bit of money, was working at Haven City, and decided to enroll in college, she came back around. I realized then it was easier to give her a little cash here or there than wait for her to escalate when I told her no. But I couldn't do it forever. Eventually she began asking for more than I could give, and the little I could manage wasn't enough.

When I told her it was the last time I gave her anything, she'd broken into our little rental house—mine and Colby's—and stolen all the cash I'd had on hand and anything else she could find. Anything she could easily sell for quick cash.

I'd been the reason Colby didn't call the cops. When we'd come home to find the place ransacked and her face plastered all over the camera footage, I'd had to pay him for the stuff she'd stolen as well as any other damages he saw fit to charge me for. It was either that or he wouldn't hesitate to file a police report.

After Colby's payout, buying myself a new laptop for classes, and my tuition—which was only partially covered by scholarships—I was broke. But I wasn't just broke. I was broke and homeless.

While lugging the sad remains of my belongings from Colby's house, I'd realized I was right being done enabling my mother. It was no longer easier to give her money—even if I only had a few bucks to spare—than deal with her rage.

It was never enough for her. The hundred bucks I gave her the week before she'd broken into our place was "an insult," as she'd called it when I confronted her. She knew I had more, so she took it. In her mind, she was my mother, and I should have wanted to help her. I owed her because she raised me.

And if I didn't help her, I was ungrateful. So she took what she felt she deserved.

My teeth ground together, and my body vibrated with cold anger.

She'd turned my life upside down, yet I'd protected her. I'd kept her out of jail, and she still had the audacity to call me afterward and ask for more. She had no remorse.

Ryder told me to file a police report, but I hoped spending my life savings to keep her out of jail would mean she'd be out of my life for good. That was all wishful fucking thinking. And, looking back on it, I wish I had called the cops.

I braced my palms on the counter and took a deep breath.

The only consolation was she still had no idea where I was. And I was going to do everything in my power to keep it that way. I could block her number and ignore her calls, but every time she showed up in person, something worse was on the horizon.

Hopped up on adrenaline and frustration, I paced back and forth between the living room and the kitchen, wearing a hole in the hardwood, until I fell into one of the large chairs near the TV.

I pushed my hands through my hair, bracing my elbows on my knees as I leaned forward. After several deep breaths and trying every other trick I could dream up, the irritation still sat heavy and uncomfortable on my skin. And I didn't know if it was the call itself or my reaction to it that frustrated me more. Hearing her voice and pleas for help wasn't supposed to affect me anymore.

At the front of the house, the door opened, instantly pulling me from my thoughts. The click of Natalie's heels echoed down the hallway, and a few seconds later, she stepped into the kitchen. Her cell phone was to her ear, several bags in her hands, and a concerned look marring her gorgeous features.

"Yes, I'll handle it on Monday," she said with an exasperated sigh and tossed her bags down by the kitchen island. Then she toed off her shoes while still listening to the person speak on the other end.

Her long, dark hair was pulled back by a clip, and the navy-blue pencil skirt she wore hugged her hips and fell right above her knees. She was breathtaking, but I could also feel the tension rolling off her in waves.

She still hadn't noticed me sitting in the corner of the living room, so I took the opportunity to run my eyes over every inch of her. Something I hadn't had the chance to do in the past three days.

Ever since she'd walked past my room after Caroline's party, we'd missed each other at every opportunity. That night, she'd stayed in her room, and I was sure she'd needed the distance to get her head around what we'd done earlier that day.

But I'd already thought enough about it and decided that I needed it to happen again. I'd already jumped off the metaphorical cliff, and I didn't have a fucking parachute. So, I might as well enjoy the fall.

I hoped she would come to the same conclusion.

"Yeah, you too," she said and dropped her phone on the counter. Bracing her hands on the island, she let her head fall forward. She sucked in a deep breath, and I heard her release it, but the tightness in her shoulders was unmoving.

"Tough day?" I finally asked, uncomfortable with watching her without her knowing.

She jumped at the sudden sound of my voice but quickly recovered with a shake of her head. "Tough week," she muttered, pulling her hair free from the clip and letting it fall in waves around her shoulders.

"Do you want to talk about it?" I offered, and the surprise on her face made me chuckle.

"You don't like talking," she said skeptically, and I shrugged, leaning back into the chair and watching her closely.

I rested my elbows on the armrests as she removed her blazer, tossing it on one of the barstools. She didn't try to hide the way her eyes raked over me or the soft smile that sat on her plump, kissable lips.

"Yeah, but you do."

Her smile widened slightly, but it was the interest flaring to life behind her blue eyes that hypnotized me. And I hoped that meant she wasn't going to keep from us what we both wanted.

For her, I would've talked about whatever was bothering her until we were both blue in the face. Or at least I would've listened and chimed in when necessary, but I didn't think that's what she wanted. She rounded the couch, her eyes fixed on me. Her steps were slow and purposeful, and my cock was already hard behind my zipper.

Even the way she walked got me hard.

"I don't wanna talk, Theo," she said, stopping in front of me, her legs barely brushing the inside of my thighs. She pushed out a long breath. "I don't want to think."

She was so close I could easily make out the quick rise and fall of her chest.

"That's something I can help with," I said, my voice unintentionally dropping an octave. "But we didn't talk about limits. Do you have any?"

She stood, thinking thoughtfully for a moment, and I could see the wheels in her head turning. It was a struggle, but while she thought, I kept my hands to myself, not wanting to pressure her to decide quickly or say something she didn't mean.

"Just don't umm…slap me in the face. I think that's really the only major one. But if you do something I don't like, I'll tell you to stop. What about you?"

I shook my head and laced my fingers through hers, pulling her closer by half a step. "Not exactly. But we need a safe word."

She nodded and narrowed her eyes like she was trying to think of one. But I'd already considered all the options.

"Red means stop. Yellow means slow down, and green means keep going."

"The stoplight system," she mused, curiosity lacing her voice.

"You've heard of it?"

"Yes."

"But haven't used it?" I added, filling in the gaps in her tentative, one-word answer.

She shook her head and let her eyes trail over my body.

I didn't mention that I hadn't used it either. I hadn't had a reason to. Ava and I had a basic safe word she'd chosen, "bananas," but we rarely did anything that would warrant its use. Same with any of my other partners.

But the things I wanted to do with Natalie. The way I wanted to explore her body, we needed more. I wanted her to feel safe with me no matter what. And a definitive system, something she could use no matter what, was a step toward that.

"If anything we ever do becomes too much, tell me. Don't hesitate."

She nodded and tightened her hold on my hand. "I trust you," she said quietly, and my chest tightened at her confession. Possession wound through me, and blood pounded south, my dick growing painfully hard.

"Good. Then get on your knees."

Without hesitation, her knees hit the rug in front of me. And the vision of her knelt between my thighs, eyes wide and eager, was nearly too much. It stirred a desire deep inside of me to take her. I wanted to claim her and make her beg.

I reached out and stroked down the smooth skin of her cheek. Whether she meant to or not, she leaned into the touch. Her eyes closed momentarily but opened again the second I took her chin between my forefinger and thumb.

"Open," I commanded, and she did so. I pushed my thumb against her tongue, and she sucked it deeper. "The things I want to do to you," I growled.

She peered up at me through dark lashes and smiled around my finger. "I want it."

I shook my head and pulled my thumb free. She let go with a satisfying pop, and my hand gripped the side of her neck. Her eyes were steady on mine, and I liked the confidence she exuded. Like she knew the power she held while on her knees. How weak she made me from that position.

"I want to fuck you," I began, deciding that she should know all of my intentions before we went any further. "But I also want to claim you, mark you. I want to make you cry, and I want to make you beg. The pleasure I want to give you, I want it to make you fucking delirious."

"Yes." She nodded, stare unwavering, and inched closer to me.

"Show me what this pretty mouth can do," I mused, and she reached for my button. There was a minor tremor in her fingers, but she easily unfastened my jeans and lowered the zipper.

I lifted my hips slightly, helping her pull the denim down my thighs just enough to expose my black briefs and the large bulge of my erection.

I pulled my black T-shirt over my head and dropped it on the floor beside the chair as Natalie dragged her nails down the outline of my cock. Even restricted by the fabric, we both saw it jump and flex.

Before she could get too far, I reached forward and tugged her blouse free from where it was tucked into her skirt and pulled it over her head. Her bra was white lace, and I traced the top of one breast and then the other with the tip of my finger. That contradiction was still impossible to miss. She looked angelic in the pure white, but she was seconds away from having my cock in her mouth.

Her eyes fell shut, and I smiled at the goose bumps that pebbled her flushed skin.

Yes, I would need to mark her before we were done. See the beautiful colors I could paint her skin.

I sat back once again, and Natalie didn't need any prompting. She ran her palm over my cock back and forth until I couldn't contain my groans any longer. Then she tilted forward and sucked the blunt head into her mouth through my briefs.

"*Fuck,*" I groaned, drawing the word out as she sucked harder.

My hands clutched the armrests, and I watched her lick my length with careless abandon. Too much longer, and I was worried I was going to come before I really felt her mouth. And just as the thought crossed my mind, her fingers dug under the elastic and tugged my briefs down.

My cock sprung free, hard, leaking, and primed for her mouth. Her eyes bounced back and forth from my cock to my face. And when she licked her lips, I smiled.

I gripped my cock at the base and pumped once hard before she struck out and wrapped her hand around my own. My movements stopped, and I removed my hand. The first brush of her fingers against my bare cock was euphoric.

She squeezed hard, and my head dropped back against the cushion. She pumped up and down, her touch unrelenting as she added her other hand. I chanced a look back down at her, but I was already staving off my orgasm with what was left of my restraint.

With measured determination, her hands worked in tandem, twisting and working me until a bead of precum leaked from my tip. She eyed the arousal and leaned forward. With her eyes on me, she licked the precum and smiled before she suctioned her mouth over me.

She lapped and sucked, tonguing the metal piercing and slowly pushing deeper. The stretch of her lips around my shaft was nearly obscene and almost as beautiful as watching her pussy spread around me. She worked her mouth from side to side, taking me deeper.

A little more than half my length disappeared before I felt the back of her throat, and she gagged. She began to pull back, but I weaved my fingers through her hair and collected it in my fist at the back of her head.

My fingers brushed the side of her face, and I trailed my touch down her neck.

"Relax your throat," I instructed and used my hold on her hair to ease her back down. She gagged once more but tried a second time and was able to take more of me before gagging again.

"Mmm," I mused. "So good. I didn't think such a pretty little slut would need instruction on how to suck cock."

The words were out of my mouth before I could think about them. With her mouth around my cock, giving me more pleasure than I ever knew possible, I worried that I'd gone too far until she looked up at me and smiled as much as she could.

She began to speak, but I tightened my fingers in her hair, and I refused to let her up an inch.

"Uh-uh. Didn't anyone teach you not to speak with your mouth full? Manners, baby."

Her growl vibrated through me, and I chuckled at her small display of defiance. But I quieted any further arguments by fucking up into her mouth, setting my own pace. And she took everything I gave her. She dug her nails into my thighs and swallowed me down like she was made to do it.

I fucked her mouth until I felt that imminent release barreling down my spine. I didn't want to pull her off because her mouth was the second closest I'd ever come to heaven. But I needed to feel the first closest—her cunt wrapped around me.

I pulled her back by her hair, and there was a line of spit leading from her mouth to my cock.

Her breathing was ragged, and her skin was flushed. The tears that streamed down her cheeks were black from the mascara that was perfectly brushed on her dark lashes. And if it were possible, she was even more gorgeous when she was panting from having my cock in her mouth.

"Take that skirt off and sit on my cock."

She was on her feet in a second, and while she did as I asked, I toed off my shoes and tugged off my jeans. Then I reached for her, grasping her hips and guiding her until she straddled my thighs. My hands smoothed down her curves, running over the sides of her breasts, waist, and hips as one of her palms flattened against my chest and the other gripped my cock, lining it up with her slick entrance.

I unhooked her bra and tossed it near her other clothes lying on the ground.

She rubbed the head back and forth over her pussy, teasing her clit and pushing down just enough to taunt me with the warm, wet ecstasy waiting for me.

"Such a little tease," I warned, and she grinned.

"I want you just as needy for it as I am," she said breathlessly.

Gripping her hip, I fisted my other hand in her hair and yanked her head back, exposing her neck. I kissed and nipped up her throat until my mouth was poised over hers.

"Do you not feel how hard I am for you? Trust me, I fucking *need* you," I growled against her lips and used my hold on her to shove her down onto my waiting cock. Her warm, wet cunt welcomed me.

She cried out at the stretch, and I devoured every single one of her sounds. My tongue dove deep into her mouth, dueling with hers as her pussy stretched and relaxed.

I released my hold on her hair and gripped both her hips. Slowly, I guided her to begin moving on top of me, rocking back and forth until her arousal dripped down my cock.

I loved the feel of her beneath my palms. Her smooth skin slipped against my calloused fingers, and she trembled with imminent release and unhindered pleasure. I pulled back from her mouth as her nails dug into my chest, and she really began to ride me.

Her eyes had fallen closed, and her mouth had dropped open. With her head tilted back, all evidence of previous worry or concern had vanished.

Her hips kept a steady, consistent rhythm, making sure my cock touched every inch of her inner walls before she pulled out and did it all again. While she drove the pace, I took the opportunity to touch her fucking everywhere. I noted how she reacted and what seemed to feel the best based on every shuddered breath, moan, and the way her pussy tightened around me.

And my conclusion was that my little slut liked a bite of pain.

"Talk to me, beautiful. Tell me how good it feels."

I returned one hand to her hip, my grip likely bruising exactly as I hoped it would, while my other hand palmed her breast. Using my thumb, I drew tiny circles around her dusty pink nipple and then pinched it with increasing pressure.

She gasped, and her eyes flew open, looking from her tits to my face.

'Tell me," I growled again, and she swallowed.

"It feels…*so* good."

"You know you're going to have to be more descriptive than that," I instructed. I replaced my fingers with my mouth, lapping at her peaked nipple before taking it between my teeth.

She cried out, and her movements over my cock became hurried. One of her hands dove into my hair and held me against her breast, and the other covered my hand at her hip, urging me to tighten my grip even more.

"It's better than anything I've ever felt before. The way you fill me and stretch me. And *god,* that fucking piercing."

I couldn't agree more. She was better than anything I'd ever experienced. I knew it would never be better than her. Our bodies felt like they fit together seamlessly, like we'd been fucking forever, already in tune with every movement, sound, and look.

I released her nipple and found her blue eyes hooded and blissed-out.

"Show me how good it feels by coming all over me. You think you can do that for me?"

She nodded and beared down on me. Her internal muscles worked and choked my cock as she rode closer to her orgasm. I knew she was right on the brink. It was easy to tell because her eyes were slightly distant.

My thumb wedged between us, I found her bundle of nerves and started easy circles against her clit as she rocked over me.

Her jaw dropped, her body tensed, and then she came all over me. Her moans were uninhibited and echoed in the quiet room. She pulsed around my cock as her nails bit into my skin at my neck and shoulders. Her eyes stayed on me until she couldn't help it, and they closed anyway.

If the way she tightened around me was any sign, her orgasm was intense and long, drawing out for several seconds and racking her body with a shudder afterward.

She was breathtaking, coming on my cock and taking exactly what she wanted. But I didn't give her a break.

There was a need clawing at every part of me, begging me to set it free. And before she'd even finished coming, I was out of the chair and placing her on the couch.

Her back hit the cushion, but she didn't have time to get comfortable. Like she weighed nothing more than a few pounds, I turned her over onto her knees and pressed her upper body down onto the armrest. I peered down at her cunt and ran a finger over her opening that was still pulsing and dripping.

"You came so much," I muttered, dipping a finger inside and twisting until I found her G-spot. One small touch and she nearly leaped from the couch. My other hand shot out, and I pressed my palm between her shoulders. "Be a good little slut and stay there while I take what I need."

I fisted my cock in my hand and pumped just once, reveling in her release coating every single inch. When I didn't immediately enter her, my insatiable little devil stuck her ass up higher and pushed back, searching for my cock.

"Look at you, presenting yourself for me," I mused, running my free hand over the curve of her ass before my palm cracked against it. She cried out, and the red that bloomed across her skin made my dick leak. I did it again and again, and by the time I was done, both of her cheeks were red and tender, and she was panting against the couch.

"Please," she begged, and I thrust into her.

"Only because you asked so nicely."

My thrusts were unrelenting and could have been considered punishing if I didn't know she wanted everything I was giving her and more. She backed up into me each time I pushed forward, and the words that tumbled from her lips were mostly unintelligible pleas and moans.

I thought I was in control. But I was sorely mistaken. Because with every second we were connected, the more she wrapped herself around every inch of me. Inside and out.

FIFTEEN

THE SWEET, SWEET FORBIDDEN

Natalie

NEVER HAD I BEEN FUCKED SO THOROUGHLY. AND NEVER HAD I imagined I would enjoy it so immensely.

I wanted everything he said he would give me. I wanted him to mark me, use me, and make me come. I wanted to be his slut. I wanted him to *make me* his little whore.

If what he was doing to me was the outcome, then I'd never be left wanting again.

Each thrust of his hips was brutal and tried to propel me forward, but his hand was steadfast on my shoulder. He held me in place with his other hand around my hip and only allowed me to move if it was to push back onto him harder. Which I did over and over again.

He was so big and long—especially in that position—and his movements were so unforgiving that there was a bite of pain in the stretch and fullness. But that made me crave it even more.

My face pressed into the couch, I moaned loudly. Delirious with pleasure and my body primed for a second orgasm, I begged, "Use me. *Please*, use me."

His hips stuttered for the first time a split second before his hand around my shoulder hauled me backward. Still unbelievably deep inside of me, he repositioned me until my back hit his muscular front.

His hand collared around my throat, and the subtle squeeze of his fingers made my eyes roll back. Suddenly, his mouth was at my ear, his warm breath sweeping over my skin like a promise. "You want me to use this cunt? Use your body for my own pleasure?"

I nodded weakly and pushed back into him. He was still moving, but his thrusts were slower, more measured, and taunting.

"Such a dirty little slut," he mused and bit down hard on my ear as he tightened his hand around my throat. "And so fucking perfect for me."

I turned, searching for his mouth, but I met his eyes that glimmered with a predatory gaze. A part of me was a little scared of what he could inflict. But that fear didn't diminish the trust I'd quickly gained, nor did it make me want him any less. If anything, it made me want him more because I knew he would make good on my request.

He slanted his mouth over mine and ran the hand that wasn't around my throat down the center of my body. His touch was hypnotizing and contradictory to the ruthless pace he set, driving into me with reckless abandon.

His fingers danced between my breasts over my stomach, circled my belly button, and finally cupped my pussy. I moaned, but the sound quickly transformed into a yelp when his touch turned from pleasurable to painful. I heard his hand connect with my skin before I felt the sting of pain against the top of my cunt.

Theo's chuckle in my ear was dark and devious. "You scream like you hate it, but your cunt is telling me a different story. The way you just clenched and gushed around me...I think you might actually like the pain, Natalie."

A sound between a moan and a sob broke free from my lips as he rubbed the tender area he'd slapped. My entire body rocked with the movement of his cock pumping in and out of me, and if it weren't for his hand around my throat, I wouldn't have stayed pressed against him.

"Do you want me to do it again?"

My vision went blurry and I tried to nod my head, but it didn't work.

"Say it," he warned, kissing down my neck. My hand clenched around his forearm, still rubbing my clit while my other held on to his powerful thigh behind me, hoping to keep myself grounded.

"Please do it again."

And he did. His fingers left my body only to reappear a second later, a sharp sting of pain in their wake. He slapped me a third, then a fourth time, and I could feel the tears brimming.

"Look how responsive you are. Such a good little whore, taking everything I give you. Are you going to make me come?"

I nodded.

"Where? Do you want me to pump you full or paint your back?" Each of his words was more forced than the last, and I loved the gravel-like quality of his voice when he was right on the edge.

"Inside of me. Come inside of me," I pleaded. The dire way I said the words sounded foreign to my own ears. I'd never begged or pleaded before, especially for *that*, but in Theo's arms, if it didn't happen, I felt like I'd combust.

"So, you're a cumslut, too. So fucking needy," he said against my neck.

The warmth of his body seeped into me as his fingers assaulted my clit. His hand around my throat shifted, and he tilted my head until I found his amber-colored eyes. They were gold with a small ring of green on the outer edge as they reflected in the last rays of the sunset streaming through the back window.

And it was with our eyes locked, breath mixing, and him thrusting into me with perfect precision that he said, "You want my cum? Then I need to feel you clench around me. Come for me. And make this cock come for you."

I fought to keep my eyes open as the orgasm ripped through me. I wanted to see him fall apart, too.

He pushed into me hard one final time and stilled, his entire body tensing behind me as I pulsed around him. With the first warm rush of his release, I saw a little part of his walls shatter. His jaw went slack, and a deep groan ripped from his chest.

He moaned my name, and it sounded so much better on his lips.

We stayed like that for a while, probably far longer than was necessary, letting ourselves find our equilibrium once again. I tilted my head forward, and he pressed an unsuspecting kiss to my forehead. Then he spun us until he was seated on the couch, and I was straddling his lap. He sat back into the cushions and guided me to lay down on top of him until my head rested on his shoulder. The steady, quick beat of his heart and his even breathing were the only sounds I heard.

He began to run his fingers through my tangled hair, and I found myself getting a little too comfortable. It almost felt too good and too intimate when we'd just been fucking like we hated each other.

"I need to clean myself—"

"No," he cut me off quickly, and I was in no position to argue. If he was fine with making more of a mess of both of us, then I was, too.

"What's happening right now?" I asked, unable to tamper my curiosity as his fingers continued moving through my hair.

"What do you mean?" Theo's voice was rough and tired. I liked the way it sounded more than I cared to admit.

"Why are you being so...sweet? That's not...I just—I wasn't expecting this."

He chuckled, and the sound took me so off guard I tried to sit up to look at him. But he pressed my head back down. "It's called aftercare," he said simply. "Have you never heard of it?"

I rolled my eyes, and he must've felt it because he tugged at my hair lightly, looking down at me like he wasn't impressed with the gesture.

"Yes, I've heard of it," I said, not mentioning that I'd just never been on the receiving end. "I just didn't think you would be interested in it."

He shrugged, and he settled farther back into the couch. His warmth and our non-sexual skin-to-skin contact was soothing. "It's just as much for me as it is for you. You let me degrade you and spank you...I enjoy doing this part, too."

For once in my life, I was at a loss for words, so we sat in a comfortable silence until the sunlight had completely disappeared. Running his fingers down my back, the darkness that fell over us was comforting.

"Do you want to talk about it now?" Theo asked quietly.

I liked his voice, I thought, and I wanted him to keep talking. But I didn't know if I wanted to talk. It wasn't really one big thing, as it was a million small things that kept piling and piling up until I was buried in an avalanche of never-ending problems.

"Only if you talk to me," I countered, and he stilled beneath me.

"What do you mean?"

I chuckled and ran my hand down the center of his chest, tracing the outline of the detailed ink. "I wasn't so caught up in my shit that I didn't miss the way you looked. Something's going on with you, too."

"I don't—"

"Don't deflect," I warned, and he sighed. He reached behind him, grabbed the blanket I kept there, and tossed it over the two of us. I hadn't realized until I was cocooned in warmth that I'd begun to shiver slightly.

"You first," he prompted.

I groaned, but I knew he was more likely to open up if I did.

"Work is just a lot. I have a lot of responsibilities and a lot of people depending on me, so when something goes wrong…"

"It's automatically your problem," he finished for me, and I nodded.

"Not to mention, something Caroline said the other day really…it's stuck with me."

He chuckled quietly. "Not Caroline again."

I smiled, and he resumed running his fingers through my hair. Goose bumps spread down my neck, back, and arms at the familiarness—the easiness—of the touch.

"She says a lot," Theo added. "She talks more than you do."

"She's the closest person to me. She's my best, and really my only, friend. So, when she says something, I take it to heart."

"What'd she say?" he asked, and I could tell that he was genuinely curious and not just asking to ask.

"She said that I've put off what I've wanted for too long. She said I stayed in a marriage I didn't want to be in for Ryder and that I deserve something for myself now."

He was quiet for a moment, then asked, "Something for yourself as in me?"

He correctly took my silence as confirmation.

"Do you agree with her?"

Over the last three days, I'd done a lot of thinking on the topic, and whether I deserved something for myself or not, I wanted Theo. Caroline's reasoning was just a convenient excuse for my guilty conscience.

"To an extent. Raising Ryder and making sure he had the upbringing he deserved was what I wanted, but now that he's older and Mark and I are divorced, I don't know what I want anymore."

"And that bothers you? Not knowing what you want?"

"Of course it does."

"That's when some of the best things happen," Theo said

thoughtfully. "When you least expect them and when you don't know exactly what you're looking for."

I accidentally brushed his nipple as I continued to trace the outlines of his tattoos in the dim light, and he jumped. I chuckled at his reaction but continued dusting my fingers over the planes of his muscled chest and stomach.

"Is that what happened to you then? With the Haven City?"

I felt him nod and continued, "Fess up. What made you look like you were going to beat someone's ass?"

"My mom," he said simply yet with enough disdain that I had to swallow before I responded.

"What about her?"

He shifted beneath me, and I could feel the tension thrumming through his body with the change in topic. For a moment, I considered telling him that he didn't have to tell me, but I didn't. I hardly knew the man who held me, who'd been *inside* of me. And I knew Theo wouldn't say anymore if he didn't want to.

"She called me," he said.

"Yes, moms tend to do that sometimes. It's in the handbook. It's required," I supplied with a laugh. But his responding chuckle was humorless and hollow.

"Except the only time she calls me is to ask for money."

My hand against his chest stopped, and he didn't keep me from rearing back and looking at him. His expression was hard, jaw tight and eyes unyielding. He stared forward, and the faint light from the lone lamp in the entryway cast shadows across his face.

"What does she need money for?" I asked softly, and a flicker of something crossed his eyes.

He licked his lips and glanced down at my shoulder where the blanket had fallen off. He replaced it and sat back, guiding my head back down on his chest.

"She's a compulsive gambler. When she can't afford it, or when she loses big, I'm usually her first call."

My heart broke for him, and I swallowed down the bubbling emotion.

"What about your dad? Didn't you say you had an older brother, too?"

My head on his chest moved up and back down as he stole a deep breath.

"My dad left when I was sixteen, mostly because of my mom's addiction," he began. "She gambled away their savings and started selling our belongings. He tried for a while to get her help but finally got fed up and just left. Not long after that my brother left, too. He was already eighteen and had graduated high school, so it wasn't a big deal for him," he said, and I sat quietly, listening intently hoping he'd continue.

"My dad got remarried and started over again. I think they have two kids, but I've never met them. My brother pretty much disappeared, too. I haven't heard from him since. After they left, I stayed for a while, going to high school while also trying to keep my mom from spiraling. But I was still just a kid, and there wasn't much I could do. On my seventeenth birthday, I left. I slept in my car for a while, showering when I could in the locker room at school before anyone else got there and finding what food I could. I got lucky a time or two and crashed on a few friends' couches. I...uh...found an abandoned house in our neighborhood. I stayed there for a while."

I opened my mouth to say something, anything, but I couldn't find the words. He glanced down at me briefly and shook his head.

He took a breath and continued faster. "Long story short, I got run out of that abandoned house and then got arrested when they found me in my car one night, and I apparently matched the description of a suspect in a robbery that had taken place nearby. The next night, I had to find a new place to park so I could get at least an hour or two of sleep, and that's when Robbie, the owner of Haven City, found me. He took me in, fed me, and gave me a place to stay. He's the only reason I finished high school and eventually started college. I took two years off because I didn't think I'd actually go."

It was no wonder Theo was so closed off—the people who were supposed to love him unconditionally had either left him or wanted to use him. I was angry for him. My heart shattered for him.

"You don't have to say anything," he said. "I know you probably want to, but you don't need to."

"I can't believe you don't talk to your dad or your brother anymore" I said quietly, and he shook his head.

He didn't want my placations or "*I'm sorry's.*" Telling him everything would be okay seemed idiotic and unnecessary after everything he'd been through. It sounded condescending in my head if I called him strong or resilient.

There was nothing I could say that he hadn't heard before. But I wanted him to know I appreciated him telling me. That he felt comfortable enough to tell me was amazing. If I had to guess, I bet one or two people knew his story.

He gave me a part of him, and I wanted to return the favor.

"I got pregnant when I was fifteen," I said, the story also not one I often shared. "Mark was a year older than me, and we'd been dating a few months. My parents were not the type to talk about safe sex, and Mark was a typical guy who didn't want to wear a condom, so we didn't. The day I told him I was pregnant, he'd come over to my house to break up with me. I didn't learn that until later, but…my parents kicked me out when I told them. No one wanted me to have an abortion, but my parents also didn't want to have a pregnant teenage daughter. So, they threw me out. Mark's parents were furious, but they let me move in with them if we got married. It wasn't like I could get pregnant again," I said with a laugh that sounded sad even to my own ears.

Theo's hold on me tightened as I continued, "I ended up getting my GED while Mark finished high school. I eventually had Ryder, which was terrible with his parents hovering over us constantly. At the first opportunity, we got our own place. It was incredibly hard for so many years, but we finally dug ourselves out of the hole. The only time my parents ever reached out was when Ryder was five. They actually called Mark and asked if they could meet him. They didn't want to see me, and I told them it was either both of us or neither of us. They didn't put up much of a fight, and we haven't heard from them since."

"*Fuck*," Theo mumbled against my hair as he ran a soothing hand down my back.

"Yeah, they were fucking assholes my entire life, so good riddance to them both." I hoped Theo didn't hear the lingering sadness in my voice. Even twenty-one years later, it still hurt. But it wasn't as sharp as it once was. The pain of losing my parents to their own egos was more of a dull ache that reared its ugly head every so often.

"At least you got Ryder," Theo said, and I smiled. Somehow it wasn't awkward or uncomfortable talking about Ryder with Theo. Apart from me and Mark, Theo knew Ryder better than anyone else. It was kind of nice to know he also cared about him.

"I did," I said, reminding myself of all the *good* memories.

"Seeing you now, I never would have suspected that you went through what you did."

"Yes, well, I don't really advertise the fact that I was a teen mom whose parents kicked her out before she could drive or before she opened her first bank account. Not that I'm ashamed, but…people tend to look at you differently."

"I know how it feels."

"Is…" I began but stopped, worried that I'd cross a line if I asked the question that was on the tip of my tongue.

"Go ahead," he instructed. "Ask."

I bit my lip nervously but asked, "Did your mom have something to do with why you had to move out of your last place and move in here?"

I wasn't sure what made me ask, but something in my gut told me to.

"Yeah," he answered instantly. "But probably not in the way you think."

"What do you mean not in the—" I began, but my question was quickly cut off with a gasp as Theo moved and rearranged me on his lap until his semi-hard erection pressed between my thighs.

Both of his hands clasped my cheeks, and all evidence of sadness, hurt, or anger had disappeared from his eyes. Replaced by a heat I wanted all over me again.

"I don't want to talk about her anymore. I want more of you."

I nodded weakly, suddenly more concerned with his rapidly hardening cock than his answers to my unending questions.

"Okay," I said breathlessly and he smiled. His tongue darted out and licked at my lower lip. I leaned forward and pressed my mouth to his, opening for him and welcoming his tongue. But the kiss was brief.

"Are you sore?" he asked with real concern in his voice.

"A little," I answered honestly and ground down on his cock to show him I still wanted more anyway.

It wasn't too bad, but there was a definitive ache that I knew would last a while. I enjoyed it—it reminded me of everything we'd done. Like he'd made good on his promise and marked me both inside and out.

"Well, we can't have that, can we," he said with a smile. Before I could argue, his hand disappeared between us and tenderly ran the length of my lower lips. He pressed a finger to my clit, and teased me softly.

Then he shifted and laid me down on the couch. My legs fell open, and he crawled between them. He inserted one finger slowly, and I gasped at the intrusion.

"Don't you have to go to work?"

He ignored my question and kissed my clit. His broad, flat tongue licked at the bundle of nerves, likely tasting a mix of both of our releases.

"My slut should always be ready for my cock, and if you're sore, I can't fuck you the way I want to. So, lie down," he instructed, pressing his hand to the middle of my chest and forcing my back to the soft cushion. "And let me kiss this pussy better."

SIXTEEN

THE WALLS ARE THIN

Natalie

I WAS SO LATE. I WAS SO LATE I DIDN'T EVEN HAVE AN EXTRA SECOND to be angry at myself for being late.

I hopped on the elevator a second after the doors opened, jabbed the button for floor twelve, and quickly hit the *"door close"* button several times. Mercifully, the doors heeded my panicked request and began to close. Only a man stuck his hand in the small sliver of space between them and got on, followed by three other people.

We ended up stopping on floors three, five, six, and ten before I finally got up to our office.

"Fuck, fuck, fuck, *fuuuck*," I sang while running to my office at the end of the long hall. Sitting in one of the chairs in front of my desk was my boss and owner of the firm, Beckett Crawford. He was my age and had taken over the firm from his father only a few years earlier. We'd worked closely ever since, and I knew he wouldn't be angry at my tardiness. But I still really hated being late.

That's what I got for staying up all night riding Theo's dick.

"I'm sorry," I said, trying to catch my breath. "There was traffic, and—" I stopped the lies and excuses when I saw the small smile on his face. "What? Why are you smiling?" I asked, knowing I'd missed something.

"Well, I was laughing at your Halloween decorations," he said, stealing a piece of candy from the bowl on the corner of my desk and motioning to the garland of ghosts hanging around the perimeter. "But now I'm laughing at you running in here."

I tossed my bags underneath my desk and jiggled my mouse to wake up my computer.

"Yeah, because we had an interview that was supposed to start five minutes ago. Wait, shouldn't you be in there? Are you waiting for me?"

Quickly, I found the young law student's resume and my notebook before frantically retrieving a pen and hoping I didn't look half as frazzled as I felt.

"He sent an email early this morning asking to reschedule. I forwarded it to Pearl"—our receptionist— "and asked her to find time next week. He copied you, but I guess you didn't see it?"

I stopped, dropped my notebook and pen on the desk, and looked around. Then I patted my pockets and bent down to dig through my bags.

"Ugh!" I groaned and turned my purse upside down, unceremoniously spilling the contents on my desk. I sifted through every single one of my belongings while Beckett looked on in curious surprise. "I must have left my phone at home or maybe in my car? I actually don't remember having it with me this morning, though," I said absent-mindedly.

"I don't think I've ever seen you this out of sorts," Beckett said, and I gave him an unimpressed look. "Could this have anything to do with—"

"No," I said quickly, which prompted his amused smile to widen. I already knew what he was going to say. Rumors had been floating around that I was dating someone. Apparently, I was less stressed and cheerier, which could have only meant that

I was getting laid regularly. At least that's what the entire office surmised.

And whether they were correct or not—because they absolutely were, about the getting laid, not the dating part—I wasn't going to feed into those rumors.

"Hmm…okay, if you say so," he added as the phone on my desk rang with Pearl's name.

"Hey, what's up?"

"Umm…I have a…" she began slowly.

"A what?"

"A guest for you," she finished, and I could hear the smile in her voice. "And I'm walking him back now."

"Wait, what? I don't have—" I began, but she hung up before I could finish my sentence and tell her that I didn't have any other meetings scheduled for that morning and whoever it was should absolutely not be there.

"Are you sure our interview rescheduled? Pearl just said I have a guest that she's bringing back here."

Beckett nodded and began to say something, but I didn't hear him as Pearl appeared at the end of the hallway, followed by a straight-faced Theo. Our young receptionist was turned around, talking his ear off while she walked him toward my office. She stumbled over her feet and waved her hands around animatedly, but Theo wasn't paying attention to whatever she was saying. All of his attention was laser-focused on me.

He wore his usual uniform—dark jeans, black boots, and a black T-shirt—except he'd also thrown on a leather jacket to protect him from the cooler late-October temperatures. There was a faint smile tugging at his lips, and it was like he was walking in slow motion as I tried to figure out what the hell he was doing there.

Him showing up didn't bode well for the rumors that were stirring. However, everyone knew Ryder's friend was staying with me, so maybe I was thinking too much into it.

And before I could fully wrap my head around it at all, there they were.

"Theo, what—" I began when he and Pearl stopped in my doorway. I continued to stutter out half-words until Beckett stood from his chair and turned, immediately offering his hand to Theo.

"I'm Beckett Crawford," he said, and Theo took his hand. "You must be Ryder's friend?"

Theo nodded and gave him a small smile before turning back to me.

Pearl suddenly put two-and-two together. "Oh, so this isn't *your* guy—"

"Pearl," I snapped, maybe a little too harshly, but she was mostly unfazed.

"What? If he's not, then maybe I can—"

I threw my hands in the air and walked toward the three of them gathered by my door. "That's enough. There are too many people in here. Pearl, I can hear the phone ringing, and Beckett, I'll see you for our ten o'clock."

Beckett's eyes bounced between Theo and me before they stopped on me, and he raised his eyebrows in silent question. I gave my head one subtle shake, and he pursed his lips in understanding.

"Nice to meet you, Theo," Beckett offered before stepping out the door.

I had to physically push Pearl to get her to leave my office, ignoring her pleas to chat with us for just a few minutes. Like the amazing boss I was, I closed the door, cutting off her arguments, and leaned back against it. I shut my eyes and took a deep breath.

"Your guy?" was Theo's first question, and my eyes snapped to him.

"Don't listen to her."

He shoved his hands in the front pockets of his jeans and

narrowed his curious milk chocolate eyes as I stepped around my desk and fell into my chair.

"What are you doing here?"

"Answer my question, and I'll answer yours," he countered, and I let my head fall into my hands. The last thing I wanted to do was to explain the rumor, which wasn't actually a rumor, to Theo.

So funny story. You fuck me so well that everyone here has noticed a change in my overall demeanor. Apparently, I was miserable without daily dick and orgasms.

"There's a rumor going around that the reason I've been less stressed and more upbeat recently is because I've been getting laid regularly," I said plainly.

He tilted his head to the side, his amused smirk turning into a huge grin before he tossed his head back. His laughter bounced off the walls of my office, and even with the door closed, it was likely heard down the hallway. The walls were thin and sound carried.

"I'm so happy I could help." he chuckled as he slid my phone across my desk. I immediately perked up. "I spotted this when I came downstairs and figured you would need it."

"Thank you. But you didn't have to come all the way down here. I could've lived one day without it."

"Of course you could have. But it gave me another excuse to see you."

My cheeks heated, and I looked past him to the door, which was firmly closed. The blinds were already drawn as well, meaning we had a little privacy. As much privacy as we could have in an office full of nosy people and paper-thin walls.

Awareness prickled over my skin, and the room suddenly became smaller. As it had for the last month every time he was around.

And he was around a lot.

Since that night we'd fucked on the couch, we hadn't

stopped. Most of our free time at home was spent together. We'd had sex on every available surface and in every possible position. We'd done things I hadn't even contemplated before I met him.

On the off chance I got home before he had to be at work, we'd make the most of our time wherever we landed. And more often than not, I'd wake up to him crawling in my bed early the next morning after he got back.

No wonder everyone at work had noticed the change. Our attraction was more than magnetic. It was utterly irresistible, and I wanted more.

We were genuinely addicted to the touch, the taste, and the feel of each other. But after we fucked, we talked. Which was bizarre. He was still a man of few words, usually quiet and observant, but when it was just the two of us, he spoke freely. Sometimes about nothing at all, but occasionally the topics would veer into deeper territory. Those deeper talks often happened after we'd fucked each other's brains out when we were both our most vulnerable.

But he never stayed. Or I never stayed when we found ourselves in his bed. At first, I hadn't understood how or why we both subconsciously agreed that we wouldn't sleep in the same bed. Then I'd almost asked him to stay one night, the words dangerously close to slipping off my tongue. And I realized it was the last little piece.

We'd so easily fallen into a routine—fucking, talking, cooking, watching our favorite movies.

Our separate nights were all that was left. We'd obliterated every other wall between us. We'd learned more about each other in a month and a half than I thought possible. We were experts on each other's pleasure, and we spent more time together than we did with anyone else.

And if we slept together too, that would indefinitely blur the lines. Waking up in each other's arms felt more intimate than anything else we'd done.

And that was terrifying. Especially since we hadn't

discussed what we were doing. We were simply living in the few moments we'd been given. Thinking about what happened after, including the repercussions or the fallout, wasn't included.

And I wasn't going to be the one to bring it up. I was enjoying it way too fucking much.

"Was that your boss?" Theo asked, motioning to the closed door behind him and drawing me from my thoughts.

"Why, you jealous?" I asked without thinking, but Theo didn't react to my provocation. Deciding to push him a little further, I stood from my chair and rounded my desk slowly until I was directly in front of him, only a few inches between us. "You don't have any reason to be," I added.

He was quiet for a beat then chuckled darkly. The little hairs on my arms and at my nape stood on end at the sound. Excitement buzzed through me, and I momentarily forgot where we were. My colleagues and coworkers just beyond the door were a faint memory when Theo took up every available inch of my mind.

"No, baby, I'm not jealous," he said, stepping closer until there was no room left between us. "I know no one can compare to what I do to you. The way you beg for my cock, there's no faking that."

Knowing exactly what would happen if I continued egging him on, I decided to do it anyway.

"I don't think I can remember the last time you made me beg." I tapped my chin, looking up and to the right, like I was trying really hard to think on it.

He snickered, and before I could react, he wrapped his hands around the backs of my thighs and hoisted me up onto the edge of my desk. His large frame towered over me as he planted his hands on either side of my hips.

"What are you—"

"Such a fucking tease," he said, dipping his head and running his tongue up the length of my neck. My eyes closed, and I automatically tilted my head to the side to allow him better access.

"Being a brat when you know I can't dole out the punishment I want. The one that you deserve."

The warmth of his body surrounded me as he continued to lick and kiss my neck. With one of my hands braced behind me, holding up all of my weight so I didn't tumble back onto my desk, the other clutched Theo's jacket, the cool leather a contradiction to the heat rolling off us both.

He kissed me hard and took my lower lip between his teeth. And suddenly his hands were on my thighs, rucking my skirt up around my hips and staring down at the sheer black tights I wore underneath.

"This won't do," he murmured and ran a finger down my center. I jumped when I heard the telltale sound of tearing.

"What are you doing?" I gasped, but he didn't answer. At least not with words. I looked down and watched him widen the hole he'd created in my tights and move my black panties to the side.

His thumb parted my folds and collected my arousal before he set to work against my clit. Forgetting myself, I moaned a little too loudly, but Theo's other hand was there in an instant.

"Shut up," he growled, his pupils blown wide with lust. "Do you want everyone to know what a little slut you are? How you fuck your son's best friend any chance you get? Or how desperately you beg for his cock?"

I panted against his hand, and on each inhale, I took in the intoxicating smell of him. Clean and masculine and the only thing I ever wanted to smell again.

"God, look at you. Falling apart, and I'm barely even touching you," he mused, and I bucked up against his finger.

Theo had become an expert when it came to my pleasure. He'd studied every one of my reactions to everything he did, including what I did to myself, to fully grasp what I liked and how he could own every part of me. He applied the perfect pressure, rubbing maddening little circles against my clit until my skin was on fire. Pleasure and an unabashed need for more made me beg against his palm, which muffled the sound enough that we weren't at risk of anyone else hearing.

"What was that?" he asked, removing his hand only enough to hover over my mouth.

"*Please*," I pleaded. "Please make me come."

He smiled, eyes flaring, and I reached out to cup his stubble-covered cheek in my hand. But my pleas didn't work. In one second, I was so close to release that I could taste it, and in the next, he was stepping back, removing his hands from me completely.

"What are you doing?" I asked as he licked his thumb and grinned down at me, still a panting mess on top of my desk.

"Making sure you remember the last time you begged."

My jaw dropped, and I couldn't believe he'd played me so easily. "You can't be—"

"Serious? Oh, I am. And if you're good today, then I'll reward you."

I leaned forward, cringing when my wet pussy pressed against the cold surface of my desk. "You can't leave me like this," I argued, and he raised one eyebrow in challenge. I knew that look—I wasn't getting what I wanted.

"What do you mean by 'If I'm good'?" I tried again.

"Don't touch yourself. Don't make yourself come, and maybe I'll let you when I get home tonight."

I growled and shoved off the desk onto shaky legs. My thighs pressed together, and the unsatisfied need still swirling through me was impossible to ignore.

"Maybe? If you want to play this game, then I'm going to need some assurances."

He stepped forward, closing the distance between us once again and cupping my face in his large, tattooed palm. "When have I ever *really* left you wanting, Natalie?"

I sighed and crossed my arms over my chest. "There's a first time for everything."

His only response was a chuckle, and then he kissed me softly.

"Be good," he instructed and stepped back.

I was so frustrated, but the idea that he controlled when and how I came was even more of a turn-on. Which didn't help the predicament I found myself in.

"You're sadistic," I breathed as he reached for the door handle.

He turned back and smiled. "Yes, but you're my little masochistic slut. You love every depraved second of it."

I was sitting at my desk, trying to work and keep my mind off Theo—what he did to me earlier and what I hoped we'd do later —when my cell phone vibrated. I looked at the screen and smiled, trying to immediately dismiss any thoughts of Theo.

"Hey!"

"Hey, Mom. You at the office still?" Ryder asked, and it was good to hear his voice. He'd been so busy that we hadn't spoken as often as we were used to. A text here or there and maybe a quick phone call was all we could manage on the best of weeks.

"Yeah, probably will be for another hour. What are you up to?"

"I'm actually going to grab a drink with some friends, but I wanted to call and check in. I miss you."

My heart nearly burst out of my chest at that, and I sat back in my chair.

"I miss you, too, kid. So much."

He filled me in on the projects he was working on and all the work he still had planned for the rest of the semester. He spoke with such enthusiasm that I worried he wouldn't want to come back.

"But there was something else I actually wanted to tell you," he said, and I immediately stiffened, preparing for the worst. "I'm not going to be able to come back for Thanksgiving."

"Oh," I said, both simultaneously relieved that it wasn't something worse and sad that I wouldn't get to see him for the holiday. "That's okay, I understand."

"I really tried, but we have a deadline for a project that falls right around that time, and—"

"Ryder, don't worry about it. I promise I'll be fine."

He sighed, and I heard commotion in the background. "Yeah, yeah. I'll be right there," he said to someone else. "Sorry, umm... well, at least you won't be alone. I'm not sure if Theo plans on going to his boss's place, but maybe you can go with him? I'm sure he wouldn't mind."

We hadn't discussed Thanksgiving, but my mind immediately went to the plans we'd made the following day for Halloween. All they consisted of was spending the day in bed, eating as much candy as we could, and watching scary movies.

It was sweet of Ryder to worry.

"Yeah, I'm sure we'll figure something out."

He apologized again, and we said our goodbyes before he quickly hung up the phone.

I groaned, folded my arms over my desk, and laid my head down on top of them. Lying to Ryder was making me miserable. The immensity of our secret was tearing me up inside. It would have been easier if I regretted it or felt guilty. But I didn't. My only regret was having to lie to my son about it. And I hated that Theo was in a similar position.

But neither of us was going to stop. Neither of us wanted to stop.

The world was a cruel fucking place.

SEVENTEEN
UNWANTED VISITOR

Theo

"IT'S PERFECT!" MY FINAL CLIENT OF THE NIGHT SCREECHED. SHE was newly eighteen and wanted a tattoo in remembrance of her mother.

It wasn't the first tattoo I'd done for someone's mom, and I didn't necessarily avoid them, but they always stirred up feelings and a tightness in my chest that I preferred never to experience. While people came to me to ink something permanent on their skin to remember their mothers, I tried every day to forget about mine.

The petite girl leaped toward me with her arms spread wide, and I caught her in an awkward hug as she continued to thank me over and over again. I chuckled at her enthusiasm and led her and her friend up front.

She was the last appointment of the night, which meant I was less than an hour away from seeing Natalie. Leaving her squirming and wanting on her desk earlier that morning was just as hard on me as it was for her. It took all of my restraint to keep from bending her over her desk, pushing up her skirt, and fucking her right then and there.

Coworkers and anyone else that might have heard be damned.

But that was how it'd been since I moved in. Since I touched her for the first time, I couldn't get enough. I'd never been so constantly hard up. Not even when I was a young, pubescent teenager. All I wanted to do was spend every free second with her, inside of her, or with my head between her thighs.

"Are you fucking smiling?" Robbie appeared beside me, nudging my shoulder and drawing me from my thoughts.

I grunted and started cleaning up the reception area after a long, busy day.

"That's fine, you don't have to tell me. You haven't stopped fucking smiling for like two months now. It's actually creepy at this point," he added, walking around the room and straightening the pillows on the small leather couch and emptying the trash behind the counter.

"It's creepy that you're paying that close attention to me."

"It's kind of part of my job," he said.

"As my boss? I don't think that's part of the job description."

"No, but you will be taking over this place sooner rather than later, so I do have reason to worry."

I chuckled and closed the register, handing him the extra cash. "No reason to worry."

He watched me for a moment, likely contemplating if I was really telling the truth until his attention moved over my shoulder and the bell above the door chimed. "Now I'm fucking worried," Robbie muttered under his breath.

And before I could turn around, a voice from behind me greeted us, "Well, hello, boys."

Every one of my muscles locked up, and every hair on my body stood on end at the sound of her voice. I closed my eyes and forced a calming breath through my nose, but it did little to help.

Slowly, I turned.

"What the hell are you doing here?" I snarled through

clenched teeth. My hands fisted at my sides, and Robbie's hand was at my shoulder, squeezing softly and silently warning me not to lose my cool.

"You know you aren't welcome in here, Kim," Robbie warned while my mom strode farther into the studio and closer to the counter we both stood behind.

The smug grin on her face was proof enough that she knew she'd been barred from Haven City. Her curly, brown hair—that was unfortunately too similar to mine—was pushed back from her face, showing off the dark circles under her eyes and her other too-thin features.

"Well, I didn't have much of a choice. My son wouldn't answer my calls and hung up on me the one time I did finally get him to answer."

I scoffed and braced my hands on the counter. "And you somehow still didn't get the hint that I don't want to talk to you?"

She shrugged, and my anger climbed higher the longer she stood there with her unbothered smile.

"I just wanted to check on you. After you suddenly moved out of your house—"

"Because you ransacked it. You stole *everything*," I seethed, and she had the audacity to look shocked.

"You're overstating it, Theo. I told you, I had collectors on my ass. I had to do something, and when you turned me away—"

"No," I interrupted her with a sharpness in my voice I never imagined I'd use on her. "You will not blame this on me."

There was no reasoning with her. I'd learned that a long time ago, yet it was always startling that the woman who was supposed to love me no matter what and who at one point seemed like she did, cared about almost anything else besides me. Especially the money. Enough that she broke into my apartment and stole anything she could sell.

"We had a deal, Mom. You leave me alone and I don't go to the cops," I said, still doing a poor job of reining in the anger simmering through my veins. "I don't know what you want from me anymore. I don't have any money! You made sure of that last time."

She looked like she was going to continue playing the concerned mother card, attempting to manipulate me and go on about how she just wanted to check in, but her mask dropped just as quickly. "I know that's not true, Theo. I'm your mother. I raised you. I just need a little bit more help before—"

"Kim," Robbie said from behind me, stepping around the counter and pointing to the door behind her. "Leave now, or I'm calling the cops. I'm not going to say it again."

"Fine, fine," she muttered, throwing her hands up in mock surrender and backing toward the door. "But just so you're both aware, threatening me with calling the cops isn't going to work anymore."

On that ominous note, her smug smile was back in place. "I'll see you soon, Theo," she said, voice laced with promise but dripping in threat.

Robbie paced across the space and locked the door the moment it closed behind her and turned to me. I kept my eyes locked on the image of her receding form, impatiently waiting for her to start her car and leave.

"I'm going to follow her," Robbie said matter-of-factly.

"You don't—"

But he waved his hand, cutting off any argument.

"We both know if she figures out where you're staying, she's never going to fucking leave you alone. She showed up here because she doesn't know where else to find you. And if she sees Natalie? It'll be a million times worse. I'm going to follow and make sure she goes straight home. Just give me a few minutes head start. I'll let you know if there's any reason you should make the block."

All I managed was a shallow nod, the words of gratitude lodged in my throat. Robbie left out the back in the next second. It was only a few moments later that he came revving around the corner of the building on his bike. My mom finally put her little beat-up car in gear.

Just as he said he would, Robbie followed her out onto the street. Both of them were out of sight quickly, but the anger and annoyance, the overwhelming frustration, didn't dissipate.

Robbie was right. If my mom figured out where I was living, it would become Natalie's problem, too. And the thought of Natalie being caught up in my shit…any anger I'd felt before couldn't compare to the rage that coursed through me. It blistered across my skin, and my temperature rose.

I stared blankly at the front door and out into the dark night beyond the glass. It was only the incessant vibrating of my phone against the counter that pulled me from my murderous, spiraling thoughts.

Seeing Natalie's name scroll across the screen instantly calmed me. Like she knew I needed to hear from her at that moment. But whatever I thought she'd send—like a desperate plea for me to hurry—wasn't what I received. Instead of a regular text, in its place was a voice note that was approximately thirty seconds long.

I turned the lights out at the front of the studio and pressed play without thinking as I headed back toward my room. Only I stopped in the middle of the hallway at the first sound that erupted from the small phone speaker. Like a fucking siren song, Natalie's breathy and hypnotizing moans echoed through the silent space.

Instinctually, I looked around, hoping no one else heard what was reserved only for my ears before I remembered I was alone. At that same moment, her sounds grew louder. She mumbled a curse under her breath, and then she was quiet long enough to hear something that sounded like…vibrating.

A devious smile split my face while my cock thickened. The last ten seconds of the message were filled with sounds I knew all too well. Her orgasm must have rocked her for how loudly she moaned. Otherwise she was putting on quite a show.

My pretty little slut...she couldn't even wait a full twelve hours without getting herself off. Ideas that bordered that sweet, thin line of tortuous and pleasurable flashed through my mind as I began to type out a response.

> Me: Dirty girl, you couldn't even wait a full twelve hours until I got home.

Her response was almost instant.

> Natalie: What else was I supposed to do?
>
> Me: You better be ready when I get home.
>
> Natalie: Ready for what? I've already gotten off.
>
> Me: Broken rules require punishment.

When the little dots didn't immediately appear, I knew my words had hit their mark.

> Me: Why did you do it?
>
> Natalie: To show you I can do the job, too. No begging required.

I let my head drop back and groaned loudly. Then I finished closing up quicker than I ever had before.

All day, the need to get to her had been nearly unbearable. And I was eternally thankful that when I got into my truck, my phone buzzed with a text from Robbie giving me the all-clear.

I threw my truck into reverse, whipped out of the spot, and sped back to her house, eager to forget everything else and get lost in her.

EIGHTEEN
"THANK YOU"

Theo

THE FRONT DOOR CLOSED SOFTLY, AND I CLICKED THE LOCK INTO place without a sound.

My steps were silent as I walked toward the back of the house. I surveyed the kitchen and the living room, but when I didn't see her, I made my way up the stairs.

The door to my room on the right was wide open, and the sheets on the bed were undisturbed. I continued down the hallway and approached her closed bedroom door. For a moment, I stood with my hand hovering above the handle, waiting to hear a noise. There was shuffling behind the door, but I couldn't make out the exact sound through the wood.

When I finally pushed it open, Natalie was standing on the opposite side of the room, digging through one of the drawers in her dresser. She gasped, nearly letting go of the towel she was holding around herself and stumbling backward into the open drawer as she turned.

"Holy shit! You scared the crap out of me."

Rather than respond, I stepped into the room and closed the door behind me. It clicked shut, and Natalie visibly swallowed.

She was freshly out of the shower, her hair still wet, and the faint light coming from the lamp on her bedside table reflected off the drops of water sticking to her smooth legs.

She was so clean. I couldn't wait to make her dirty again.

Knowing that my indifference and nonchalance made her squirm, as did my silence, I tucked my hands into the front pockets of my jeans and openly raked my eyes up and down her body. Even with a towel tucked around her, I could make out the curve of her hips and remembered how good she looked wet.

Just as I wanted her to, Natalie grew more nervous the longer I stood unmoving. My expression neutral and not giving away a single one of my dirty thoughts, she pivoted from one foot to the other and tried to tighten the towel around herself without letting it fall. She licked at her bottom lip before she bit it, and her attention darted to the right for a fraction of a second.

It happened again, and I followed her line of sight to the table beside her bed. My interest peaked when I spotted the item I knew she'd been glancing at.

Tucked between a half-empty bottle of water and her phone was a pretty purple wand vibrator. I'd seen it in the drawer where she kept all of her toys once or twice, but we hadn't had the opportunity to use it yet.

And after what I planned to do with it, I couldn't imagine she'd ever want to use it again.

I could feel her eyes boring into the side of my face as I stepped toward her bed and picked up the lightweight toy. The silicone was soft against my palm, and I held down the bottom button for a few seconds until it flashed. I pressed another button right above it, and the toy came to life. I touched the large, rounded end into my other hand and pushed the button again and again. The intensity of the vibration steadily increased until the center of my hand was nearly numb.

I turned it off, not wanting to waste the battery and flipped it in my hand as I spun back to Natalie. She was pressed against her dresser, towel straining to stay closed around her tits, and the nervous expression on her face unwavering.

"Is this the one you used?"

Her eyes bounced from the toy to my face as she slowly nodded.

"Hmm," I mused and stepped around the bed. "I thought I made myself pretty clear when I said don't touch yourself until I get back."

Some of her hesitance dissipated, and her shoulders dropped as the corners of her mouth tilted slightly upward. More and more over the past month, we'd experimented with different dynamics and scenarios. But we hadn't yet explored the excitement that was bratting. She'd never explicitly done the opposite of what I'd told her to do. Occasionally she'd tried to rile me up by demanding that I *"make her"* do something, but the resolute defiance shimmering in her blue eyes was new.

And I couldn't wait to fucking decimate it. The need to touch her and have her was blazing within me.

"Technically, I didn't touch myself. The toy touched me," she said, motioning to the toy still in my hand.

Oh, she was definitely in for it. I matched her mischievous smile with one of my own. Hers instantly faltered, a little of the earlier worry filtering back in.

"That's a nifty little loophole, baby. But what was the rest of my request?"

She thought for a minute, chewing on her bottom lip until her eyes widened.

"How would you know if I came or not? All you heard in the message was me moaning. I could have been edging myself. Or maybe I was pretending to get a rise out of you," she argued, and I commended her attempt.

Slowly, I stepped forward. She tracked each of my steps, her chest rising and falling quickly. With nowhere to go, her back flattened against her dresser.

I tossed the toy into the air and caught the thick head in my palm. The pointed end I brought to her chin and ran the length of her jaw with it. I traced down her neck and along her collarbone. It was the same path my lips liked to take.

"My pretty girl, you don't think I can tell the difference between when you're moaning for show, when you're moaning from pleasure, and when you're coming?" I asked, tracing the curve of her breasts.

She swallowed hard, but I didn't wait for a response.

"Do you remember your safe word?" I asked. It was both a warning and a checkpoint, so she knew exactly what I planned may require it.

But she nodded, need flaring to life behind her eyes.

"Yes, red means stop, yellow means slow down."

A low groan vibrated up my throat at her eagerness.

"On the bed," I commanded, and she hesitated. So, I tried again, dropping my voice and gripping her chin between my forefinger and thumb. "You don't want to test me right now, Natalie. Get. On. The. Bed."

The second time I asked, she moved immediately. The moment I let go of her chin, she was perched on her knees on the edge of her bed.

"Lose the towel," I said as my knees hit the bed frame.

She whipped the towel from her body and tossed it away. Although I wanted to, I didn't glance down at her body. In my peripheral, I could see her nipples were already hard and waiting for my mouth.

"Look at that. My slut *can* follow instructions."

Her eyes narrowed, but the argument I was sure was poised on her tongue didn't come. I smiled and let my hand rest at the base of her throat. Her skin was warm and soft, and I wanted to touch every inch of her.

"I would say I want you to be a good girl for me, but I know that's not likely. You're only capable of being my dirty little slut. Aren't you?"

Again, I didn't wait for a response as I crashed my mouth

against hers. Instantly she was putty in my hand, yielding to every unrelenting stroke of my tongue. I pulled back quickly though, and if it weren't for my hand around her neck, she would've tumbled forward.

Motioning with her vibrator that was still in my hand, I pointed to my waist.

"Take me out."

I let go of her throat and stayed still as she unfastened my belt and unbuttoned my jeans. She freed my cock, dropped her hands back to her sides, and licked her lips.

I momentarily dropped the vibrator on the bed and pulled my T-shirt over my head and stepped out of my boots. A second later, I discarded my jeans and briefs next to where my T-shirt fell.

Her gaze swept over me hungrily, and my cock twitched at her outward appreciation.

"Turn around and lay down on your back. Let your head hang off the edge of the bed," I instructed.

She dropped to her hands and knees and crawled to the edge of the bed where she flipped over to her back. I peered down at her and was in awe of the trust she put in me. Her willingness and desire to give up control to me and let me guide her pleasure.

I'd never take those moments for granted.

I swept my hand under her head and freed her long hair so it fell down the side of the bed. I cupped the back of her head and stared down at her perfect features—expressive eyes, high cheekbones, and full lips.

I held her head with one hand and pumped my cock, poised just above her face, with the other. Beneath my length, she wetted her lips and watched my hand move up and down. I shifted slightly to the side for a better view of her face and tightened my hold on her hair.

"Open your mouth and stick out your tongue."

She visibly shivered at my command but did as I asked,

fisting her hands in her sheets and opening her mouth. Her stare didn't waver from me as I leaned forward and spit in her mouth.

She sucked in a breath, mouth still wide, as I rubbed the head of my cock through the mess I'd made on her lips and tongue. Carefully, I let go of her head, and she let it fall back while I eased myself deeper into her mouth. She moaned as her lips stretched around me, and I cursed as the warmth of her mouth enveloped me.

I shouldn't have started like that, with her mouth around me, sucking me deeper and licking at my cock with reckless abandon. The punishment I had in mind would take a while, likely hours, and I already felt my orgasm taunting me. Coming within the first five minutes would not bode well for the rest of the night, but I ground my teeth and retrieved that purple toy from beside her.

"Open those gorgeous legs and show me how wet you are."

Her legs automatically parted, and I ran an appreciative hand down the center of her chest and her stomach until I grazed her clit and parted her folds. She was dripping, her arousal already coating the inside of her thighs like I imagined it would be. She enjoyed being told what to do, being degraded and used, as much as I enjoyed dishing it out.

We were a match made in filthy fucking heaven. Except we worshipped each other and got on our knees to do anything but pray.

Even so, it was still a holy experience.

Quickly, I turned on the toy and set it to the lowest setting as I rocked into her mouth. Physically unable to tease her any longer, I pressed the large head of the vibrating toy to her clit. Her resounding moan filtered through the air around us and vibrated up my cock.

"Tap my leg twice if it gets to be too much, okay? Squeeze my thigh if you hear me," I said over the quiet buzzing of the toy and the pounding of my pulse in my ears.

She squeezed my thigh and I thrust into her mouth deeper.

Even when she gagged, I continued pushing forward.

No tap, no mercy.

She eventually released the sheets from her grip and raised her hands to grab my ass, urging me deeper. She did what she could in her position to set a rhythm, and I let her take over momentarily while I focused on her own pleasure.

Her legs were wide but her heels dug into the bed. The low setting was likely just a little tease, but that was exactly what I wanted. Her hips bucked up to meet the toy, and I trailed it down to her entrance and back up to her clit until she was panting around my cock.

It was filthy how wet the toy already was. Her arousal smeared all over the rounded head as she shamelessly chased that euphoric high.

Below me, I watched her lips stretch and her throat accommodate my length. Her warm mouth swallowed me over and over again, and I was having a hard time hanging on. In that position, with her head thrown over the side of the bed, she could take me deeper than I ever imagined.

When most of my length disappeared down her throat, I growled low in my throat and added more pressure to the toy between her thighs. She bucked and groaned. Her nails dug into the skin of my backside, and I knew she had to be close. I encircled her throat with my free hand and squeezed slightly.

"Come for me. Don't hold back. Rub your pussy against the toy just like you did earlier. Show me exactly how you fell apart."

And several seconds later she did just that. She writhed and shuddered as the orgasm swept through her, moaning around my cock until she was panting.

I stepped back, letting my cock fall free from her mouth, and tilted her head up so the blood would flow back where it belonged. I only removed the vibrator long enough to flip her around and onto her back, lining her cunt up with my cock.

"So fucking pretty," I muttered, running a finger through her wetness. "So perfect and made just for me."

I placed the vibrator back on her clit as I prodded her entrance with the blunt head of my length. She immediately tried to shy away from the overstimulation, but a firm hand around her waist was enough to keep her in place.

"No, you're not going anywhere. I told you if you break the rules, you'll be punished. And this is it."

She was shaking, hands tangled in her hair, and jaw slack with astonishment. I made sure her hooded eyes were still on me when I continued.

"This little toy has thirteen different vibration settings, each one stronger than the last. You're going to come for me thirteen times. One orgasm for each setting. And after each orgasm, you're going to thank me because it's fucking polite."

"Thirteen?!" She began to sit up, but I pushed her back down with a firm hand against her chest. "I don't think I can—"

"You can, and you will," I clarified, leaving no room for any other arguments.

I turned up the speed on the vibrator and pushed into her at the same time. She cried out and reached for my hand holding the toy. The thick ridges and veins of my cock glistened as I pumped in and out of her pussy.

"You can't give up yet. And you haven't said thank you for the first one."

There was a split second of indecision in her eyes at hearing my entire plan, and I stilled inside her. Her hand hovered over mine holding the toy, and I thought she was about to call it quits. I didn't want her to, but if she really didn't want to continue, I wouldn't have.

But she didn't tell me to stop.

"Color?" I asked, checking in.

She fell back onto the bed and gripped the sheets above her head. She arched her back and ground against me.

"Green," she breathed and added a second later, "Thank you."

NINETEEN

HOW MANY ORGASMS IS TOO MANY ORGASMS?

Natalie

"THANK YOU," I SCREAMED AS MY NINTH ORGASM CRESTED.

My entire body was covered in sweat, and my muscles were exhausted. I felt like I was hovering outside of my body with four more orgasms left in Theo's sick game.

Theo had fucked me through the second, third, and fourth orgasms at the edge of the bed. For the fifth and sixth, he'd put me on my side and fucked me from behind.

Then I'd ridden him through the seventh, eighth, and ninth with the wand tucked between my clit and his pubic bone. My entire body went limp, and I fell on top of him. The vibrator was awkwardly positioned between us, and it fell away from my clit. I was thankful for the momentary reprieve because I knew it would only last a second.

He'd lasted nine of my orgasms before finally coming himself, emptying inside of me with a manly groan. I didn't know how he was able to resist for so long, but it was also the last thing I was worried about.

My head lolled against his shoulder, and his cock slipped

free. Both of us were breathing hard, and I could have easily fallen asleep right then and there.

Theo's fingers dragged through my tangled mess of hair and rolled over me until my back hit the bed. I peeled my eyes open long enough to see him grab the vibrator—which by some miracle was still working—and gaze down at me.

I knew he was likely to dole out some form of punishment when he got home after receiving my voice note, but I wasn't expecting Mr. Pleasure Dom to make an appearance.

I both simultaneously loved and hated what he was doing to me, especially seeing him derive so much pleasure from my own. But I didn't know if I could keep going. I knew if I told him to stop, if I used my safe word, all of it would cease in an instant. The knowledge that the option was there was enough for me to keep going, though.

One of his large palms pressed against the inside of my thigh, and he dragged the vibrator higher up the other leg.

"You're taking your punishment so well," he murmured against my skin, kissing up my neck and along my jawline before pressing his lips to mine. "I'm so proud of you. Only four more."

He continued the same pattern, massaging the inside of one thigh while running the vibrator up and down the other. I cupped his face with my hands and directed the kiss, tilting my head to the side and pushing my tongue past his lips like I could taste the depravity lingering within him.

The rough stubble along his chin scraped against my palms, and I'd never felt so unbound yet fully connected to another person.

As our kiss continued to ramp up, Theo's hand slipped down my thigh and through my slit. He circled a finger at my entrance and slowly pushed inside of me, using a mixture of my arousal and his own release as lubricant. The sound it made was obscene. The vibrator quickly joined the onslaught, and my moment of reprieve vanished.

I didn't think it was possible, but my tenth orgasm was easily the quickest.

The pulsing vibrations on my clit and the targeted, easy movement of Theo's finger inside of me too much. As was each sweep of his eager, firm tongue through my mouth.

Pressed against my leg, his cock was rapidly hardening once again, and I moaned a muffled "thank you" into his mouth as I fell apart. At least that was what I thought I'd said, but I couldn't be sure. My thoughts were no longer coherent, and my voice was hoarse.

"You still with me, baby?" Theo asked as he tilted back and peered down at my sated and sensitive form.

I nodded and wetted my dry lips, tasting the remnants of him. His smile was beautiful, and so was the devious intent in his eyes.

He kissed his way over my jaw, down my throat, and paused over my chest before he took one delightfully sensitive nipple between his teeth. He sucked and licked a heady pattern until he moved to the other side and repeated the process.

My mind barely aware of my surroundings, I could barely comprehend what was happening when Theo flipped me and dragged my hips up as he positioned himself behind me. My face was pressed into the sheets, and my fingers gripped the blankets beneath me.

A soft hand with a careful touch caressed the skin of my ass. He mimicked the touch on the other side, and I melted further into the bed. It was such a stark contradiction to our earlier rough and savage fucking that I felt emotion sitting heavy in my chest.

He was so good at doing both—flipping between soft and sweet, nearly reverent, to ravenous and untamed. It was a dangerous combination that made me lightheaded.

He'd said before that that was his favorite type of sex.

"My favorite kind of sex is the kind that combines dirty and deep, savage and sweet."

There was still that incessant, faint buzzing in the distance, but the first sensation wasn't the toy as I expected, it was the blunt head of his cock pressing against my cunt.

I'd been so thoroughly fucked and used, yet my body still welcomed him. He pressed inside of me slowly, dragging his thick head against every one of my inner walls until his hips were flush with my ass.

My moan was barely stifled by the sheets, and Theo's hand around my hip tightened at the sound.

"That's it, moan like the fucking whore I know you are. So thoroughly used, yet you still can't get enough," he murmured.

He drew back only an inch or two before he methodically pushed back in. Setting a tortuous tempo, I was useless to do anything but take what he wanted to give me. And with the thick fog surrounding me, his deep strokes were the only thing keeping me grounded.

So consumed by the way he filled me and the warmth of his body behind me, I jumped when the vibrator grazed my clit.

"*Fuck*, Theo, *please*," I begged. For what, I didn't know, but Theo redoubled his efforts and slammed into me harder until it was only his vice-like grip on my hip that kept me in place.

"Say my name again, Natalie. Tell me who the only person is who can make you feel this way." His voice was low, and it sounded like he was having to force every word out through clenched teeth and between grunts and groans. Like he was enjoying it just as much as I was.

"*Theo!*" I nearly screamed. "It feels so good. *Fuck*, your cock feels...so good. You feel so good."

"Yes, there you go. Now, reach down and hold the vibrator for me."

"I—I can't. I—"

"Yes, you can. I know you can, sweet girl. Grab the vibrator so I can make my pretty little slut feel even better."

I groaned and reached my hand down between myself and

the bed until I grabbed the vibrator. My first thought was to throw the thing at the wall and hopefully kill it in the process.

But like he was reading my thoughts, Theo warned, "Move it an inch away from your clit and I add another orgasm."

My whine morphed suddenly into a gasp. Theo's thumb brushed against my ass, circling the puckered hole with a soft touch and a low groan. The vibrator was suddenly heavy in my hand, and there were so many sensations—sensations that felt too damn good—that I couldn't focus on just one.

"Don't drop that toy. I know you can follow that simple instruction, right, Natalie?"

"Yes, it just feels so…"

"I know it feels good," Theo crooned, petting my asshole and pumping into me. "This little hole is just begging for my fingers."

A second later, I heard him spit and felt the wetness glide down my crack. I shuddered at the depravity and only tensed a little when his thumb collected the spit and breached the tight outer ring of muscle.

"*Fuck*, there you go. Relax for me."

Theo's strokes slowed while he worked his thumb into my ass. It was a new feeling, one I wasn't certain I would enjoy but quickly learned I really, *really* loved.

With his other hand wrapped around my waist, Theo fingered me until my body fully relaxed and let him in. That was when pleasure rocketed through me, and each overwhelming sensation was nearly too much to bear.

Unintelligible words and sounds of pleasure spilled from my lips as I held onto the vibrator with one hand and mercilessly gripped the sheets with the other. The room was a cacophony of sounds: the bed colliding with the wall, our skin slapping, and echoing moans of pleasure. A light sheen of sweat covered my entire body, and I thought it was dripping down my face until I realized those were tears.

I was crying.

It was all too much. It was too good and too much, and I couldn't hold back the onslaught of emotion that whipped through me. Like I was stripped down and exposed and completely out of control.

With nothing left to do, I gave myself over to the feeling and came. My cunt squeezed Theo's cock harder than ever before, and my ass clenched around his finger. His thrusts didn't stutter as he fucked me through the orgasm of my life. My legs shook as my body convulsed.

Drowning in ecstasy, I closed my eyes and gasped, "Thank you."

Only my orgasm didn't stop. The eleventh immediately turned into number twelve, and I screamed into the sheets. It was sharp, verging on the edge of pain, the pleasure only an undercurrent.

Before I knew it, Theo flipped me onto my back and slammed back into me, the aftershocks of two orgasms still thrumming through me. I opened my eyes only to see his blurry form above me. I blinked a few times, gasping for air I couldn't find, and was taken aback by the intensity in his eyes.

"Look at those tears," he said, his voice finally cutting through the fog around me. "You look so pretty when you cry."

Theo's curly hair fell forward as he leaned down and licked at the salty tears that had fallen free. He kissed each of them away until my cheeks were dry, and he pressed his lips to mine. His thrusts resumed as our tongues tangled, and I whimpered into his mouth.

"Have you found your breaking point?" he murmured. His nose skimmed across my jaw and down my neck as he waited for me to respond.

When I didn't immediately say anything, he reared back, his cock stilling inside of me and his hand cupping my face. His thumb brushed my cheek, and his eyes softened.

"Natalie, tell me," he demanded quietly, and with those few words, I relaxed.

"One more," I said without hesitation, and he smiled down at me. He licked his lips and kissed me again, reaching for what I knew was the vibrator as I grasped his face and tangled my fingers in his hair.

I released a harsh breath from my tired lungs as he pressed the vibrating head to my clit. He eagerly consumed every uncontrollable sound I released. My overstimulated body was simultaneously arching toward and retracting back from the pleasure.

More tears slid down my cheeks and collected in my hair that was fanned around me.

The warmth and strength of Theo's body covered mine as he dropped to one of his elbows and gripped the nape of my neck in his fist. With the toy still poised on my clit that was screaming for relief, the position allowed him to fuck me deeper. Each thrust was greedy and rough yet specifically designed for my pleasure.

My hands roamed his body, able to really touch him for the first time in a while. I drug my nails down his chest and then his back, loving the way his muscles tensed with each brush of my fingers.

"You're so perfect. My perfect slut crying for my cock. I need one more. Give me one more," he said, his voice strained and raw. Seeing him so undone by me renewed my energy, and I palmed his ass, urging him deeper and lifting my hips to meet his thrusts.

"You want me to come?"

"Yes," he growled.

"Fuck, Theo," I moaned, eager to see him even closer to the edge. "You feel so good. I'm so close. Keep going just like that."

I drug my nails down his chest and stole the vibrator from his grip. He willingly gave it over and wrapped his now free hand around my throat.

I smiled with the pressure and the lightheadedness that fell over me. The desire in his eyes shifted at my reaction, turning crazed and uninhibited.

"Please come with me. Please, *please*," I begged and shook with the release that was clawing and tearing at my insides.

A low growl ripped from Theo's throat. "That's." *Thrust.* "My." *Thrust.* "Good." *Thrust.* "Little." *Thrust.* "Slut."

The last word was punctuated with a deep moan, and I felt his hot cum coat my inner walls, shooting deep into me as my cunt tightened around him in a vise grip. It felt like hours of falling as we both let our orgasms overwhelm us.

I'd fractured into millions of glowing little pieces.

I immediately turned off the vibrator and tossed it across the bed, likely done with it forever. Theo chuckled and caught himself before his arm gave out, and he dropped all his weight on me. Slowly he lowered himself on top of me and buried his face between my neck and chin.

"Thank you," I muttered, and he wrapped his arms around me until there wasn't a part of us that wasn't connected or touching.

He kissed my neck, his lips lingering for several seconds before he blew out a breath and said, "No, thank you."

TWENTY
DEAD OR ALIVE

Natalie

THEO BREATHED DEEPLY, LIKELY INHALING THE SCENT OF SWEAT AND sex stuck to my skin, but it didn't seem like he minded. He took a second deep breath before climbing off the bed.

"I'll be right back," he stated. "Don't move."

And honestly, even if I wanted to, I didn't think I could have. My body felt lightweight yet exhausted. I heard him walk into the bathroom, and water began running before my bedroom door opened and quickly closed. But all I could do was stare up at the ceiling and watch the fan spin idly.

My brain was still foggy, and a rogue tear spilled free, but I couldn't contain the faint smile on my face.

Theo was back before I'd even fully registered he'd left. He hooked an arm under my thighs and another around my upper back, easily lifting me from the cloud-like bed. He carried me into the bathroom and over to the tub that was already filling with water. I wasn't much of a bath girl, instead preferring the dark and cozy shower, but the smell wafting up from the water drew me in.

Carefully, he set me on uneasy legs and bent down to test the water. The only light in the bathroom was a small lit candle between the sinks and the faint light streaming in from my closet.

Theo was still naked, his toned and tattooed back and powerful thighs on display as he knelt.

"What did you put in the water? It smells amazing."

He smiled and stood, holding one of my hands as I stepped in, the warm water sloshing around my legs.

"It's eucalyptus epsom salts. I'm sure you're going to be sore, so hopefully this helps."

"That's umm..." I cleared my throat, trying to dislodge the emotion clogging it. One act of kindness, and I was lost for words. "Thank you," I finally said as I dropped into the water. It was the perfect temperature, not too hot and definitely not cold.

I scooted forward slightly and glanced over my shoulder before I looked back up at Theo. Immediately understanding my silent invitation, he slid in behind me and gathered my hair in his hands. He awkwardly tied it up with a scrunchie, and I smiled at the gesture.

The bathtub was just big enough for the two of us. His muscular thighs cradled my own, and I leaned back into him. My head rested against his shoulder, and his arms wrapped around me.

I stuck my feet under the water as it continued to fill, and we sat there in companionable silence. Theo's hands ran over me, massaging every muscle he could touch without jostling me around too much.

The only word I could use to describe it was perfect.

"How do you feel?" he whispered into my hair.

I shut the water off with my toes and leaned farther back into him. "So good," I said as he ran his fingers over my breasts, brushing over my sensitive nipples that he'd nipped and pinched and lathered with attention only minutes before. "How do you feel?" I asked.

He chuckled at my question and kissed my temple.

"Fucking incredible," he said simply, then added, "and exhausted."

"Me too," I groaned and sank deeper into the water. "But it's a good exhaustion. I feel so…"

"Well-fucked?" he supplied.

"I was going to say used, but I like well-fucked better," I said with a laugh.

He was quiet for a moment, massaging my hips with an expert touch. "I didn't go too far?" he asked in a voice that was barely above a whisper and laced with concern.

"Just far enough."

"Good. I was worried when I saw the tears."

"You loved the tears," I said with a smile, covering his hand on my hip with my own.

"I did," he said, tightening his hold on me. "But there was a moment of concern."

"I trust you."

Theo stilled behind me, and I felt every one of his muscles tense. I turned slightly and peered up at him, only for his attention to stay fixed on his hand beneath the water where he held me. I smoothed the deep furrow in his brow with my thumb and let my hand fall back down his chest.

When his eyes finally met mine, I knew there was something more going on in his head. The man I once thought was aloof and guarded had lowered his walls around me. He was so much easier to read now. And I was so lucky to know him.

I didn't want to ask for fear that it was something I'd done or said that made him suddenly retreat back into himself. But he didn't leave me hanging for long.

He sighed, his chest rising and falling underneath my palm as he glanced back down. "My mom stopped by the studio tonight."

I straightened and turned until both of my legs were draped over one of his, and I sat awkwardly in the tub. "What did she want?"

"The same thing she always wants: money."

His hand came to rest on my knee, and I could feel the way the short visit from his mom had affected him. It was no wonder he'd come into my room ready to dole out a punishment. A punishment I loved, but that was beside the point.

He'd been impatient, nearly feral when he walked in. I didn't believe that it was his main goal to use me to escape his reality, but it was likely still an unconscious decision. And I was okay being that for him. We'd escaped into each other a lot over the past two months.

"Did she tell you why?"

He shook his head, and I could tell there was more he wanted to say. Rather than try to pull the information from him, I laid my head against his shoulder, and he wrapped his arms around me. He pressed a kiss to my hair and inhaled before he settled deeper into the quickly cooling water.

"She never tells me why," he finally said. "She just shows up and thinks that because I'm her flesh and blood that I'll give her whatever she wants. She thinks that the only argument she needs is to remind me that she's my mother. It worked up until a couple months ago, and she's having a hard time taking 'no' as an answer. I'm worried she's going to rely on lesser methods when she gets too desperate. Like last time."

"Like last time?" I asked tentatively.

My hands brushed over the top of the water. Patiently I waited for him to expand, or better yet, hoped that he would. He hadn't opened up again about his issues with his mom. The last time he'd said anything about it was also the first and only time he had. It was killing me not to know the entire story, but I'd tried my best not to pry.

"She broke into my house," he finally said with a long sigh. "She stole literally everything I owned that was worth more than a hundred bucks. She stole a bunch of my roommate's stuff, too. Laptops, TVs, even our coffee maker—she took it all. That's… that's why he kicked me out. I would've probably done the same in his situation, but I didn't call the cops on her. I just paid him back for everything she stole, and in return, he didn't call the cops either."

It was everything I could do to stifle my initial reaction. I wasn't usually the violent type, but the anger that flashed through me was swift and brutal.

"I told her that I wouldn't call the cops if she stayed out of my life for good. She obviously didn't think I meant that."

"That's how you ended up…"

"Here?" he finished for me, and I nodded.

"Yeah, I spent pretty much my last dollar trying to keep her out of jail. If I could go back, though, I would've called them. No matter how many times I tried to help her, she always comes back asking for more. I thought…" He shook his head and chuckled dryly. "I thought that after not turning her in and letting her take our shit, she would leave me alone at least for a while. But three months later, she's back for more. Unfortunately, I don't have any more to give."

The hurt and betrayal clouding his eyes and weighing heavy on his shoulders was too much. With a deep breath, I laced our fingers together and stared at our intertwined hands as I found the confidence to say exactly what was on my mind.

"I'm so sorry that you had to go through all of that, but…I'm not sorry that it led you here."

My heart was suddenly trying to beat out of my chest as I focused on where my legs were slung over Theo's. The details of his tattoos were distorted by the water, but it was something to focus on rather than the significance of my words or the weight of his silence.

It was the closest either of us had come to saying that maybe the thing between us was more than just sex. It was a topic we'd done well to steer away from, yet I felt like I'd nose-dived straight into it.

Just when the panic was beginning to set in and I was prepared to start rambling, Theo's hand brushed against my cheek. His forefinger hooked under my chin, and he tilted my face until our eyes locked. His lips were only slightly tilted, yet there was enough of a smile in his eyes to ease my worries. His thumb brushed against my jaw before he leaned down and pressed his lips against mine. Without words, he'd told me he felt the same. Because that's all it took with us.

It was a brief kiss, and I found myself chasing his lips when he pulled back. He chuckled, and I rolled my eyes. His hand shifted and tightened around the side of my neck.

"Roll your eyes at me again, and there will be a less pleasurable punishment in store."

Even after thirteen orgasms and hours of nearly painful pleasure, a thrill shot through me. I shivered at the intensity of it and leaned into his touch.

"I think you like watching me come too much to make it not at least a little pleasurable."

His wet hand fisted in the back of my hair and yanked hard enough for my head to snap back. His teeth dug into my lower lip, and the moan that ripped from my throat was uncontrollable.

"I *love* watching you come. And lucky for both of us, you like the pain just as much as you like the pleasure."

Another shudder rocked through me, but it wasn't only the desire that made my body shake.

"Water's cold. Come on," he murmured against my mouth with another kiss. He stood, pulling me up as well and wrapping a towel around my shoulders before he began to drain the water.

I stepped from the tub and ran the towel down my legs and over my stomach as Theo came up behind me. In one swift movement, he lifted me into his arms and walked back into the bedroom.

"You know I am capable of walking, right?"

"I never doubted that. But I...I like having you in my arms."

He kissed my forehead, and I didn't even have time to react

to his sweet words before he dropped me on the bed. I bounced off the mattress with an uncharacteristic giggle, the blankets tossing up around me.

"Get comfortable. I'll be right back," he instructed and sauntered toward the door, one of his hands holding up the white towel draped around his waist.

He left the door slightly ajar, and I leaned over, tossing my wet towel back into the bathroom, and found Theo's shirt discarded on the floor along with the panties I'd been about to put on when he'd barged in earlier. I pulled on the panties and threw the shirt over my head, pressing the collar to my nose as I settled back into the pillows. My exhaustion was bone deep, and I was more sore than I ever remembered being, but I wasn't ready to go to bed. I wasn't ready for our night to end.

I found the TV remote buried under the blankets and turned on the mindless show I'd fallen asleep to the past few nights. I was about to snuggle deeper into the bed when Theo pushed open the door. The towel around his waist had been replaced by a pair of gray sweatpants, and he held a bowl in each of his hands.

"I thought you might have fallen asleep already," he said, smiling and kicking the door closed behind him. I sat up, his T-shirt pooling around my waist as he crossed to the bed and placed both bowls in front of me.

One was full of freshly popped popcorn, the scent of which hit me before he set the bowl down, while the other was filled with M&M's. It was my favorite late-night snack, and it was one that Theo had quickly grown to love as well.

Or at least tolerated because of me.

"What are we watch—oh, not this again," he groaned, lying down next to me.

I scoffed and grabbed a few pieces of popcorn and a couple of M&M's, creating the perfect salty and sweet bite.

"You were invested the other night. You can't pretend like you don't care now," I argued.

He popped a piece of popcorn in his mouth and pushed his unruly curls back as he looked up at me. "That's my issue: I got too invested, and now, I care too much. I dreamed about it for the past two nights."

With a hand over my mouth, I tried to suppress my laughter but ended up choking on a piece of popcorn. I laughed and coughed as I downed the rest of the water from the bottle on the nightstand nearest me.

Theo's expression was unimpressed, but I didn't miss the way the corners of his mouth ever so subtly tilted upward.

"What was the dream? Were you one of the contestants?" I asked, then quickly added, "Wait! Did you get kicked off the first round?"

He scoffed and threw a piece of popcorn at me, which I skillfully caught in my mouth.

"We were both on the show except you didn't pick me, and since I didn't pursue anyone else, yeah, I went home week one."

My eyebrows shot to my hairline as my hand froze mid-air in front of my mouth. Theo turned back to the TV, leaning his weight on his elbow, his forearm brushing the exposed skin of my thigh as he shifted.

I wasn't usually someone who searched for a bigger meaning in everything. It wasn't a sign from God when I got stuck at a red light, and it wasn't the universe trying to tell me something when it rained and I had somewhere to be.

But dreams were different. Dreams were a direct line to a person's subconscious. Which made me think Theo's subconscious was, what? Worrying?

"I also only spoke in weird accents and refused to wear any pants, which probably contributed to why you didn't choose me."

He laughed, and I finally ate the popcorn I'd been holding.

"Even if you were speaking in different accents, I still would've chosen you. And the no pants thing probably would've helped your cause."

"Are you saying my dick is my best quality?" A playfulness I'd grown fond of and saw more and more of lit his eyes as a small, coy smile lifted his lips.

I was so used to seeing that side of him—playful and flirty—that I sometimes forgot that it was a side of himself he reserved only for me. Or so he said, and honestly, I hadn't seen anything to the contrary. He was still gruff and stoic and quiet, but when we were alone, he was freer.

I pursed my lips and narrowed my eyes like I was really considering it. which made him scoff. He turned away, acting offended until I ran my nails through his curly hair and across his scalp. Instantly, his shoulders relaxed, and his head dropped onto my thigh.

"It definitely doesn't hurt that you have a really nice dick *and* you know how to use it," I murmured, settling back deeper into the pillows. "But I wouldn't say that's your *best* quality."

He chuckled and moved the snack bowls to my other side so he could settle between my outstretched legs with his head against my lower stomach. His arms wrapped around my left leg, and my hands went to his hair once again.

Our conversation continued. We talked about the absurdity of the show, and Theo told me about his classes and his clients. I told him about my conversation with Ryder and how he wouldn't be coming back for Thanksgiving.

No matter how hard I tried, there was no hiding the disappointment in my voice. Theo lifted his head and peered back at me. There was a softness in his brown eyes that saw right through me.

"I'm sure he didn't make that decision lightly."

I nodded and shifted until I was lower on the bed, my head cushioned against the pillows. Theo moved until he was lying next to me. He tugged me into his side, and I threw one of my legs over his waist. I tucked my face into the crook of his neck and breathed in the faint eucalyptus scent still clinging to his skin. The scruff along his jaw brushed my cheek, and I sighed contentedly as his hand found the hem of his T-shirt I still wore and began caressing my bare skin.

Goose bumps instantly pebbled my skin from head to toe.

"But without Ryder at Thanksgiving, that just leaves more for us. And…" His words trailed off as his other hand gripped my leg and pulled it tighter across his waist. "I already know what I want for every single course."

The very tips of his fingers trailed over my skin, closer and closer to the edge of my panties. He slipped two fingers underneath the thin fabric, making it known exactly what he was thinking about *"eating."*

I chuckled and pushed his hand back down my leg. He returned my laugh and kissed my hair as he tightened his hold on me.

"Maybe I'll be ready then, but I can't even think about you going anywhere near—" I motioned to the lower half of my body, and I felt his chest rise and fall quickly with laughter.

"Kissing your pussy better worked pretty well last time," he murmured into my hair.

And although I didn't think it was possible, my body reacted to his words, especially when memories from the last time he used that method bombarded me. I readjusted on his lap, and of course he didn't miss my reaction or the movement.

He chuckled and I shook my head.

I trailed my fingers over the ink covering his chest, as I'd grown used to doing. I outlined the shapes and detailed art permanently inked into his skin with intrigue and fascination.

"I can't believe I've never asked you about your tattoos before," I murmured against his skin, finding a particularly sensitive spot against his ribs. He squirmed, moving my hand back safely to his chest, and I laughed at his ticklishness.

"Which ones do you want to know about?" Theo asked.

I tapped my fingers over his chest, eyeing each tattoo carefully. "All of them."

"That would take forever. And some of them are random—they don't all have a bigger or special meaning."

I traced the intricate mane of a lion that was inked on his left pec, its mouth wide and teeth sharp. "This one?"

"Mmm," Theo mused, glancing down at the tattoo and rubbing his palm over the artwork. "This was my very first tattoo actually. Robbie designed it and tattooed it. I couldn't give you the exact reason he had for choosing it, but he said it reminded him of me."

"That's a huge tattoo for your first," I said.

Theo shrugged and settled further into the bed, kissing the top of my head. "It hurt like hell, and sitting there for that long was miserable, but most of the others were easy compared to it."

I ran my fingers along his collarbone and over a pair of broken, battered wings spanning the width of his upper chest before I picked a tattoo on his side. It was a small, empty bird-cage, the metal bars of which were bent and broken in some places. "This one?"

He peered down, lifting his arm for a better view, and smiled softly. "That one's random. It was something I sketched early in high school and thought it would be a badass tattoo."

Lower down on his hip, there was a snake that began at his back and twisted over his side and down his leg, wrapping around his right thigh. The scales, the shading, it all must have taken hours to complete.

But it was the one next to the snake that caught my eye. Just above the band of his sweats was a pig with wings wearing a top hat. The tattoo couldn't have been more than an inch and a half big, and there were so many other tattoos surrounding it that I'd somehow never noticed it before. Laughter bubbled out of me, and I motioned to it. "Why?" was all I could manage to ask.

Theo sighed and shook his head. "I lost a bet. And one of the apprentices at the time asked when he would be able to tattoo me, and I made the mistake of saying, 'when pigs fly.' So, when I lost the bet, he got to decide what I got. Hence the pig with fucking wings on my body for the rest of my life."

I giggled again. "Hence."

I suppressed 'the yawn that was clawing up my throat as I remembered one of my favorite tattoos on his arm. I wiggled out from underneath his hold and examined the outside of his bicep.

The only light in the room was streaming in from the bathroom, and under the partial darkness, the ink was even more insidious and unnerving.

Half of it was a skull, the cheekbone and jawline sharp and stark, while the rest of it was hollow. The shading in the space where its eye should have been was so deep and dark that it looked like it went on forever. A black hole with nothing on the other side.

The other half of the art was a human face. The top of the face was mostly normal, apart from the scars and cuts set above an eye that was similarly empty. But the bottom half was melting away. The skin dripping and tearing below the cheekbone until it altogether disappeared.

The tips of my fingers danced over the ink, and Theo sucked in a sharp breath. My eyes met his, and I opened my mouth to apologize, thinking I might have nicked him with my nail. But he was staring down at the tattoo, lost in thoughts I knew were likely just as severe as the ink on his arm.

His brow was furrowed, and his jaw flexed.

"You don't have to tell me," I said at the same moment he began talking.

"I've never talked about this one. Robbie did it for me because that's a weird angle, otherwise, I would've done it myself." His words trailed off as he ran his thumb down the center where the two faces met and melded together.

"I'm serious, Theo. You don't have to tell me if you don't—"

"I want to," he said, finality in his tone.

I sat quietly, watching his eyes scan over the tattoo on his arm like he was mustering the courage to talk about it. I was about to say, once again, that he didn't have to tell me anything he didn't want to. I swore I could feel the pounding of his pulse where my fingers wrapped around his wrist and then again when I clasped the crook of his arm.

"Dead or alive, that's what it represents," he said, looking up to stare across the room at nothing in particular.

I waited for a moment, and when he didn't continue, I said, "The alive half doesn't really look alive at all. He might be alive, but he still looks half dead."

Theo glanced back down at his arm for half a second before his distant eyes snapped back up. "Yeah, being alive doesn't always feel that great, does it?"

The question settled over me, and I tightened my hands around his arm. I laced my fingers through his, and I hoped he could feel the care and comfort radiating through me. Tears pricked the backs of my eyes, and my poor heart wanted to burst for him. There was so much pain behind those words, I couldn't catch my breath.

"Especially when no one cares if you're dead," he added with a deep breath. He straightened and plastered on a small, fake smile before he looked back down at me. That smile faltered when he read my expression and saw the unshed tears gathering in my eyes. But he quickly corrected himself and softened his eyes.

I couldn't let the moment pass without saying something. I wouldn't let it pass without him knowing. "I care," I said, and quickly added, "Ryder cares."

His smile, although sad, morphed from forced to genuine, and I smiled back, blinking back the tears that thankfully didn't fall.

He tucked a strand of hair behind my ear and kissed me softly. Butterflies replaced the anxious mess that was my stomach.

"I know," he whispered against my lips. He wrapped his

arms back around me, and I burrowed deeper into his chest, inhaling the clean scent of his skin.

"This show just keeps getting worse," he mused, drawing patterns with his fingertips against my back.

"You are—" A yawn suddenly slipped from my lips, cutting me off mid-sentence.

"Go to sleep, baby," Theo whispered, and I could hear the smile in his voice.

And hearing him say that, I couldn't continue fighting the exhaustion that swept over me. He settled back into the bed and I let my eyes fall closed.

But I couldn't fall asleep just yet. I wanted to live in that moment a little longer because I knew he'd be gone when I woke up.

And it was on the tip of my tongue to ask him to stay.

I

TWENTY-ONE
GROCERY STORE HELL

Natalie

MY VERSION OF HELL? THE GROCERY STORE THE DAYS LEADING UP TO Thanksgiving. And anyone who disagreed with me was just flat wrong.

I parked at the back of the lot and stood near the trunk, staring at the front doors and the hoards of people constantly going in and out.

I braced myself with a few deep breaths and started the long walk. All I needed was a few cans of pumpkin and graham crackers. We were having a potluck at work, and I had everything else for the recipe, yet those two ingredients were nowhere to be found.

This was my third grocery store. And if I didn't find them there, I was giving up on pumpkin pie cheesecake bars.

I bypassed the carts, not even stopping to grab a basket, and beelined straight for the canned foods. Weaving between people and their carts, I nearly collided with a tower of boxed stuffing mix when a group of children came out of nowhere. I choked down the curse that nearly flew out of my mouth and continued down the aisle until I could see the shelf I needed.

The shelf that was surrounded by at least a dozen other shoppers.

Patiently, I waited for people to clear and considered the millions of things I'd rather be doing at that moment.

Like waxing my eyebrows or doing my taxes.

At least I had something to look forward to after I was done.

The other day, I'd surprised Theo by dropping to my knees the moment he stepped through the door. He'd returned the favor by eating me like his favorite meal on the kitchen table. But it was afterward, while we were cooking and discussing our days, that he said he wanted to do something together.

Outside of the house.

I was reasonably hesitant and proceeded to argue that it was an unnecessary risk. I was nervous as hell that we'd be spotted by someone one of us knew and it would get back to Ryder.

But Theo wasn't taking no for an answer. He said he had a plan, and I should be ready at seven thirty. I had no idea what his *plan* entailed, except that we would be leaving the house.

We were going on a date. He hadn't called it a date, but I figured that's what it was. Although a date also blurred those lines that were seeming more and more vague every day.

Too caught up in my Theo-filled thoughts, I nearly missed my opportunity to squeeze between a few people in front of the pie filling. But I managed to snag two cans of pumpkin and slip out without colliding with anyone else.

I hurried down to the other end of the aisle and stopped in front of the graham crackers. The shelves were already sparse, so the choices were limited.

As I scanned for the regular crackers, a woman several feet away at the end of the aisle caught my attention. With so many people crowded in the small space, I didn't understand why she stood out until I glanced at her in my peripheral twice and realized she was, in fact, staring directly at me.

I looked ahead and tried to ignore her stare, but my curiosity got the better of me. I peeked in her direction again. Her eyes were still fixed on me, and the longer I stood there, the more uncomfortable I became.

Mentally, I considered my hair, my outfit, my face and wondered what, if anything, could be out of place. Her unwavering attention made me more and more self-conscious as the seconds ticked by.

One final glance, and I noted her brown hair, faded jeans and large sweater. And her openly hostile expression. My fight or flight response was flaring to life, and I didn't want to fight in the middle of the damn grocery store. I wasn't really a fighter anyway.

Flight it was.

Quickly, I reached for the first box of crackers and almost dropped the cans in my hands. But I managed to keep a hold of everything as I turned to quickly escape.

Except I ran directly into the woman I was trying to avoid. In the two seconds my attention was elsewhere, she'd managed to walk around to my other side and stop less than a foot away from me.

"Oh, shit," I mumbled, stopping short only an inch or two before I ran straight into her. "Excuse me."

I pivoted to step around her, hoping she'd give up and move along, but she didn't. She stepped to the side as I did. I tried the other side, and she mimed the action.

Fuck my life. I had no idea who this woman was or what she wanted with me.

"Umm…" I stuttered. I was way out of my depth and had no idea what to do. Turn around and try to walk away? Confront her?

But I didn't have to make the decision.

"Natalie Calaway," she said, and my full name was the last thing I expected to hear. Apparently, she knew me, at least. I'd tried to refrain from making eye contact like she was a damn wild animal. But hearing my name made me look up.

"How…?" I began, and her smile was condescending.

"I have my ways, but the better question is," she continued, tilting her head to the side and narrowing her eyes. "Do you make it a habit of taking advantage of young men?"

"Wha—" I started, only to be immediately cut off by her sharp voice.

"Don't play dumb. You know what I'm talking about," she said. She crossed her arms over her chest and planted her feet like she was prepared to wait as long as it took for me to figure out what the hell she was talking about.

My mind reeled, and I was struggling to put together a single, coherent thought. It wasn't every day that a random woman approached you in the grocery store, knowing exactly who you were and looking for a fight.

Except she wasn't a random woman. She raised her eyebrows expectantly and tucked a lock of her curly brown hair behind her ear. I'd seen that look before, and I couldn't believe I hadn't instantly noticed the resemblance.

I straightened my spine and tried to make myself appear taller. She had at least a few inches on me, and I was already intimidated.

"Kim. You're Theo's mom," I said, and she nodded her approval. Now that I'd figured it out, it felt obvious. The eyes, the hair, the facial expressions were all so similar to her son's.

I immediately liked them better on him. On her, they were hollow and dismissive.

"Great, now that we know each other, we can move on to the real reason I'm here."

Irritation swept through me at her condescending tone. Not normally a confrontational person, I still couldn't hold my tongue. "You mean you don't make a habit of confronting random women in the grocery store?"

Surprise flitted across her face, but it was gone in the next second. I was happy I'd caught her off guard, but she was still standing in front of me, so I hadn't ruffled her feathers as much as I would have liked.

I didn't even know this woman, yet I despised her for the pain and torment she'd put Theo through. I was angry on his behalf.

"Interesting," she mused. "Anyway, I know my son is staying with you. I'm not sure how that happened, but I need you to undo it."

That anger roiling through me was simmering closer and closer to the surface the longer she stood there. She knew how and why Theo had ended up living with me. And she knew it was her fault.

However, the last thing Theo wanted was for her to know where he was. Or that he was staying with me. He kept all comments about his mom very brief, but he had told me that if she ever found him, she wasn't likely to leave us alone. *Ever.*

"Don't look at me like my request is unreasonable. My son is pulling further and further away from me, and I'm sure, as a mother yourself, you understand how difficult that is. So, if you could just send him on his way, that would be great. I will take it from there."

"Are you really asking me to kick him out? With nowhere else to go? All because he's not giving you—"

She raised her hand and firmly said, "No," loud enough that a few people around us turned to look.

Money, I finished in my head.

"He will have somewhere to go. He'll come back home and live with me."

I opened my mouth to argue, but she took a step closer, crowding my space and leaving me little choice but to back up into the shelves.

"And before you try to argue, you should know that I know what the two of you have been doing. I also know you're struggling to keep it a secret. If I figured it out, how long do you think it'll take before everyone else does? So let me make this really easy for you. If you do not kick my son out of your damn house, there will be consequences. Maybe I'll tell *your* son that you've been fucking his best friend. Or maybe I'll just make your lives hell until you finally give in. Either way, I want my kid back."

She didn't wait for a response. She merely turned like she hadn't just threatened to blow up our entire lives and strutted back down the aisle.

I didn't move until she was out of sight. And even then, it took me several seconds to wrap my mind around what had just occurred.

She'd threatened me. In broad daylight with a ton of witnesses. Although no one noticed anything out of the ordinary, all of them were too caught up in their own shopping to realize what was happening. To realize that I was shaking.

It wasn't until a woman kindly asked me to move so she could get a box of graham crackers behind me that I was able to overcome some of the shock and surprise. I handed her mine and replaced the pumpkin on the shelf before I beelined for the front door. I wasn't hanging around long enough to try to navigate the checkout lines that were wrapping around the place.

My head was on a swivel, and I knew I looked paranoid, but I couldn't shake the feeling that Kim was still watching me.

I didn't stop until I was sliding into the driver's seat of my car and locked the doors. My heart was racing, and my mind was struggling to keep up. My first instinct was to call Theo and tell him that his mother was on a rampage. And to revel in the calm he created. But I couldn't, I knew that much.

I was still scanning the parking lot when my phone vibrated. I glanced down and saw Theo's name appear. My breath caught in my throat as I opened it.

Theo: Be ready by 7:30.

Without hesitation, I responded.

Me: I'm still not sure this is a good idea.

Actually, I was absolutely positive it wasn't a good idea at all. It was a horrible idea, only made worse by what just occurred.

Theo: I promise no one will recognize us.

Theo: I have a plan.

I squinted down at my phone screen, my fingers hovering over the keyboard, and contemplated how to get out of this date.

Knowing their history and how he'd reacted when his mom came into Haven City almost a month before, I didn't want to tell him about my run-in with her. The effect it had on him wasn't something I ever wished to witness again. The hurt radiating from him was too much to bear.

So, I wouldn't tell him.

At least not yet.

Going out together was already a bad idea—who knows who we could run into and what questions they would ask. But now that his mom knew and was eager to break us up, to make our lives hell as she put it, I wouldn't put it past her to do whatever was necessary to make that happen.

And outing us was one easy way to make that hell our reality.

Still considering how I could convince him that leaving the house wasn't the best idea, my phone buzzed again.

Theo: Please.

My heart dropped into my stomach, and my forehead connected with the steering wheel.

Theo: Trust me.

I groaned into the silent car. Trust wasn't the issue. I trusted Theo implicitly, which was already terrifying enough.

I didn't trust other people. I didn't trust Kim.

She seemed like the type of woman to make good on the promises she'd made. She was desperate enough.

But I knew how much this meant to him. How much he wanted to get out of the house and act normal.

I hoped one night wouldn't hurt. One night and I'd worry about blowing our world up with the truth tomorrow.

There was always tomorrow.

TWENTY-TWO
PROM NIGHT

Theo

I FELT FUCKING STUPID. I WAS STANDING AT THE BOTTOM OF THE stairs patiently waiting for Natalie to appear like I was about to take her to prom.

But I didn't know the proper protocol when the person you were taking on a date lived in the same house as you. Actually, I didn't know most of the normal date protocol.

I couldn't remember the last time I'd taken someone out on a date. It was likely back in high school when I was still living with my parents. When I hadn't had to worry so much about where I would live or staying alive. Since then, I hadn't been interested in dating in the traditional way. No one had intrigued me enough to really try.

Until Natalie.

We'd spent all of our time together cooped up in the house. And although neither of us were complaining, I suddenly wanted to do more. It was a foreign feeling, but one I wasn't going to second-guess.

Going out together was a near impossibility when we were bound to run into someone who most likely knew Natalie. Especially if we stayed in that little suburban area. So, I'd planned a night that would hopefully assuage her worries from the get-go.

I lifted my head and caught my first glimpse of her at the top of the stairs.

God, she was fucking gorgeous. She'd curled her long, black hair and darkened the makeup around her eyes enough to make the blue pop. She was wearing a black dress that was reminiscent of the one she'd worn when I'd first touched her in the kitchen. She was the definition of sultry, sinful sex.

If I didn't have bigger plans for the night, I would've tossed her over my shoulder, marched back upstairs, thrown her on the bed, and made her ride me until we were both exhausted and completely sated.

My eyes raked over her body, taking in every inch of her as she slowly descended the stairs. I committed that moment to memory.

"We're never going to leave the house if you keep looking at me like that," she said, crossing to where I stood next to the kitchen island.

Her heels were dangling from her fingers, so she was still nearly an entire foot shorter than me. I leaned down and let my intrusive thoughts win as I tangled my fingers through her perfectly styled hair and tugged.

Her eyes locked on mine, and I whispered a kiss over her lips. I didn't want to disturb her lipstick, but I needed to feel her mouth beneath mine. Even if it was just a ghost of a touch.

"Looking as perfect as you do, you're testing every fiber of my self-control right now."

Her tiny breaths against my mouth were nearly my undoing, and her breathy laugh went straight to my half-hard cock.

"And we wonder why we never leave the house," she murmured, and I tightened my fist in her hair as I remembered the little toy I'd left on her bedside table.

When I saw it in the store, I knew we needed it. It had only taken a little experimenting to learn that Natalie loved when I played with her ass. And the vibrating butt plug I picked up—one that I could conveniently control from my phone—was perfect for our night.

I didn't want her to feel pressured to wear it, so I left it next to her bed with a note that said she should use it for the night *if* she wanted. Just the thought that the toy could be squeezed in her tight little ass was enough to make my cock stir all the way to life.

I wrapped a hand around her waist and marched my fingers over the top of her ass.

"Did you?" I asked.

She licked her pretty, pink lips and paused for a second that seemed to stretch on infinitely before she finally nodded.

A groan I couldn't hold back slipped from my lips as I tilted my head to the ceiling and prayed for even more restraint.

"How does it feel?" I asked through clenched teeth. My entire body was vibrating with the effort it took not to spin her around and bend her over the counter to look at that little toy peeking out from between her round ass cheeks.

"Good," she said on a breath, and I had to step back. I kissed her forehead and released her from my vise-like grip.

One more second that close to her and I would've relented.

She smiled, noting my difficulty, and slipped on her heels. She smoothed down her dress, peering in the mirror in the entryway as I turned out the kitchen lights and headed for the door. I held her coat open, and she slipped her arms inside.

"Is this okay?" She motioned to her dress.

I didn't know if it was nerves from us going out together or what, but I sensed something was off. I reached forward and pulled her hair from where it was caught in her coat collar. My fingers lingered on the back of her neck, and I tilted her chin up with my thumb.

"You are stunning. Utterly perfect. *'Okay'* is never a word I would use to describe you."

Some of the tension in her shoulders dissipated, and her smile appeared genuine.

Happy with the effect my words and touch garnered, I led us out to the driveway. I turned to lock the door, and when I stepped off the porch, Natalie was already climbing in the passenger side of my truck. I slipped into the driver's seat and cranked the heat after tossing my bag of supplies I'd stowed by the front door in the backseat.

Natalie followed the motion with her eyes and then raised her eyebrows at me in silent question.

I only smiled in response, and she didn't question it further.

"Where are we going?"

I backed out of the driveway and started down the street. "To dinner."

"Okay, but where?"

I shook my head, and she rolled her eyes. I reached for her hand, laced our fingers together, and rested our joined hands in her lap.

She settled back into the seat, and we both sat in quiet contentment as I drove further into the city.

I pulled into the parking lot of the restaurant, and Natalie glanced at the unsuspecting building and then back to me.

She was cute when she furrowed her brow in confusion.

"Where the hell are we?"

I wasn't surprised by her reaction. I would've been more surprised if she knew where we were.

I didn't answer her. Instead, I hopped from the truck and cringed against the cold wind. The cooler temperatures were normal for the end of November, but I still hated it all the same. No matter if I'd grown up learning how to plow snow or not—I fucking hated the cold.

When I rounded the truck, Natalie was already halfway out the passenger side, an uneasy look plastered on her face.

"What the hell are you doing?" I questioned, stepping around the door and offering her my hand.

She slipped her fingers between mine and hopped the rest of the way down. "I'm getting out of the truck, Theo. What the hell does it look like I'm doing?"

I scoffed and closed the door as she straightened her dress. "I was coming around to open your door for you. That's customary on a date."

Natalie's stormy eyes shot to mine, and it was impossible to miss the surprise in her gaze. I'd thought the word, but I wasn't sure I'd said it out loud to her until that moment. Her uneasy expression morphed into something more playful, and my lips quirked at the change. That one look confirmed my suspicion: I hadn't actually called it a date until now.

"A date?" she asked. A faint, amused smile danced across her lips, and unable to resist, I bent down and kissed her. A small sound of satisfaction emanated from behind her lips as I gripped her waist in my free hand.

I kept the kiss chaste and pulled back only a second later. Her eyes fluttered back open, and I peered around the parking lot, making sure we were alone before I said, "Yes, a date."

She went to say something, likely to argue based on the defined set of her features, but I shook my head.

"I planned the entire night, and I plan to pay for everything, too. And when we get home tonight, I'm going to remove that little toy from your ass and fuck it until I make you come so many times you're crying. Again."

The prettiest blush darkened her cheeks, and she bit into her lower lip as her eyes dilated.

"Okay, but...I don't know how comfortable I am with turning it on..." Her words trailed off, but I knew exactly what she meant.

I hadn't turned it on yet because I knew when I did, my razor-thin restraint would snap in an instant. I also had some serious rules about playing in public.

"No one will know. I promise. None of these people consented to being part of this, so I won't turn it on here. Okay?"

She nodded, relief evident in her eyes.

I had to try to forget about the toy until we were done with dinner at least. I wouldn't make it through if I continued imagining her face when I turned it on the first time. Or imagining what my cock would feel like in its place.

"Let's go," I said quickly, clasping her hand and shutting the truck door.

"But really, where are we?"

"Somewhere no one will recognize us."

Not the answer she wanted, she huffed out a breath and tightened her coat around her.

We crossed the small parking lot, and when I opened the door, she gave me an unsure look before she stepped inside. I led her around the wall and into the main dining room with a hand at the small of her back.

She stopped just in front of the hostess stand.

"Wha—" she stuttered, peering around the colorful, dimly lit dining room.

"Good evening. Two?" the young hostess asked.

"Yes, we have a reservation under Wilde."

The hostess's eyes lit up and she smiled, eagerly grabbing three menus and motioning for us to follow her. There was soft music playing in the background, and Natalie was busy eyeing the art along every inch of the walls and the colorful decor.

It was fairly small—the entire restaurant was no more than a couple hundred square feet. But the moody lighting, quiet music, and hushed whispers filling the quaint space made it almost romantic.

It smelled freaking amazing, too.

The hostess led us to a table in the corner of the restaurant and the farthest away from the rest of the patrons. When I made the reservation, I specifically requested a table with a little more privacy knowing that Natalie would appreciate not being too out in the open.

"Here you are. Does this work, Mr. Wilde?"

"Yes, thank you."

I pulled Natalie's chair out, and she barely suppressed her laughter as the hostess placed our menus on the table and hurried off. "What's so funny?" I asked as I took my own seat.

"*Mr. Wilde*," she mocked, and I narrowed my eyes at her as I shook my head.

"That's my name."

She shrugged and pulled her menu into her lap. She cringed slightly with the movement and readjusted in her chair for a second.

"Uncomfortable?" I asked. She rolled her eyes at the smile in my voice. I didn't want the toy to make her too uncomfortable. I just wanted it to remind her that it was to stretch her and prepare her for my cock later.

"No," she answered instantly. "It's just…the chair is hard, so there's some *pressure*." Her cheeks flushed as she whispered the last word. She looked around again, and the faint candlelight danced in her eyes. I was mesmerized by the awe and surprise lighting up her face.

"Where did you find this place? It's so cool in here."

"Robbie recommended it when I mentioned I wanted to take you somewhere where we wouldn't be recognized. And that you liked Mediterranean food."

Her eyes widened and she looked down at the menu. "It *is* Mediterranean," she said, her surprise apparent in every word.

I nodded. "It's your favorite, and I've never had it."

A look I couldn't quite decipher passed over her face. Her eyes softened, and she opened her mouth like she was about to say something else as our waiter approached.

I would've paid him all the money in my account—which wasn't a lot—and all the money I would ever have in the future if he would've come by a few minutes later. I wanted to know the thoughts behind that look. And what spurred such raw honesty in her expression.

It made my heart erratically collide with the inside of my chest.

Our waiter took our drink order and ran through their specials. Natalie was nearly bouncing in her seat as she perused the menu. I asked her about her favorite dishes and items she loved.

She pointed out a few that stuck out to her, and I ordered all four when the waiter returned along with the appetizer he mentioned during his earlier spiel.

"Theo, that—that's a lot of food. I didn't mean we had to order all of that," Natalie said, straightening her napkin in her lap and smiling kindly up at the older woman refilling our waters.

I waited until she left to say, "How will you know if this place is any good if you don't try a little bit of everything?"

She shrugged and sipped her wine. My eyes tracked the movement of her tongue over her upper lip as she licked the excess and set the glass back on the table.

I so badly wanted it to be my tongue licking at her lips, tasting the wine on her tongue mixing with her warm and intoxicating taste.

"We could always come back. Try the things we didn't try this time," she offered. A playful yet slightly hesitant smile tugged at her lips.

The future. She was considering the future, and that wasn't something either of us did. It was something we'd actually both pointedly kept from doing. Because the closer we came to the end of the year, the closer we came to the end of…us.

Or at least that was what was supposed to happen. It was what *had* to happen.

Ryder would be back, and I would have to find somewhere else to live. I'd put off finding something else for long enough. Much longer and people would begin to question why I was sticking around. I was surprised Ryder hadn't already asked me about it. Especially since I was so reluctant to stay there in the beginning.

I couldn't very well continue living with my best friend's mom, even if it was the closest I'd ever felt to home.

Or somewhere I'd wanted to stay.

My thoughts were quickly spinning out of control, which was exactly why I didn't mention the future—it had a way of impacting the present, too. And our present was something I really wanted to enjoy.

I mimicked her posture, setting my elbows on the white tablecloth and leaning forward until I could see her eyes dilate. I'd thrown my leather jacket over the chair when we sat down, and she eyed the sleeves of my black button-down shirt. The fabric strained over my forearms and biceps, and although it was unintentional, I enjoyed the way she openly stared at me.

"We could," I said. "But I love giving you everything you want. And often the things you don't even know you want."

Heat flared in her eyes, and my eyes immediately shifted down to her cleavage as she pressed her tits together. I fisted my hands to keep from reaching out and hauling her across the table.

She noted my reaction and her quiet laughter pulled me from my daydream. She sat back as our waiter slid our appetizer onto the table in front of us.

"Enjoy," he said and hurried off.

"That smells *so* good."

The small plate of fritters he placed between us did smell amazing, but I was transfixed on the look on Natalie's face. The happiness that exuded out from her and wrapped around me, wrapped around everything when she was near.

The waiter returned a moment later with two small plates, and I motioned for her to go first. She scooped one fritter onto her plate and dug in while I chose one as well. She groaned low in her throat, and I swore the sound went straight to my cock.

I realized I'd been watching her eat, transfixed by the way her lips curved around the fork and struck by the way her tongue collected any remnants, only when she cleared her throat. A knowing smile tilted her lips.

I finally took a bite of my food and immediately understood her little sounds.

"Why did you want to do this?"

I stopped chewing, and my eyes shot up to hers. She'd set down her fork and sat back in her chair, the half-eaten fritter still on her plate. Her hands were in her lap, and I could feel her leg bouncing beneath the table.

As usual, when she was nervous, her bottom lip was caught between her teeth.

I thought for a moment, searching for the words that would settle her anxiety and accurately explain the emotions that I didn't fully understand myself. Words that would describe why I suddenly wanted to do more. But words often fell short where I was concerned. And anyway, words were meaningless without action.

Before I knew what I was doing, I was leaning around the small circular table and grabbing the edge of her chair. She let out a tiny yelp as I yanked her closer to my right and into the corner I occupied.

Her eyes were wide, and she gripped the sides of her chair with white-knuckle force. Like I'd ever let her fall.

Settled beside me, I moved my leg until it brushed one of hers. Beneath the table, I reached out my hand until I found her thigh. I clasped that perfect place where the soft fabric of her dress kissed her even softer skin.

I brushed her hair over her shoulder and leaned forward until my lips were poised next to her ear. "Do you often question when people do something nice for you?"

"No," she quickly rushed out, turning her head so she could look me in the eye. "I just wanted to make sure," she continued, but her breath caught in her throat. We were so close—my head still bowed to speak into her ear—and our proximity was affecting us both. "I wanted to make sure that you weren't doing all of this because you felt like you had to or something. I would have been content spending the night—"

"I know." My voice wasn't purposely sharp, but the words came out like they were poised at the end of a blade.

"You are fairly easy to please," I said, hoping the innuendo and softness in my tone helped counteract the harshness. "I have zero doubt in my ability to make sure you enjoy everything I do. But there's nothing wrong with switching it up. Besides, the idea of showing you off is a fucking turn-on."

Her dark brows shot to her hairline like she didn't believe me. "Showing me off?"

I nodded, and she was shaking her head before I could say anything more.

"That's sweet, but no. They're probably wondering what the hell *I'm* doing here with *you*."

My initial reaction was to throw her over my lap, lift up her skirt, and spank her until she relented and never again doubted her appeal and draw. She was striking, captivating, and it wasn't just me who noticed it.

Without moving my eyes from hers, I whispered, "There's a man at a table to my left. He's wearing a dark blue shirt and has not stopped looking at you since we sat down." I tilted my head slightly in the general direction. "Look."

She waited a moment, then lifted her gaze. I watched her blue eyes search, but it only took a second before recognition registered on her face. She immediately averted her attention to her napkin still in her lap, and the pleased smile that crossed my face was beyond my control.

"There's another man two tables to the right of him who could only see the back of your head until a few seconds ago. Yet he also can't seem to control himself from looking over here every minute. Even with his wife—or the woman I assume is his wife—sitting across from him."

She glanced in the direction of the other man. The second time, she didn't let her reaction play out as loudly over her face. A blush bloomed across her cheeks, but nothing more was noticeable.

When her eyes met mine once again, there was a challenge reflected back to me. "Fine, two men have noticed me. That doesn't mean anything," she argued.

I sighed and glanced up only long enough to make sure our waiter was occupied with something else and wouldn't be interrupting us anytime soon. When I spotted him refilling the drinks of a couple across the dining room, I leaned in closer to Natalie.

My fingers tangled in her hair at the base of her neck. I'd already decided I had an unnatural obsession with her hair, especially how it felt around my fist. And I enjoyed the little gasp that left her mouth when I tugged just hard enough to expose the long line of her neck.

Her chest was heaving, each breath shallow and rushed. And the quick movement only accentuated the curve of her cleavage.

It was enough to bring any man to his knees.

"Watch his face and tell me he doesn't envy me. That he doesn't wish he was the one touching you," I whispered into her ear.

I watched her only long enough to see her eyes slowly raise then I kissed her jaw and her neck. My lips lingered over her heated skin with each kiss, and it was an effort to have to pull away.

Releasing my hold from her hair and running my fingers down her arm until I could hold her hand, I sat back in my chair, and I enjoyed the way the blush had spread down her neck and chest. And the way goosebumps had appeared across her chest and down what I could see of her arm.

Quickly, I glanced to my left and met the man's eyes. He was as transfixed as I knew he would be, and he had the wherewithal to immediately avert his attention to the plate in front of him.

"You made your point," she muttered. Her voice was devoid of humor, but a small smile flirted on her lips.

She sipped her wine, and we fell into easy conversation. The quiet hum of the restaurant and the music filtering around us created the perfect background noise.

It was easy. Fuck, everything was so easy with Natalie. No matter what we were doing—talking, cooking, playing or fucking—there was an easiness, a contentment that shook me every time.

It wasn't something I'd felt before, and I never wanted it to end.

The waiter returned to take our empty appetizer plates and to let us know our food would be out shortly.

"Have you, um…heard from your mom recently?"

Startled by the abrupt change in topic, I stiffened in my chair and gripped my glass so tightly I was surprised it didn't immediately shatter. Even the slightest mention of my mother was enough to mess with my entire mood. Something Natalie knew all too well.

Curious why she would ask, I answered simply, "No. Why?"

Natalie nodded and quickly averted her eyes. "Just curious."

But there was something in her expression that made me stop. I couldn't quite decipher it, but it was like she'd expected a different answer. I considered asking why she'd brought her up, but the waiter arrived with our food. And the smile that split her face was too perfect to disrupt.

TWENTY-THREE
DEVIL IN DISGUISE

Theo

I PUT THE TRUCK IN PARK, AND OUR CONVERSATION CEASED. Natalie glanced over at me and narrowed her eyes.

"The movies?"

I nodded as I parked the truck toward the back of the packed lot.

"It's a first date classic. And you mentioned the other night that you hadn't been in a while."

I found a higher-end movie theater in the city that boasted luxury seats and a full-service bar. It was also far less likely for us to be spotted in the middle of the city and in a dark theater. I'd tried to think of something a little more original, but with her already being hesitant about the entire night, I thought simple and classic would be best.

I wasn't sure who I'd turned into—or, better yet, who Natalie had turned me into—but I'd tried to think of everything.

Including the bag of goodies in the back seat.

"You remembered that?"

I reached into the backseat and retrieved the bag. "I remember everything, beautiful. Now, here's the fun part."

Her sweet expression turned to something closer to astonishment as I dropped the bag into my lap.

"What?" I asked as she glanced between me and the bag and back to me.

"I've just never seen that smile on your face before. And I'm not sure whether or not I should be terrified or excited."

Rather than answer her question, I instructed her to close her eyes. She only hesitated a moment before doing as I asked. Her eyes fluttered closed as she exhaled, and yet again, the trust she put in me made protectiveness rumble through my chest. But I ignored it for the time being and dug through the bag, grabbing out the items I'd selected for myself and making sure they were perfectly arranged before clearing my throat.

The things I would do for this woman.

"Open."

Her blue eyes met mine, and she immediately doubled over in hysterical laughter. She gripped her stomach, and I swore I saw a tear slip from the corner of her eye. The sound was nearly as perfect as any sound could ever be.

"I'm not sure why you're laughing. You were worried about people noticing us. This"—I motioned to the tangled blond wig, thick sunglasses, and black mustache—"fixes that problem."

She wiped at her eyes and peeked into the bag.

"Is there a disguise for me too?"

I fished the neon pink wig from the bag, and she fell into another fit of laughter. My smile was hindered by the stupid, itchy mustache fixed to my upper lip, but I would've sat there forever if it made her laugh like that.

Her contagious laughter wrapped around me, and the melodic sound hit me right in the chest. There was a rapid tightening and unmistakable pull. Like she was the sun I was supposed to be revolving around.

It felt so right.

I cleared my throat and tried to dislodge the rising panic.

But Natalie reached for the bag the moment it all nearly

became too much. Her soft hand against mine jarred me out of my chaotic thoughts, and her smooth voice calmed my frayed nerves. She reached into the bag and retrieved the wig and her own pair of red heart sunglasses. She set the wig precariously over her dark hair and donned the glasses.

"If we're going to be in disguise, we have to change our names. I can be..." She thought for a second, looking into the distance. "Phoebe, a semi-famous, semi-professional model that does charity work for underprivileged dogs. And you can be...Kristoff, my tall, scary assistant," she finished with a giggle.

"Kristoff? I look like a Kristoff?" I managed to ask through the emotion gripping my vocal cords.

She shrugged and fingered the mustache above my upper lip. "With the blond wig and mustache, yes."

I shook my head and tugged at the pink strands of her wig. She swatted my hand away and laughed again. God, that fucking sound was going to rip my heart out of my chest.

"Pink could be your new color."

"I actually had pink hair once. It was just highlights when I was in middle school, but..." She tugged off the wig, playfully tossing it to me. "I don't think we need disguises. Although it was a really sweet thought."

I placed my own wig, mustache, and glasses in the bag and tossed it into the backseat, mentally reminding myself to return it all to Ava the next time she came into the studio.

"Great, because that was fucking itchy," I said, turning off the truck. "And we would've been more conspicuous wearing them."

I hopped out of the truck and rounded the front to the passenger side. Finally, Natalie waited for me to open the door. She gingerly slid from the seat and shivered against the cold. She pressed herself against me, searching for warmth, and I held her close. Something inside of me softened at the way she did so without hesitation.

She tilted her head back, black hair draping down her back

and tickling the backs of my hands that were pressed to the outside of her coat. Her eyes bounced between mine for a moment until she gripped my jacket and pressed onto her toes.

I cupped her jaw and tugged her closer, stooping and meeting her halfway. I kissed her softly at first, her cold lips meeting mine and warming with every slip and slide of our tongues. As was usual, our kiss didn't remain chaste or sweet.

With no one else around, I shifted my hand on her hip and underneath her coat until I palmed her ass, and she sucked in a sharp breath against my mouth.

"Theo," she breathed, not a reprimand but an outward expression of all the sensations tumbling through her wrapped up in my name.

And with that whispered plea, the lust coursing through my body skyrocketed to a level that was nearly unbearable. I knew she could feel my hard length pressing against her stomach. The slight tremble in my fingers as I held back, but the confidence in my lips and each stroke of my tongue. She could feel just how much I wanted her.

I kissed her one last time and groaned, straightening and adjusting my erection so it didn't press uncomfortably against the zipper of my jeans.

"Hmm…" she mused, glancing down between us and smiling. "I've been turned on since the little stunt you pulled at the restaurant. Actually, I've been turned on since I saw this toy on my bedside table. And I love that this is going to be just as hard for you as it is for me. To sit there through the entire movie without being able to *really* touch me."

Her smile was devious as we began walking, hand-in-hand, toward the front of the theater.

I shook my head and held the door open for us, the warm air welcoming.

"It's going to be impossible. But," I said, dropping my voice to a whisper as we passed a family heading out of the theater. "I enjoy delayed gratification. It makes it all the sweeter in the end."

I took her hand once again as we walked toward the concessions, and she peered up at me out of the corner of her eyes and through her long, dark lashes. That beautiful blush began on her cheeks once again, and she opened her mouth to say something before we heard—

"Natalie!"

Both of us froze at the sound of her name, and my heart began beating overtime.

Of all the fucking places in this goddamn city.

Our heads snapped up, but neither of us had a moment to react. Caroline was striding toward us, some guy I'd never seen trailing behind her. Natalie stiffened beside me and loosened her grip on my hand like she was prepared to let go. But I only tightened my hold.

Her eyes flashed up to mine, widening in confusion and glancing quickly to Caroline like I didn't also see her coming, silently urging me to let go. But Caroline was the one person who also knew about me and Natalie. And like hell was I letting go of her hand unless absolutely necessary.

It was complicated, but I felt pride at being able to claim her out in the open. That this beautiful woman wanted me, too.

"And Theo…" Caroline said with a surprised smile as she glanced between the two of us and down at our joined hands. Natalie fidgeted again, and I squeezed her hand once.

"Date night?" Caroline continued, and Natalie nearly choked as she fumbled for an explanation. Her words were jumbled, and I didn't hear a single one of them as Caroline narrowed her eyes at me. I stood stock-still, letting her judge me as she wished, as I willed my expression to remain neutral and unbothered.

Her own expression was as unreadable as I hoped mine was, but I didn't fidget under her scrutiny.

Next to me, Natalie continued rambling, and I could tell the longer one of us didn't interrupt her, the more nervous she was growing. Finally, I dropped her hand and brushed her hair over her shoulder, wrapping my palm around her nape. She shivered and let out a long breath, her words falling away.

"Who's this?" Natalie asked after taking a deep breath and pointing to Caroline's date, who was standing almost completely behind her, an uncomfortable smile perched on his lips.

"I'm Kevin," the man said with a quick wave.

Caroline acted like he hadn't spoken and continued, "It's a shame we aren't seeing the same movie. We could've—"

"Yup!" Natalie interrupted. "Such a shame. Anyway, we should get going. Our movie starts soon. I'll text you later, Caroline!"

She hugged her best friend, waved to her date—who was still standing awkwardly at her side—and stepped around them. Before I could react to the sudden change, she was tugging me along toward the bar.

"Whoa, babe. What's the rush?"

"No rush," she said quickly with a smile, averting her eyes. She grabbed a menu off of the bar top and stared at it like it was the most intriguing piece of literature she'd ever seen.

I studied the side of her face for a moment and watched her pretend to read. Her mind was working overtime, and she was too expressive to hide it.

I brushed her hair back over her shoulder and leaned down until my mouth was next to her ear. "Don't lie to me, baby girl."

Her eyes shuttered closed. She drew in a deep breath and finally looked back up at me. "I'm not lying."

I chuckled and replaced my hand at the back of her neck as I stood up straight and plucked the menu from her hands.

"Theo, what—"

"Hey, guys, what can I get you?" The bartender approached us, wiping down the bar top and looking slightly flustered from the crowd he'd just finished serving down at the opposite end. They were a rowdy group that I hoped wouldn't be walking into our movie.

I ordered myself a whiskey cocktail and Natalie one of their signature gin drinks.

"I could've ordered for myself," she mumbled after the bartender stepped away.

"I know. But I ordered what you wanted."

She glared at me from the corner of her eyes and fought the smile trying to pull at her lips.

"That's not the point," she said. She chewed on her lower lip and glanced behind us. I followed her line of sight and watched Caroline and her date head into their theater.

"Tell me why you rushed away. If someone was going to spot us, I'd rather it be her." I tried again, and her attention snapped back to me.

She sighed and glanced back in their direction one last time before she said, "Yeah, better her, but Caroline just has a lot of…concerns."

I nodded and handed the bartender my card as he slid our drinks across to us. Taking a shot in the dark, I asked, "Concerns about us?"

Her blue eyes went wide as she sipped her drink. I left a tip and retrieved my card from the billfold. I sipped my drink and waited patiently for her to answer.

"Yeah, about us. She's my best friend, and honestly, I care more about her opinion than I do almost anyone else's. And… she's worried. Actually, she calls it 'supporned': concerned yet supportive," she explained with a short chuckle and shake of her head.

I nodded and considered how to respond. Natalie was right, Caroline was opinionated. The few times I'd been around her, she'd had no issue telling me exactly what was on her mind, and I'd respected her for it.

I also knew she had Natalie's best interests at heart and was fiercely protective of her best friend. But I didn't want Natalie second-guessing anything about us. What "*us*" was exactly, I had no fucking clue. But I didn't want it to stop. We still had a few weeks until we had to figure that out.

"I could probably guess, but what is she concerned about?"

Natalie peered down at her drink and took a breath before she said, "Everything you're thinking and everything we've both been thinking about this entire time. That we're in over our heads and that we're in so deep that when Ryder comes back..." Her voice trailed off, and she squeezed her glass tighter. "She's just worried about this...about *us*."

I set my drink on the bar and took hers from her hands, sliding it next to mine. I stepped toward her, crowding her space until she bumped into the barstool behind her. She had to crane her head back to meet my eyes, and when she did, I didn't like the uncertainty I found in her expression.

Her chest rose and fell quickly, and from my position above her, I could see a sliver of her black lace bra from between her breasts. With one hand, I cupped her cheek, running my thumb back and forth over her soft skin. With the other, I pushed her coat out of the way and gripped her upper waist just beneath her breast.

Our breaths mingled, and suddenly, we were the only two people in the place. In the world.

She licked her lips, and her eyes bounced back and forth between mine.

"Are *you* worried about us?" It was a simple question. One that I hoped would warrant a simple answer. Yet my voice shook with anticipation at her response.

And she instantly, without hesitation, said, "No."

I smiled and stepped closer, until the front of her was pressed against every inch of me. "That's all I care about, baby girl."

Remembering we weren't alone, our kiss was quick. When I pulled back, she was smiling, and some of the tension she'd been holding had vanished.

"Now, let's go play," I said, grabbing her hand and my drink and leading us back into the theater.

. . .

We settled into our seats at the very back of the theater minutes before the trailers started. The movie we'd chosen had come out weeks ago, so there were only three other people in the theater. One lone guy sitting way too close to the screen and another couple whose seats were in the middle row furthest away from us.

Next to me, Natalie kicked off her boots and settled back into the large, black leather chair. She tucked her legs underneath her and cringed slightly when I assumed she settled back and felt the plug still in her ass.

"You okay?"

"Yes, I just kind of got used to it at the restaurant and while we were standing, but now that I'm sitting again…" She continued to squirm for another second or two before she found a position that seemed somewhat comfortable.

"Just wait until I turn it on."

Her eyes widened, and she swallowed hard as the lights dimmed around us.

"Color?" I asked. I wanted to push her out of her comfort zone, but I wasn't going to do anything more if it was a limit.

"Green," she whispered immediately.

Between us, I lifted the armrest and scooted closer, placing my hand on her thigh. The large screen illuminated, and I settled back into my seat.

Natalie was sitting stock-still, her spine straight, and her eyes locked on the trailer that had begun playing. I squeezed her thigh, and when she didn't look in my direction, I dug my blunt nails into her skin hard enough to draw her attention.

She gasped quietly and finally looked at me.

No words passed between us, we didn't need them. She knew by my expression that I was silently asking her to relax.

She leaned back and covered my hand, still gripping her thigh, with her own. I shifted even closer to her and relished the calmness that fell over me every time she was near. It wasn't something I'd ever experienced before, but nothing about me and Natalie was normal. At least what I'd begun to think was normal.

Natalie was different.

I couldn't spend enough time with her or inside of her. I'd talked to her more than I'd talked to anyone my entire life, and somehow the silence was just as comfortable.

Her quiet laugh pulled me from my thoughts. A trailer for a new romantic comedy was playing, and she giggled again as it ended.

She leaned closer to me. "That looks so funny. We should go see it," she whispered.

The release date flashed on the screen: *New Year's Day*. Ryder's internship would be over by then, and the happy little bubble we'd been living in would finally burst. That moment, when what we'd been doing was bound to come crashing down around us. Reminders that it would eventually happen were everywhere.

After he came home. *After* I moved out. *After* life went back to normal.

It was like the past few months had been a vacation from my real life. A vacation I was desperate not to see end.

But there would be an after. No matter how hard I hoped it would never come.

The movie began, and I glanced at Natalie. She sipped her drink and was intently watching the screen. The light cast shadows across her face, highlighting the curve of her lips and her long lashes.

She caught me staring and smiled in my direction before setting her drink back down and getting a little more comfortable in her seat, shifting closer. My hand still resting on her thigh, she wrapped both of her arms around one of mine and laid her head on my shoulder.

Loving the feeling of her against me, those thoughts of *"after"* began to take root once again. But before they spun out of control, I reached for my phone. Eager for the distraction and to watch her squirm, I pulled up the app that controlled her toy.

Fully engrossed in the film, Natalie didn't notice the dim screen of my phone. I hid it next to my opposite thigh and squeezed her leg. I leaned forward until my mouth was next to her ear, and I knew I had her attention. "You ready, baby?"

I barely heard her sharp intake of breath over the action on screen, but I didn't hesitate to click the button on my phone. She startled, lifting out of her seat for only a moment and gripping tighter onto my arm. Her nails dug lightly into my forearm, but it was the only sign that anything had changed.

I glanced down and watched her capture her lower lip between her teeth and her eyes flutter.

"Good?" I asked, and she nodded instantly.

With a smile, I tapped my phone again and upped the vibration. Her reaction was the same: eyes still locked on the screen, she jolted from her seat, momentarily caught off guard by the sensation, and dug her nails deeper into my skin.

She was bound to leave small, half-moon indentations on my skin, and I loved that she was marking me similar to how I often marked her.

When we'd sat down, she'd tossed her coat on the seat next to her, and without it, I could easily see the rapid rise and fall of her chest.

My cock was angrily hard and pressing mercilessly on the seam of my jeans. I adjusted in my seat, but there was no relief. There wouldn't be relief until I was inside her again, and that relief would only last as long as the orgasm.

There was no relief where Natalie was concerned. I wanted her more and more every fucking day.

"Theo," she gasped, leaning into me and muffling her moans against my shoulder.

"Watch the movie, baby. We don't want anyone turning around and seeing how fucking filthy you really are."

Her lust-filled eyes were hooded and slowly rose before settling on my face. With some effort, she turned back to the movie and rested her cheek against my upper arm.

The way she clung to me settled something inside of me. Like she was experiencing something new and nerve-racking yet she trusted me to guide her through it.

Everything else faded into the background. I kept my eyes peeled for anyone glancing backward, but the few people in the theater were focused on the movie. The sounds of bombs detonating and rapid-fire gunshots that would normally be difficult to ignore vanished. Natalie was my only focus.

I tapped the screen again, and Natalie's hand flew to cover her mouth. She squeezed her eyes shut.

"Open your eyes," I instructed.

"Fuck, Theo. Someone is going to notice," she groaned quietly.

"I'm watching, baby. I promise no one is going to see you. Just stay still and watch the movie."

Somehow she managed to roll her eyes even through the onslaught of sensations.

"I can't," she panted, her jaw dropping open and her face contorting in pleasure. "I can't stay still."

She'd begun sitting in her seat with her legs crossed underneath her, but as I turned the toy higher, she'd pressed herself closer to me and shifted to her knees. I opened my mouth, poising near her ear to give her further instructions when I felt her body begin to move subtly. Her tits brushed my arm, and her thigh tensed underneath my palm.

It took immense strength not to move my hand higher or shift her onto my lap. Especially when I glanced down her body to find her hips moving of their own accord. She hovered above the seat and eagerly rocked her hips over nothing, searching for some sort of relief.

"*Fuck*, look at you. Such a brazen little slut, humping the fucking air where anyone could see," I murmured through gritted teeth.

What I wouldn't have given in that moment to put my head between her legs and taste her fucking cunt. Her whimper at my words made me suck in a sharp breath. It was a struggle to control my own breathing or to maintain the composed, unbothered exterior I was supposed to portray when all I wanted was to bury myself so deep inside of her that she'd never be rid of me.

I glanced around us once again, and I buried my nose in her hair, breathing in her clean, warm scent. I could feel the tension in her body coiling tighter and tighter. She was on the brink of release, and I wanted to watch her fall over the edge.

"I can feel how close you are," I whispered, and she choked back any sound before she cried out.

"I-I need," she stuttered, and I shook my head.

"You don't need anything else. You're going to come just like this."

A little bit of my restraint snapped with that thought. My right hand tightened on her thigh. I wanted to hold her, but I didn't want to slow her movements. I had to muffle her moans with my other hand over her mouth. Her eyes widened as the theater was plunged deeper into darkness, the action on screen picking up in the background.

"Now," I muttered low enough that there wasn't a chance anyone else could hear. "You're going to come, you're going to keep your eyes on me, and you're not going to make a *fucking* sound."

Her moans were silent, but I could feel the vibrations against my palm. Her long lashes fluttered momentarily, but she didn't close them. She kept her eyes on me, and I watched the ecstasy cross her face.

Her hips continued to move back and forth, and my hand tightened on her bare thigh. I was likely holding too tight, trying to keep myself under control, but she didn't seem to care.

Her lips moved behind my hand, and I dropped it.

"Too much," she half-choked.

Reaching for my phone, I turned it off, and she sagged back in her seat. My hold on her loosened, and I cupped her cheek, brushing my thumb at the corner of her mouth where her lipstick had smeared.

The theater around us suddenly lit up. White light from the screen momentarily blinded us, and the change allowed me to see the blush staining her cheeks and a light sheen of sweat glistening across her forehead and upper lip.

"How much longer is the movie?" she asked, pushing a hand through her dark, disheveled curls and doing what she could to right herself. But she still looked like she'd just come. There was no changing that.

I glanced up at the screen, but I hadn't been paying attention, and I had no idea what was happening. People were fighting and running and panic had ensued.

"Actually, I don't care. Can we go?" Natalie continued before I had a chance to respond.

"Don't you think that would set a bad precedent if we left our first date early?"

"No, I don't."

"Why are you so eager to leave?" I teased.

She leaned forward and ran the tips of her fingers down the inside of my arm. I sucked in a sharp breath, and my cock twitched. Her eyes brightened with a stirring desire and glanced down to my lap. "Because this toy is really great, but I need *you* inside of me. Nothing feels as good as you. And I need you. *Now.*"

In the next second, I was out of my seat, grabbing our coats, and reaching for her. She immediately slipped her hand into mine and intertwined our fingers. I led us quickly down the stairs and out of the theater.

TWENTY-FOUR
POOR PICTURES

Natalie

THE WIND WHIPPED AROUND US, AND I SHIVERED AS THEO QUICKLY unlocked the front door.

We were inside in a second, but the chill in the air felt like it had already burrowed bone deep. I didn't have time to think about the cold, though. Theo pushed open the door and stepped to the side so I could walk in first.

The house was thankfully warm, and I turned to say something as he walked in behind me. The door shut, the lock clicked in place, and the heat of his body was pressed against my back. Every thought faded from my mind and was easily replaced by him.

He ripped my coat off and tossed it somewhere behind him as he urged me forward with his large, commanding frame. His hard body pressed against me, and he pushed me forward until my hips were flush with the table right inside the door. With one firm hand in the middle of my back, he forced me lower until my cheek was pressed against the surface. All of the photos propped on the table fell and clattered against it. The commotion was loud in the otherwise dark and silent house.

His hand on my back slid higher until his fingers twisted in my hair and pinned me in place.

My dress was short, but in that position—leaned over the table with my ass in the air—it was completely indecent. He flipped the bottom of it over my ass, exposing the cheeky black lace underwear I'd put on with him in mind.

His grip in my hair tightened, and the pain made my cunt throb with hope that he'd fucking touch me there soon. Reflexively, hoping for some relief, I pushed my ass back as much as I could.

One skillful and precise finger slid underneath the fabric at the curve of my ass and brushed tenderly against my skin. The soft touch was so suddenly different from his harsh, determined movements that I shivered.

Like he was admiring the lace, his finger brushed back and forth, up and down. And with each pass, he grew closer and closer to my pussy.

His fingers suddenly disappeared, and I began to whine at the loss until they reappeared between my legs. He dragged his thumb down the obvious wet spot on my panties, and my eyes rolled back when he pressed against my clit. He didn't move, but the pressure was enough to make me buck backward again.

"Did you leave a wet spot on the seat in the theater?" His voice was low and gravelly, and I barely heard his question over the sound of his belt loosening.

I forced air into my lungs over and over again, each breath fogging up the table beneath me. The hard surface was as unforgiving as Theo's grip on my hair. And it was all I wanted.

I squirmed against his hold, and he tightened it like I knew he would.

"My little pervert. My little exhibitionist. I bet you loved every second of that, didn't you?" He pushed my panties to the side and ran his thumb down my slit.

Between moans, I somehow managed to say, "Yes, but so did

you—" My words were immediately cut off when he slammed his cock inside of me in one quick thrust. All of the breath escaped my lungs, and I cried out at the sudden intrusion.

"*Fuck*," he moaned as I clamped around him. He steadied himself, and my body quickly accommodated his size. Fucking every day didn't do much to help; he still felt huge inside of me, and the toy in my ass only made him feel that much bigger.

Ever so slowly, he pulled back, but my inner walls squeezed around him like my body was unwilling to let him go.

He withdrew completely, and I braced myself against the table. His hips snapped forward again, and waves of euphoric pleasure crashed over me. Again and again, he fucked me into the table. My hips met the edge, and I knew I'd be bruised, but all of it was too carnal for me to care.

Behind me, Theo said something, and I was trying my best to focus on what it was when the toy came to life. The vibration was low, but it was enough to light every one of my nerve endings.

"Yes, that's so good. Tell me how good it feels, Nat."

I opened my mouth to agree, but all that came out was a desperate whimper.

"It's okay, you don't have to say it. Your body tells me everything I need to know about how much you love being filled and fucked."

The vibration continued to increase until I was clawing at the wall and the table. Pictures fell to the floor, the sound of shattering glass mixed with the melody of our combined moans, but I didn't care.

Suddenly, Theo's hand was at my throat, and his other arm was around my waist, hauling me off the table and back against him. We were both still fully clothed, and for some reason that made it all the hotter. That we couldn't wait long enough to rip our clothes off was just proof of how desperate we were for one another.

"God, I can feel the vibration," he said between thrusts.

I moved all my hair to one side and tilted my head so he had full access to my neck and mouth. Fingers pressed against my jaw, he turned my head and captured my lips in a punishing kiss, nipping my lower lip and exploring my mouth with his tongue. That perfect piercing at the tip of his cock brushed inside of me, and I ground back on him, fucking him as much as he was fucking me.

His lips were replaced by his fingers, and his eyes bored into mine as he traced the outline of my mouth. Then he slipped two of his fingers between my lips and shoved them deeper until I gagged. His thrusts grew more measured as his fingers fucked my mouth.

"So fucking full," he muttered.

Tears sprang to my eyes, and my hands fumbled for something to hold onto. One hand reached behind me and gripped his ass, pressing against the fabric of his jeans and silently willing him to keep fucking me just like that. My other hand wrapped around his wrist, and I let myself fly over the edge.

Full was right. I'd never felt so full or so totally consumed. My orgasm shot me higher and higher until I was spiraling back down, free-falling into oblivion. I cursed and cried out around Theo's fingers, tears streaming down my face and my cunt clamping around his cock. My ass even tightened around the toy, letting the incessant and strong vibrations ratchet the pleasure higher.

"Fuck, fuck, *fuck*," Theo moaned into my ear. And I was sure I was going to drag him over the edge with me, but somehow he held off.

He pulled out of me and spun me around. His eyes devoured my face quickly, and then he licked and kissed away the tears still staining my cheeks. My hands found their way under his shirt, and my nails clawed down his abs.

He took my bottom lip between his teeth, and I dug my nails

in deeper. His muscles jumped and tensed under my touch. He sucked in a sharp breath and reared back.

"Upstairs. *Now*."

I immediately turned on my heels, my dress falling back around my thighs as I strode farther into the house and began up the stairs. Halfway to the top, I heard Theo's boots thud against the steps. The sound made me move faster. My heart raced as I pushed through my bedroom door and unzipped my dress in the same motion. It dropped to the floor in the doorway, and I easily stepped out of it.

Loud steps still chasing me, I didn't turn back until I heard the door close.

Left in the black lace matching set and my strappy black heels, Theo stilled in the middle of the room. His eyes raked over me, and I shivered at the desire and hunger reflected back at me.

Somewhere along the way, he'd shed his leather jacket and his black shirt, displaying the tattoos covering most of his upper body. Tattoos I'd spent hours studying and memorizing. His jeans were unbuttoned, and his boots had disappeared. My hands itched to touch him, and I stepped forward the same moment he did. Instantly, he ate up the space between us and fitted his hand around my throat.

His mouth slammed down on mine, and I quickly pushed his jeans and briefs down his legs. Without breaking our kiss, I reached between us and wrapped both of my hands around his hard cock. I pumped him hard and ran my thumb over the head, smearing the thick bead of precum down his shaft. The manly groan that emanated from the back of his throat vibrated through me. I tightened my hold and teased the piercing at the tip.

"Fuck, Natalie," he murmured against my lips. I smiled at hearing the awe in his voice and slipped my tongue past his lips again. In the next breath, he pushed me back until my thighs hit the edge of the bed, and I tumbled on top of it. My heels fell to the floor as my back hit the comforter, and I released a surprised breath.

He ran a hand down the center of my body—his touch was soft and reverent—while his eyes stayed fixed between my spread thighs. His thighs were poised between my legs, pressing against them to keep me spread open. His fingers glided down my panties, and all I wanted to feel was him inside of me again.

"These are pretty," he said, pressing a finger inside me through the lace fabric. "I'll buy you new ones."

My brow furrowed, and I looked down just in time to watch him easily rip them from my body. I gaped at him and swore when I remembered the price tag. But watching him rip them from my body all because he didn't want to move from between my legs, that was priceless.

He gripped his cock in his hand and rubbed the tip between my lips. He spread my arousal up and down and teased my clit with the cool metal piercing. My hips moved of their own accord, and the smile he shot me was laced with every devious, depraved desire tumbling through his head.

"There you go, rub yourself on my cock while I tell you what I want to do with you."

Unable not to, Theo held himself still while I did exactly as he instructed. He didn't begin speaking right away, instead watching me pleasure myself with only the broad head of his cock. And every time I tried to notch him at my entrance, he shook his head and tsked like I'd broken the rules.

"You may be a horny slut, but you know how to listen," he chided, and embarrassment heated my skin. I contemplated stoking the fire, but I was more curious to know what he had to say than I was eager to wind him up. At least for now.

"There's one last place I haven't fully explored yet. I want to replace this little toy with my cock. I want my mouth, my hands, and my cock to have explored every inch of you, both inside and out," he said, pressing the wide base of the toy with his free hand.

A strange nervousness and excitement hummed through me. He had used his hands and his mouth back there on more than one occasion. but we hadn't graduated to his cock. But *god*, did I want it.

My safe word sat at the back of my mind just in case I needed it. I knew I wouldn't, though. I wanted it. And it was overwhelming how much I trusted him. How all my nerves disappeared when he gazed down at me. All I could manage was a weak nod and a hissed, "Yes."

"That's my good little whore. You don't care where it is as long as you get my cock, right?"

Another nod, and he gripped my hips, flipping me onto my stomach. I planted my hands and pushed up onto my knees as he rounded the bed and retrieved the lube from the bedside table and a towel from the bathroom. My body was trembling with anticipation by the time he returned, and he smoothed a hand down my back.

"If you ever want to stop, you have your safe word. If you want to slow down, tell me," he instructed.

"I will."

I lowered my chest down onto the bed and spread my thighs, pushing my ass higher. I flipped my hair over my shoulder and peered up at him. His expression was unreadable.

There was a small smile tugging at the corner of his lips, but his eyes were slightly narrowed. As quickly as it appeared, his expression morphed, and his eyes dropped to my ass.

I heard his hand connect with my skin before I felt the sting of the slap.

"Oh, *fuck*," I cried and buried my face in the blankets as he landed another smack on the opposite side. Sharp pain bloomed over my skin, and he gripped me hard.

"I love when your skin turns red. It's my favorite color." He smacked my ass again and smoothed his palm over my tender skin. "And your moans are my favorite sounds. The way you smell is my favorite scent, and my favorite view is your face contorted in pleasure when you come."

"Then make me come again."

I took a deep breath and glanced back at him again with a smile. He returned my smile and landed another smack in the same spot as before.

He quickly unhooked my bra and said, "Happily."

He pressed against the base of the toy, and the pressure inside of me intensified for a moment. I'd actually grown comfortable with it inside of me, and when he pulled the toy free, I was suddenly empty.

But he didn't make me wait long. The click of the lube bottle was followed by the press of his fingers against my ass. I was prepared for the sensation, but that didn't keep me from tensing up. Theo felt it the moment my body went rigid and stilled. His fingers continued to tease my hole as his other hand brushed against my ass, gripping my hip and massaging lightly.

"Take a deep breath and relax for me," he murmured, and I did as he said. "There you go, baby. Let me in."

I took a deep breath and let every intrusive thought filter from my mind. I focused on his touch—both on my hip and my ass.

"Such a good slut. You listen so well."

He eased two thick fingers inside of me, and I barely felt the stretch. The toy had prepared me for more and he slipped a third finger in only a minute or two later.

I groaned and fisted the blankets beneath me. He pushed deeper and twisted, stretching me wider and readying me for his cock. That thought—that his cock would soon replace his fingers —made me clench around him.

And eventually the burn and the stretch morphed into some-thing good. He scissored his fingers inside of me, and my hips pushed back, meeting them.

"Fuck, Theo," I mumbled through a moan.

He withdrew his fingers from my ass, and I heard the lube

bottle again. I looked back long enough to watch him massage the liquid over his length. The head of his cock notched at my ass, and he slowly breached the tight outer muscles. With another deep breath, he pushed inside another inch.

"That's it, take my cock. You're doing so good." His voice was gravelly and low, like he was barely hanging on to the little restraint he still held.

His dick was so much bigger than the toy or his fingers, but I leaned into the pain and every other sensation. I focused on the way he held me, on every place we were connected, and how right it felt while he guided his cock inside me.

Another inch and then another, and *finally* I felt his hips meet my ass. It felt like an eternity before he was completely sheathed inside of me.

A string of curses left his lips, and both of his hands grabbed my ass, spreading me wider. I imagined him staring down at where his cock disappeared inside me, where my ass stretched obscenely around him. And I had no doubt that the awe my mind conjured was written across his features. I loved how dirty and depraved it all felt. And how I was completely at his mercy.

"Beautiful. Tell me how it feels."

"Big. And so good," I said immediately, and he chuckled. He still hadn't moved, and I knew he was allowing my body time to get used to him.

His hold on me tightened, and I leaned forward, putting my weight on my forearms, before easing back and impaling myself on him again. It was a different, deeper stretch, but slowly the burn dissipated and pleasure had taken its place.

I repeated the motion, bouncing back onto him, and he groaned. His palm connected with my ass, and I clenched around him. He did it again, and I mumbled a plea for more into the sheets.

"I knew you'd love my cock in your ass. My pretty little slut takes it so well in every single hole."

He set an unrelenting pace, pounding into me with enough

force I knew I'd feel him for days. With each slap of his hand against my ass or the side of my thighs, I grew closer to a climax I knew would alter everything.

He soothed my tender skin and reached around until his fingers found my swollen clit. His body draped over my back, and the warmth of his toned, muscled front seeped into me. His thrusts grew deeper and more measured as his fingers played a perfect rhythm between my legs.

Theo buried his face in the crook of my neck, and I barely caught the words he pressed into my skin. They were mumbled praises that lit me on fire.

"*Fuck*, my perfect little slut. My perfect girl. I love...*Fuck*, I love..."

I thought how much I loved the weight of him on top of me when he was suddenly gone. He pulled free from my body, and I couldn't feel him at all.

My attention shot over my shoulder just in time to feel him grip under one of my legs and effortlessly toss me onto my back. I exhaled a breath and watched him drip more lube on his hard and angry cock.

He lazily stroked himself from base to crown, eyes devouring my naked form as his fingers found my clit again. I gasped and forced my eyes not to roll back in my head. He groaned at my reaction just the way he groaned when I wrapped my lips around him for the first time. Like giving me pleasure was just as intense for him as it was for me.

He stepped forward, eyes never leaving mine and notched his crown at my ass. He pressed into me achingly slowly, yet the small circles he drew over my clit were targeted and quick. The perfect pressure and the perfect recipe for my ultimate undoing.

His eyes shuddered when his tip breached my tight hole once again, but he quickly recovered, his gaze finding mine. "Reach down, hold yourself open for me."

Eagerly, I pulled my knees to my chest and gripped my ass, stretching myself open. His smile was reward enough, and the humiliation that followed was only icing on top of the cake. My nails dug into my skin yet I held on until he collapsed on top of me. The stretch and fullness were freeing.

Slow, deep strokes were paired with an intense clashing of our mouths. I took his unruly, curly hair in my fingers and pulled enough that his breath caught in his throat. He gave it to me harder, and my back bowed with the power behind his movements.

"Such a brave girl taking such a big cock."

He pressed higher onto his forearms and snaked one hand between us, finding my clit again and rubbing relentlessly. My thighs shook, and I could barely hang on.

"Do you want to come with my cock in your ass?"

"Yes!" My answer was somewhere between a moan and a scream. The intensity of it all pressed down on me enough to make me feel like I was going to explode.

He brushed away a few stray strands of hair that stuck to my sweat-slick face and muttered against my lips, "Beg, then. Make me believe that you want it."

"Please," I gasped. "Please."

He shook his head and slowed his fingers and hips. I barely heard him ground out, "Not good enough," over my frustrated groan.

I didn't mind begging, and better yet, I loved what it did to him to hear me beg for something we both knew only he could give me.

"Please, Theo. It feels so good. Please fuck me so good that I have to come around your cock. Please, *please* make me come."

And my begging must have been sufficient because he resumed the intoxicating rhythm on my clit and pounded into me so perfectly that I cried out immediately and shattered in waves and waves of release. My entire body shook as I wrapped my arms around his neck. Falling was so easy when he was there to hang on to.

Seconds later, he followed me over the edge. I palmed his

face as it contorted in blissful ecstasy. His whimpered moans blanketed over me, and I tried to catch my breath.

His forehead connected with mine and my fingers trailed down his tattooed neck and chest until my hand flattened against his frantically beating heart. The pace perfectly matched mine.

TWENTY-FIVE
WHAT A PAIR

Theo

NATALIE WAS LIMP IN MY ARMS, WHICH WERE SHAKING ALMOST AS violently as her legs.

Until I could control my shaking limbs and my breathing, I laid there, poised above her.

The last thing I wanted to do was pull out of her, but eventually my cock slipped free, and I stood on unsteady legs. Watching my cum spill out of her stretched hole was almost enough to make my cock stir back to life. But the mascara running down her cheeks and the red blooming across her chest and thighs made me think twice.

Instead, I scooped her into my arms and walked us into her bathroom. Without letting her go, I stepped into the dark, luxurious shower and turned on the water. While we waited for it to warm, I held her closer and buried my nose in her hair.

She still smelled like her—sweet and warm—but she smelled like me, too. And god, it would be a shame to wash away that perfect scent that was the essence of us. But the warm water was calling my name, and I stepped under the stream and carefully set Natalie on her feet.

I tilted her head back into the water and drug my fingers through her hair. She kept her eyes closed as I pumped shampoo into my hands and lathered it into her dark locks. With steam surrounding us, I washed her hair and her body, and she returned the favor. She demanded that I kneel down so she could wash my hair, and while she rinsed the shampoo, I ate her pussy until she came all over my tongue.

I shut the water off and wrapped her in a towel, carrying her back to bed between her giggles and arguments that she was capable of walking. She crawled under the comforter, and I followed her with the intention of only staying a few minutes until she undoubtedly fell asleep like I usually did. But her sweet voice, her soft, warm body curled against mine, and her idle hands tracing the patterns of my tattoos were too tempting.

Each night it had grown harder and harder to leave. Somehow, I managed to convince myself that slipping from her bed was best for us both. It was that final line, the last boundary we had yet to cross for our own good.

For the past week or two, I'd awoken with my hands searching the bed beside me, slipping over the empty sheets for something that wasn't there. *Her.* And each time I realized she wasn't there, it was nearly impossible to fall back asleep.

If I could, I would have built a wall so thick and high that nothing could touch us. A wall so impenetrable that it wouldn't matter what we did behind it or what happened on the other side.

But it was a dream and the furthest thing from reality I could imagine.

Until Natalie fell asleep on my chest, and I lay there awake for nearly an hour trying to will myself to leave. I did as I always had, running through the reasons why I couldn't stay for both her sake and my own. And what it would mean if I did stay, especially for the first time after all this time. It would be a statement, a claim that I was dying to make on the woman in my arms. But I wasn't sure if she wanted me to.

Through clouds of thick emotions, I considered maybe she'd want to be mine. Maybe she'd decide that it would be worth it.

But that felt like another far-off dream.

Finally, I decided. I began to slip from the bed, my muscles fighting with the wrongness of it all. I circled my fingers around her wrist and started to lift it away from my chest when she tightened her hold on me. Then she mumbled something I didn't quite catch. I froze when she said it again.

"Stay," she muttered sleepily, her black hair a dark halo across her pillow.

I already didn't want to leave and her subconscious, sleepy plea obliterated what little fight I had left.

She told me to stay, so I stayed.

When I woke up, I was greeted by Natalie's warm lips against my jaw. Her nails followed, dragging through my stubble, down my neck and my chest.

I reveled in the feel of her hands on me, and when I opened my eyes, I found her staring up at me. Blue eyes still bleary from sleep, I could faintly make out the smile curving her lips with the help of the small stream of sunlight filtering through the window.

She held me hostage in those moments when we were both still waking, letting the sleep fall away. As we both realized that I'd stayed and what that could mean.

"You stayed," she whispered so quietly I barely heard it over the pounding of my heart.

I breathed out through my nose and pushed her hair from where it caught on her lower lip. "I did."

I brushed her nose with mine and whispered my lips over hers. She hummed softly, and I tasted the little sound. It was so sweet, and I went in for more, wishing to stay in that perfect, quiet, peaceful moment forever. But too soon, that moment shattered when a door somewhere else in the house slammed and raised voices followed.

Both of our eyes went wide, and I was sitting up, about to jump from the bed, when the bedroom door swung open.

Ryder stepped into the room, and his eyes bounced between us. We were both still beneath the covers so we weren't exposed, but we were caught in the one position that we couldn't deny.

Guilt churned in my gut while shock and shame washed over me in enormous waves.

The rage brimming behind Ryder's eyes was palpable, and his white-knuckle grip on the doorknob was telling of all the vengeful, murderous thoughts running through his head.

I'd decided several months ago that if it came to this, I wouldn't stop him. Ryder wasn't a fighter, but if he wanted to beat the shit out of me, I wouldn't swing back.

But he didn't get a chance to even take another step in the room.

Another man, dressed in a police officer's uniform that he didn't deserve to wear, shoved past Ryder. A cop I didn't recognize was hot on his tail.

"Theodore Wilde." Not a question but a statement said with an easy, brazen arrogance. He knew exactly who I was, and he was relishing what he was about to do.

"Officer Needledick," I quipped, the insult rolling off my tongue with the same disdain I usually conjured in his presence.

His chubby face turned beet red and his fingers tensed, reaching back for his gun like he was contemplating pulling it on me just for insulting his manhood. "Get up," he said through clenched teeth.

Out of the corner of my eye, I watched Natalie, surprise blazoned across her features and her attention bounced between everyone crowded in her room.

"Whatever you have planned, at least let us get dressed first."

Still standing in the doorway, half-hidden by the other cop, Ryder visibly tensed at the reminder that I was naked in bed with his mother. I internally cringed at the thought. But the anger already simmering in my veins strengthened when I considered that there were three other men in the bedroom and only a thin sheet hid Natalie's naked body.

"Knowing you, I wouldn't be surprised if you tried to leave out the window. I'm not letting you out of my sight," the officer explained.

"Fine," I growled and ripped the sheet off. They all averted their eyes as I quickly stood, naked as the day I was born, and scooped up my briefs.

"Hey, watch it," my favorite officer chided. He glanced back long enough that I caught his eye and couldn't resist the opportunity to rile him up even more.

"You like what you see, Officer?" I said ruefully as I tugged on my jeans.

"Still such a fucking asshole. Hurry the hell up."

My anger turned white-hot when he dared to glance at Natalie, who was still clutching the sheets to her chest. I contemplated ripping his eyes out right then and there. I might have thought Ryder would have my back. But he was still glaring unwavering daggers at me.

Natalie's clothes were too far away for her to reach, and she looked like she was about ready to rip the sheet from the bed and tie them around her body. Her confusion and concern made me spring into action.

"Turn around," I growled and stepped around the bed.

I brushed past Officer Dumbass, and he opened his mouth to argue, but I cut him off with a snarl. I got in his face, noting the sweat forming on his forehead.

"Try it. *Fucking* try it," I warned.

His partner took a step toward us, but the officer raised his hand for him to stay where he was. He appraised me up and down, a rebuttal on the tip of his tongue before he thought better of it and snapped his mouth closed.

He didn't try it again as I continued around the bed,

collecting a T-shirt and shorts from the floor. The two officers turned around, and Ryder dropped his eyes to the floor.

"Come on, baby girl."

Natalie eyed my outstretched hand and glanced over my shoulder. Her eyes hardened, and she tugged the blankets tighter around her before she stood and walked into the bathroom to my left.

"Do not follow her in there, son," Officer Shithead warned from behind me.

I handed the clothes to Natalie and reached to close the door. She took the clothes with one hand but stopped the door with the other.

"What are they doing here?" she asked, and I intentionally didn't look at her. Instead, I stared down at where her small hand and red-painted nails shook as she held the clothes I'd just given her.

I knew that this was it. It was the end. It had come sooner than I'd hoped, but we couldn't resist it now. And it would be easier to let the end pass if I didn't watch the same realization cross her face.

"I don't know but get dressed. I'll figure it out."

I tugged on the doorknob, but she pushed against the door harder.

"Theo." She'd only whispered my name, but the emotion within it nearly made me push her back into the bathroom and kiss her until she was moaning my name instead. I clenched my jaw so hard, fighting against the urge, that my teeth ached.

"Get dressed," I said and tugged on the door again. She stepped back and let me close the door with a soft click.

The kind officer barely gave me a second to turn around before he was stepping toward me, cuffs in his outstretched hand. "I've been waiting to do this again for a while," he drawled with a smile, and I should've been more surprised with what he said next. "Theodore Wilde, you are under arrest for breaking and entering and attempted arson. You have the right to remain silent. Anything you say…"

I tuned him out after I heard—and felt—the cuffs click closed. He made sure they were extra tight, and Ryder seemed to enjoy my pained expression when the officer walked me down the hallway and right past him.

The officer shoved me down the stairs, muttering something about me being worthless and a waste of space.

The perp walk out the front door and down the sidewalk would surely be the talk of the neighborhood for weeks to come. Especially with Ms. Morris peeking out her living room window and another one of the neighbors conveniently trimming their rose bushes at a little past six in the morning on a Sunday.

"Get in," the officer instructed, and he didn't miss the opportunity to shove me inside the car. Without my hands to catch me, my head slammed into the top of the frame before I fell onto the seat. The door slammed closed behind me, and my head immediately began throbbing. I struggled to sit up as he climbed in the front seat. He was talking about how meaningless my life was again, but I wasn't listening.

I'd caught sight of her. Natalie was standing on the front porch, arms wrapped around her middle, only wearing the thin T-shirt and cotton shorts I'd shoved at her. The despair and regret plastered on her beautiful face were enough to make my withered and dead heart shatter in a million pieces.

"What a pair the two of you are," the officer muttered as he pulled away from the curb. "Lying to your best friend and her son. You're a stupid punk, and she's just a fucking whore."

TWENTY-SIX

WAS IT WORTH IT?

Natalie

THE COLD, EARLY MORNING NOVEMBER AIR WHIPPED AROUND ME AS I stood on the porch and watched the police cruisers disappear at the end of the street. I barely registered the chill that settled in my bones.

Helpless. I felt helpless and devastated and so confused.

One second, we were cocooned in pure fucking bliss, and in the next, reality was banging down our door. Literally.

I sucked in a shaky breath and tried to calm myself, even with the nervous, relentless pounding of my heart. It wasn't just my breath that was shaky, my entire body was shivering from the cold and the anger.

I didn't know what to do. Half of me wanted to immediately follow Theo to the police station and find a way to clear up the obvious misunderstanding that had led them to our home.

Breaking and entering? Attempted *arson*? I swore I hadn't heard them correctly through the bathroom door.

Between working, going to school and spending time with me, Theo didn't have time for anything else. Even if I thought he had it in him to commit those crimes, he wouldn't have had the opportunity.

I wanted to take out all the anger brimming inside of me on the piece of shit officer who didn't attempt to hide his blatant contempt and disdain for Theo. I wasn't sure how they knew each other, but it was obvious they did.

I wanted to right this wrong for him. But awareness was tugging me back into the house. One tear slipped free, and a second soon followed.

Ryder's heartbroken, disbelieving expression would forever be imprinted on my memory. The anger that pulsed from him and the confusion that clouded his eyes as he stared unwavering at Theo was torture.

The wind surged again. My teeth chattered at the fresh gust of cold air, and it was that that finally drove me to move.

With an uneven breath, I pivoted and refrained from looking up and around the street. No doubt the police cars had caused enough of a commotion that everyone was curious.

Pushing open the door, the heat hit me. But rather than wrapping me up and soothing my chilled skin, it was thick with tension.

The door clicked closed behind me, but when I turned to walk down the hall, I stopped. Ryder was sitting at the bottom of the stairs. His elbows were braced on his knees, and his hair was fisted in his hands.

Hair that was several inches longer than it was last I saw him. And maybe it was the weight of what he'd just witnessed heavy on his shoulders, but he seemed older too. Much older than twenty-one. And much older than he'd looked the last time I'd seen him a few months ago.

My steps were loud in the silent space, and I walked farther into the house. Everything inside of me was urging me to fix it. To take away the sadness and frustration that was permeating the air around us and emanating from Ryder. But I didn't know how, especially since I had been the one to put it there.

That thought rocked me. To be the cause of your child's pain was the last thing any parent—any *good* parent—ever wanted.

Stopping in front of him, I knew I had to try to remedy some of it at least. The only thing I could do was try to fix it.

"Ryder," I whispered his name, the shame and guilt heavy in my voice. And like he heard it too, he looked up.

Emotion was swirling behind his blue eyes, which were so similar in color to my own. As I had every time he'd been upset, I could feel his pain like it was my own. It shredded through me in sharp slashes, ripping and tearing me open until I was bleeding with him.

I held my breath and impatiently waited for what he'd say. It was on the tip of his tongue as his eyes brimmed with unshed tears. I wanted to wrap my arms around him and tell him it would all be okay.

But it was a lie. I didn't know if it would be okay, and my comfort would be anything but comforting to him.

"How long?" he asked through clenched teeth.

Like a coward, I closed my eyes, unable to look at him as I spilled all our secrets. "Labor Day weekend."

He scoffed, and I opened my eyes to see him stand and pace into the kitchen. He flashed me an incredulous expression as he brushed past. His hands went back to his hair, fisting it tightly before he scrubbed both down his face.

"Almost three months. You've been—" He stopped abruptly, cringing like the words physically pained him to say. "You've been sleeping together for three months?"

"Yes," I said quietly. There wasn't anything else I could say. I wasn't going to lie to him, and although it hadn't been exactly three months, we were only a few days short.

He choked out another hollow laugh and nodded, staring through the windows at the back of the house and into our backyard. "I have so many questions, but I don't think I really want to know the answers."

I understood that. "You can ask me anything, and I'll answer it the best I can. Ryder, I'm so, so sorr—"

He whirled with one hand raised. "I swear to God, Mom, if you apologize right now, I'm leaving. I come home to surprise you yet I'm the one that's in for the surprise of a goddamn lifetime."

"This isn't how any of this was supposed to happen. I swear, we...god, we did not want it to happen like this."

"So, you're speaking for both of you now? I guess Theo can't speak for himself since he just got toted off in fucking cuffs." He gestured toward the front of the house with a dismissive wave.

"Whatever *that* was is wrong, he didn't—"

"You don't think I know that, Mom? He's my best friend," he said with a sigh. "At least I thought he was," he added, and another tear slipped free. If we couldn't fix this, if it ended up tearing the two of them apart, that would forever be my biggest regret.

"I'm so—" I began, but Ryder shot me a sharp look. All I wanted to do was tell him how sorry I was, but he didn't want to hear it.

"What are you so sorry for? Sorry that you did it? Or are you sorry that I found out? Maybe you're sorry that you've both been *lying* to me for three months?"

Throwing caution to the wind, I began speaking a mile a minute, trying to explain the best I could while he was still listening.

"I'm sorry that we lied to you. I'm sorry that I hurt you. It was the very last thing I wanted to do, and it wasn't intentional," I pleaded with Ryder as he circled the island and planted his hands on the butcher block surface like he needed the help standing. I stood on the other side and hoped he was hearing me. "I wanted to find a way to tell you that didn't involve you walking in on what you did. I understand how fucked up this is, and I'm just so, so sorry. And I love you so much."

He straightened, stuffing his hands in his pockets, and I

sucked in a stuttered, broken breath at the resolute indifference reflected back at me.

"That's all great, but you still did what you did. And I don't think I can have this conversation right now." His voice was flat, and he turned. He swept his keys off the counter and stalked to the front door.

"Wait, Ryder. Please don't leave. Just…talk to me." I rushed after him but stopped in my tracks when he threw open the front door with all the anger I knew was stewing just beneath the surface.

Cold air rushed inside, and I wrapped my arms around myself again. Hiding from the cold and trying against all else to keep myself together.

He slammed the door, and I hurried toward it. I pulled it open and stepped back out onto the porch.

"Do not follow me." He turned and seethed the warning through his teeth.

I stopped, knowing that space was likely exactly what he needed at that moment. He'd always been like that—needing space to think through a problem before coming to terms with it or settling on a solution.

That space scared me, though.

His next words pierced through me, impaling my heart with their weight and sadness.

"I hope it was worth it," he said before continuing to his car and slamming the door behind him. He sped off down the street, and I was yet again left alone on my front porch.

Anger at myself, at the situation, at the cruelness of the fucking world made me push hard back through the front door.

"*I hope it was worth it.*" Those potent words rang through my head once again and debilitated me completely. Unable to stand any longer, I slumped onto the stairs behind me and dropped my head into my hands. The sobs I could no longer hold back rocked my body.

My heart had been severed. Ryder held one half and Theo the other.

Ryder didn't come back.

I sat on the stairs for a while, crying and feeling sorry for myself, before I found the strength to take a shower and get ready for the day.

After I'd gotten myself together, I called the only other person in the world I could talk to. Caroline picked up on the third ring and talked me off the very precarious ledge I found myself on.

I didn't fully believe her when she told me that everything would be okay and that I hadn't royally fucked up my entire life or my relationship with my son, but it was nice to hear someone say it. Especially with as much conviction as she held in her voice.

I tried to heed her advice and give Ryder a little space, but I was worried, and I could only wait so long before I gave in and called him. When it rang twice and went to voicemail, I knew he was purposely ignoring me.

Then I proceeded to call the police station and anywhere else I could think of to find information on Theo. I hit dead end after dead end. And rather than sit around and wait in a house that was haunted with new, chaotic memories, I got in my car.

I stopped to see Caroline, who was acting suspicious, until I realized she was hiding a man in her bedroom. I left promptly after that, not wanting to ruin her fun with my own disasters.

Driving around aimlessly was how I ended up at the police station, sitting in the parking lot for almost an hour, staring at the front door before I found the courage to walk inside.

The interior was sparse and decorated in various shades of brown and beige. It was dull. The only welcoming aspect was the heat they were pumping through the place.

"Can I help you?" the officer behind the counter asked as I approached.

"Umm...I'm looking for—"

"Mom."

I whipped my head from left to right until I found Ryder seated in one of the wooden chairs lining one side of the station. Cautiously, like I was approaching a wild animal, I walked over to him and took a seat.

He didn't look up, continuing to stare unwavering at the linoleum floor beneath his shoes. He looked tired and worn down. His hair was mussed like he'd been running his hands through it all day, and his shoulders slumped.

"How long have you been here?"

He settled back in his chair and crossed his arms over his chest. Blue eyes glanced at me quickly before he returned his attention to the receptionist's desk across from us. It was busy, people bustling in and out and talking loud enough that I almost didn't hear him.

"A while." He took a deep breath, and his head rested on the wall behind him. "They said he'll be out"—he glanced down at his watch and back toward the hallway where I assumed Theo would walk out—"any minute now."

I nodded, prepared to let him lead the conversation or not talk at all. But I couldn't stand to sit there in silence when there was so much to say. "Ryder, I—"

He held up his hand, effectively cutting me off, and took another deep breath. He dragged his hand down his face and through his hair before he leaned forward. Bracing his elbows on his knees, he looked at me.

"Mama, when I tell you I can't do this right now, I mean it. I cannot talk to you about this right now."

Mama. I'd been Mom since he was at least ten. But Mama was reserved for the few times he was serious or when he was upset. The times when he really needed me. The smallest amount of relief, of hope, welled inside me. Unshed tears clouded my vision, but I heeded his tone and sat back, prepared to wait in tense silence for as long as it took.

Several minutes passed without either of us saying a word. Thirty minutes later and the station wasn't nearly as busy as it had been. My knee bounced, the nerves having no other place to go, and I peered over at Ryder to see his leg bouncing just the same.

Like mother, like son. The thought was almost enough to make me smile. But my attention was quickly split when Theo appeared at the end of the hallway.

I think I stopped breathing. Neither Ryder nor I moved as Theo walked toward us.

Out of my peripheral, I saw Ryder's eyes pinging back and forth between me and Theo, and I knew he was observing every reaction, movement, and expression. Aware of the anxiety rolling off my son, I sat still.

Until I saw the angry red cut on Theo's forehead and was immediately out of my chair. Heart racing, I met him halfway and stood on my toes to get a better look at the injury. It had been bandaged, but not well, and was deep enough that I thought it might scar.

Feeling Ryder's eyes on my back, I stopped short and refrained from reaching out to Theo like I was itching to. "Are you okay?"

His downcast eyes flashed to mine for a second before he nodded. Ryder stepped up behind me and cleared his throat. Theo's eyes darted around the nearly empty police station as he shoved his hands in his pockets.

"Not in here," he muttered.

Over my shoulder, Ryder jerked his head to the door leading outside. He didn't wait to see if either of us followed.

The jacket I'd grabbed quickly on my way out of the house wasn't enough to protect me from the harsh November night. And absolutely didn't help me against Ryder's cold stare.

A few feet away, Theo should have been shivering. He wore

only the T-shirt and jeans he'd been able to grab when he was escorted from the house. But he wasn't shivering. He stood stock-still, unfazed by any of the harshness surrounding us.

I wanted to move closer to him. My fingers longed to reach out to him and *really* make sure he was okay. Not just physically but emotionally, mentally, everything.

Ryder paced back and forth in front of us. Hands clenched and face marred in a permanent scowl, he stopped suddenly, still looking down at the ground. "Since Labor Day?" he asked.

"Let's go home. We can talk there," I said, trying to keep my voice calm.

"No." His answer was immediate, with no space for argument. "I've had all day to think about *this*"—he waved his hands in front of him like he couldn't come up with a word to describe *us*—"and I want answers from him, too. *Now,* when did this start?"

"Labor Day," Theo answered smoothly.

"Labor Day," Ryder repeated and scrubbed a hand down his face. "Labor Day. You waited an entire two weeks before pursuing her? Wow, I'm honestly shocked, Theo."

"Ryder—"

Like he'd done to me, Ryder immediately cut Theo off, but this time, it was with just one menacing look. "Breaking and entering? Attempted arson? How did that happen?"

Still stoic and straight-faced, Theo answered quickly and succinctly. "My mother accused me of breaking into her house and then trying to burn it to the ground. They questioned me all day, kept me in a holding cell, in a room for questioning, but it didn't take them long to corroborate my alibi and confirm... where I was last night."

"They would've asked you for your alibi before arresting you."

Theo shook his head. "Not when the cop has been gunning for my ass since I was seventeen. And is now dating my fucking mother. He wasn't going to ask a single question before carting me in here. He's been dying to see me in cuffs again for years."

"It's the same cop?" I asked.

Theo nodded solemnly, again without looking at me, and I sighed. That story had stuck with me long after he'd spoken it. Of the cop arresting him for trespassing while sleeping in the abandoned house and again while he was sleeping in his car because he might have resembled someone who'd just burglarized a nearby business.

Uncaring of the reaction it may have drawn from Ryder, I stared daggers into the side of Theo's face. My eyes bore into him, and I pretended like if I tried hard enough, I could will him to look at me. Or to at least acknowledge my presence with more than a shallow nod of his head.

"So, I guess you really got to know each other then?" Ryder surmised from my question.

Behind us, a couple, the woman crying in the man's arms, walked out of the police station. Ryder stepped out of their way and gave them an apologetic smile, and it was more proof that this was not the ideal location for this conversation.

Not that anywhere else would've been great, but there were at least places that were better.

"We...I..." I stuttered, unsure if I could really say *"we"* anymore. Or if I ever could.

I stepped forward. "Let's go home and do this. We will tell you everything you want to know. Whatever questions you have, we'll answer. But I don't think—"

"No!" Ryder whipped toward me, raising his voice in a way I hadn't expected or had ever heard. My immediate reaction was to tense. Automatically, I took a step back and nearly ran into Theo, who moved past me.

There was instant regret in my son's eyes, but Theo didn't stop.

"Ryder." Theo's voice was even, but I watched the muscle in his back flex through his thin cotton T-shirt. There was anger quietly thrumming just below the surface, and if we weren't careful, I worried they'd both explode. "I know emotions are high, and you're hurt. But you're not going to speak to her like that."

My heart tumbled through my chest. Falling and expanding all in one swift movement.

Hearing the protectiveness in Theo's words was the acknowledgment I'd craved, but I knew Ryder's actions were a product of the tense situation. Like Theo said, emotions were high, and everyone was on edge.

Tears that I'd held back since I'd stepped out of my car were stinging the backs of my eyes. I was so fucking stupid to have put any of us in this situation. Stupid and selfish. An award-winning combination.

"I thought I was ready to have this conversation, but…I don't think I can."

Ryder took one step back and then another.

"Ryder, please don't," I pleaded, worried that if he walked away again, I wouldn't know the next time I'd see him.

"Ryder," I said again. But his long legs ate up the short distance to his car.

I didn't have a chance of stopping him. My kid was hard-headed and headstrong. He'd made the decision to go, and so that's what he'd do. But that didn't mean I didn't still try to persuade him not to.

"I'll…" he began to say as he opened the door. But he didn't finish his sentence.

He'll, what? See me later? See me at home? Never fucking speak to me again? The possibilities and their implications were endless.

The sound of his door slamming made me flinch. And those tears I'd held back readily began to fall. The engine turned over, and he backed out of the spot. A few seconds later, he was out of sight. I sniffled and barely kept myself from falling to the ground.

I watched the parking lot where Ryder's car had disappeared for several long seconds before I pivoted. Theo hadn't moved a muscle. His eyes stared blankly at the spot where Ryder once stood, an emotionless mask deforming his features.

One slow step closer and then another, and the honey-colored eyes I'd begun to associate with warmth and humor and lust and dirty desires were all but dead. Hollow and vacant.

I didn't register the sleek black truck pulled to the curb a few feet away until the man behind the wheel rolled down his window. I wasn't sure how, but I knew the older man with a salt-and-pepper beard and tattoos covering every inch of his exposed skin was Robbie.

"You called Robbie," I muttered the observation.

I wasn't sure what I expected him to do. He'd been dragged from my bed early in the morning while my son, his best friend, watched on in surprised horror. He'd been sitting in a police station all day, being questioned for a crime he didn't have the opportunity to commit and stewing over the events of that morning.

And I was the cause of it all.

I knew that wasn't necessarily true—his mother was to blame, but I felt the weight of the secret I'd been keeping on my shoulders.

"She confronted me yesterday," I said, trying to wear a stoic mask that mimicked his for at least as long as it took me to get the words out. But it didn't work, and a stray tear slipped down my cheek.

That broke him out of his trance, and he finally looked at me. A deep furrow wedged between his brows, he shook his head. "What?" he asked.

"Your mom told me that she knew what we'd been doing, and if I didn't kick you out last night, she'd tell Ryder. Or make our lives miserable. She said you'd been pulling away from her, and I was the issue."

Theo scoffed and didn't seem half as surprised as I expected he would be. Which was a testament to the lengths his mother would go. "I'm sorry she confronted you."

"It's not your fault."

Theo didn't like that response and let loose a derisive laugh as he tugged at his messy hair. He shivered like he finally realized the windchill was nearing twenty and looked at Robbie's truck. Robbie was patiently waiting in the driver's seat, the window partially rolled down and music humming from the speakers inside.

Still staring at the truck, I didn't see or hear Theo step toward me until he was a few inches away. I tilted my head back and watched his eyes grow distant once again. He was looking at me, but his mind was miles away. Tender fingers brushed away my tears, and his warm lips pressed against my forehead.

My eyes closed against the sensation, but it was gone the next second.

By the time I'd opened my eyes, he was sliding into the passenger seat of that stupid black truck, and Robbie was giving me an apologetic look I wanted nothing to do with.

I felt behind me and dropped onto a metal bench as the truck pulled away from the curb. I was keenly aware of the cold air seeping through my jacket and into every part of me. I knew I should go to my car and crank up the heat and then drive home to my warm, empty house. But I couldn't move just yet.

TWENTY-SEVEN

WORDS ARE HARD

Theo

THE WEIGHT OF THE DAY WAS ENORMOUS, AND I FELT LIKE IT WAS laying directly on my chest.

I'd betrayed my best friend, lost the one woman I'd ever truly cared for, and been arrested and held on trumped-up charges all in one day.

Laying on Robbie's couch, staring up at the ceiling, and watching the light of the passing cars dance along the walls, I couldn't stop my mind from replaying the entire day. But with the first flash of Natalie's face, crestfallen expression, and eyes tender with hurt, I couldn't stop the onslaught of memories from the past few months.

The good, the bad, the struggle, the desire—it all flitted behind my eyes.

A good part of my day had been spent in an interrogation room. When I wouldn't say anything and finally they heeded my demand for a lawyer, they gave me my one phone call, which I'd used to call Robbie.

He found an attorney, and I waited a few hours for the guy to arrive. After he did, things began moving faster. They had to check my alibi and quickly realized that I could not have been at my mother's house. One phone call to the restaurant and another to the movie theater—the smallest amount of investigating required—and they had their answers.

Once the attorney arrived, Officer Needledick disappeared, likely realizing that his and my mom's plan had been foiled. It had been a half-cocked plan in the first place, but I would've loved to have seen the angry look on his face when they let me go.

But the time I'd spent in that quiet, comfortless room, I'd spent alone with only my thoughts as my company. And they were really shitty company.

I thought about the people in my life, especially those that I truly let in, and the list was *very* short. Both by design and due to events that were completely out of my control.

Robbie and Ryder had been on the list for years, their positions cemented and unchanging no matter what.

Natalie was a new, surprise addition, and rounded it out at three. *Three* people was all I had.

The moment my dad left, followed by my brother, and when my mom began looking at me as a burden unless I was financially contributing to her habits, they fell off the list. I wished I could have discarded them as easily as they had me, but that wasn't how it happened.

It took years, but I finally decided I had no room in my life for people who didn't want to permanently be there.

Investing time in someone who could so easily walk away was counterproductive and a waste of time. They could one day wake up and decide I wasn't worth it, especially with my airplane hanger full of baggage.

Anyone was capable of it. A shared past, love, familial relation, none of it was enough to keep a person from leaving if they really wanted to. My loving family taught me that.

The list never expanded because it was easier to never let people in. A shrink, if I saw one, would probably tell me I had trust issues sprinkled with a large dose of abandonment issues. I was self-aware enough to realize that.

But it was hard to be abandoned when you didn't give people the power to abandon you.

Letting people get close enough to have that kind of power over me, to hurt me if they decided to walk away, was what I'd been trying to avoid for the past six years.

But it would hurt more than I could imagine if Ryder walked away. It would be agony, pure and simple.

And losing Natalie sounded like the worst kind of torture. Like what it might feel like to walk around with my heart shredded and torn from my chest, hanging outside of my body, still connected only by the memories of our few months together.

Fuck. I'd turned into a goddamn sap, and yet I wouldn't change it for anything if I got to keep her.

But I couldn't forgive myself—even if Ryder somehow forgave me—if Natalie and Ryder were estranged because of the choices we made. Or the desire I'd willingly given into, ignoring all the horrible possible outcomes for a taste of her.

I couldn't regret her, but I wouldn't be the reason that they lost each other either. The way Ryder walked away tonight, I worried that was exactly what would happen.

Anxiety turned my gut, but I felt steadfast in my decision. I sat up on the couch and reached for my phone on the table in front of me. Before I lost my nerve, I unlocked it and tapped my best friend's name. It rang once, twice. It made it almost three full rings before he sent me to voicemail.

I'd expected as much, so I didn't let it deter me. I ignored the twinge in my chest and opened our text thread. Our last text was from a little more than twenty-four hours ago. He'd sent me a video of some guys acting stupid, and I'd promptly responded with a text that said, "us." He'd sent back a laughing emoji, and then he'd shown up in Natalie's bedroom.

With a deep sigh, I stared at the blank screen and the flashing cursor for so long my eyes went dry. I was too in my head. There were so many things I wanted to tell him, but every thought sounded worse than the last.

Words were hard. And rather than spend any more time second-guessing it, I started typing, hoping Ryder would understand.

It took some convincing, but Robbie finally agreed to drop me off at Natalie's to get my truck and extra clothes when I knew she'd be at work.

The night before had been the longest night of my life. I'd been awake for most of it, staring at my phone and waiting for a response from Ryder that never came.

Now, I was sitting in my truck, parked a few houses down from Natalie's. I was behind another, larger truck where she wouldn't be able to spot me. But where I could see her.

It was a little past six in the evening, which meant she should be home any minute.

I felt like a fucking stalker, but I couldn't help it.

Although Ryder wasn't home, I wanted to give them the space they needed to fix their relationship without me in the way. They deserved that much, but I couldn't leave without getting one last glimpse at her.

Just when I thought all was lost and she'd decided to change up her schedule, her car pulled down the street. She parked in her usual spot in the driveway and climbed out.

I held my breath as she rounded the car and collected her bags from the passenger seat.

She did so efficiently, grabbing a bag in each hand and bumping the door closed with her hip. Her hair was thrown in a messy bun at the top of her head, and her black coat was pulled tight around her. I was still too far away to make out more than those few details.

She walked up the walkway and climbed the stairs, and I

swore the further she got from me, the more wrong it felt. Our inexplicable connection was pulling at my chest and telling me we were too far.

The front door shut behind her.

For several seconds—or maybe it was minutes, I couldn't tell —I stared at that front door. The green door with the gold knocker. The flowers that were wilting in the cold but had once been vibrant pinks and reds surrounding it. It was everything that had begun to feel like home.

Even thinking the word made my throat constrict with emotion.

Lifting my hand to put the truck in gear and finally leave, I stopped when my phone began ringing. One swift glance and the device was in my hand. I shouldn't have, but before I could stop myself, I was jamming the "answer" button. I didn't say hello, let alone breathe.

She broke the silence first. "Theo," Natalie murmured tentatively. And my entire body relaxed at the sound of my name on her lips.

"Baby girl," I whispered without thinking.

I heard her small, sharp intake of breath, and I internally chastised myself for the slip. Not knowing exactly where she stood—or where we stood—the term of endearment probably wasn't appropriate.

"I—uh," she stuttered. "I wanted to call and check in."

Her voice sounded so sad, I had to close my eyes and collect myself before I could respond. But she spoke again. "Your truck is gone," she said.

As usual, I stayed silent. Only I didn't want to. I wanted to tell her about everything I was thinking, no matter how chaotic, jumbled, and messy it was. But I couldn't.

"But it was here this morning. And I have a feeling if I go upstairs, your room will be empty, too." She choked on the last words.

"Yes," I said, refraining from further explanation.

"You didn't have to leave," she whispered, and those soft words were so genuine and unbidden that I felt them crack me open, leaving me raw and exposed.

"I did," I finally managed to say after several seconds. I swallowed hard and forced the next words out. "You and Ryder need to fix things. That's what's most important right now, and you won't be able to do that if I'm still living there."

She was silent for so long I'd thought she'd hung up until she cleared her throat.

"You're right," she said, then added, "but I didn't want you to leave."

I would give anything to stay, I thought. But I choked the words down, worried that anything more I added would only make it harder for her. Harder for both of us.

"Do you have somewhere to go?"

"Yeah," I confirmed, my voice hoarse with emotion. "I'm going to stay at Robbie's for a little while."

"Okay."

"Okay."

More silence and I swore I could hear her crying, which was confirmed when she sniffled and cleared her throat. Instinctually, I wanted to comfort her. I wanted to take away the pain and shield her from being touched by it ever again.

"Bye, Theo," she said, and I was gripping my phone so hard I nearly shattered it.

I hated how final it felt and how definitive that word sounded. I searched for anything else to say that didn't make me want to barge into that goddamn house and never fucking leave.

"I can't say goodbye, Natalie. This isn't goodbye," I ground out before hanging up the phone and throwing it down on the passenger seat. I threw the truck in drive and sped down the street. Hoping it wasn't the last time I saw that house or the last time I heard her voice.

I

TWENTY-EIGHT
BE HAPPY

Natalie

ANOTHER SLEEPLESS NIGHT. THAT WAS ALL I HAD TO LOOK FORWARD to for the past three days.

I'd gone to work on Monday but had taken the following two days off for the Thanksgiving holiday. Which meant I had no distractions and more time than I ever wanted to think.

Everyone at the office could tell something was off, but thankfully no one pointed it out. Instead, they went along as usual, throwing me lingering glances and whispering their theories when they thought I wasn't listening. It could have been worse.

Worse was coming home to an empty house for the first time in months. When I pulled up and saw Theo's truck was gone, my heart sank. When I walked into the house, I didn't even have to walk upstairs to know all his stuff would be gone, too.

That's what had prompted the one and only call we'd had since everything happened. He wanted to stay away, to give Ryder and me space and time to figure it out for ourselves and hopefully salvage what we could of our relationship.

I hated that I understood, and I hated that it made sense.

I couldn't breathe without him there. My only comfort was that it seemed to be just as hard on him as it was on me for him to leave.

Ryder went to his dad's house across town, so I at least knew he was still in the city. I wouldn't have put it past him to go back to Texas and try to put as much distance between himself and the mess we'd caused.

I also assumed he hadn't mentioned to Mark why he was staying there since I hadn't received a phone call from my ex-husband telling me what a shitty person and a shitty mom I was.

I already knew it; I didn't need my ex to tell me. That would have been the icing on top of a really fucked up cake.

Although I hadn't been doing much, my body and my mind were exhausted.

Crawling out of bed, I meandered into the bathroom, not stopping to look in the mirror. I didn't need to look in the mirror to know how awful I looked.

I used the restroom, braided my hair, and found my glasses next to the sink. Ambling through the motions as had become my norm.

I swung the bedroom door open and felt the smallest twinge of excitement for the only thing that I had to look forward to: coffee.

To make matters worse, it was Thanksgiving, and with the way things were going, it would be Caroline and I curled up on the couch with take-out.

It wasn't until I was halfway down the stairs, lost in thought, that I heard a sound from the kitchen.

Immediately, I froze.

My pulse skyrocketed, and my instinct was to sprint back upstairs. But I stood still and waited to see if I heard it again. A second later, someone cursed, and something clattered to the floor.

My eyes widened, and I was hurrying down the stairs before I knew what I was doing. I hit the third step that always squeaked, and Ryder turned around from where he was standing at the stove.

"Did I wake you up? Sorry, the lid fell when I pulled the pan out of the cabinet."

"No, umm…" I stuttered, still trying to get my mind around the scene in front of me. "I was already awake. What are you—what are you doing here?" I cautiously walked down the last three steps and prepared for Ryder to vanish like he was a figment of my imagination.

Ryder didn't respond to my question. He set the frying pan on the burner and turned on the heat, reaching for the butter he'd already pulled out of the fridge. He had that ridiculous apron that had been hanging in the pantry for years tied around his neck and waist and was cautiously moving around the kitchen like he hadn't grown up here.

"Ryder," I said through a lump of emotion.

He turned to face me, and I tried to swallow.

"I figured we should talk."

I nodded and couldn't find the strength to respond or move or do anything besides freak out and begin to hyperventilate. At least until I knew exactly what he was thinking.

"Do you want to go first, or should I?" he asked, and when I didn't say anything, he said, "I'll go first."

I nodded again because apparently that's all I could do before I slipped into one of the barstools at the counter. The shaking in my arms and legs made it difficult to position myself in the seat.

He blew out a long breath and stared down at his shoes. There was less tension in his shoulders than there was the last time I saw him, and he didn't appear as angry. But that wasn't saying much when the last time I saw him it looked like he was about to rip Theo's head off.

"Are you happy?" he asked abruptly, and I stilled in my seat.

Completely caught off guard by the question, it took me a second to formulate a response. "I'm happy you're here," I said hesitantly, and he was shaking his head before I could finish.

"No, I mean, are you happy...with Theo?"

That made more sense, and I didn't hesitate to answer the second time. "Yes," I said with a sigh, and if he heard the longing in my voice, he didn't react.

Ryder nodded like that was the answer he expected and turned back to the stove. He shut off the heat, and the melting butter in the pan quickly began to cool.

"He texted me," Ryder said without turning around. "It was a long, kind of chaotic message, but it was...interesting."

"Interesting? What did it say?"

Ryder shook his head, turning back to me with a small smile tugging at his lips.

"I'm sure he would probably prefer to tell you himself, but I'm glad he sent it. I wasn't in the headspace to listen to either of you on Sunday, but it cleared some things up."

"Like what?" I asked again, my voice laced with panic and concern I couldn't keep contained any longer. I was immensely curious what Theo had told him, but I was more concerned in that moment how Ryder felt about it.

The new emotion in his eyes was unmistakable, which didn't help my anxiety. But he didn't keep me hanging for long.

"He's happy, too. Happier than I think he's ever been. At least in the time I've known him. Not sure if you noticed, but he's not very emotive."

I was glad to hear that Theo was happy, it lightened a part of me to know it, but it didn't tell me much about what Ryder was thinking. And that was what I was most focused on at the moment. I needed to know that my son was okay. That we were going to be okay.

"I'm so glad, but Ryder, I want to know how you're feeling."

He sighed, and I held my breath.

"I've spent the last three days trying to figure that out. There's a lot...it's a lot."

"I know," I placated.

"I was so angry and pissed, and then I felt betrayed. I don't know, it's a lot to process. This is such a fucked-up situation. My mom and my best friend? How did that even happen?"

I raised my eyebrows in silent question, wondering if he really wanted me to answer, but he shook his head and waved his hand.

"That was very much rhetorical," he clarified and scrubbed a hand down his face. "I was really upset. Honestly, I still am. The two of you lied to me for *months*. I feel like an idiot for not having figured it out earlier."

"How would you have known? You weren't here. You couldn't have known. You're not an idiot."

"I know, I know, but that doesn't help anything. Actually, it kind of makes it worse. You both knew you could get away with it since I was eight hundred miles away."

My heart constricted, and I swiped away the tears that had begun to fall.

"We—it wasn't like that. I swear. We didn't want to lie to you. That was horrible and awful, but when it was just us," I stopped, trying to think of the most diplomatic way of saying it that wouldn't make Ryder want to puke and storm out of the house. "It was like the rest of the world didn't exist. He wasn't your best friend. He was just…*Theo*."

Ryder considered me for a second, and I worried I'd said too much. Gnawing on my bottom lip and picking at my nails, I considered if I could physically stop him from leaving a second time.

"I get it," he said, surprising the hell out of me. My expression must have belied my shock because he chuckled softly and continued, "That doesn't mean I'm suddenly over it, but Mom, I can't deny that you deserve this."

He braced his hands on the butcher block counter between us and said earnestly, "You deserve to be happy."

More tears fell, and suddenly, I was holding back relieved sobs.

"I know you tried to hide it from me, but I knew, Mom, that

you weren't happy with Dad for quite a while. Yet you stayed together for me. And I also know that you only got married because of me."

"It wasn't necessarily because of you," I argued halfheartedly.

"It was, but it doesn't bother me. You were great parents, and I'm honestly glad things happened the way they did. But Mom, you've never done anything for you. And as strange and confusing as it is, I know that Theo is *that* for you."

"Caroline said the same thing," I muttered.

"Why am I not surprised?" he asked with a tentative smile.

"And as strange as it sounds, the two of you together make more sense the longer I thought about it. I can't quite explain it, but you've both been through a lot. And you both deserve some good." He rounded the island and stopped in front of me. "You're going to have to give me some time. Actually, a lot of time before I fully come to terms with the two of you being together. And I'm still upset that you both lied to me and went behind my back, but I'm never going to stand in the way of your happiness."

Quickly, I stood from the chair, giving up on wiping away the tears, and threw my arms around Ryder's neck. He hugged me back, and I started muttering, "*I'm sorry,*" over and over again.

He pulled back and smiled down at me. "I heard your first million apologies, and I know you're sorry. So, you don't have to keep saying it."

I nodded, and he squeezed my arms before returning to the stove and his forgotten pan of melted butter. Somehow, I'd been blessed with the most understanding kid. And I would never take that for granted.

"I'm making your scrambled eggs," he said, glancing over his shoulder with a smirk. "But better."

Laughter bubbled out of me, and I felt lighter for the first time in days. He'd already made coffee, and I retrieved a mug from the cabinet directly above the coffee maker as I sniffled and wiped away the last of the tears.

"You wish. My scrambled eggs cannot be made better because they're already the best."

He cracked a few eggs in a shallow bowl as I poured my cup of coffee, and I felt like it was all too good to be true. Things were back to the way they were supposed to be.

Mostly.

"We'll see about that," he challenged as he retrieved the whisk and got to work.

I sipped my coffee and took a deep breath. I'd thought I'd lost him. I'd thought I'd lost them both.

But he was back. Although Theo was still gone.

TWENTY-NINE
BREAKFAST?

Theo

DRIVING DOWN NATALIE'S STREET, I WAS REMINDED OF THE FIRST time. When I nearly ran over the toddler on his trike and contemplated turning around.

I think I contemplated turning around every second of that day and considered leaving the house altogether—promise to Ryder be damned—until I saw her.

It had been three miserable days waiting and hoping to hear from either Ryder or Natalie that they'd worked it out. I'd refrained from reaching out again after I'd left Natalie's house and after I saw that Ryder had read my text. Or at least opened it.

It had been three of the longest days of my life, but I knew I did the right thing.

And I'd woken up that morning, Thanksgiving morning, to a text from Ryder.

Ryder: We should talk. Come over this morning.

I'd jumped out of bed—well, off Robbie's couch—and gotten

dressed faster than I ever had. It was barely eight in the morning, and Ryder hadn't acknowledged my text letting him know I was on my way. Sent only twenty minutes after his came through.

I parked on the street, and my heart began beating overtime. Natalie's car was in the driveway next to Ryder's. They were *both* here, and I had no idea what I was walking into.

Over the past three days, I'd thought up every worst-case scenario my imagination could conjure. Most of them included Ryder beating the shit out of me and telling me he never wanted to speak to me again. In others, he'd promised to never forgive either of us. In almost all of them, I'd lost not only my best friend but Natalie, too.

With that thought, I began moving. I hopped from the car and strode up the walkway. Bounding up the porch stairs, I didn't hesitate until I pushed open that bright green front door and heard...*laughter*?

I stood in the open doorway, the cold air wafting in behind me, and waited a second until I heard the sound again. Shock was replaced by confusion as Ryder's deep chuckle was followed by Natalie's bright laughter. I closed the door behind me with a quiet click and stepped inside.

"Yeah, now turn the heat down and push them around so they don't stick to the pan," Natalie instructed. "Ryder, they're going to burn if you don't keep moving them."

"Mom, I know how to make scrambled eggs. I've done it a few times, actually."

They were both in the kitchen so I couldn't see them, but I imagined the eye roll Natalie would give Ryder for that response.

"You said you were making them the way I make them, so I'm telling you how."

I continued down the hallway, my steps light and nearly silent against the wood floor. It wasn't until I was at the bottom of the stairs, the living room to my left and the kitchen opening to my right, that I saw them.

Ryder was standing at the stove, spatula in one hand, a glass of orange juice in the other, and an apron tied around his torso. Hearing me enter the room, he turned, and I wasn't surprised that printed on the front of his apron was an image of a man—from the shoulders down to his knees—wearing small red swim trunks and flexing his abs.

No, that image didn't surprise me. What did surprise me was the easy smile tilting his lips. The dark circles and irate expression had disappeared. As had the tension lining his shoulders and radiating off him in endless waves. The Ryder standing in front of me was my best friend and the version of him I never thought I'd see again.

"Hey," he said, waving the spatula like it was a normal day. My confusion kept me silent, as did the torrent of emotion ripping through me.

His smile dropped slightly, and I imagined he was reminded of everything that happened the day before. His carefree, unbothered demeanor was not as easy as it appeared. But he quickly recovered, stepping to the side and revealing a sleepy, yet smiling Natalie.

All the air and energy was siphoned from the room when she looked at me. My breath left me in a quiet whoosh, and my chest expanded, filling with all the warmth and light carried in her eyes.

Her dark hair was braided and fell over one shoulder, and her simple wire glasses were sitting on her nose. She was still in her pajamas—a matching navy-blue set I'd seen her in a time or two, and I knew was one of her favorites. A light flush that was my favorite shade of pink colored her cheeks and complemented her rose-tinted lips.

So quickly that I barely realized it happened, she looked at Ryder, and a silent conversation passed between them. The entire interaction occurred in the few seconds it took me to take a deep breath. Like nothing had happened, Ryder turned back to the stove, and Natalie walked around him.

She rounded the island, one of her hands skating over the butcher block counter as she came to a stop in front of me. I held my breath as she folded her arms over her stomach and pushed to her toes. I didn't move a millimeter when she pressed a light kiss to my cheek and dropped back down onto her heels.

With one final gentle smile, she continued around me and up the stairs.

"Breakfast will be ready in a few. Do you want orange juice or coffee? I also bought champagne for mimosas. I'm not sure what kind of vodka we have, but a Bloody Mary also sounds good. Maybe we could—"

He turned from the stove, reaching for some spices on the kitchen island behind him. He must have caught my expression, which I was positive looked as dumbfounded as I felt, because he started backtracking.

"Sorry, I know you've been living here for months, so I guess you can help yourself to whatever. I didn't mean—"

"What are you doing?" I asked abruptly, cutting off another rambling tangent. My tone was a little harsher than I meant for it to be, but I couldn't keep the disbelief from my voice. It was like nothing had happened. Like the days before were a cruel nightmare with the way he was acting.

"I'm cooking breakfast," Ryder said with a shrug.

His nonchalance frustrated me, and I opened my mouth to say as much but caught myself. I ran a hand through my hair and stepped farther into the kitchen, bracing my palms against the countertop and waiting to see what he'd do next since I couldn't begin to predict my best friend's next move.

He didn't do anything, though. He just stared at me, his usual smile in place.

"And acting like nothing happened."

I didn't want to bring it up, but I knew if I didn't, nothing would ever be resolved. And part of me hoped that his attempt to make everything feel normal—or as normal as it could feel—was a sign that he wanted that.

My statement broke him from his elation. His eyes dropped to the spatula in his hand, which he turned over and over again in his palm. It was odd seeing Ryder lost in thought. I didn't talk much, yet he was never at a loss for words.

He reached for the glass of orange juice in front of him and knocked back the rest of it.

"Not just orange juice, then."

He chuckled and shook his head as he swallowed. "Gin," he answered simply, and I nodded.

The anxiety churning in my gut wasn't something I was used to. But I was ready to be done with it. I wanted to know what he was mulling over so intensely and what the future of our friendship would look like.

And when I finally felt like I couldn't take his silence a second more, when the anticipation felt like it was going to strangle me, he said, "I read your text."

That was progress, but it could have also meant a plethora of things. I'd reread the text once that morning on the way over to their house and it was more chaotic and jumbled than I remembered. There wasn't a single coherent thought or reason.

I nodded, at a loss for words.

"It cleared some things up. It—umm…it made me see things a little differently, too."

I nodded again. I felt like a bobblehead, but I didn't have anything to add. My text, although a compilation of unorganized and messy word vomit, had a very clear overall message that was hard to miss.

"I was fucking pissed," he said, and I nodded.

"I know. And you had—*have*—every right to be."

Ryder leaned against the counter next to the stove and folded his arms over his chest. I tried not to stare, but the stupid apron was too much of a distraction. He followed my line of sight and chuckled as he untied it from around his waist, lifted it over his head, and tossed it behind him.

"Now we can talk since you're not staring at my abs," he quipped.

"They were a little distracting. Not the best attire for a difficult conversation."

"No, not a difficult conversation."

I straightened, miming his posture. "No?"

He shook his head. "I'm still angry," he said, looking down at his hands as he continued. "And I hate the fact that you both lied to me and snuck around behind my back. It makes everything worse that *you're* my best friend and she's my mom. The two people in the world I was supposed to be able to trust, and you do this? I felt *betrayed*. But..."

I held my breath as the single word trailed off, and he lifted his head to meet my eyes.

"I can't lie and say that it doesn't make any sense. Because when I think about it, the two of you together...it *does* make sense. Sort of."

"You're serious?"

"Yeah, but it's still really fucking weird, and I'm not sure how to handle it. I've spent the past few days trying to wrap my head around it, and I'm not sure what the hell I'm supposed to do now."

I nodded, and I could tell he was contemplating what he wanted to say next, so I stayed quiet.

"I opened your text when you sent it, but I didn't actually read it until last night. Like I said, after three days of feeling like you both betrayed me, it gave me a new perspective." He said the words like he wasn't quite sure if that's what he meant. "I guess, for some reason, knowing that it's more than—" He stopped abruptly, waving his hands around. His face screwed up in a disgusted, uncomfortable expression. "I don't even want to think about it, it's so gross. But knowing that it's more than, you know, *that*."

Sex, got it.

"That helped. I thought this was just another classic Theo move. No strings, no emotions, no thought of the woman beyond the bedroom. Or the back of the car," he added. "But it's not."

"No," I agreed quickly. It was strangely easy to admit the realization I'd come to only a few days before and had been slowly understanding for months: she was so much more.

He nodded slowly and for several seconds before he continued. "Your text made that clear."

"I can't believe you understood a word of that," I joked, my laughter still tinged with caution.

"Oh, it was a fucking chaotic, stream-of-consciousness nonsense. But I got the idea."

"Okay," I said, at a loss for words and overwhelmingly thankful for a best friend who understood even when he had every reason not to.

He raised his dark brows and narrowed his eyes. "That's all? Just okay?"

I stuttered out a response. "I just wasn't expecting to have this conversation. I thought I'd walk in here, you'd tell me what a piece of shit, horrible friend I am—maybe beat the crap out of me—and then tell me to never come back."

He chuckled and crossed to the bar cart where he retrieved the half-full bottle of gin.

"I'm not a big fighter."

"Looked like you were ready to beat my ass a couple of days ago," I said as he found the orange juice and started mixing his cocktail.

"I definitely was, but that's why I left the police station. If I stood there for another second, I would've caved your face in. And that wouldn't have been good for anyone. It would've made a complicated situation even worse."

He motioned to the drink, silently asking if I wanted one, and I shook my head. I already felt drunk. My best friend was forgiving me. Or at least he was accepting the fact that what I felt for his mom was beyond what he'd initially thought. That was a good first step.

"I wouldn't have fought back," I confessed quietly, and he eyed me over his glass as he sipped.

He set it back down with a soft tap and pressed his palms into the wood.

"I know, and that's another reason I didn't want to do it. You knew you fucked up, and that made it even harder to be mad at the both of you."

"I'm sorry," I finally said out loud. I'd said it several times in my text to him, but it felt good to say it to his face.

"I know."

I took a breath and tilted my head to the ceiling. Searching for the right words, I went with the unbridled truth.

"I'm sorry for lying and putting our friendship on the line. And I'm sorry for putting you and Natalie in this position, too. The last thing I'd ever want is to drive a wedge between you two. Your relationship...it's what any mother and son would want. But..." I had to collect myself before I confessed it out loud. "I'm not sorry that it happened. I could never regret her."

It was the moment of truth. If he couldn't forgive me for lying to him, then I wasn't sure how our friendship would make it. And I couldn't imagine my list getting any smaller.

His smile was tinged with caution, and he took another sip before he said, "Good answer. But umm...it doesn't mean that I'm suddenly *over* it. I'm still pissed you lied to me, and honestly, I'm going to be upset for a while. It's going to take time for me to really get on board with it, but I'm not going to stand in the way."

Relief, cool and quick, washed over me. I couldn't remember the last time I cried, but knowing that we'd eventually be okay, I felt the telling prick behind my eyes. It was the most I could ask for.

"Thank you," I muttered and straightened as I cleared my throat.

"And I will thoroughly beat your ass if you hurt her. You have higher standards now because it's my mom. You better be fucking perfect. Anything less and murder is on the table."

"Understood," I agreed.

We stood there for a moment, neither of us knowing exactly what to do next when Ryder finished off his second drink and pointed to the stairs behind me.

"So, you should go up there, and I'm going to make myself scarce."

He turned and double-checked that all the burners were off. He then returned the ingredients to the fridge and pantry as I stared at the stairs. Natalie was up there, and based on Ryder's instructions, she was waiting on me.

"You talked to her?"

"Yeah," he said, slipping his phone into his pocket and grabbing his keys. I figured he had since I walked into them laughing together, but I wanted to be sure. "We talked this morning. That wedge you thought you could drive between us, it's going to take more than your dumbass for that to happen."

He knocked his shoulder with mine as he pushed past me. "Now it's your turn. Go smooth shit over."

I swallowed around a new emotion sitting in my throat and worked my teeth together. "Did you show her my text?"

He took a deep breath and shook his head. "No, I didn't think it was my place. But I did tell her that you texted me, and it helped me see the situation in a different light."

That made me feel a little better at least. The things I told Ryder were things I wanted to tell Natalie myself, not through her son. I wanted to see her face and gauge her reactions.

"Thanks. I'm gonna—" I said, motioning to the stairs behind me with a thumb over my shoulder.

"Yes, you should do that. Talk and do whatever else—" He cringed like he was in excruciating pain and shivered dramatically. "Okay, yeah, this is weird. I'll be gone for an hour or two. I'll text you when I'm on my way back."

Ryder left, and I didn't move until I heard his truck start up.

I stared at the dark second floor. There were only thirteen stairs between me and everything I'd ever wanted.

THIRTY

A LANGUAGE ALL OUR OWN

Theo

MY STEPS WERE HEAVY ON THE WOODEN STAIRS. EACH FOOT FELT like it weighed a hundred pounds as I walked closer toward the unknown.

Ryder had somehow forgiven me for sneaking around with Natalie behind his back, and I had full confidence we'd get back to how we were before.

It would just take a little time. And I'd wait for however long.

But I had no idea where Natalie's head was. The kiss she gave me wasn't very telling.

I could've asked Ryder how their conversation went, but it was something I wanted to hear from her. Her son being my best friend was only one of the many obstacles we'd have to overcome if we wanted anything…more.

Our age difference hadn't been an issue, but it also wasn't something we could ignore, and my mother would undoubtedly show up again. Although, after the day before, my motivation to rid my mom of my life completely had been renewed.

I paused at the top of the stairs and inhaled a deep, grounding breath. It didn't work, but it was worth a try.

Her bedroom door was closed at the end of the hall, and I wondered if I should knock. I hadn't knocked in months, her room essentially becoming our shared space.

I imagined her wearing a groove into her bedroom floor, pacing endlessly, and preparing what she'd say when I finally came in. Her lower lip caught between her teeth, and fidgeting with the hem of her T-shirt.

That was what I was considering when I started down the hallway and immediately stopped.

My bedroom door was ajar. From inside, hazy sunlight peeked from between the curtains around the window and reflected on the floor in the dim hallway. My eyes followed the stream of light upward until I saw her.

My heart faltered.

She was seated in the middle of my bed. One of my pillows in her lap, she stared straight ahead, perfectly posed in that ray of light.

The entire scene was eerily familiar. For a second, I reminisced about the first time I found her on my bed. I remembered the white dress, her flushed cheeks, her sweet yet confident demand for *"more."* I could only be so lucky to have her that way again. To hear those words from those perfect lips one more time.

My heart rate skyrocketed, and I couldn't wait another second. She was there, waiting for me, and hope bloomed in my chest.

I pushed the door open, and she startled when it quietly hit the wall. Her eyes went wide for a moment before she realized it was me. And the surprise was replaced by a soft, welcoming smile.

Stepping farther into the room, I shoved my hands in my pockets. They tingled with the need to touch her and remind her of the many reasons why we were so good together. Although it went against every base instinct, I knew we had to talk first.

Patience, where she was concerned, was not my fucking

virtue.

"This might be the sweetest, best déjà vu I've ever experienced." Somehow my voice was steady, although my insides were in turmoil. And her responding smile did more to settle me than I realized it could.

"Just without the towel this time," she said, subtly squeezing the pillow tighter to her chest. I stopped at the end of the bed.

Silence stretched between us. And the air swirling around us was heavy with all the words we wanted to say. But I didn't feel the weight of them. I was too busy looking at her to pay them any attention. Because in her eyes and in the open, hopeful expression settling on her features, I knew how this would end. Those words were just noise.

"Did Ryder leave? I heard the door and thought maybe…" Her words were faint and cautious as she broke the silence.

I easily read between the lines: she'd thought I'd left.

"Yeah, he said he'll be back in a few hours. He wanted to give us some time."

"So, you talked?" She sat up straighter, moving the pillow out of her lap and recrossing her legs.

I nodded. "And so did you."

Fuck, I didn't know how to start the conversation. Similar to what I experienced when talking to Ryder, I couldn't form the chaotic storm of thoughts and feelings into cohesive ideas. But with Natalie, it was worse. Those emotions were tenfold. They were big and daunting, as were the consequences if I didn't get it just right.

"Theo," Natalie said, drawing me from the mess in my head. She scooted to the side and patted the spot to her left.

I didn't hesitate when I rounded the bed and sat down next to her. She turned to face me and placed her hands in her lap.

Yes, that was better, but it was also worse. Things made more sense when she was near. When I could feel her and smell her and touch her if I wanted to. All the thoughts in my head quieted except for one. The only one that mattered.

Well, that one thought and the million of others that demanded I pin her to the bed and claim her. Mark her until she was covered in me, and there was no way she'd ever be able to scrub me off.

I leaned back against the headboard and settled deeper, letting her calming presence wash over me. It filled all the cracks and smoothed the worn, ragged edges.

"What did your text say?" she asked, taking my hand in hers and dragging her nails down my palm. "He said that whatever you sent him helped him come to terms with...this."

A shiver worked its way down my spine at her careful touch and cautious words. I contemplated if I should tell her everything, knowing I couldn't predict her reaction, but I wouldn't censor myself. It was all important, and she deserved to know.

"I told him everything."

Her dark brows shot up her forehead, and she gaped at my admission.

But I continued quickly, "Well, within reason."

She settled with a nod and continued tracing patterns on my palm.

"I told him about how I fought it. How we both fought it, but it was useless. We both knew it was useless after the first time. I told him how far gone I was since I first saw you in the kitchen. There was never any other ending. You were always going to be mine."

I took a breath, readying myself for the next part and bracing for her reaction. Her blue eyes were too much to bear, and I instead studied the movements of her hand and the contradiction of her small, unmarred fingers to my large, tattooed ones.

"I told him that I'd leave. For good."

She sucked in a sharp breath, and her fingers suddenly stopped. I could feel her preparing to pull away, but I gripped her hand. It was enough to keep her in place for the moment, and I hurried to finish before she could pry herself out of my hold.

"When I saw how much it hurt you when he walked away, I would've left if it meant you never experienced that again. I told him that if he couldn't find it in himself to forgive you with me in the picture, then I'd stay away. I told him that I'd give anything to protect your happiness and joy because you let me experience it for at least a few months. You reminded me what life could feel like, what *home* is supposed to feel like. And that would've been enough, it had to be enough, if he wanted me gone."

My voice broke on the last word, and Natalie shifted next to me. She swung her leg over my lap and straddled my thighs, settling on top of me. Her warm hands gripped my cheeks, and she forced me to look up at her. Her eyes, brimming with unshed tears, bounced between mine as her thumbs caressed my skin. She felt so good on top of me, even closer than before. She disintegrated all my walls with one look.

A tear finally fell, and I reached up, brushing it away.

"You know I love it when you cry for me, but not like this," I said, trying to distill the heaviness with any sort of levity.

It did the trick, and she chuckled. But her laughter turned into a sigh that held all the uncertainty lingering between us.

My arms wrapped around her, one fitting around her waist and forcing her closer to me while the other traveled up her back, clasping around her nape. She willingly fell into me and circled her own arms around my neck. In return, I buried my nose against her neck and breathed in her intoxicating scent.

I never wanted to leave her. Ever since she walked into my life, I couldn't imagine a scenario where she wasn't in it, where she wasn't the center of it.

I wanted to be closer. I wanted to feel her everywhere, and I wanted to start again.

Putting it all behind us, I wanted to shed the secretive, forbidden life we'd led for the past few months. And I wanted to love her out in the open.

It felt odd to think those words when I hadn't said them out loud yet, but I could feel them. They were as physical and real as Natalie was on top of me.

We must have both had the same thought, because Natalie released me and ran her hands down my chest until her fingers settled over my belt. Her eyes were drowning in desire, lust flaring live and real within her blue irises. Reflexively, my hands grasped her hips, so supple and pliant under my palms. We could talk and talk and talk about the past and the future, but being together, moving as one, and deriving pleasure from the other, that was the language we both spoke fluently. The one that weeded out all the noise and filled in all the gaps where those words couldn't.

Over her hips, her hands covered mine. She tangled our fingers and lifted until my arms were stretched out above my head. A wicked little smile crossed her lips, and she slowly let go.

"Hold onto the headboard. Don't move until I say." Her voice was lilted with a devious intent, and although I didn't usually like to sit back and watch, I loved seeing her like that. The power dynamic shifted for the moment, and I went along with whatever she had planned.

I gripped the headboard like it was my lifeline and nodded. I would have done anything if it meant she kept going.

Knowing I was game, Natalie deftly undid my belt and unbuttoned my jeans. She curled her fingers under my waistband and pulled my jeans along with my briefs down, only far enough for my cock to spring free.

She palmed me and pumped once, letting her thumb circle the head and collect the pearl of precum that leaked from the slit. My hips jerked up into her waiting hand, and a deep groan vibrated through my chest and clawed up my throat.

She made a pleased little *hmm* sound in response. I needed to taste that sound. I leaned forward, eagerly seeking her mouth, but all I found was one of her slim fingers pressed against my lips.

A new groan, one of frustration, rumbled through me. She pressed harder with her finger when I surged forward again. The headboard creaked as it moved with me, and I momentarily considered letting go.

But I managed to maintain a little bit of control as she stood on the bed and stepped out of her flimsy sleep shorts. For the briefest moment, her pussy was directly in front of my face, level with my mouth that watered at the sight. Just the memory of her taste made me leak more arousal and throb with need. Her plump lower lips were taunting me, begging me to run my tongue along her slit and lick until she was panting for me to do dirty, indecent things to her body.

She slipped back down onto her knees and poised my cock at her entrance. Wrapping her other hand around my neck, she held my stare while she began to lower herself onto me. My attention bounced between her tumultuous look and where the flared edge of my crown breached her entrance.

She wasn't nearly as wet as I liked her to be when I slid inside for the first time, but if I knew Natalie at all, I was sure my little slut was enjoying the pain. Her eagerness to get me inside her matched my own. We were feral for it, and nothing would stand in the way.

Inch by agonizing inch, she slowly slipped over me. Her warm cunt stretching to accommodate my size, I gritted my teeth to keep from pushing up into her.

Her pupils had dilated to twice their size, and each of her panted breaths tickled my skin by the time her skin was flush with mine.

"*Fuck,*" I groaned, willing my eyes not to close so I could watch the pleasure play out over her face. Natalie did the same, sucking in a quick gasp and then moaning. It was a throaty and desperate sound that made my entire body ignite with pulsing need.

"I need to touch you," I ground out before she even had the chance to move.

She choked out a breathy laugh. We moaned in unison as her cunt constricted around me. She was driving me mad, and the pleasure was making me delirious, because suddenly I was begging, "Please."

With both hands running through my hair at the base of my neck, Natalie sat back and ground down over me. My tip prodded her cervix, and I growled.

My heart was chanting a foreign beat, a warrior's call: claim, possess, consume. Natalie riding me with careless abandon, touching me everywhere, and taking her fill while driving me fucking wild.

"Say it again," she instructed.

"*Please*, let me touch you," I said without hesitation. Although it was more of a growl than a plea, she didn't care. I was going to break the fucking headboard with the way my hands grasped it.

Her hips began a taunting rhythm as she fucked herself over me, ignoring my pleas and prioritizing her pleasure. I wanted that, too. I wanted to help her get there the way only I knew how.

She stared down between us where my cock disappeared inside of her and picked up speed. With the new flush to her skin and panted breaths, with the way she clawed at my neck and grew louder with each movement of her hips, I knew she was falling headfirst into the abyss.

"Yes," she hissed, and with that one word, I let go of the headboard, more than ready to be done with the game that tested the very foundation of my restraint and control.

The bed creaked when I released it, and then my hands were everywhere. I ripped off my shirt and then her own, palming her breasts. Rubbing her nipples with my thumbs until they were hard, little points, I wrapped my arms around her.

With a gasp, she sat forward until every part of her warm, naked body touched mine. My hands traveled up and down her back, grabbing at her hips and gently spanking her ass to feel the recoil and urge her to continue moving over me.

Even if I could touch her everywhere, all at once, it still wouldn't be enough. She held me hostage with every jerk of her hips, every whispered word, every pleading look. And it was only in her that I found any sort of freedom.

Her smooth cheek pressed against my stubbled one, and she groaned in my ear as I pumped deep inside of her. With each thrust, I drew the prettiest sounds from her parted lips. I slowed slightly, making sure each stroke was intentional and thorough, grazing every inch of her swollen cunt.

It was intoxicating and liable to make me crazy the way her body responded to me. She grew more and more wet, slipping over my length with ease.

Suddenly, she sat back, her eyes wide and desperate-looking.

"I feel you…everywhere," she breathed, punctuating the statement with a gasp.

She slammed her hips down, and I sealed my mouth to hers. And if I wasn't already fully gone before, that kiss was my ultimate undoing. She willingly parted her lips, and my tongue dove inside her mouth, tasting all of her and devouring every sound she made. I held her in place with a hand around her throat and an arm wrapped tightly around her waist.

"Natalie," I whispered against her mouth. I was so bombarded by emotions that for the first time with her, I was beyond words. All I could think was, "Natalie."

It was good before, but it was even better now. I didn't think it was possible, but every sensation was magnified by the intimacy of the moment. We were just fucking before, the feelings simmering between us hidden behind a thick haze of smoke to try to ward them off. But now, with those feelings out in the open, shining bright in her eyes and zapping into my skin with every brush of her fingers, it was better.

It was everything.

Sex had always been good. I'd always *loved* sex. But nothing would ever compare to this.

The mesmerizing woman in my lap rode me hard, meeting every one of my thrusts with a quick snap of her hips. And every second that passed, she burrowed herself deeper and deeper into me. Until I couldn't breathe without feeling her.

"Stay." Her breath tickled my wet, parted lips as she whispered against them. Her voice was so quiet I barely heard the word. "I know there's so much more to talk about, but I want you, Theo. I want you to stay."

She whispered it a second time, and my eyes slid open. I sucked in a sharp breath as her hips slowed and methodically rolled over my cock. She was intoxicating, and I felt both drunk and high on her. The heady smell of sex surrounding us and untapped desire pulsing through my veins, she bumped her nose with mine and ghosted her tongue over my lower lip.

"Stay."

"Yes," I said with conviction.

"Stay." She kissed me, and I tightened my hold around her. She continued whispering the word, "*Stay, stay, stay,*" like a plea against my lips, a prayer she was willing to be answered as we tumbled back into our ruthless pace.

And to her plea, I responded with a promise of my own.

"*Fuck*, Natalie. I'm not going anywhere."

"Yes," she cried. Her cunt constricted around my length, and my guttural groans mingled with her resounding moans. We both plummeted into that blissful abyss I knew was just on the other side.

My forehead dropped to her chest, and her cheek rested on top of my head. She let out a satisfied "*mmm*" sound that vibrated through her chest. Her heart was pounding and matched the chaotic rhythm of my own.

Hands exploring exposed, sweat-slicked skin, neither of us dared to move for several minutes. I would've bet anything that her thoughts matched mine. The moment was too perfect to break. But there were things I needed to make sure she knew.

Settling back against the headboard, I looked at the woman who'd become my sun. Her eyes were just as hopeful and eager and open as they had been the first day I saw her. Not holding back, I let the smile tugging at my lips take over my face and the happiness bubbling in my chest well to the surface.

Only her. This feeling was exclusively Natalie.

Her own smile was bright, and when I cupped her cheeks, her hands covered mine.

"You," I said through a shuttered breath, brushing my thumb over her bottom lip like I could feel her joy. "You are everything I didn't know I wanted and everything I wished I could be good enough for."

Her mouth slid open to argue, but I stopped her with a quick shake of my head.

"You make me feel good enough," I said softly. "You make me want things I never imagined for myself, and like hell am I giving that up. I want to make you come so fucking hard you forget your name. I want to wake up beside you every morning and plan the future. *Our* future. I want to be the one to put that smile on your face."

She sighed and kissed me. "You are not disposable, Theo," she murmured against my lips, and I drew back. She placed one hand on my chest and the other against my cheek, brushing her thumb back and forth against the thick stubble. "You leaving wouldn't make our lives easier or better. Life would be *worse* without you. I don't want you to go…anywhere."

Her voice broke over the last word, and I held her closer. I kissed away the quiver in her bottom lip and brushed my nose against hers. Her smile widened like I hoped it would, lighting up her entire face the way I loved.

"Baby girl, you are everything to me. You've given me somewhere I *want* to stay."

THIRTY-ONE
WORD VOMIT

Natalie

THEO'S ARMS WRAPPED AROUND ME FROM BEHIND, AND HE SMILED at me through the mirror.

"Take your time," he muttered into my neck, dropping a kiss just below my ear. "I'm going to start cleaning up the mess Ryder made with breakfast and start on the food."

"Okay."

He kissed the top of my head and ran his hand across my lower back as he walked out of the bathroom, glancing back before he rounded the corner like he didn't really want to leave.

My cheeks hurt from smiling so much. It was a welcome change from the swollen eyes and red cheeks I'd been sporting the few days before.

I put my moisturizer back in the drawer and braced my hands on the counter.

I couldn't believe it had all worked out the way it had. I had truly believed I'd lost them both. And it felt like a miracle that they'd both come back.

I threw on a pair of jeans and a sweater before I headed

downstairs. There was an extra pep in my step, and I couldn't help the smile that tilted my lips when I stepped into the kitchen.

Music was humming in the background, and Theo was quietly singing as he leaned over the stove, stirring something that smelled amazing. His muscles jumped and tensed under the black T-shirt stretched across his back, and my eyes lingered over his ass wrapped in a pair of dark jeans.

Something about watching a man cook in my kitchen was so attractive. And it was even better that it was Theo. My house felt so much more like a home with him in it.

Theo reached across the counter and grabbed the salt, twisting the top and adding the seasoning to whatever he was making.

Butterflies took flight in my stomach, and my chest tightened watching him move around like he was meant to be there. Because he was.

And then suddenly my mind was spiraling. There was something about Theo cooking our Thanksgiving dinner and looking perfectly at home that made me pause.

Then I remembered what he'd said earlier. That he wanted to plan our future. But what did that future look like? What did he want it to look like?

My pulse raced as he turned around, and the room spun with my thoughts. He noticed me immediately, and a gorgeous smile graced his lips.

"Hey, I didn't hear you come down," he said, reaching for his phone and turning down the music.

My hands trembled and my mouth went dry. He stepped toward me, and the moment the music stopped, I blurted, "Do you want to get married?"

It took me a second to register the words that had flown out of my mouth, and when I finally did, I felt the blush heat my cheeks and crawl down my neck. The butterflies in my stomach turned murderous, and nausea replaced the excitement from only moments before.

Theo's brows hit his hairline, and his jaw went slack.

I opened and closed my mouth several times as we stood staring at one another. His expression was unreadable, and the longer the silence stretched, the higher my panic climbed.

"I—what—we—" I stuttered, swallowing around the rock in my throat when I couldn't manage a word or even a coherent sound.

That's not what I meant exactly. It had come out more abruptly than I'd wanted it to, and I wanted to take it back. There were just so many questions swimming through my head that I couldn't contain them all.

Theo's indecipherable expression morphed into one I knew well. Amusement played at the corners of his mouth, and he ran his tongue over his lips like he was trying to hold back a smile.

I rubbed my sweaty palms against my jeans and shuffled awkwardly on my feet. I knew Theo pretty well, but I couldn't imagine what he was thinking.

He scrubbed a hand over his mouth and took a cautious step forward. "Baby girl, did you just ask me to marry you?"

I scoffed and tried not to appear as ruffled and nervous as I felt. "What? No. Well, I know it sounded that way, but I just meant…" My words trailed off and Theo gave me an incredulous look. I steeled my spine and took a deep breath.

"You just meant, what?"

"I meant, would you want to, or do you want to get married? *Eventually*."

He didn't immediately respond, and I got the itch to fill the silence with my nervous rambling. I stared down at my hands and couldn't stop the word vomit.

"Not right now or even in the next couple of years, but you know, this is just something that we should probably discuss. We kind of went about things a little backward since you were already living here, and we decided to make it permanent after the fact. But I think it's probably a good idea to discuss it before we go any further. But if you don't know, that's totally fine. You don't have to know right now. You could…"

Still staring at the floor with unwavering intensity, my words trailed off when Theo's boots appeared in my line of sight. His tattooed fingers skated down my cheek and tucked under my chin. I didn't fight it when he urged my face upward.

My breath caught when I saw the look on his face. That one much easier to read than any before—happiness that I felt as much as witnessed.

I craned my head back for a better view and relaxed into his touch.

"Do you want my answer?" he asked, and I nodded slowly.

Like Theo felt my nerves too, he reached up with his other hand and cupped my cheek. With my face cradled in his hands, and his warm, honey eyes holding me hostage, he said, "Without a doubt."

"Really?" My voice jumped an octave or five with the question, and I reared back to make sure his expression matched his definitive answer.

He chuckled and nodded. "If you want that, I want that. Imagining you as my wife…"

He closed his eyes and tilted his head back to the ceiling. His Adam's apple bobbed as he swallowed and a groan, deep in his throat, ripped through his lips. "Just thinking about that makes me fucking hard."

I gasped as he gripped my hips and yanked me toward him. Even with layers of fabric between us, I could feel his hard cock pressed against my lower stomach.

I wasn't necessarily shocked by his response, but I was surprised by the confidence with which he said it. Although his birthday was in a few months, he was still only twenty-three. He was young, and I didn't want him agreeing just because he knew I wanted to get married again.

He lifted his hand and smoothed the furrow between my brows. "What are you thinking about?"

A lie sat on the tip of my tongue, but it wouldn't do me any good. If I didn't ask right then, it would eat at me until I blurted it out at the most inopportune time.

"You think you're ready for that?"

He scanned my face, eyes settling on my lips as he tugged at my lower one with his thumb. "Honestly?"

"Yes, of course."

He shook his head but continued, "Not yet. But in the not-too-distant future, I want to marry you. I want you to be my wife. I already know I'm not fucking letting you go. We'll just have to make it official."

"Do you want to live here? Or would you want to move? Since you're staying, I think you should have a say."

He shook his head. "You've made this house a home. This is your home."

"I lived here with Mark. This was our home…once."

"Yes, but now it's yours. And I'd love to share it with you. I'm not insecure, that doesn't bother me."

It was the perfect, most honest answer I could have asked for. To show my appreciation, and because I couldn't hold back a second longer, I pressed up on my toes and kissed him.

His lips were soft and pliant, and for a moment, he allowed me to lead the kiss. I wrapped my arms around his shoulders, pressing myself against him, and before I knew it, he cupped my ass and lifted me off the floor.

Instinctually, my legs wrapped around his waist as he stepped back and began moving around the kitchen. He set me down on the edge of the butcher block island in the same position and location from our first night together.

Brushing my hair behind my shoulders and gripping the sides of my neck, he used his thumbs to tilt my face just how he wanted it. His wicked tongue explored my mouth, and with each lick, I grew wilder and more frantic.

He wanted to get married. He wanted to marry me.

And I was overjoyed at the realization that we were both on the same page. At least about two things.

But we'd just touched the surface of my questions.

If we ended, my heart would be shattered. But I would rather know now, before we went any further, if we weren't compatible in every single way. I needed to know if what he wanted out of life aligned with me.

I knew he had dreams and goals. He wanted to take over Haven City and make it even more successful, possibly even open another studio on the other side of the city. And now I knew he also wanted to get married.

But there was more.

"Kids," I mumbled between kisses, and he kissed me one last time before he leaned back with his eyebrows raised, silently waiting for me to expand. "Do you want them?"

His answer wasn't as automatic as it had been about the marriage question. And whether I was expecting that reaction or not, it still made me anxious. It didn't keep me from holding my breath or chewing my bottom lip and preparing to nervously ramble.

But Theo contemplated my word vomit and stopped it with a thumb pressed over my parted lips.

"For God's sake, Nat." He chuckled. "Just give me a second."

The humor in his voice made my shoulders sag in relief.

He took a deep breath and squared his shoulders. Both of his hands fell to my thighs, and he pressed his palms into the denim. He stared down at his tattooed fingers and dragged them up and down, massaging my legs and creating a warm friction that was filled with uncertainty.

"Kids...is not a topic I've given a lot of thought to," he began, and I refrained from interrupting. "With the way my childhood ended, I don't know how keen I am to even put myself in the position to repeat that for a kid of my own."

"You wouldn't," I added quietly.

His responding smile was soft yet unconvinced.

"Right now, it's a maybe. Maybe I could see myself as a…*dad*." He stumbled on the word as he said it. "Or maybe not. I think I would be fine either way."

I covered his nervous, fidgeting hands with my own, and he finally looked up at me.

"Same here. I like the possibility, but I already had one really good kid. If you didn't want any, I wouldn't feel like I was missing anything."

The relief he felt with my confession was apparent in every part of his body. The cocky, devious glint in his eyes returned as he cupped my ass and tugged me to the edge of the counter. The outline of his cock pressed between my legs, and I unabashedly ground against it. But with the denim between us, it did little to ease the growing ache.

"We could practice, though. Practice for when, or if, we decide to do the real thing."

I smiled into our kiss and let myself fall into his arms.

"What are we practicing for?" A voice abruptly interrupted from behind us.

I nearly jumped out of my skin and off the counter as I whipped my head in the direction of the voice.

Caroline strolled into the kitchen first, a large bowl covered in Saran Wrap in her hands, completely unbothered by the fact that Theo and I were nearly humping on the counter.

Ryder cautiously turned the corner only a second behind Caroline. With one hand covering his eyes and his head tilted toward the ground, Ryder bumped into the edge of the refrigerator and then ran straight into the back of Caroline.

"You're a hazard," Caroline said, setting the bowl on the counter.

Ryder dropped the bag he was carrying next to the bowl.

I pushed lightly against Theo's chest, and he reluctantly stepped back. I slid off the counter and hit the floor on unsteady legs.

Ryder slowly raised his head and lowered his hand, peering

up at us with a cautious half-smile. "I'm a hazard? They're a hazard." Ryder pointed toward me and Theo.

"Shit, I forgot the desserts," Caroline muttered.

Ryder peered around the kitchen at the pots already on the stove and the ingredients Theo had laid out, along with the large bowl and bag Caroline set next to the fridge.

"You all do realize it's just the four of us, right? We have enough food for at least ten."

"Yes, but the leftovers are the best part," I added, stepping over to the stove and stirring the vegetables that were beginning to soften.

"You're going to have leftovers for the next two weeks," Ryder mumbled. "And if you keep doing that," he said, waving his hand out in front of him like he couldn't even begin to describe what he'd just walked in on. "Then I'm not going to have an appetite at all."

Caroline rolled her eyes and took his wrist. She unceremoniously tugged him toward the door.

"Come on, grumpy pants. Help me with the desserts."

They argued back and forth as they headed toward the door. I couldn't suppress my laughter as Caroline called him "grumpy" again and Ryder said something along the lines of the pot calling the kettle black.

The door shut at the same moment Theo stepped up behind me, wrapping his arms around my waist and nuzzling my neck. I leaned back into his embrace, enjoying the warmth and hardness of his chest.

"We are going to have way too much food," he muttered against my skin.

"Not you too. I'd rather have too much food than too little."

Theo took a deep breath, dragging his nose up the side of my neck and holding me closer.

"It's going to be amazing, but you're the only thing I want to eat. My mouth is watering just *thinking* about eating your perfect pussy."

I sighed and let my head fall back against his chest. Peering up at his desire-stricken, deep brown eyes, I wanted to take him up on that suggestion immediately.

Although I was confident in Theo's ability to make me come in minutes, Caroline's house was only just down the street. Even walking slowly, it should take no more than a few minutes for her and Ryder to get there, grab the food, and get back.

I turned in his arms and urged him backward with a hand at the center of his chest until his back hit the island.

"You were doing just that like an hour ago," I said.

"Mmm," he mused. "Feels like forever."

"If you can hold off just a few hours, until Ryder goes to his dad's tonight and Caroline inevitably gets tired of us and escapes, I will let you tie me to the bed and do whatever you want to me."

His pupils dilated with my promise, and he shook his head to hide the smile teetering over his lips. He dropped his forehead to mine, and I slid my hands beneath his T-shirt, scraping my nails against his tattooed stomach. His muscles clenched, and he sucked in a sharp breath.

He was so fun to tease. Especially when he gave up control long enough to let me do so. I traced the waistband of his jeans, dipping below the fabric enough to make his breath come out in a ragged gasp, but I swore I heard a sound from the front hall-way. I cursed Caroline for being so quick and efficient, but no one appeared around the corner. Knowing we were still alone, I began to turn back to Theo, but not before my attention landed on his keys on the counter.

But it wasn't so much the keys that caught my attention as much as it was the keychain that was still attached to them: a dark pink heart with my name printed in the center.

He followed my line of sight and chuckled when he noticed what caught my attention.

"You never changed it," I said. It was kind of pointless to say; we could both see that he'd never thrown it away or removed it, at least. But he knew what I meant. That it meant something he'd never gotten rid of it.

"No, I didn't."

"Any reason?" I asked with a flirty smile, anticipation filling my chest with a nervous lightness.

His smile was sweet and soft. "I think I knew then," he said. "That I would...you know...*Fuck*," he sighed. "I..." he tried again, but his voice trailed off. His expressive eyes were steadfast on mine and were a window to his thoughts.

Like he was exhaling for the first time in a long time, he finally said, "I think I knew then that I would fall in love with you. Fuck, I'm so in love with you, Natalie."

My hands stilled, and my heart picked up speed, pounding over time like it was trying to escape my chest. "I love you, too," I breathed, loving the weight of his arms and his distinctly masculine smell surrounding me. Enjoying the way those words so easily fell from my lips and how right it felt to finally speak them aloud.

He leaned down and softly brushed his lips against mine. And if he always kissed me like that, with more love and desire than I ever thought I'd feel, I'd never want for anything.

"Thank you," he whispered against my lips.

I chuckled and nipped at his bottom lip. "For what?"

"For nothing...and everything."

I leaned back, my eyes devouring his face and the uncharacteristically tender look that slipped over his features.

But just as quickly as it appeared, it morphed. He threaded his fingers through my hair and tugged until my neck was exposed. The kisses he trailed down my throat were intoxicating. Goosebumps appeared up my arms, and a shiver of desire ran down my spine.

"And tonight," he said in a low voice. "To show my gratitude, I'm going to tie you up and make you beg like the filthy little slut you are."

"Yes, please," I begged, my voice cracking over the word. His eyes found mine, and he kissed me again. "Always."

EPILOGUE
CAUTION: DANGER AHEAD

Ryder

"Stop calling me grumpy," I muttered under my breath.

Caroline pushed through her front door and gave me an unimpressed look over her shoulder. The door swung closed, and I had to catch it before it smacked me in the face.

I had a right to be a little grumpy, as she called it. It had only been a few days since I found my mom in bed with my best friend.

The shock still hadn't worn off.

And whether I had accepted it for what it was and realized that maybe they would be good together after all—no matter how strange it was—I still had a right to be a little confused and irritated about the entire situation. Walking in on them dry humping on our kitchen counter also didn't help matters.

I followed the click of Caroline's heels on the white tile floor as she moved deeper into the house.

Her house was immaculate. Decorated mostly in white and black, the space was open and minimal. Compared to the home I grew up in where knick-knacks were on every shelf and black and white were scarcely seen, it was the polar opposite. And it was a representation of the put-together, perfect woman Caroline presented to the world. The facade few were lucky enough to see behind.

I was one of them.

"Your mom is happy. *We* should be happy for her," Caroline said as she pulled open the fridge. She retrieved a dish from the back, hidden behind a carton of almond milk and a container of Greek yogurt.

She spun back around, glass dish in hand, and leveled me with a stare that would make any man weak at the fucking knees. Gray-blue eyes stormy with determination, I was far from immune.

I'd tried really hard for the past seven years not to waver when she was around, but not even time and a shit ton of willpower were enough to stave off the immensity of feelings that pounded through me when she was near.

God, I was such a fucking sap. But it was just for her.

The first time I saw her at that ridiculous block party on the Fourth of July, I never dreaded a neighborhood event again.

"I am happy for her," I said, and the words sounded unconvincing even to my own ears.

Caroline raised her eyebrows and set the dish on the counter.

"It's not that I'm not happy," I continued. "It's just going to take some time before I'm as gung-ho about this as you are."

"Sure, I guess you have improved since you were here on Sunday."

"You mean when you hid me in your room when my mom showed up?" A grin split my face when she stopped at my words.

Her shoulders stiffened, and she slowly turned back around. "I mean when *you* showed up here freaking out about your mom and Theo."

"And then you hid me in your room like I was a dirty little secret. You also didn't correct her when she caught on to the fact that you had a man hidden away."

Her eyes widened. That cool, unruffled façade falling away ever so slightly. "You heard that?"

I nodded.

"I didn't argue, because she was technically right," she said. Then she added quietly, almost to herself, "Although right now you're acting less like a man and more like a *boy*." I didn't have time to respond and make a crack about how much of a *man* I was before she said, "And I knew she'd leave quickly if I didn't argue."

"Yes, but you knew what she was implying. That you had—"

"Don't," she cut me off, and my smile widened. I really fucking enjoyed ruffling her feathers.

"Don't what, Caroline? Insinuate that we could have been doing something more?"

"Yes, because that's ridiculous. It's *insane*."

"Is it, though?"

She threw her hands in the air and whirled around. Even from the other side of the kitchen, I could see the fire brimming in her eyes. "What the fuck, Ryder? Yes, it's the most ridiculous thing I've ever heard."

"More ridiculous than pigs flying or people denying climate change? What about kids believing in a magical man sliding down their chimneys to leave them gifts? Or is it more ridiculous than my mom falling in love with my best friend who is fourteen years younger than her?"

Her lack of response was enough confirmation that my words rang true. I chanced a step toward her, and when she didn't retreat, I found the confidence to take another. My boots were silent against the tile floor, and I kept my steps tentative and cautious. But I continued moving forward until there were mere inches between us.

I held my breath as she stared up at me from beneath lowered lids, her gray eyes more uncertain than I'd ever seen them. My eyes dropped to her full, pink lips, and my entire body vibrated with anticipation. Anticipation to *finally* feel how perfect her mouth felt on mine. I knew it would. I knew her blonde hair would be soft and slip easily between my fingers, and her skin would be smooth and warm beneath my hands.

I could imagine it so clearly, I could almost feel it.

Almost.

And as good as it was in my head, I knew it would be even better in real life. If only she would give me a chance.

I lifted my hand so, *so* slowly, and reached for a strand of hair that had fallen from the tousled bun on top of her head. Each of my movements were purposeful and deliberate, providing her with more than enough time to move out of reach if she wanted to.

But she didn't. The thin strand of hair was delicate between my fingers. And her eyes stayed locked on mine the entire time I pushed it behind her ear. Her eyelids only fluttered closed for a moment when my finger brushed against her cheek.

Her sharp intake of breath was so faint, I almost missed it. But I was so close that I thankfully heard it and saw her chest rise and fall quickly with the inhalation. Her eyes slid open, once again settling on me with a new, darker look.

"You," she said in a breathy whisper before she paused to take a much-needed deep breath. Her dark look turned unsure, and she licked her lips before she continued. "You, Ryder Calaway, are *very* dangerous."

What?

Her confession threw me, and it took several seconds before I realized what she'd alluded to. In so many words, she'd acknowledged that this thing I'd been feeling wasn't one-sided at all. That maybe she wasn't as unaffected as she appeared. Maybe she was just damn good at pretending.

Maybe there could have been another meaning to her words, but I liked my definition too much to consider any other option.

With that knowledge, new confidence pumped through me, and I bowed my head enough to brush my nose along her cheek.

Her responding shudder was like a gallon of lighter fluid to the fire already burning inside of me.

My lips poised next to her ear, I took the opportunity to breathe her in. She smelled like cinnamon and sugar from baking all morning, and I wondered if her skin tasted just as sweet.

Somehow, I managed not to steal a taste and instead said, in a voice that left nothing to the imagination and belied all my dirtiest desires, "You say that like it's a bad thing, Caroline. But isn't it the dangerous rides that leave you breathless? They leave you panting, your heart racing, and your thighs weak. Danger is so much fun."

The End

ACKNOWLEDGMENTS

I love age gap romance, and I knew I really wanted to write a *reverse* age gap; however, the circumstances surrounding the relationship were extremely important to me. That's how Natalie and Theo came to be.

These two are freaking *hot*, but they are also so damn sweet. When one of my beta readers said that they were the sweetest couple I'd written, I didn't believe her. But once the tension finally snaps, she's definitely right! I love how Theo melts just for Natalie. That could be my favorite romance trope of all time…maybe.

Anyway, thank you to everyone who made this book happen. Mayhem Cover Creations kills it every time, but this cover? It could NOT have been better!

My Brother's Editor is always a gem to work with and really makes my crappy draft sparkle.

And as always, my beta readers and family are essential to my writing process. Their patience and feedback are invaluable.

Thank you so much for reading! I hope you enjoyed Natalie and Theo as much as I loved writing about them.

And get ready, you won't want to miss Ryder's story!

ALSO BY GRACE TURNER

If you haven't already, check out the Murphy's Law series:

Unexpected (Murphy's Law book 1 – Hazel & Luke)
Unforgettable (Murphy's Law book 2 – Amanda, Josh & Reed)
Undeniable (Murphy's Law book 3 – James & Ivy)
Book 4 coming later 2024!

And to stay up to date on everything else Grace has to come, sign up for her newsletter at graceturnerauthor.com and make sure to check out:

instagram.com/graceturnerauthor
facebook.com/graceturnerauthor
tiktok.com/@graceturnerauthor
amazon.com/author/graceturner
goodreads.com/graceturner

ABOUT THE AUTHOR

Grace Turner lives in Houston, Texas with her husband and two rambunctious pups and has a revolving door full of friends and family always visiting. By day, she works as a paralegal, and by night she reads, writes, and breathes contemporary romance.

www.ingramcontent.com/pod-product-compliance
Lightning Source LLC
Chambersburg PA
CBHW072024020726
47501CB00006B/1935

* 9 7 9 8 9 8 7 6 2 2 5 2 0 *